Night Swimming in the Jordan

Yaara Lahav Gregory

LEAF BY LEAF

Published by Leaf by Leaf
an imprint of Cinnamon Press,
Office 49019, PO Box 15113, Birmingham B2 2NJ
www.cinnamonpress.com
The right of Yaara Lahav Gregory to be identified as author of this work
has been asserted by her in accordance with the Copyright, Designs and
Patent Act, 1988. © 2023 Yaara Lahav Gregory.
Print Edition ISBN 978-1-78864-971-1
British Library Cataloguing in Publication Data. A CIP record for this
book can be obtained from the British Library.
Designed and typeset in Adobe Caslon Pro by Cinnamon Press.
Cover design by Adam Craig © Adam Craig
Cinnamon Press is represented by Inpress.
This is a work of fiction. Names, characters, places, events and incidents
are drawn from the author's imagination or used fictitiously. Any
resemblance to actual persons, living or dead, or to actual events is
coincidental except when citing historical incidents.

About the Author

Yaara grew up in a Kibbutz in Israel, a socialist farming
community on the banks of the river Jordan. After two
years of compulsory military service in the Israeli Air
Force she moved to Devon in the UK where she still lives.
Yaara has spent many years as a teacher of both children
and adults. She loves to swim in rivers and in the sea.

More Praise for *Night Swimming in the Jordan*

In *Night Swimming in the Jordan* Lahav Gregory opens the door on a world under-represented in fiction. Hers is a sensitive coming-of-age story told with real warmth about a young girl hungry to explore everything the world has to offer beyond the confines of the kibbutz. But as she begins to enjoy the thrills of first love, political unrest rumbles louder in the wings, and the events of one protest march will send shockwaves across the continent for decades to come.

Delphine Gatehouse, editor, Daniel Goldsmiths Associates

A wise and daring novel that sensitively explores the Israeli-Palestinian conflict, told by Abbie, growing up on a kibbutz and drawn into the waters of youthful desire and politics. Swept along in the maelstrom that engulfs her family and friends as they struggle to find stability, it will be her daughter, Yasmin, who tries to unravel the past. Yaara Lahav Gregory sheds humane light on this important subject, which she understands because she has lived through it.

Rebecca Gethin, poet and novelist

This book is dedicated to the memory of my father, Moshe (Mousa) Lahav 1928-2013. A lone child refugee during WWII, he was sent from Novi Sad, Yugoslavia to British-colonised Palestine. He made a home for himself in a community by the Jordan, and never saw his parents again.

Night Swimming in the Jordan

PROLOGUE

Torquay, England, March 2008

Yasmin picked me up from the hospice today. She helped
me into the passenger seat of the car, and we drove down
to the bay. There was a chill wind at the seafront, and we
stayed in our seats, looking out. The water was vast and
grey, restrained with quiet, slow waves. Yasmin held my
hand.

Does it upset you that I'm driving your car, Mummy?

Not in the least darling, I'm glad it's being used rather
than gathering rust on the road.

Gathering dust, not rust. And it's a car, Mum, not a
horse, it doesn't need to be exercised.

We laughed a while and were quiet.

On the beach, two women left their clothes in neat
piles and walked into the sea. Yasmin talked about the
children she works with at school, about wanting to train
as a teacher. I'm so proud of you, darling, I said, and
thought of Queenie. Beautiful, vibrant Queenie, not yet
thirty years old and a student at the Teachers Seminar
when she died all those years ago. Queenie, who was too
young to be our mother but loved and looked after us as a
mother should.

I told Yasmin teaching was wonderful, a noble

profession, but tears were in my voice. She said, Mum, what are you crying for, we're talking about something good. We sipped milky tea from a flask as the two swimmers made their way along the coast, leaving faint foamy trails.

I said, I'd like to go in the sea one more time. My words were steady without pain, but Yasmin cried, Oh Mummy, and squeezed my hand. So I hastened to add, But I'm too soft now for the open water with all the hot baths they give us.

Don't make light of it Mum, you miss it, it's okay to be sad. And I wondered, where did she learn such kindness. Not from me. After a while she said, I used to love your stories about swimming, about the Jordan.

Ah. I sighed. The Jordan, yes, there was not much else one could do in the heat in those days.

Remember that tortoise you found on the riverbank?

Oh yes, I wrote about it, it's in one of the diaries.

Tell me again.

I will darling, another time, I'm tired now.

In the afternoon Ivanka pushed my wheelchair to a sunny bench in the garden. Shall I stay with you a while, Abbie, she asked, but I dismissed her, Go on now, back inside, you've better things to do than hang around here. Sitting among bees and dragonflies, primroses and bluebells. I look over the bay and wait for Queenie to arrive, to sit by my side.

Do you remember the story I wrote, about the tortoise?

I think so, though you never did let me read it.

I was going to but then you died.

Ah, yes. Did the tortoise run away?

It did. I was upset and Ester called me a baby.

She shouldn't have done that, it's okay to cry.
I know that now. Doesn't the sea look peaceful?
Beautiful.

Oh the gladness of seeing my Queenie once more, and talking about the days.

Chapter 1: Jordan Valley, Israel

5 April 1969

After lunch I went to the library to borrow *Anne Frank* again. Queenie had turned the air-conditioner on in the children's house, which meant it was 43 Celsius outside. Or more. Hot enough to fry an egg on a car bonnet. Apparently. I would like to check whether this is true, but Father doesn't own a car. He drives Community-shared ones, and you can't break an egg onto one of those, whatever the weather.

Normally in the summer, no one can sleep after lunch, we toss and turn, sweating into our beds, until Queenie says it's three o'clock, the end of rest-time. But occasionally it gets so hot she takes pity on us and turns on the air-conditioners, only for an hour; it's like throwing hundred-shekel notes into a bonfire, she says. Then the children fall asleep, even Leo and Saffi do. But today I just couldn't drop off, however many songs I went through inside my head. And Queenie said I may go to the library instead. Only me. Even though it was rest time!

I love Queenie, she looks after all us children. She's too young to be our mother, but she can make you feel precious with a flash of her smile. Sometimes she kisses me goodnight. Just me. She is the most beautiful woman

I have seen in real life. Her hair is dark and straight, soft and shiny, and sometimes she wears it in loose plaits. I've tried to plait my hair the way she does but it's so thick and stiff the plaits look like bunches of straw. Queenie wears cut-off jeans and rings with big stones. When she walks, her hips move up and down, up and down. I practise walking that way too, Mother saw me once and said I looked ridiculous, as though I was desperate for a pee. I love Queenie as much as I love Mother. Sometimes more.

In the library, I borrowed *Anne Frank* and was reading as I walked back. The afternoon wind crept among the houses, a cockerel crowed beyond, a tractor was on its way home to the shed. The pavements are quiet at rest-time. Community Members are in their rooms. But today, a voice said, That book looks interesting.

I looked up. It was Micah Ashkenazi, Saffi's brother. Wearing army uniform, crumpled and dirty. Shoes dusty, I noticed that straight away. His eyes were squeezed nearly shut against the sun, so his face seemed like a smile. First, I looked around, wondered whether he was talking to me or maybe to someone behind me. But there wasn't anyone else. Still, I wasn't sure. He's even older than Ester, that's my older sister, maybe twenty years old, why was he talking to me? What's so interesting about what I'm reading?

I stood still, we both did, and the moment stretched like a piece of pink Mastic gum you pull out of your mouth with two fingers, teeth holding on to the other end and it gets longer and longer, you can't pull it any further, your arm is too short, and you lose. But here, today, the Mastic snapped.

It was him who spoke first. I was saying that's an

interesting book. He was still grinning.

I know, I said. I've read it. Twice already.

And what do you think of it?

That put me on the spot if I wasn't on it already. Anne is so clever and nice; she laughs even when her life is so hard. I want to be able to write just like she does. Though I know how her story ends, I never can help hoping she will be saved instead of die in the Nazi concentration camp. But I wasn't going to say all this to Micah, he'd only tell Ester, and together they'd laugh and call me silly. Also I was feeling nervous with his nearly-shut, staring eyes. So I said, It's good. Then I smiled, and walked on, still reading.

I'm going to keep a diary just like Anne Frank and if I die in the next war or in a Syrian bombardment my diary may be published and I will become famous in death. And if I don't die first I may be a famous writer like Jules Verne or Enid Blyton, or my very favourite, Erich Kästner. In his books children always sort things out themselves, the adults never have time to notice what's happening around them. I love Erich Kästner, but I would never be able to write like him, or even near.

My name is Abbie. I'm nine years old and nearly a half. I can skip two ropes on the double, which my brother Tommy still can't and he's twelve already. I'm good at swimming, and next year Father and I are going to swim the Annual Crossing of the Sea of Galilee, three kilometres long! I live in a Kibbutz Community by the river Jordan. We are Socialists, and everything is shared like it should be in a big family.

If I become a famous author I will just keep writing more and more, and children all over the world will wait for my latest book to be translated from Hebrew into their languages and their grandmother might bring them my books as presents when she comes to visit. That's what I really want. And for Josh Pasternak to love me (but I know *that* will never happen).

3 May 1969

I will never be rich like most famous writers because my money will belong to our Community. You can't have a private income at the same time as being a Socialist and that's why after my grandfather Arthur died and left Mother an Inheritance she gave it all away.

Her brother, Uncle David, lives in Tel Aviv with his wife Betty, where he is a big businessman selling air-conditioners. He offered to open a bank account for Mother where she could keep the Inheritance and no one in the Community need even know. And she need never use it, he said, but Ester, for example, may one day want to go to university and then Mother would be able to help her out. But no, Mother wouldn't have it. The Community would pay for Ester to go to university, as long as she becomes a Member, and as long as she studies something useful such as book-keeping or even medicine, Ester is that bright and clever she could be a doctor if she put her mind to it.

Ester says she won't go to university, even though she's the best in her class at all the difficult subjects. After military service she's going to live in Tel Aviv and do a Working Class job, where you work long hours for hardly any money and have dirt under your fingernails. Being Working Class is a step towards The Revolution, Ester says. But Mother and Father think she will change her mind. Like Micah Ashkenazi did; everyone had been worried when he joined the Communists, and look at him now, an officer in a secret crack unit. Mother and Father say Ester *will* go to university, whatever she thinks or says now.

Uncle David said that their father, my Grandfather Arthur, would not have been happy for Mother to hand over her Inheritance to random strangers. But Community Members are not random strangers. And Mother is not permitted to be in possession of private money, stashed in secret bank accounts or not. Also, Grandfather Arthur most certainly *did* know what Mother would do with her Inheritance. But David doesn't believe this, not for a moment. He himself had been certain that Mother would—yes, he was going to say it whether she liked it or not—he had been *certain* that she would grow out of it. But Mother is a grown woman in her thirties, how *dare* David suggest she doesn't know her own mind? In any case, it was too late—the money was already in the Community Treasury; David may as well stop haranguing her.

So then there was relief or a ceasefire, Mother said, as they all went right back to normal, which is David keeping quiet, and Aunt Betty dominating every conversation. Betty has many friends, all with important jobs like running half the army or being surgeons, or otherwise they don't work at all but meet with their girlfriends at cafés and eat shop-bought cake. Shop-bought cake is something I'd like to try one day. But Mother can't abide sitting at cafés, being served by low-paid workers. She did not leave London and come to live here, in The Back of Beyond, only for her children to grow up spoilt and *bourgeois*. Besides, she says in English, which is so embarrassing when there are people all around. Besides, you know, money doesn't grow on trees.

But the issue of Mother's inheritance didn't go away. Every time she and David talk on the phone he just can't let it rest. Mother and Father don't have a telephone in their room, but our neighbours Jacob and Ruth do, because Jacob stood on a mine in the Sinai War, 1956. It was a miracle he didn't die, and he still has metal pieces all through his body. So to make sure he has a comfortable life after doing his duty to our country the government gives him a telephone and a car. And because he is 79 per cent disabled he doesn't have to hand over these luxuries to the Community. So David sometimes telephones Jacob, after nine o'clock, cheap time, and they hang up straight away, to save on David's bill, and then Jacob's wife Ruth walks over to call Mother. And Mother goes to wait by the phone until David calls again after five minutes, or longer if the lines are busy, the whole Nation uses the telephone at nine o'clock, cheap time.

The next day Mother has news. Manu, Betty's brother, stood up during Passover meal and declared himself a homosexual. Being homosexual means you might leave your wife and children and run off to live with another man; Father's friend Jonathan did this and was never seen again.

But Manu never married in the first place and he hasn't run off, so I don't know how he is being a homosexual. Mother said she will explain when I'm older. But Leo knows and he told me, it means Manu likes kissing another man. On the lips—which is disgusting. I

15

sometimes imagine myself giving Josh a kiss on his cheek and holding his hand. I must close my eyes when I think of that.

Now Mother says she won't talk to David on the phone anymore, the man is obsessed, he is obsessed with money, Father will have to do it instead. Father hates the telephone. And he hates to talk about money. He was a child in Yugoslavia when the Second World War started and his parents sent him and his sister Deborah to safety in Palestine. They themselves stayed behind to make more money before going to Palestine also. Then the Nazis invaded their town and shot them into the Danube, the same river Father and Deborah had learned to swim in when they were small children. All the Jews in the town were shot into the river. The fish must have thought Christmas had come early, Manu said at New Year. Mother and Betty frowned. Neither of them likes Holocaust jokes.

Father thinks if his parents hadn't been greedy for more money they would have gone to Palestine sooner, with him and Deborah, and been saved. So now he won't answer David's calls either. It's her inheritance, her brother, Father says, as he sits outside on the boulder for a smoke without inhaling.

10 June 1972

Last night there was a bombardment from across the Syrian border. Queenie came to the children's house to take us down to the bomb shelter. She said to stay calm, as though we wouldn't, and to take just a pillow, but I stuffed my *Anne of Ingleside* book inside the pillow-case, and the torch Grandma Rose gave me for secret reading.

We went down to the bomb-shelter, where I got a bunk next to Saffi. We lay in the darkness, listening to the bombs, like far away thunder. In the bunk above, Leo was making strange noises, pretending he wasn't scared. In the end Josh rolled over and flicked him hard on the head and that was that, quiet, except older boys snoring.

With my torch under the blanket I read *Anne of Ingleside*. I cannot get enough of Anne. Last Friday, it was family time, half past four, I was still reading and didn't go to the parents' room. So Father and Tommy went looking for me, searched all around, even took a tractor as far as Abudiya, the Arab village on the other side of the Jordan. Then Saffi's brother Micah told them he'd seen me by the pine grove behind the children's house, and there I was, sitting on top of the bomb-shelter, reading without a care in the world. Tommy came up behind and twisted my arm so it hurt, said he'd wasted a whole hour looking for me, and I must say, Sorry, Sir! But I know Tommy loves driving the tractor, Father always lets him even though he's only fourteen.

I finished the book but couldn't sleep. I thought of Anne, long ago and far away in America, knowing nothing of wars, while we have already known two.

Anne Shirley is my favourite person. I wish my name were Anne Shirley instead of A-bi-gail-Bos-ko-vitch, jagged and long. Anne Shirley sounds like a smooth pebble, bouncing once, twice on the water, then sinking silently, no fuss. She could be a line in a romantic poem. You wouldn't use "Abigail Boskovitch" in a poem, except maybe a limerick. Anne hated her red hair, but when she grew up it turned a beautiful auburn. Rita dyes her hair a colour called Auburn Sunset; Leo told me it comes from America where they have time to make up such names. But Rita's hair is orange, like the persimmon father brought home from army reserve duty, and it's a waste of money, says Mother; she should let it go grey like all the other Members do. One of my eyes is brown and one grey, and that's worse than having red hair. Queenie says no one's perfect, and to stop looking down all the time, you'll have a hunched back and who would marry you then, eh?

Look at me when I'm talking to you, Mother chides, people will think you have no manners! By "people" she means the English side of our family; here in Israel no one is bothered by such things. But I don't care about the English and what they think of children with bent necks and abnormally coloured eyes.

In books, I love Gilbert Blythe who loves Anne Shirley. She only realises that she also loves him at the very end, lucky he proposes to her again after she's turned him down. If Josh ever asks me to walk out with him I would say yes. He is the one I love in real life, and thinking of him lying in the next bed but three pushed sleep even further away. I lay awake until all the sighing and creaking had stopped, though not the snoring, and not the far away bomb-thunders.

In the morning I woke up to see Leo's leg dangling through the gap between the two bunks. He was prodding me in the ribs, so I squeezed his toe, tight until he begged for mercy. After lunch Mother came by to say Father had been called up in the night, to join the fighting. The bombardments had stopped and we were allowed outside. Lessons were as usual except history—Solomon had also been called up. Solomon is our history teacher and

Father's commanding officer in the Infantry. He's a lieutenant colonel, and Father only a captain.

15 July 1972

The night we buried Lady I lay awake in bed, thinking about her life, how she broke her leg and Father drove us to the veterinary's big house overlooking the Sea of Galilee; how I used to check her for ticks, behind the ears, between the toes, pull them out, burn them until they explode in a puff and good riddance. I remembered the litters she had every year, we would fill a canvas sack with grass to make her comfortable, and give the puppies names. And then how upset we were when they were taken away by Chaled the Arab builder, to live in his village, according to Queenie, but actually he had them drowned, we found that out later; you can't have dogs running around procreating without control and giving us all rabies, Tommy said sagely.

Lady died in the big dog clear out. There had been a rabies case, and everyone was told to keep their dogs indoors while the strays were rounded up. A notice had gone up in the Dining Room. But us children were away staying in another kibbutz by the sea. No one at home thought to take Lady in, not Mother or Father, maybe they don't know I'm the one who's always feeding her and looking for her when it's time for her vaccination. She belongs to all the children in Squill Group but no one takes care of her like I do. Did. And that's how she ended up being shot like a stray. Mona found her in a bin. We gave her a solemn burial in the eucalyptus grove outside the security fence, it overlooks the bridge over the Jordan so a nice view for her. Instead of a headstone Ori put up a cross over her grave, he'd seen them in a photograph that shows how many American soldiers died in Vietnam. It's a Christian thing, but we didn't mind, the adults don't know, or they might tell us to take it down. At least, Ori's parents would, it was Christians who killed their family in the Holocaust. Father doesn't hold a grudge against Christians even though they also murdered his parents, he's been an orphan since he was eleven, that's younger than I am now. I miss Lady every day, but that's not why this summer has been a sad one, which I will write about next and pray to G-d even though I know he doesn't exist that no one ever reads this diary but me.

That night, after the burial, as I lay awake, remembering Lady's life, a secret thing happened. The moon was up and then someone was standing in the doorway, a tall broad shadow. Leo and Sara were asleep. The shadow was still, but after a while he stepped in and stood over my bed.

It was Micah, Saffi's older brother. I thought perhaps he was looking for her but he wasn't. I didn't answer when he sat on my bed and said Hello Abigail, no one else calls me Abigail, only Grandma Rose, and How are you? I said, Okay and he carried on asking questions in a quiet voice, about my day and favourite subject at school, a hushed close voice, as though we were friends and always did have conversations in my room after lights-out. He said, it was difficult to find you; he had gone into another room first. Someone, maybe Anya, was awake, and he told her he was looking for Saffi. Who *was* he looking for, was it me I didn't ask, just lay there, quite calm.

It was Friday, he was home for the weekend. There had been a party in the Dining Room, he said. Next year when we're thirteen my class will be allowed to go to such events, but I didn't say so, it was embarrassing that Micah was sitting on my bed, he's Saffi's brother, also Ester's friend, ten years older than us, what if Leo or Sara wake up, what if someone saw him walking into the children's house, bold as brass. All I could do was sit up a little and pull the sheet over my pyjama top, it had got tangled between my thighs in the heat of the night. He noticed pretty soon that I was hardly saying anything and so he stopped talking too and sat quietly and I lay in my bed wishing he'd go away quick but saying nothing. It was exciting too.

His hand dug in under the sheet and held my hand; was this instead of asking me to be his girlfriend I wondered, will I say yes even though I'm still waiting for Josh? The skin on his hand was rough and hard near the knuckles like Father's, and my hand was lying there as though it were a wet floorcloth after Queenie had pulled it out of the bucket and wrung all the bleach water out with her strong hands; I didn't move at all. Numbness crept up my arm and my shoulder stuck to the pillow. I lay quietly, breathing shallow, in-out carefully, quietly in-out, what shall I do, nothing, look away, nothing, just lie back. We sat like this a long while, the moon crept off my bed, across his lap.

What were we doing here, what's next, and then he held on tighter to my hand and also moved forward, he was going to kiss me maybe even on the lips his face was close up, I could smell cigarette smoke, Grandma Rose smell, but not so nice, also his lips were thick and fleshy, I didn't think I wanted them to touch me and my head went back into the pillow I was holding my breath he was too close, so close in the end I had to move, to use my right hand, the one he wasn't holding, to hold him back slightly, which meant my hand on the front of his shoulder, I did it gently, weren't we friends? And he sat up again but looking at me straight in the eyes, smiling, finally I breathed in and the air filling my lungs was light like a relief.

So I was quite still, and he was holding my hand, the left one, and my right was on the front of his shoulder, not really holding him back anymore, just resting, I wanted to take it away, not to be taking part in this thing that was going on, what's going on here Queenie says when she walks in on us and we've done something wrong, what's going on here anyway I didn't know, but also had to be so still like a statue not move a muscle so I left it there, my hand. And his shoulder was thick and hard not bony like the shoulders of boys I know, Leo or Tommy. Because he is a man with a man's shoulder. Micah smiled a Cheshire Cat smile; what did it mean? I was confused just as Alice was in the Wonderland wood. Was he happy sitting here with my hand upon his thick man shoulder? Was he thinking, this is what I want to do now with this very girl called Abigail? My stomach made a knot and squeezed it tight, I let my hand fall onto my lap. He smiled that confusing smile. Then he moved towards me again.

Was he going to kiss me again, was it because I let my hand fall off his shoulder instead of keeping it there and being still? And he was not as handsome now, his head too big, ears out to the sides, his nose weighed him forward, some of his curls touched the side of my forehead, thick lips smiling, seeping smoky breaths onto my face.

I've seen such scenes before, in the movies Ester calls "romantic". But this was not a movie. What would they say if they saw us? I turned my head. He sat up again. The hand holding mine let go and then he sighed.

Not smiling anymore, he stood up, walked out of the room. The moon out in the pine grove was toying with some fireflies. Afterwards, looking at the sky getting lighter behind the trees, I wondered if the thing had happened at all.

The next day was Saturday. I went to help Father feed the cows. We took out the green John Deere, and I sat by him on the fender. Father was talking about engines, why you must check the oil level every single morning, when I saw Micah coming towards us on a bicycle. I looked away feeling tight in the stomach, if he is here, in the Community, then last night did happen in real life. My cheeks felt hot.

I prayed to the God I don't believe in that he should ride his bicycle right past us but Father saw him too. Ah, he called, Look who's here, and he turned off the engine, they talked for an absolute age, what was Micah doing in the army, he's just finished officers' training course, with distinction, well done, good, and where next; and what he thinks about the inter-party talks, will they form a coalition, will a Labour government continue to build Settlements in the Occupied Territories, yes certainly, Micah says, if they want to hang on to power, Father nods his head then shakes it. Father thinks all building projects in the Occupied Territories should stop right away, the Settlements are a thorn in our side, also a waste of money, well, Micah agrees, of course, but he's a realist, we must accept the status quo, hmmm, we'll have to disagree on this. Etcetera.

They were talking and talking and I was trapped. Micah was there, leaning against the bonnet, ignoring me as though he hadn't sat on my bed the night before and tried to kiss me not even once but twice. I wondered, should I walk away, my heart was beating, beating from having him near, but also that paralysed floor-cloth feeling from last night. So I sat, stupid and small. I'm twelve years old and know about how people have babies; but kissing on the lips I've so far only seen in films.

Hello Abigail, Micah is saying and his eyes, light blue in the sun, smile at me. Again. I smile back, but only with my mouth, I think. Father is also looking. They are both smiling. Aren't you going to say hello? says Father. Another knot in my stomach, squeeze.

Hello, I say. Pause.

Father chuckles into the silence. Well, we must get on or we'll be late for lunch. He turns on the engine, and we speed towards the cow sheds. Ah, Micah, Micah, he says, Micah is my kind of lad. But there's no need for me to answer, Father has lost half his hearing defending the Jordan Valley from the Jordanians in 1948, barricaded in the police station the British abandoned during the War of Independence, leaving us to fend for ourselves against seven Arab armies. Mother wishes he'd been more careful when blowing up that bridge which stopped the Jordanians driving their tanks straight into the Jordan Valley, he was the one who carried the dynamite over to the bridge. I'm so proud of him but now Mother has to suffer, Father can't hear half of what she's saying or is it that he's just not listening. Oscar are you listening to me she says and I do not know what's so annoying about someone being a little deaf sometimes like right now Father is intoning, *Micah, Micah my man*, and I didn't have to say anything, he couldn't hear me anyway over the engine roar.

Since that day, Micah has not been back. Saffi says the army is on High Alert, tensions at the borders, so his weekend leave was cancelled. I don't care when he takes his leave, but I keep imagining seeing him in the distance through the corner of my eye, especially on Friday nights.

4 August 1972

Anya joined our class after the last bombardment. She's from Odessa. That's in the USSR, not Russia, says Ester, Odessa is in Ukraine, which Russia has oppressed since the Revolution and still does. Ester never misses a chance to give me a lecture. What a shock Anya had, coming to live here! First, the heat. It's June and already forty degrees, Mother simply cannot face another summer like the last one, she *longs to,* spend August with Aunt Rachel in London. If only she could get Committee Approval to travel. If only we had money. It's been fifteen years, she truly does miss England, where people like to complain when it rains, instead of being grateful. A short stay in Hampstead would be something to look forward to in this hellish oven where only mosquitoes thrive.

Mother has had twenty years to get used to our summers and she hasn't managed yet. But Anya is here for the first time. Her white skin turns red in the sun, and when we go to the Sea of Galilee she has to sit in the shade instead of bouncing pebbles or playing Bulldog in the water. Collecting mussels from the sea bed she wouldn't do anyway, because she can't swim. And she wouldn't eat them afterwards, mussels aren't kosher, she said, and we tried not to laugh.

In Odessa, Ukraine, as well as sending her to secret Hebrew lessons, her parents bought her a pair of sandals in preparation for coming to the "Holy-land". The sandals are a townie sort with covered toes, and if that's not ridiculous enough, they are also shiny red, which is a colour only babies wear. Leo sniggered when he saw them, but I told him it's not her fault. In the afternoon, she came out to play barefoot like the rest of us but it's too late in the year to get used to the heat on your feet. You should start about Passover when it's not yet hot, then by June you can walk on the pavements even at noon. Black tar roads are the worst. You must run across quickly or you'd get blood blisters. So Anya had to wear her embarrassing sandals until Queenie took her to Dov the Shoemaker for a pair of biblicals, brown, now she looks normal.

Then, after lunch, Queenie asked me to take Anya to the clothes store so she can get summer clothes. Why me? I was looking forward to our *Siesta*. Queenie calls it *Siessstahh*, in a rolling winding kind of way, like the Spanish say it—that's our reading-in-bed time and my book is *David Copperfield* by Charles Dickens, Agnes is my third-favourite character after the two Annes—Shirley and Frank. She's patient and graceful, waiting and waiting for David Copperfield to notice her, just as I wait for Josh. Why me, I asked, but Queenie said she has a headache and to please not argue. Why can't Anya go alone? Because I asked you to go with her, Queenie snapped and turned away, continued washing the shower floor. Sometimes she can be mean or angry but it doesn't mean she doesn't love you anymore.

The clothes store isn't a shop, it's where all our clothes are kept, and every new season the oldest children go there to check which clothes still fit, and which they have grown out of, those they give back to the store. I explained this to Anya as we walked along the pavements, she was wearing her new sandals but not me, I was barefoot. The heat at noon makes you breathe carefully and walk slowly, it presses down, wraps around you like a too warm woollen blanket you can hardly bear. So we rushed from one ficus tree shade to another, slowing for the cooler air, then fast through the next sun patch to another shade. Slow, fast-fast-slow, even stand still, wait for the fire on the soles of my feet to go out.

Anya said, What if I don't like the clothes she gives me? My dad says short shorts look cheap. What is she… religious or something?

Is your father religious?

No. But my granddad was a rabbi, an underground one; before we ran away from Odessa he used to hold prayer meetings in our house.

Well, Sara is the only one who makes a fuss over clothes. That's what she's like.

What?

No one likes her.

I think she's nice.

She's always in trouble and annoying everyone. Even swore at Mona, once.

Why do you share a room with her?

Queenie decides where we sleep. It'll be someone else next.

In the clothes store Miriam gave Anya an up and down look and offered her a pair of pioneer shorts with elasticated thighs and button fastening on one side, home-made. Anya didn't look happy, she was probably thinking about what her dad would say, but she said nothing; Miriam looked sour, her face was puckered, she always does look like that, but Anya doesn't know that. And in that vein, she received two pairs of work-shorts, two for evenings and the same with shirts. Also a hat. And Miriam stares at her still-small breasts.

Do you need any underwear?

Anya went bright red. No, thank you.

Miriam said, Well, if you do have any of your own clothes, I'll have them marked for you so they don't get lost in the laundry. She looked a little less cross when she said that.

Things have moved on in our Community in the last years. Children are allowed to keep their own clothes now, if someone buys them any. When Ester was in kindergarten, Grandma Rose brought her a pair of sandals from Tel Aviv, but she had to share them with all the other girls, by rota; her Nanny said it would be unfair otherwise. That's Socialism.

Ester says, Why should I have had more just because my grandmother can afford to buy it for me? I think so too, most children don't have grandparents because they stayed too long in Europe and were killed in the holocaust. Like Father's parents, Irene and Morris. Or some children's grandparents are Community Members, and so have no money of their own. This is a Socialist ideal: *To each according to his needs; from each according to his ability.* Or her.

Maybe because she's a baby, or hasn't yet got used to all the sharing and being equal, Anya cried as we walked out of the store. Or maybe she was missing Odessa, far away in Europe, or her Mother, working in the kitchen or having an afternoon rest, but Anya can't see her until family time at half past four. Or did I upset her instead? I sometimes do that without meaning to and people think I'm rude. Mother told me so. But crying where people can see is being selfish which is a bad thing. After all, she did get to keep her nice shop-bought pants, whereas the rest of us wear home-made cotton ones, white and loose.

We walked back to the children's house. Anya was still crying. I did suddenly want to comfort her, but couldn't decide what would be a helpful thing to say, maybe nothing was best. Queenie was in the kitchen helping Ori and Shira wash the lunch dishes but when she saw Anya she put her arm round her shoulder and they walked off together. Queenie would have the exact-right words to make Anya feel better. But to follow them would be eavesdropping which you mustn't do, people will think you have nothing better to think about than other people's business which is none of yours. So I went to bed, it was rest time, Leo was reading and Sara was pretending to sleep, in a minute she'll start her fake sleep-talking, for attention. Suddenly I could hear Queenie, she and Anya were in the classroom, next door. Lucky that my bed was by the door. I opened my book. If you're trying to read you can't be accused of eavesdropping.

And it was terrible, Queenie was saying, I hated

everything: the heat, the food, the communal showers. The other children, they already had each other and didn't need a new friend, a strange townie like me.

Queenie had never told us that coming to live here had been difficult. You assume everyone loves our way of life. Our Kibbutz is the best place. There are no poor people; the garbage collector is valued as highly as the factory manager. It's true the farmers are the highest value, but they are the ones safe-guarding our land. We are the defenders of our Country's borders; every few years our enemies try to destroy us in an all-out war, and between wars they send infiltrators across the border to terrorise our nights. When we are in our beds in the children's house, with no adults to watch over us, we aren't afraid of made-up nonsense like witches or giants. We lie awake, listening to hyenas in the fields, and imagining an infiltrator has crept over the Jordanian border two kilometre away, or Syrian border five kilometres away. We think of him lurking in the pine grove outside our window, then we might call out for the night-guard through the intercom box on the ceiling, and if she hears us, after a while she might appear, and might walk over to our parents' room and tell them I want my mother, but Father would turn up instead, tired and silent, and lie down on the cold marble floor next to my bed and go straight to sleep; he has to be up at four o'clock, and guilt would sit inside my forehead, poor Father, selfish to have got him out of bed; eventually I wake him up and he goes back to bed in the room he shares with Mother by the banana plantation next to the security fence, and finally I can fall asleep.

And the boys of our Country's Communities are the

fighters and officers of our Defence Forces, the IDF. Lots of town-people spend their military service as non-fighting job-nicks. But in our Community, a job-nick without a good excuse, such as polio, or only one arm, would be in disgrace and his parents would not hold their heads high for the shame of it. For example, Gideon Goldberg. He pretended to have a limp, spent a week walking with one leg on the pavement and one off, to make it look real. And now he is a cook (a cook!) in a base one kilometre away, by the Sea of Galilee. Every evening his mother has to get his food from the Dining Room, he's too ashamed to show his face on weekdays while his classmates are pulling their weight far away in secret locations.

In the afternoon, after talking with Queenie, Anya was smiling and asked to learn how to skip a long rope till it was half past four and family time.

23 September 1972

Last summer, when Lady died and Micah came into my room the night we buried her, was my worst summer so far. The reason it got to be my worst came near the end, after Anya and I became best friends. Her skin was creamy now, and her accent not so strong. Sometimes she laughs too much when there are boys around, but friends are friends, you can't go around criticising or you'll end up on your own. We had just moved into our new house in the big secondary school. The school is outside the perimeter fence, beyond the swimming pool. Anya and I share a bedroom. The week before school started, she asked if I wanted to swap secrets. I first thought about the

Micah-secret but didn't want to tell, these words are too hard to say. Then I thought I could maybe tell her about Josh. My love for him is unrequited, he's never talked to me apart from joining in with Tommy's teasing, sometimes; Tommy is an absolute idiot who shows off when Josh is around—worships him, he does. Sometimes, I forget about Josh even for two days in a row. But then I see him, and he presses on my chest, tight around my neck. Would sharing him lighten my load? Would his name on my lips carry him off and out from inside me where he perches on top of my heart like a kingfisher? I cannot say it, cannot say, Josh, only in a whisper, alone under the sheets. My mouth watered, my tongue laboured through thick cement, and, hoarsely, shyly, it came, Josh. I didn't think Anya had heard, but it felt good, and I was working my mouth up to saying more.

But she did hear, and she said, how did you guess it was Josh, he was *her* secret, he'd asked her to be his girlfriend. Surprise was the least of it. Could she be talking of anyone, anyone at all, other than him? She couldn't know. I would have said something, but my mouth was numb. Dumb.

She asked, what do I think, should she say yes, she wasn't sure, her father would go mad! It would have to be a secret and she didn't know if she could be bothered. Yes, she knows he's popular and clever, quite good looking, but not really her type. She has a *type*! She just went on and on, he's too loud, always thinks he's right, always assumes everyone wants to listen to him. You know, he never even spoke to me before, not once! And now he wants us to be *friends*. What do you think? Abbie? And, hating myself for being the worst most disloyal friend, I said so maybe say no? But she wasn't listening, was thinking maybe give it a try, but is it fair? You know Abbie, as I don't really like him that much? And I do want to have a boyfriend, don't you? Now we're in high school, and no bed-time, we could go for walks, sit under trees. It's quite romantic now I think about it. And it doesn't bother me that he's two years older. You know, Ori and I used to kiss, quite a lot when we were walking out; so I know what I'm doing.

Anya was going to be Josh's girlfriend because she feels sorry for him. I said, But do you like him?

It's okay for you, Anya said, you have Leo. And—you're a *Sabre,* a native here. But, you know, it's not so easy for me. I miss the home we had in Odessa. We were a family then. We didn't have much food, but we ate it together around a table; and my mother would put me to bed, and take me to school. Here, it's like I've lost my parents; although I still see them every day. And, nothing ever happens to just me. It's always Us and We. I probably sound stupid to you. But, I don't know, with all this *together* and *solidarity* I often feel quite alone.

I said, Leo? He's not my boyfriend! I don't even like him—very much!

Later, in bed, I could see the heavy cloud pushing the air aside and engulfing me with a chill, like an evil cradling, slowly suffocating. I stayed in bed for two days after that. The second afternoon, Mother came to see what had happened to me. She made me a cup of lemon tea, stayed a bit, then went home to Father. It's stupid. I've been in love with Josh since I was seven years old, since the day the Six Day War ended and Queenie took us all down to the river. But I'd never thought Josh would want me anyway. I'm not nearly so pretty as Anya with her light brown, hazel eyes and her perfect skin. My skin has turned to spots, my eyes are two different colours and I can't even wear a bra yet. I have no right. Except, however often I tell myself it's hopeless, there's a little bit of stubborn hope. A hope that if, incredibly, miraculously I'm wrong, Josh may one day love me back.

So this is why this summer has been my saddest so far. A week later, Anya and Josh started to walk out together. I've seen less and less of her since then.

The Tortoise—a story by Abbie Boskovitch

In the spring of 1967, just before the Six Day War I found a tortoise on the bank of the river Jordan. Talia, Goldie and Saffi were waiting in the water below as I climbed to reach the swing rope which hung from a high eucalyptus branch. Grasping at a tree root that jutted free of the slippery mud bank, and heaving myself onto shore, I came face to face with its wrinkled head, so close our noses nearly touched. Startled by the encounter, I let the root slip through my hand and fell crashing back onto the other girls. Laughing and spluttering, I recovered myself and again clambered up the bank in search of the creature. It had attempted to avoid detection by slipping sideways amongst the reeds, but I found it and carried it back up the hill.

I made a home for the tortoise in an old grapefruit crate Tommy and I found behind the silo. We filled the crate with straw, added fresh grass and a carrot and placed it outside my parents' room by the red stopcock. Let it go, Ester said, the poor thing must be terrified, she often spoke of things like Justice and Politics. We ignored her. The tortoise would want for nothing. The next day after lessons I rushed over on my bicycle to see it,

34

but the crate was turned on its side and the creature had gone. It's hardly surprising, Ester said knowingly, wouldn't you want to break free? I am free, I retorted fiercely, fighting back tears. Ester raised a dismissive eyebrow. Abbie you're not, she said. None of us are.

I remembered the tortoise again the next time I swam in the river. The war had just ended, the Six Day War in which our paratroopers conquered Jerusalem and handed it back to the Jews. That morning, the children were let out of the bomb shelter and in the afternoon, Queenie took us all down to the Jordan. Up and down stream we swam, first grabbing onto submerged boulders, pulling ourselves against the current, past the stepping stones and swing rope to where the water was so shallow that when we stood up again our fronts were smeared with black riverbed mud. Then, turning onto our backs, we gave ourselves to the current and, arms stretched over our heads, floated down-stream, squinting into the afternoon sun that drifted in and out through the reeds. Gently, slowly, the river carried us back to the bridge, where our clothes hung like colourful bunting on eucalyptus branches, out of the reach of scorpions and ticks. Back to where Queenie lay snoozing on a flat bank.

Queenie, we're back! Goldie called cheerfully, beating her naked chest with two fists like Tarzan King of the Apes. Queenie sat up, smiling indulgently at us, the children of Quill group. Everyone okay? She called out. We are, Goldie cried excitedly, All present and correct! Stay nearby, and don't go near the sluice, Queenie said, already lying back in her sunbathing position. Why shouldn't we go to the sluice if we want, Saffi muttered, we can look after ourselves, we're not babies. Queenie's hearing was so good she could tell when a cockroach was scuttling inside a closed cupboard. She said,

Saffi, in future you'll do whatever you want, but right now I'm in charge. Mildly, she added, There'll be plenty of time to look after yourself, don't worry about that. All afternoon we played in the river, basking in the June sun, in our new freedom, in the knowledge that war had been won. Our country was invincible and so were we.

As the sun lowered over the old Arab village, turning its ruins to silhouettes, the teenagers came walking down the hill. Ester, Micah and the others were almost grown up and allowed to do anything, even stay out till nightfall. While the younger children had to go to their parents' rooms at family time, half past four. Ten minutes, Quills, Queenie called from the bank, then we go back!

Let's see who can get to the shallows with one breath, I told Talia and Saffi. I hadn't notice Tommy and Josh sitting high above us on the bank. Tommy shouted, Don't make me laugh little ones, you'll never do it in one, even Josh and I can't do that! The two of them were smirking and carving sharp points into branches with pen knives. Then Josh jumped to his feet and threw his pointed stick over our heads and onto the opposite bank. It flew smoothly through the air and landed in the reeds. Yes! They both cried, and Josh ran across the bridge to retrieve it. Holding the stick high over his head as though he'd just won the Olympiad he called out, No one makes javelins like Josh Pasternak!

They're so stupid, I muttered, my face hot. Yeah, they are, Saffi said, ignore them. Okay, then, I whispered, let's do it in two breaths. Ready? And the three of us plunged into the green-brown darkness. I reached the shallows and lifted my head out of the murky water. Gasping for air, I rubbed my eyes open and found myself lying prone between Micah's feet. He was sitting in the shallows, legs spread, heels braced into the mud. The wet, muddy shorts he wore were just an arm's length away. A long bamboo stick was balanced across his knees like a staff. I thought, does he look like an olden day traveller at rest? Or a muddy buffalo I'd once seen a photograph of in a magazine? Hastily, I stood up, searching for balance as my feet sunk through the soft riverbed. Then I could think of nothing else but to stare at Micah, who stared back with an inscrutable face.

Time seemed to stop. Where did Saffi and Talia get to? The older children were lounging in the shallows nearby, chatting and laughing. No one saw me standing over Micah, our eyes locked in a staring match. At that moment I noticed Micah's shoulders were stooped, steep slopes like the flanks of the Golan Heights which dominate our eastern skies. I noticed his neck surge forward at a precarious, comical angle, his eyes squeezed nearly shut against the evening sun. And I realised he looked much like my old runaway tortoise. That thought made laughter bubble up in my stomach, spreading into my chest, up my throat and I started to giggle. Micah's expression was unchanged and I looked down at my mud-smeared stomach.

Finally, reproachfully he said, Do you know who I am? Of course, he was Saffi's big brother, Ester's friend, our mothers had been schoolgirls together in Krakow and still visited each other's rooms often. I would sit on the floor, listening as they laughed and talked and shifted to Polish when they thought I was hearing more than a child should. And I would pretend to be absorbed in my game when they cried for their long dead families, brothers, sisters and parents murdered by the Nazis, when they dried their tears and laughed some more over plain biscuits and cardamom coffee. Yes, I told Micah. I knew who he was.

As though I hadn't spoken, he said, Micah, that's my name.

He picked up the bamboo from across his knees and pointed one end at my chest. Carefully, he rested it where my ribcage undulated under the skin, and I watched as he slowly guided the point down to my stomach, then diagonally up, ploughing a skin-coloured farrow through the black mud, and gradually revealing five pale letters. Transfixed, I stood still. There, he said. His mouth twitched into the semblance of a smile as he placed the bamboo down and leaned back to admire his doing. Actually, he added, as in an afterthought, frowning and gesturing at my chest, Actually, you're only six, aren't you? I mean, can you read yet? Do you even know what it says? I'm seven, I said. And you've written your name. Micah. He seemed pleased. Good, he said, then you'll remember me now. And at this he sprang to his feet and walked over to join his friends.

Abbie, what are you doing? Josh's voice was behind me. Come on, he said, Quills have to go back now, Queenie is waiting for you. I turned and saw him tread water in the deep. What's this on your front, he asked, squinting in the dimming light, you've got something written there. Nothing, I said, wading towards him. It's nothing, I'm coming. I stumbled and Josh caught my elbow. Squeezing it gently, he held on and said, So we don't lose you again. We let the current take us back towards the bridge. As we floated past the swing rope where I had found the tortoise before the war I whispered, Micah did it, he wrote his name with a stick in the mud. I didn't think Josh would hear me, his ears were submerged in the water but he said, Micah? What, Micah Ashkenazi? Why? Why did he do that? I don't know, I said and wondered if he noticed the tears in my voice, but he laughed, Ya'Allah, he's so stupid, isn't he? Yeah, I said, Yeah, he is.

That night, in my bed I woke with a start before dawn. I

lay flat on my back, watching shadows glide over the sleeping forms of my friends. Listening to the owl crying in the pine tree outside the window, I held onto my elbow just as Josh had done on our way back the bridge, to Queenie. And I wondered whether it had been the bamboo or Micah's own finger which ploughed pale, skin-coloured letters through mud on my chest.

14 October 1972

Since last summer and Anya walking out with Josh, I spent more time than ever in my parents' room. Mother: Is everything alright, darling? They think it odd I should be hanging around with them in the evenings instead of with my friends, being normal. I said, yes. That was the end of the conversation. Normally, Mother would absolutely insist on having an answer. She grew up in London where it's bad manners not to make an effort at answering questions. People would think you rude. Mother herself is a wizard at small-talking which is an English way of passing the time without allowing the silence in; silence is what they are afraid of. She is driven to destruction when we children forget to say please, is mortified that getting us to write a thank you letter is like milking stones. But everyone knows the Pioneers rejected the European ways and etiquettes when they turned their backs on their old lives in the Diaspora. And that's like throwing the baby clear out of the bath water, Mother says. She has so many funny phrases she brought over from England along with her strange accent and politeness.

When we're getting on Mother's nerves by being *Uncouth* she says, This Country is too hard for me. She means Israeli natives like us are too hard, that's why we're called *Sabres* which is a prickly cactus pear, thorny on the outside, sweet inside. Obviously, she doesn't mean everyone. Not Queenie. Queenie was born in Kurdistan, is graceful as grace itself, graceful as Grace Kelly, Mother says though the joke only works in English. Or Father, she doesn't mean him either, he's a true Gentleman, she's looking at him side-ways now, you can kick the man out of Europe, she says, and they did, kicked him right out those Nazis and their Hungarian sword bearers; but you can't kick the Europe out of the man. She doesn't mean everyone, but we understand, don't we? And that's why Mother is desperate to go back to England, even for a short visit, she misses passing the time of day with complete strangers, people in the park discussing the weather, shop keepers asking whether she's on holiday, because they haven't seen her before, people to talk to who then walk away, you don't have to see them again. Here in our Community everyone stays and stays. Or comes back and keeps coming, like Micah, and every time he's here at Friday Reception meal in the dining room I don't know whether he's going to turn up in my room at night or what.

Not to mention that the English would rather be strung up and fed to wolves than neglect to say please or thank you, Mother misses this every day. When you shop in London even if it's just buying bread there are at least five of each, Mother says. That'll be three-pound six'ee, please. She does a shopkeeper's voice, he didn't go to a good a private school when he was a child and that's why he can't be bothered to say Sixty properly, with a 't'; and he forgets to put an 's' on the end of Pound. Turning a

40

word to plural in English is a children's game, add the 's' and you're done, this person would have no chance in Hebrew where you must consider gender, time and numbers. Mother still gets it wrong quite often; she says Hebrew is going to get her before she gets it.

Thank you! Mother is the customer now, handing over the money. The customer went to a proper school which made her Posh, she sticks her chin forward and her voice is loud and mumbly at the same time, she looks as though her mouth is full of too-hot potatoes. And so on, *thank you* for the money, *thank you* for the change, *thank you* once more, as you walk toward the door, *Cheerio, madam, and thank you, come again!* We fall about laughing when Mother does English accents—Professor Higgins-posh, Eliza Doolittle-Cockney.

The English are obsessed with Class, and with what type of school you went to. The Class System is a complicated code, called *Stereotype*. Or *Prejudice,* according to Ester. We have Prejudice here, too, Ester says, for the different nationalities that make up the melting pot of our Jewish state, the German has his pernickety ways, everything just so; the Moroccan carries a sharp knife in his pocket, Romanians are thieves, Poles like to horde food, Georgians are stupid and that's why it takes ten of them to change a light-bulb. Etcetera. Of course, none of it is true, as everyone knows. But the English, they take their class system so seriously it's a great big thing if anyone ever moves up or down; they'd be as famous as Cinderella after she married the prince. And that's why Professor Higgins will never marry Eliza Doolittle even though they love each other.

Mother said, Abbie will be alright in England, foreign

accents fall outside of the class system; she can be herself. But Father said, if Abbie goes to England, she's sure to marry a tall-dark-handsome man, she's that pretty and clever, and he will keep her inside his castle in the rainy countryside, where she'll do nothing but write letters and hunt on horseback. All Englishmen are impossibly tall and most are filthy rich and where will he, Father, be without me to get him through his days. Mother laughs, English men may be tall and rich but they have pale skin and weak chins and hairless chests, and they've all been to *Posh* boarding-schools which stunted their emotions and made them extremely difficult to live with, she's had to travel all the way here to find a kind, straightforward, hairy-chested man after her own heart, he simply swept her off her feet and everything was lost, she gave up her place at Oxford University, her career as a doctor, breaking Grandma Rose's heart in the process. And she came to live in this God-forsaken furnace she now must call home, and instead of being rich and working in Harley Street she is a poultry farmer and that must be the come-down of the century, you know.

Father says, Rifka, a come-down? Of the century? Just that, but in a tone, she's gone too far. Mother was never a Zionist before she came to visit Uncle David in Palestine the summer after her first year at medical school. But then she met Father and that was that. She still gets sad about the life she left behind, and the things she says would make people in the Community talk, if they heard her. We know she doesn't mean it; she believes farming is our saviour, without it we would still be a nation of pawn-brokers and tailors, living in European ghettos or maybe made extinct by the Nazis.

But she's smiling at Father now, and he is smiling too and walking over to where she's standing by the kettle in the kitchenette. She says, You know, there are compensations for this *in-ex-pli-ca-ble* life choice. She hasn't noticed Father is right behind her now and she's speaking loudly as though he's still in the other room. There are, I promise you, you know, to do with—*Oscar, let me down! Not-in-front-of-the-children, Oscar, put-me-down.* But she's laughing because Father has picked her up and he's dancing, practically on the spot because the *kitchenette* is by far the smallest room in the house, more corridor than a room actually, but with energy, and he's singing, *We're gonna hang out the washing on the Siegfried line*, it's one of her old favourites and the only song in English he knows the words to. Tommy and I make disgusted faces and beg them to stop before it becomes any more embarrassing. Ester says nothing just looks disapproving, but it's too late, Mother isn't protesting anymore, she's singing along:

Whether the weather may be wet or fine,
We just scrub along without a care!

Then we all three of us give up the protest, it's better to sit it out:

We're gonna hang out the washing on the Siegfried line,
If the Siegfried line's still there!
Which I doubt, all right, coming sergeant.

The last line Father says in his own version of an English accent, which is a sort of Russian mix, and he carries Mother off, onto the balcony, there's nowhere else to go except outside. They come back, smiling and exhausted and we stare at them from the sofa, you look like the three monkeys, Mother says as she sits down with a sigh.

Ester can't let anything go. She says, But the shopkeepers, the people in the park, they aren't your friends, Mother, they care nothing for you, however politely they speak. At least here people don't pretend to like you when they don't.

Mother says, There's no harm in a little pretence from time to time, Ester. One day, when you finish staring at your own navel, you might think so too.

Chapter 2: Jordan Valley

28 October 1973

Yesterday we came out of the bomb-shelters. The war had been over for some days, but we weren't allowed out until it was quite safe. It was Thursday but there was no school because most of the men-teachers were still with the army, and the women-teachers were doing the men's jobs milking the cows and driving tractors in the fields. Queenie said we should soak up some sun, maybe go down to the Jordan, the cyclamens should be out, it had rained a lot while we were underground. The late autumn sun was shining through the casuarina trees, too strong for my eyes. It had only just stopped raining, you could smell the ozone in the air, and the grass was ready for cutting just as though everything was normal and nothing much happened in the last two weeks. As though we hadn't had a war. We children wandered on the central lawn, not sure what to do, it wasn't a Saturday so you couldn't go to your parents' rooms during the day either. Then Josh said let's all go on an expedition. To *Abudiya*. Tommy rushed off to get our father's camera even though he's not allowed to use it on his own but Father is away fighting so won't find out. Anya said she wasn't coming, but Saffi brought apples from the kitchen and about twenty of us went off without water or sandwiches, we had to be back by three o'clock for the funerals.

Abudiya is on the other side of the Jordan, nearly where the mountain starts to climb away from the valley. By the narrow gate in the perimeter fence there's a path down to the river. Past Lady's grave, walking down the slope, you can't see the water yet, the river is screened by eucalyptus trees; but you can smell it from the top. I love the smell of the Jordan, it's a home-smell. Tommy says it's sewer but I don't care. And I don't think sewer smells quite like the Jordan does. It's musty, mixed with the strong-tea smell of eucalyptus leaves.

The Jordan has been here forever—even Joshua led the people of Israel across it in the Bible. And Gideon, he was a biblical Judge, made his troops drink from it, and those who drank softly-softly, kneeling gently, capping the water in their hands politely, those he threw out of his army straight away; but those that drank like dogs, gulping as quickly as possible, they were the ones he chose to be his soldiers. This story tells us that manners are all very well in the king's palace or at a Viennese restaurant having your hand kissed by gentlemen (Mother says they do that in real life), but such manners won't always serve you right. It also shows there was a time when it was fine to drink water straight from the Jordan. You can't do that now; it really is full of sewer.

We ran down the slope, not stopping to find snails or eat the sweet hearts of the thistles that materialised by the path since before the war. Let's not stop for anything, Leo said, his father will kill him if we're late for the funerals. Actually, everyone is going to the funerals, except the ten-year-olds, they aren't allowed, not even Tali even though her father, Alex, is one of the soldiers being buried.

Alex used to do lunch duty at our children's house on Saturdays. He was a nice man, often singing Sabbath songs at Friday Reception Meals and once, after the first rain, he drove us all in a tractor and trailer to the Northern Pasture to look for mushrooms. He knew all the different types, whether they are poisonous or good to eat.

But when we got to the bottom of the hill everyone did stand and look. You can't walk across the river without stopping, you can't ignore it, not when you haven't seen it since the first rain, and you can't ignore it when they have just opened the dam and the water—oh, instead of trickling slowly around the base of each stone, the water gushes fast and furious, rising nearly up to the bridge itself! We leaned against the railing on the side of the bridge, and we watched.

Until Josh broke the silence. Well I tell you, friends, you can go all around the world, twice, and still you won't lay eyes on a magnificent sight like this one.

A silent agreement. Then, Have you ever been abroad, Josh? It was Daniel. Daniel joined Tommy and Josh's group last summer. His father is a Son of our Community, which means he was born here. But he married an English woman (a Gentile, Rita has told Leo!) and went to live in London. There Daniel was born, and then the English woman turned to alcohol or ended up in a mental home, or maybe both. And Daniel got into trouble with the London police, Rita wouldn't tell Leo what sort of trouble, probably to do with drugs, and when I asked Tommy, he said to mind my own business, so he doesn't know either. The London police said Daniel must go to children's prison, but his father had a better idea and asked if Daniel could be shipped off to a Kibbutz Community instead. And the police evidently didn't mind because here he is, living with us. Daniel doesn't understand Josh. He says, Ever seen Buckingham Palace? Walked down St. James Park

Josh ignores him. We're all quiet, waiting for him to continue. He says, The Jordan originates in the north, it gathers water from the Lebanon, icy springs and rain water, and flows down through the Syrian-African Rift valley, until it reaches us, here in the Jordan Valley. Two hundred metres below sea level. He raises his voice, but only slightly, In and out of our lake Kinneret, (turning towards Daniel), otherwise known as the Sea of Galilee, and on to this very spot, under this bridge, and down, down, towards the centre of the earth, the Dead Sea; the lowest place in the world. Think about it, friends. Still facing Daniel, It is ever changing. This water has just arrived, yet it has always been here. Cherish this moment.

I love listening to Josh. He's only fifteen, but always knows what to say. And he loves our Country. I love our Country too, and the Jordan Valley where we live but I don't have such beautiful words to describe them. Josh had been walking out with Anya for a year when the war broke out. In the bomb-shelter he told her that having a girlfriend was "too frivolous" in war time, and that was that. Hence why she didn't come on this walk, probably. He still never looks at me, or talks to me although he does of course know who I am. Everyone knows everyone in our Community. Not like in London or New York where you can fall in the street and people will step over you and continue walking. No one is safe in London or New York, and that's why Daniel's mother kept a whistle round her neck in case of an attack so she can blow it and the attacker would run away. And this must mean she's not a patient in a mental institution but only an alcoholic after all.

Saffi and I scrambled down the bank to get eucalyptus leaves for tea. Then we ran after the others. We were running and laughing, lifting our faces to the sunshine. It was good to be out of doors. We caught up with them by the Apple of Sodom tree. Daniel was laughing; a tree called Sodom. People in England know next to nothing about the Bible, which they call Old Testament. So all they can think of when they hear Sodom is homosexual sex. Whereas the point is that the Sodomites were sinners but even so Abraham tried his hardest to save them and he even argued with God Himself to do that. I hope I would have the courage to do what Abraham did, if ever I need to. Not everyone would. Noah, for example. God told him that his family would be saved from the Flood, and he didn't try to save a single other person. Just got on with building the ark.

We ate the bitter-sweet flesh of the Apples of Sodom. They are not actually apples; some of the stones are so big and the flesh so meagre there's really nothing but skin. You wouldn't think to put them in a fruit bowl at home, but there's a special kind of fun in finding food on walks. Mother calls it food-for-free, something she brought from London, England, here all food is free to us. Usually, I walk as near as possible to Josh, he's always pronouncing facts I never knew and having an opinion about everything. He listens to the radio and discusses newspaper articles with his father Dov, our shoemaker. They do this over coffee-and-biscuits at family time,

Tommy told me, he and Josh are best friends. Tommy would rather skip coffee-and-biscuit altogether than talk about the news; except maybe football news.

But today Josh didn't talk much. Tommy was practising his English on Daniel, and maybe there was no one else worth having a conversation with. So I was talking with Saffi, one of the Arab builders had puppies before the war, we were wondering if Queenie would let us adopt one now Lady was dead. And I noticed Josh had fallen into step with us. Saffi knows I'm in love with him, she's the only one, and so she made herself disappear from view practically in mid-sentence and we, Josh and I, continued to walk, but in silence.

The other children were still talking but I couldn't hear what they were saying, the silence between us was screaming in my ears, and my throat pressed down on my stomach so that even if I could think of something to say, I wouldn't have been able to say it. And my right arm, the one closest to him, was aching. He wasn't close, you have to keep to one of the deep tractor wheel tracks on the path, quite far apart, the middle is piled-up mud. So we were walking in the two tractor tracks, and silence was hovering in the middle, and I looked ahead only, and to the left away from him, thinking, if it's a chance he's walking next to me, he'll just drift away in a minute. But he didn't, all the way to Abudiya.

Some people say this is where the Garden of Eden actually, *actually*, was. The mound of earth called Abudiya used to be a thriving Arab village which spread down and along the little valley called Fijas. Archaeologists had been digging here before the war, because buried beneath the abandoned village are six other villages, going all the way back to the Stone Age. Last spring when we walked down here to look for daffodils, I found a chiselled stone knife. Mona said it was a true Stone-Age Article.

When the Pioneers of our Community first came to live here in 1927 the Arab villagers were their neighbours. But then 1948 came, and the War of Independence, and the Arabs ran away and never came back.

Why not? says Daniel. Why haven't they come back? No one answers him, we're waiting for Josh to explain, but he says, Let's go to the mayor's house.

Tommy climbs up, gathering wood for a fire, and we follow him like a conquering army, Joshua's Army storming the city of Jericho after the walls came tumbling down. We're spread across the side of the hill, fighting thistles with sticks as we go. With Josh at their helm, the boys are sword-bearing soldiers. They shout and fight imaginary Arabs defending their fallen fortress. They advance in formation, slaying the enemy with a stroke of their arm and move quickly on and up to the top. Here they pose for a victorious photograph which Tommy takes an age over, measuring light intensity, adjusting shutter speed, telling them to look this way, no, the other way, just as Father does. By the time we girls get to the top, they are in full occupation of the village, sweaty and pleased.

The Mayor's House is the only one still standing in the village. The rest are in ruin, ragged stone walls of various heights. We sit inside the house, which is just a room. The boys break the sticks for a fire and Tommy takes out a pot and water for eucalyptus leaves tea. Its smell hovers in the still air, lovely and strong. But its taste is bitter. One hot cup goes around the room. No one talks much. And it turns out no one has a watch so the boys go outside to check where the sun is in the sky, stand around discussing what time it probably is. We mustn't be late for the funerals.

Imagine if they came back, Saffi says.

Who?

The Arabs. The ones who lived here.

They're probably dead already.

Not all of them, it was only, maybe, thirty years ago. Some of them were children.

Maybe they have new homes.

Still—

Well, they can't come back; just let them try. It's Josh, he appears in the lit open doorway; all eyes are on him. He says, This is ours now. All of it! From the Jordan to the sea. Get it? If they come back, we'll say, *Ruch min hoon!* Get away! He stands like a great Commander, berating the enemy for not accepting defeat gracefully. This is life, see? He says to all of us. You have to get it into your heads: it's them or us. Pause. And when I'm old enough I'm going to help make sure it's not them. I'm going to be a fighter pilot. I would not sit around and let *Ahmed* or *Abdullah* take my land away from me.

Well, there's no answering Josh when he's in this mood, not that I would know how to argue against him even if he were in a different mood. He just always has the right words to put yours down. Then Tommy said he thinks it's time to go. So we hurried down the mound, along the dirt track by the river, across the bridge and up the hill, walking fast in case they got the sun wrong, in case we were late for the funerals.

These were my first funerals, not counting the one we gave Lady two summers ago. We were now in secondary school, so old enough to go. Everyone was congregated by the western entrance to the Dining Room, standing in silence or speaking quietly. Many of the Members had rushed home from work to change into Saturday clothes. Mother wore the weddings-and-funerals black dress she bought in Oxford Street, London, years ago. It makes her look lady-like. Also foreign. Which is embarrassing. She was standing next to Father; heads together; they didn't notice me. Father was in army uniform, an M16 on his shoulder, I hadn't seen him since before he joined the fighting two weeks ago. The coffins were perched on tables, draped with Israel flags, pale blue and white, a Star of David over the top.

There were three coffins at the top of the Dining Room steps, set on three Dining Room tables; in them lay Joseph and Ella's son Ehud, Tali's father Alex, and Noam, who was a year younger than Ester. Noam had been so quiet I don't think I'd ever heard him talk and now I never will. I stood with Saffi and Anya. Watching.

Why are they burying them in a coffin? Anya's whisper in my ear.

How else would they be buried? I asked. Sometimes it's annoying to have Anya around, how she understands nothing.

Isn't this a Jewish burial? They should be shrouded not shut in a box like *Goys,* she retorted, like gentiles. Is anyone even going to say *Kaddish* over their graves?

We were still waiting for the funerals to get underway, and obviously she did need to understand. So even though I don't care whether we live by the rules of Judaism I said,

No one is going to say *Kaddish*; we don't pray. I was almost certain that was the case. And, I added, religious people in our Country try to control us secular Jews.

But why not give Jewish men a Jewish funeral?

The point is, I said patiently, but firmly, we refuse to abide by their rules. It's to do with the Socialist Revolution. We rejected the old ways. And we keep God out of everything. That's what we do.

The coffin bearers lifted the coffins. They walked slowly towards the cemetery and we followed, a procession towards the Community gate and along the security road which rings the outside of the perimeter fence. Anya said, You mustn't talk like that about God, Abbie.

She doesn't get it. God has chosen us of all nations to be a Light Unto Others. But we are secular Jews, and we refuse to live by His rules, such as praying three times a day or eating *Kosher* food. That's why religious people disapprove of us; say we Seculars are worse than the *Goyim*, the Gentiles. They even think we're worse than the Arabs, because we have a choice and they don't.

Religious parties have been in every one of our Country's governments since 1948, independence, when the British were kicked out and good riddance. So even though the religious are in the minority, they get to tell us how we live, what we learn at school, who can get married, who is a proper Jew and may come to live here. Because of them there are no buses or open shops on high days or holidays, and that's why the War we've just had was started on *Yom Kippur*, Day of Atonement, holiest day of the year. The Arabs chose this day, knowing there would be no radio service in the Country, no way to let everyone know about an emergency, and so they marched through every border, killing our regular border guard soldiers, and it took hours and days to bring in all our Reservists; and that's why we nearly lost the War and now Golda Meir will have to resign and we won't have a woman Prime Minister anymore. All this I thought Anya ought to understand; but in the end all I said was, Why not? I don't care about God.

Shhhh! Saffi's elbow in my ribs. We were walking behind the three coffins. They had been placed on a flat trailer borrowed from the banana fields, it was draped with a huge black cloth. I wondered whether someone had swept it clean; banana stains never come out however much you try to wash them. The green John Deer towed the trailer and the bearers walked alongside it, one arm resting on the edge, making sure no coffin fell off, and no dead body rolled out for all to see. There was silence now among the people, only the tractor purring up front, and the starlings screaming their hearts out in the trees.

The cemetery is on the edge of the hill. It overlooks the bend of the Jordan where the Pioneers settled in the 1920s, where they lived in mud-huts until it was time to move to a permanent spot which is where our Community is. Standing in the crowd with Anya and Sara, I looked behind us, down at the palm plantation. It's not the usual angle, normally palm trees tower over you, and the sky paints the spaces around their canopies bright blue or grey, maybe ten or more metres high. There were about two hundred trees, impassive in dead-straight rows. At the top, their green feather-leaves jutted out in all directions, like Josh's unruly hair. Beneath the leaves, partially hidden were bright orange date-laden fronds, hanging like frowns or tears. The canopies were balanced delicately on single long slender legs, leaning slightly towards each other here and there, as though heads-together mourning the dead. But the people of our Community did their mourning alone.

The Members gathered around Ehud's grave; it was the first to be filled. Joseph and Ella stood at the front, flanked by Amalia and Nira, their twin daughters. Joseph is one of the first Sons of our Community, born when the Pioneers worked all day and then danced all night with the joy of living the Zionist dream and of being young together. And in between working and dancing they had passionate debates about equality and justice, and the evils of bourgeois values.

Mona read the eulogy. It wasn't long, Ehud was only 25 when a piece of Syrian shrapnel lodged into his brain through his left eye. She'd been his teacher at school. A good-looking boy who had turned into a handsome, popular young man. She had spoken to him only a few weeks before. He was about to be discharged after serving as an officer in the standing army. He was looking forward to coming home and getting back to working in the palm plantations, the ones we can see below us in the valley. He'd already agreed to join the Members Committee with a view to chairing it after a couple of years. He was a principled man, standing up for the underdog at every opportunity; a natural leader loved by friends; a superb officer worshipped by subordinates; a shining light; a great future ahead. Heartbreakingly, in that last conversation he had told her that in all the years of living away, what he missed most about home was walking down to the Jordan and among the palm trees. Now will he rest in peace in this earth, overlooking the landscape he so loved. Mona was quiet then, I thought she was finished. The grave-diggers looked around and clutching their shovels, wondered whether it was their turn, whether it was time to shovel the mound of earth that lay in wait by the side of the grave. But then, Mona's voice again reciting a prayer. *God full of mercy* is a prayer for the dead, but there's a twist and the poet throws it back in our faces, if God were not so full of mercy there would have been mercy left over for the rest of us down here in the world.

We stood still, stony faced. Ella had her hand on Joseph's arm. Her shoulders were hunched, her face stricken. No one was crying, except Ehud's girlfriend. They'd actually broken up six months ago, said my sort-of-friend Sara, so inappropriate, she didn't really know Ehud at all. Gun shots in the air, military honour style, the coffin is lowered, earth shovelled in, some rocks make hollow sounds on the wooden lid. Then people move towards the grave, mostly placing a stone or flower onto the fresh earth, but some just stand for a moment. It was a slow procession. I turned my head away, towards the valley below and the palms again. Now the sight of those trees, each a work of nature's art, grabbed at my heart and for a moment it was hard to keep seeing so much beauty. I felt tears well in my throat and had to swallow hard to stop them, this sadness is not mine and it's not my place to cry. Joseph and Ella continued to stand in front of the mound. Members filed slowly past, then headed for the next grave. Some stopped briefly to touch one or both gently on the shoulder. Joseph and Ella were still, never said a word or moved a muscle, like two pillars of salt.

Then Tali's father was being buried in the plot next to his sister Annushka. She'd died of heart failure. I remember the perfume she wore to Sabbath reception meals in the Dining Room on Friday nights, how Father would get impatient if we were late, Come on, Rifka, if we don't leave now Annushka will be walking ahead of us and I'll be stuck smelling her soap all the way to the Dining Room. And Mother, I can't do up my necklace, Oscar, why don't you help me instead of complaining about Annushka. She's a holocaust survivor, you know, we shouldn't begrudge her indulging in a little luxury on a Friday night, God knows she's endured enough suffering! ...and it isn't soap, you know, it's perfume. Mother always speaks in paragraphs when she's pointing out why people are wrong to think as they do.

I felt incredibly tired. I wanted nothing more than to sit down but who would dare in the middle of a triple funeral? People shifted and shuffled, adults standing in the way of my view. Solomon stepped forward to the grave, holding sheets of paper in his one hand, trying to fish a pair of reading glasses from his shirt pocket with the same hand, he lost the other one in Suez, 1956. This was taking quite a long time and people shifted and shuffled some more, until one of the sheets got away and Solomon tried to retrieve it, but dropped the other one in the process, and the afternoon breeze came creeping through the crowd and lifted them both so for a moment they floated peacefully above the people's heads, lined sheets of paper, crowded with dense, black-ink writing, like a message from God, or something. Somebody caught one sheet, but it looked as though the other was going to float into the open grave, then a brave person would have to go down and fetch it, everybody was imagining this terrible eventuality and watching, paralysed by the horror of it, as the paper glided slowly over the mouth of the grave and landed on the edge the other side. The corners continued to flap a little as though it were not quite finished, was trying to take off again but at the centre you could see a wet patch forming, it was stuck to the damp rained-on earth. Mona took a small step, picked it up and handed it back to Solomon. Now he was ready to start.

He talked about Alexander, Tali's father, how as a very young child living in a Polish town near Warsaw, he became ill with smallpox and was sent to stay with an old couple who had worked in his father's bakery business before retiring to the country. Alex was one of seven children so it was considered too dangerous to let him stay in the house with the smallpox contagion. The old couple lived on their own, and Alex's parents paid them money to house and feed him while he was ill, and they made Annushka who was fourteen and the oldest girl go with him so she could look after him. The two stayed with the old couple for a month and Alex recovered and was very homesick indeed but then Annushka became ill and so they stayed another month. Those were the two months in which the world of the Jews in their home town was shattered because the Nazi invasion took place. Everyone was taken out of their homes, given one hour to pack, and lined up and made to walk to the train station where cattle trains waited to take them to the Warsaw ghetto where they stayed for a time, some dying of disease or starvation, and some still living when the ghetto was cleared and it was off to the Auschwitz extermination camps, their last station stop.

But Alex and Annushka knew nothing about what had happened to their family, they were with the old couple, staying in a remote and cut-off part having hardly any contact with the outside world. So, when Annushka finally felt well enough to go home, the old couple took them in a horse-drawn cart to the nearest village and they waited for the train, it was a long wait and it was dark by the time they got off at the station in their home town. The two children walked hand in hand, taking the same steps as their parents and brothers and sisters, their uncle and aunt and cousins, their neighbours, friends and teachers in the little Jewish school, the same steps they all took, only they were going in the opposite direction. Annushka said later she was always and forever haunted by this walk home from the train station, a terrible cold heavy dread coming over her and she felt a great weight on her heart but dismissed those feelings, thinking maybe she was still a little ill, not quite recovered, but then little Alex, chattering and excited to go home, went very quiet as though he, too, sensed the catastrophe in the air.

Solomon was telling the story of how Alex survived the holocaust as the afternoon western wind picked up and it became difficult to hear his cigarette-crackle voice. I was straining to see him so I could watch his mouth moving, craning my head, when the shuffling and shifting from moments before resumed next to me, a tall soldier in dusty uniform was standing too close. Alex and Annushka arrived at their home, their family had to leave in a rush and some supper dishes were still on the dining room table, the house had been looted after they'd gone and there was a dreadful mess. They knocked on their Jewish neighbours' door, house after house, but they were all empty and so in the cold dark night they walked to the other side of town to the house of their cook and their gardener who were married to each other and were not Jewish. When she opened the door, the cook looked like she'd seen two ghosts, and she pulled them into the house for fear of someone recognising them and knowing them to be Jewish.

She told them what had happened to the Jews of the town, and they cried together, Annushka hanging on to Alex, Alex hanging on back, and the cook hugging both, saying through her sobs, poor children, poor little children, poor little wretched children. But then she wiped her tears and went back in the kitchen and soon returned with food parcels. She said they had to go; she had already taken a great risk letting them in her house. The children cried more, they had no idea where to go, but the gardener came in and said he would walk them to the edge of town and he did and they carried on walking at night, hiding and sleeping by day, and then their food ran out and it looked as though that was the end, but a miracle happened and they found themselves outside the little village where the old couple had taken them to the train station all that time ago, and made their way to the old couple's house and the old woman opened the door and she looked as though she'd seen two ghosts and this time they really did look like ghosts, they were thin and pale and dirty. The old woman took them in and that's how Alex and Annushka were saved. And in the Avenue of the Righteous Among the Nations in *Yad Vashem* there's an olive tree with the old couple's name on.

Solomon paused, it looked as though he might have finished, but he was just swapping the two sheets of paper so he could carry on. After what had happened earlier, he was being extra careful and taking a long time.

Really, I ask you, what's Solomon thinking of? Rita's voice was behind me, sighing and whispering loudly.

Huh? Shshsh was her husband Ezra's response. It wasn't time to talk yet, anyone could tell that.

My feet are killing me, is he never going to end it? Rita continued.

Well this *is* the end, Rita. Of *Alex*. And Solomon has been *asked* to write a *eulogy*. Ezra kept his voice down at *piano*, doing *pianissimo* reverse-emphasis of some words.

This isn't a *eulogy*, Ezra, it's a *biography*. It's *inappropriate* and *you-know-it*. We have *three* funerals to get through before dark. Rita used the same reverse dynamics, *pianissimo, piano, diminuendo*.

Shhhhhh. Quiet! It was Leo, *mezzo-forte*; he stood next to Ezra. Poor him for having such embarrassing parents.

Solomon was not going to let either of the sheets of paper get away this time—he took the back one between his teeth and swapped it to the front without incident, but it turned out the manoeuvre had caused the front sheet to be up-side-down and there was a further pause for shuffling and murmurings while he dealt with this new problem.

This is what Righteous Among the Nations is: Most Europeans just sat back and watched us being murdered by the Nazis. Some even collaborated, like the Hungarians who went into Yugoslavia and killed Father's parents with all the other Jews of their city, Novisad. But others were different, and they are those Righteous people. The price for helping Jews was death, sometimes for the whole Righteous family, or the whole village for good measure. If I were a *Goy* in Europe during the holocaust, I would be a Righteous person. Whatever the cost.

Solomon was ready again. He cleared his throat.

Hello Abigail. The dusty soldier standing too close was talking. It was Micah. His eyes were smiling and they were pink. Had he been crying? I remembered he and Ehud were about the same age. They'd probably been friends. He said, Come on, let's get out of here.

Night Swimming

We walked out of the cemetery, Micah and I. *Micah and I?* It sounds quite, *quite* different to what this actually was. We turned down towards the river, past the palm trees, then to the bridge, where I'd stood with my friends earlier that day. I didn't look back to see if anyone had noticed us slipping away. It was fine for me to miss the third burial; I didn't know Noam at all and two funerals in one day was enough. But I didn't think I wanted anyone to ask what I was doing walking out with Micah. How would I answer that question? What was happening? What on earth was going on between Micah and me? I have no idea. We were not boy and girlfriend; I'm almost certain about that. We had hardly ever talked before, even including the night we buried Lady two summers ago. When I was younger and Ester was still at school, he used to sometimes come to my parents' room in the afternoons with her. But then he'd only ever look at me and smile while Ester told me off for doing something normal like playing my recorder or getting all my own books out, I have seven, not including the *Noddy* ones Grandma Rose used to give me for my birthdays when I was little. Ester can be so mean when her friends are around. Tommy once said she was in love with Micah. Don't be ridiculous, she snapped and twisted his ear till he cried; they were just friends, she said. And plus, in case Tommy hadn't noticed, she already had a boyfriend.

I'm not even sure I like Micah. Not that much. And he isn't good-looking like Josh, but that may just be because he is quite old, maybe twenty-five even, and besides, Josh isn't here with me, is he? And his breath smelled of cigarette smoke, like it did that long-ago night. Normally, I like the smell, especially on Grandma Rose. She smokes like a train engine and lets me light her cigarettes for her by myself, she even showed me how to blow smoke rings. You do that without inhaling. But on Micah, the smokiness is a little bit repellent. Yellow teeth are also not a good look in a younger man, it doesn't matter so much if you're as old as Grandma Rose.

And yet... and yet it was thrilling he was walking next to me, as though right now there was nowhere he would rather be. We were silent for the longest time. I don't like silences; they are oppressive to me. Usually, I try to break them, say something, anything, even if it's inappropriate. I get this habit from Mother; I mean the habit of breaking silences; inappropriateness I learned all by myself.

I thought about Mother doing her polite English performance the summer before, how Father carried her in his arms, and they sang the Siegfried Line song; how we laughed with joy and embarrassment, not knowing that Mother really does miss England, that she misses her family deeply and sadly; and not thinking that there will soon be another war, just assuming Tali will always have a father and Joseph and Ella will always have a son. This scene of fleeting family happiness was nothing to do with the Here of Micah and Me, down by the Jordan; it had nothing to do with the Now of everything being confusion and wonder. This safe, long-ago time was a comfort in the cold silence.

What song is that? Micah was talking. I had been humming *Hang up the washing on the Siegfried Line,* my heart smiling with Mother and Father's love for each other. Will anyone ever love me so well? Micah keeps catching me by surprise, crashing like a bulldozer into the space around me.

Oh, nothing. Just an old English… a war song. I didn't feel like saying anything else, didn't really feel like helping him make our silence less oppressive. That was his job, didn't he say, Come on, let's get out of here? I was a passenger in this drama bus, this event he had created, for yet unknowable reasons. The conversation was his responsibility now. And yet, I did want to ask him, to ask what he wanted me for. What was he doing here? Why me? Probably this would expose how young and naïve I am, and maybe he would be forced to say, I just want to lie with you, that's what I brought you here for, no big deal; we're both grown up, aren't we? And then I would die. Of awkwardness. On the spot.

Which war? Him again.

Second World, I said. It's Mother who calls it A War Song. In England, the First World War is The Great War, and the Second is simply The War. You couldn't do the same in our country without getting very confused. Even in my own thirteen years, we've had three already, and Mother and Father have lived through three more on top of that. But Micah wouldn't want to know any of this, would he; does he wonder what I'm thinking, he hasn't asked a single question of me, yet? None. And I thought, shouldn't I be with Saffi, or Leo, even Anya, now she's not walking out with Josh anymore. I felt lonely and small. It was exciting too. Like being a pioneer, a traveller in a foreign, new-found land.

How does it go? Sing it again. He smiled.

I smiled back. But I'm not going to sing to him. Not in English or any language. No way!

So I asked if he was, had been, a friend of Ehud's, is that why he came to the funeral? He said they'd been in the same group from when they were babies. And he talked about something that happened when they were younger, about my age, oh, that's *years* ago, when *I* was not even *born!* He said a couple of older boys bullied Ehud, called him names, and in the end, he wouldn't go to the Dining Room in case the bullies were there, and Micah took food for him and went up to the two boys and told them to cut it out even though they were older and stronger than he was, he stood up to them and they did, they stopped. He looked at me then, and the smile in his eyes, I think I was meant to appreciate this, but I was thinking, that's showing off. But also, I was wondering, so is he trying to impress me? Does he care about what I think? Is he? Does he? And I thought I should stand up to Leo, he can be mean to Shira. He's my friend and would probably listen to me.

We reached the river and stood on the bridge, leaning

over the railings, looking west through the trees at the hills and the sinking sun. The Jordan was fast and furious, its murky water dark, the round black granite stepping-stones menacing among the ripples, like evil spirits. I wondered if it was time to go back next, in a minute, but Micah said, Shall we have a swim? I know a pool downstream. And when I hesitated, he said, Come, it's not far.

We walked along the bank; round the bend the river broadened and the water looked calm. I sat on a eucalyptus tree root. He took his clothes off. All of them. And waded through the mud and reeds, stood briefly still, knees-deep, shadowy now in the ebbing light. Then he leaped in, head first, with a big, inelegant splash. I wondered whether he was wondering what I was thinking, if I was admiring his dive, his bravery in winter cold. It was a while before he emerged again, splattering, brushing the hair off his face with one hand like an old man, not the cocky sideways flick of the head our boys think so manly.

I hit a stone on the way down, he said, fingering his head, looking for a wound.

Does it hurt?

Yes. No. No, it doesn't, I'm fine, I'm going to be fine. Come in. The water's warm, really. He laughed.

I'm wondering about whirlpools, I said, and thought of Queenie. She is terrified of whirlpools; has made us all promise not to swim when the dam is open and the river high. Tommy and Josh got into trouble last winter when they took Daniel swimming, he's never learned to do it properly, and was swept downstream and over to the other side and instead of walking the extra kilometre to the bridge they persuaded him to swim back, they knew what to do in a crisis, had already started training as assistant lifeguards, had two first aid lessons and one practical in a pool. As they told Father. Father was furious. He was speechless, just speechless, which wasn't so, because he did go on talking.

They were irresponsible, *wholly! And completely!* irresponsible. Their behaviour was truly beyond, *beyond...* endurance. That's how Father talks when he's upset, which is very rarely. Taking a new boy out of bounds was bad enough. But! But insisting he should swim back across! That was... it was *idiocy!* Daniel might have drowned, do you realise?! Do you, I don't think so, I am... I'm speechless, he said again, because by now he'd had his say and the room was too small for both him and Tommy to be in at the same time. He put on his coat and looked around for the cigarette box.

In fact Daniel nearly did drown, he was so weakened by the second crossing and swallowing litres water, they had to carry him all the way up the hill and into bed where he stayed a whole week, he also had flu from being cold and wet.

And Tommy and Josh were barred from Tuesday night films for two weeks and that's how they missed watching the best film ever. Full stop. It was *Dr. Zhivago*, they were devastated. And the next week they were going to miss *Bonnie and Clyde* with Warren Beatty, the best-looking man in the world. Full stop also. Even Father felt sorry for them, he had time to recover from being so angry. Well, missing two such great films, that was too much, so they sneaked out of their room and watched, hiding under the filming hut where Josh saw a snake, but kept very still till it slid away.

Don't worry, Micah was saying, no whirlpools here; but if it pulls you down, just go with it to the bottom and kick off on the diagonal.

Everyone knows what you're supposed to do in case of a whirlpool. I listened to his watery snorts, swimming away. In the thickening darkness I took my clothes off, and waded in. The muddy bottom was laced with broken reeds and branches. Plunging was easier than walking on that mess. The water, black and soft, welcomed me with a gentle sigh. It was strange and wonderful, swimming in the near darkness; stranger to do it without the other children, my friends. And strangest that the person who was there was Micah. I tried to pretend I was alone. The thought of him, in the water quite close, was so curious and thrilling.

But he was circling me, quietly, from a distance, and I circled back. We were catfishes, sleek, at ease in our watery home, round and round, slowly, slowly, no time except the Now. When the circles got too small, I dived down. Silence. Gliding along the bottom, my stomach brushed lightly against a branch. I hung on, hovering in the cool peace. I can hold my breath for two minutes or more, but way before then the murky darkness was closing on me. Will I find the surface of the water again? What if I get entangled in reeds? My naked body will be discovered down river and my parents will never know. They'll never understand what took me here tonight. My heart beat fast and I could feel the warmth of tears before the river took them in. It was romantic, even poetic. Would I be a poet when I'm all grown and know what men and women do once they had walked into the setting sun? My poem will be called, *River by moonlight*. I was pleased with that. Then Micah was behind me, his brief, light touch on my catfish back. Just that.

I kicked hard against the branch, eyes open, floating up, up, the unsuspecting surface breaking in my face, and I was breathing. The moon was out. The trees silhouettes against the nearly-blackness of the sky. I trod water and the surface broke again, he was right there. I could hear the effort of his breath, feel the currents of his thrashing arms.

Are you cold? His breathless wet whisper, so close. The weight of what might be about to happen made my head spin.

Yes, I think so. I'm going out now. I glided past him, Catfish-like. An arm collided with my waist, turning chance into a momentary stroke.

When he came out, I looked away. Dressed, we walked back to the bridge and stood still for a moment. The moon had climbed above the trees. It shone onto the reeds we had just trodden. We looked towards where the water was assembling its broken light shards. I thought, we'll probably go back now, I'm ready to return. I thought, this wasn't bad, maybe I like him more than I'd imagined. I thought, it's nice to stand this close, perhaps we'd do it all again sometime. But then, quite suddenly he turned my head towards him and we kissed, it was not so disgusting at first, I had to breathe in through my nose and the weakness in my shoulders made my arms drop to the sides. Round and round my stomach turned like an audition for the circus, I had to hope it doesn't bounce right up my throat. It was confusion, thrill and drama. I thought, still not so bad, that's it then, my first kiss. I thought of Josh. I thought, I've done it now, like they do in the movies, and the feeling was coming back into my hands, it was a while, and it was fine. But then. Then he opened his mouth, lips to lips still and his tongue. Oh, I took five seconds, or straight away I staggered back, two steps, he knew I'd been surprised. He looked at me. His face a shadow. I couldn't see his smile, if it were there. The river held our secret in its gentle flow.

Come, he said and caught hold of my hand. We headed off, not home but in the opposite direction, for the valley. I wasn't scared. The darkness was whole, except around the moon, a large wheel of slow-receding light, and the hyenas were lamenting in a field nearby. Ahead rose Abudiya, the Arab village, its houses silhouettes against the sky. You couldn't tell they had no roofs. You couldn't tell their people went away so many years before. It might have been an ordinary hill with ordinary families, fast sleeping in their beds.

I wonder where they're sleeping tonight, the Abudiya people. My voice surprised our silence, we hadn't spoken since the bridge.

They're in Syria. Or Jordan. That's where they went.

Something made a splash in the water, an owl or a bat. I thought of the Arabs, the villagers, leaving; how they crossed the river in the dead of night, 1948, all those years ago. It was before the bridge was built, and so they crossed by foot and the sound of their feet walking through the muddy water, was a constant, lingering lament. And in the silvery darkness I could almost see them, a great long convoy, with their old and young and livestock and their horses and donkeys pulling carts of furniture and crates of bedding. And I could hear their feet striding doggedly through the water, and the splashing of their steps spelling out the words, Remember us, Remember us, Remember. It took three days for all the villagers to cross the river. And after three days nothing was left behind except the stone-built one-roomed houses on the hill.

But why did they? Go, I mean.

Were we having a grown-up conversation, Micah and I? It wasn't that I had previously thought they left simply to oblige us Jewish people, to give us more space to build our Promised Land. It was just it hadn't occurred to me to ask before. They had been there, now they're gone, the end.

Micah said, They ran away because they were afraid of being slaughtered by us, once the British went back home. Of course, that was a fallacy, Arab propaganda; we would never have treated them so.

It's sad, having to leave your village behind, I said, thinking of Father, whose old house in Yugoslavia is now home to three strange families. My aunt, his sister Hermina, went to see it a few years ago, with her husband, Uncle Aaron. The woman who opened the door wouldn't let them in when they told her who they were, she was afraid they were there to claim their house back. But Uncle Aaron is a lawyer; they don't need any more money.

Sad, yes, Micah said and his thin smile, his eyes were on me again. But, you know, they did have a choice; and besides, that's war, Abigail; bad things happen.

It is. They do. We turned off the path to the river again, by the ancient flour mill. Looking up at the village and the moon behind. It was beautiful, not in a picture-postcard way, but heavy, rough; jagged like a fatal wound. We sat by the river bend, flat like a beach. Just for tonight, the weight of what had passed between us drew us near in a familiar peace. I wasn't scared.

You know, they're digging here for Stone Age presence, he said, and I thought about the chiselled stone I had found there last year, probably a knife or spear head, quite small. I still have it in my drawer at home. Maybe it was used for fishing, at the end of a long reed. He lay back, both hands behind his head. Long pause, deep breath, then sigh. Aaaah—all the stars are out tonight.

I lay next to him. They were. Big Bear and Orion, Little Bear, the Northern Star, I know them all.

He said, They think this is the Garden of Eden, the actual one.

We were talking to and fro, as if normal, as though he wasn't a man and I wasn't just a child, too young, scared of tongues-in kissing. This was a place of longing, of regret.

I said, So Adam and Eve were exiled like the villagers.

Don't forget the ancient Jews, he said. They lived here much before the Arabs came. They were exiled too, this was our Promised Land. Still is.

His hand crept over to hold mine. And it was comfortable, no fuss, no too-wet kiss, no shuddering dark watery pursuits. Just fine.

Tell me something, Abigail. His head turned towards me. I could hear the air going up and down his nostrils.

What?

Something… anything. What did you think of the funerals?

It was another age-gap reminder. I said, Well I haven't been before. And I liked what Solomon said about Tali's father, I mean, Alex—and Annushka in the Holocaust. I was trying to remember it so I can write it down later. When I get back.

I hadn't meant to tell him about my diary. But he didn't notice.

Yes, incredible survival. He chuckled, I tell you, Solomon is a strange man, but he can tell a story—it's a gift. He had us all in the palm of his hand, didn't he? The right one, of course. The right hand.

And at that, he snorted, it was a joke. My brain raced in search of more words, but nothing turned up. Nothing suitable.

Solomon lives near my parents. He lost his left arm in the Suez Operation of 1956. When not teaching us history he tends the gardens of the neighbourhood, my parents' too. Father is a farmer and has no interest in non-productive plants. Like roses. And mother is too tired after working all day in the henhouses, lifting and carrying, it's the worst thing for her back, you know, she really should change to something less demanding, Father says, but she won't. Ester says farming is Mother's way of Realising the Zionist Ideal. Mother thinks she needs to justify her choice in following this dream to our country, because it's what made her leave so much behind in England.

Ester always sees the worst in everybody. As though they are automates, following predetermined destinies. She watches people like an anthropologist would, Mother says. With detached scientific interest. She knows so much she's impossible to ever argue with. But of my two siblings, Tommy is the more annoying. By far. So, anyway, after work, Mother has us children to cope with. Even though no one else in my group is in a family with fewer than four children, she only had the strength for three. And committee meetings and what-not in the evenings. And that's why she has no energy for gardening. So they leave it to Solomon.

It's not clear what Solomon spends his gardening time doing. He is out there afternoons and evenings, most days, but still, the garden looks—well, second rate, neglected, wild even. Two massive pecan trees take up half the space between the house and pavement. The rest is lonely, indistinct beds of roses, sweet peas and violets, with wasteland in between. More roses and gerberas at the front, and a Wondering Jew covering up the rest. That's all. Mainly, he seems to irrigate.

Aunt Betty finds Solomon, whom she calls The Gardener, hilarious. What does The Gardener do there, hour upon hour? she asks in a hushed voice. It's gone dark, soon she and David will return to Tel Aviv. But Solomon is still rustling about outside our window.

Who do you mean? Mother is so used to him being in the garden she doesn't think it strange or unusual anymore.

The Gardener, Rifka. You know, *Sisyphus*, Betty replies. And she bursts out, laughter gushing like water from a burst pipe, high and loud, head tipped back.

Mother is laughing too, but holding back, the walls are thin. Her face contorts; she's shaking silently with Betty's metaphor. Sisyphus—oh, Betty you are priceless, they are good friends again, the business with my grandfather's inheritance has long been swept under the carpet. If not forgotten.

I know about Sisyphus being made to push a great rock

up a hill and at the top the rock would roll back down. Forever. I see the joke, not why they find it quite so funny. But I keep my head down and mouth shut. If they notice me, they're sure to stop the conversation straight away. Children are not meant to hear adults criticising other adults.

They both shake with giggling now. Mother calls out, Oscar, the house is sinking, the walls are cracking, the foundations are floating away—he's going to sink us all! Oscar, do you hear me? She's shrieking silently into her chest, tears rolling down, nearly choking with the effort to resist an all-out roar.

Betty, through tears and gasps: Oscar, do something, he's drying out the Sea of Galilee!

Mother is recovered now; enough to say, Betty, last night, I couldn't sleep, he's breeding mosquitoes right outside my bedroom window, in the violets bed. Fresh shrieks, they're helpless again.

Then she sees me, sitting in the corner, looking through my stamps collection. She coughs significantly. And so they go back to discussing Ester, Mother is worried about her, politics are becoming extreme, and she's threatening not to take up her place at university, where she is set to study accountancy. Says she has no time nor money for bourgeois paper-chasing, is going to work in a factory instead, the proletariat way. And plan the Revolution between shifts, no doubt, says Father. Mother is in despair, truly she is.

Ester left our Community for Tel Aviv as soon as she was discharged from the Forces, so now she's not entitled to any Community help. And Mother and Father don't have the money to support her through university. For which Betty graciously doesn't mention they only have themselves to blame. Later, quietly, on their way back to their car, Betty tells Uncle David, This communality idea, really, I tell you, *really*, it's bound to get young people confused. *Especially* the clever ones.

Earlier, Betty tells Mother, Oh, Rifka, what a shame. Ester's such a bright girl, and she is patting Mother's arm. Danna, Betty's own eldest daughter has an engineering career and one child already. My other cousins are all also doing The Right Thing. Poor Mother.

I smile at the memory of mother and Betty's friendly laughter. Micah might think I'm smiling at his joke, the one about Solomon holding the audience in his right palm, but I don't think it's very funny. Solomon may be an inept gardener, but he is a good teacher, and he had once, when he was still a junior officer, years before he lost his arm, saved Father's life.

Okay, my turn to tell you something now, says Micah. Did you know, this mound, Abudiya, is made of seven villages? They lie one beneath the other. It goes right back to the Stone Age.

Or right back to Adam and Eve.

Yes, which might amount to the same thing.

We sat up. There was a figure, a person standing on top of the mound, framed by the moonlight. Standing very still. Instantaneously, Micah went quiet, his shoulder moved closer against mine. I knew he'd seen it too. Quick heart beats, stomach churning, listening to the footsteps that separated us from the moon-lit houses on the hill. He was breathing steadily, alert. The figure disappeared. Have we been seen? Was it possible to make out two shadowy bodies merged in darkness at such a distance?

He might be a homeless person. Or a fisherman, sleeping rough in one of the ruins, Micah murmured.

But we could hear him scrambling in the overgrowth, stamping his feet, clapping his hands, it's what you must do at night so as not to surprise sleepy snakes. He was coming our way.

Don't move, Micah said as though I even could. The figure re-emerged at the bottom of the mound, was briskly walking down the dirt road, heading in our direction. A man, quite old, maybe Father's age, quite tall, carrying a small bundle in one hand, walking towards us, I could feel Micah squaring his shoulders. He sat up, then moved onto his feet, but crouching. The man was nearly up to where he'd either notice us or else keep walking past. His clothes were loose, ill fitting, he wore an Eastern kind of hat. Maybe a Bedouin from the Golan heights; or a hippie religious man; an Eastern Jew? Two more steps and he'd be gone, we wouldn't need to know if he is friend or foe. I held my breath, shut my eyes, keep walking, I pleaded. But Micah was standing up. The man had stopped.

Good evening, Micah said, coolly. The man froze. *Salam aleichum,* Micah tried again, in Arabic.

The man was still and silent, a pillar of salt. You could hear his breathing, quick and shallow. He was scared.

Shu bidak? What do you want? Micah said. This is our land, he was trespassing.

In response came a deluge of Arabic. The man was pointing at the mound, then flailing his hands, point again, this time to the hills of the Golan, hand to mouth,

I understood some words, he called Abudiya by name, but I couldn't make out what he was saying, regretted not having paid more attention in Elisha's Arabic lessons. Micah was nodding sagely, saying, *Aywah… aywah,* yes, yes, then, *Anna arref…*— I know; and *Bukra,* tomorrow, *Tfadal, tfadal, ya saidi,* you're welcome, sir, because the man was thanking him profusely. And finally, *Ma'asalame,* goodbye. And we were walking back then, quite quickly, leaving the man and the village behind. What's just happened?

What happened down there, with the Arab man? I asked once we crossed back over the bridge and started up the hill.

Oh, nothing, Micah said, he was lost. But I knew that wasn't so and said nothing the rest of the way, leaving him the space to change his mind about letting me in on the secret, to show me the trust I feared he couldn't have for a thirteen-year-old he didn't even know. Who wouldn't even do tongue-kissing.

10 November 1973

After the evening with Micah down by the Jordan I didn't hear anything more about the Arab man for about two weeks. Then, on the Friday afternoon we walked down to the old village, to Abudiya, Leo, Ori, Saffi and me, Anya came along too, now she wasn't walking out with Josh anymore. We settled in the mayor's house, the one that's less of a ruin than the rest, and got out our sandwiches, yellow cheese and tomato, no margarine for Saffi, and hard-boiled eggs. There was coffee smell and some spills in a corner, it looked like someone had been there and stayed the night. The boys got excited and talked about who might have been sleeping there, was it a homeless person, or maybe a spy or a terrorist infiltrator from across the border, or a Syrian soldier who lost his unit in the war and has been living in the countryside ever since, hiding, maybe he doesn't know how to get back home. Leo said there were Second World War soldiers still hiding in Japanese forests, not realising the War was over. Maybe our man hadn't heard about the ceasefire either. Saffi and Anya said we should tell an adult when we get back, it could be dangerous. And I had to keep quiet. I longed to tell them what I knew; that I had seen the man. But I didn't know what I would say about how I came to be here when the squatter (surely, it *was him*) turned up, that it was Micah who talked with him for five whole minutes in quick Arabic which I didn't understand. It would have been bad enough without Saffi being Micah's sister. And that made it all the more embarrassingly... what? It was so... I'm not sure what it was. Somehow it was not quite right. Sordid, even. Maybe shameful. But why? I didn't know.

So that's when I found out what happened after my evening with Micah down by the Jordan. When we got back from our picnic Leo went back home and spoke to his father, who told him, and he told us. It was Friday evening, after the Sabbath meal, and we were piled up on the grass under the great ficus tree by the cinema screen, head on thigh, head on stomach, friends together. There was nothing much to do and it was a beautiful November night, warm enough to be outside, too cold for mosquitoes. Leo reported that on the Monday night two weeks before Micah woke Ezra, Leo's father. It was two o'clock in the morning and he told Ezra that he'd just been out for a night walk down by Abudiya (a night walk!), where he came across a man, unarmed, or at least not brandishing a weapon. The man didn't speak any Hebrew, so they talked in Arabic and it seemed as though he was a 'Palestinian', living in a refugee camp in Syria. He had been in the area for a couple of days, and was out of food and clean water, Micah thought, although his Arabic was limited, and he didn't understand anything else that the Arab said. Ezra oversees safety in our settlement, and he knew exactly what to do, which was to get help and go down looking for this man, there was no way he could be allowed to roam the banks of the Jordan, it was a major security risk which needed sorting straight away. So a group of men, Micah too, went down with their M16 rifles or Uzi sub-machine guns or whatever weapon they keep under their beds, and looked for this Arab until dawn, and then told the border-guard police, who intensified their patrol routines, but he was gone.

According to Leo, Ezra thought Micah had been brave and calm under pressure. When he met with the Arab and it was one-on-one. When he was faced with an explosive and potentially even lethal situation, confronting an Enemy face on. Micah had no way of knowing what the Arab was capable of, whether he was desperate enough to do something… well, something desperate. Though it's not surprising he kept his cool, he is after all an officer in Staff Patrol, an elite intelligence commando unit, and they pick their soldiers with extreme discrimination, vigilance and caution, Leo said. He was looking at Saffi with new-found reverence. Probably he's going to begin worshipping Micah next, he's always got to have some idol or other.

Saffi was unimpressed with all this accolade bestowed on her brother, she said he was usually a complete idiot, showing off all the time about what a brilliant military career he's having and swapping girlfriends like socks, she really can't understand what they find in him. She was annoyed Micah hadn't mentioned any of this drama to her. No doubt he just thought she was too young and stupid to bother with, she'd love to swap him for a proper, older, sister like Ester. And she was taking the conversation right off course, the others haven't even nearly finished describing the matter in hand, and so they went on talking and speculating about the enigma of a refugee from Syria ending up in our very own Abudiya. But I wasn't listening anymore, I was thinking, Girlfriends? I didn't know he had lots or even any. And also, where do I fit into this story? Why did he say nothing about the Arab in all the time it took us to walk side by side along the river and back up the hill? Am I too young, too stupid to be let in on a secret? And, anyway, has he got a girlfriend, or have all the socks gone in the Saturday early morning wash?

After that, nothing; and it's been months. Micah went back to the army, and I haven't seen him since, except the odd incidental comment from Saffi, who is completely unconcerned whether he comes or goes. I daren't ask her about him except in a most oh-so-casual way. So I know he's gone on a jeep tour of the Sinai desert with squad mates. The Sinai was taken from the Egyptians a few months ago, in the war, and Israelis are swarming into it, in their thousands, snorkelling in the Red Sea and trekking the interior. I want nearly more than anything to see the Red Sea reef. It's known to be the most beautiful in the whole world. Father said we might go there on holiday, next year, he and Mother have not taken a vacation in years, so they are owed one by the Community. But, I don't know, I don't think my parents really see the point of holidays. Also, Mother is talking about visiting England; more seriously than before.

17 November 1973

I don't know why I bother to think about Micah so much. Sure he spends no time thinking about me. He's got under my skin and is burrowing this way and that, like some parasite, causing irritation and pain. Except occasionally the pain is also pleasure. It's become part of me. Like a persistent scratch, or a sneeze that comes only at last. Without it, I would be lost. There would be not very much to think about. So I hang on. Besides which, I'm in love with Josh, have been for such a long time. Unless. Unless the time has come to give up on the Josh thing. Maybe I'm growing too old for harping after someone who is yet to notice me even though he's my brother's best friend and has known me since I was born. I'm going to be fourteen in the Civil New Year, only eight weeks away.

So I make myself think about something else. Which is not Micah. I think about the Arab man, sleeping in the one house still standing in the old village. Leo called him a 'Palestinian'. Palestine is the name given to this region before it became Israel. But it doesn't exist anymore, except in the minds of terrorists, who want to drive us all into the sea. That's why they murdered eleven Israeli athletes in the Munich Olympics last year. They want

Palestine to be Liberated, that's the P and the L of P.L.O. What they don't understand is that violence never gets you anywhere.

According to Father, there are refugee camps in Syria, Jordan, Lebanon and Egypt—all our neighbouring countries, which I know nothing about. At school we study Jewish history, and world events like the American Civil War, the French and Russian revolutions. Nothing about the Middle East. Or Islam. All I know is that Mohammed is their prophet, that Mecca is their holy city, that so is Jerusalem, that the Quran is their holy book.

Father said the Arab leaders want a refugee crisis. They want refugees to be a thorn in the side of the Jewish state. And that's why they have kept those people in camps since the War of Independence. Instead of allowing them to integrate into their countries. Which would have been the humane and right thing to do. So this is why Palestinian refugees are a problem for us today and forever. Or until peace comes.

24 November 1973

When will peace come? I asked Ester on Friday evening. She'd wanted to know what to get me for my birthday and I was going to say, a book, like I always do. I do love reading and because of planning to be a writer it's important to check out what other people are doing. That way, I can make up my mind about what sort of writer I want to be. Also, it's exciting to have a book on my shelf, all of my own. I can keep it as long as I want, and fold the corners of the pages which I know is wrong, you certainly absolutely mustn't ever do that to a library book, you'll be called *a brazen vandal*; that's what Talma the librarian said about Sara once. Sara doesn't care what anyone says, and she doesn't read books anymore, only magazines for teenage girls, but I do—I care and I read lots of books. Of course, a book is not the most exciting birthday present. But I know Ester has hardly any money, she wouldn't even come to visit if Father didn't pay her bus fare every time. She and her boyfriend Gill live in a flat with a kitchen and shower they share with other tenants, in the south of Tel Aviv. Her neighbourhood is full of criminals, single mothers of future criminals, prostitutes, drug addicts and welfare scroungers, Mother says in one of the long laments she's fond of treating us to these days. It is such an undesirable neighbourhood that she, Mother, daren't describe it to David. Aunt Betty would simply have a fit and the whole business of their father's inheritance would rear its ugly head again. Ester is a student and also a metalworker in a factory, it's part of being a proletariat. So they have not enough money, especially with Gill at university. And that's why he's going to quit his studies. Which is the same as throwing all your life chances down the drain.

For my birthday, I wouldn't even ask Mother and Father for something so expensive as a record player. Let alone Ester. Anyway, it would only mean having to find somewhere in my room to put it, there isn't space, with my bed and Anya's taking up the two long walls, the wardrobe in between and two chairs already there. I would also have to start buying records; I only have one so far, by Simon and Garfunkel, which I can very well listen to in my parents' room, or Leo's. It would make no sense for me to ask for a new bike or a radio of my own, I've never even

seen a new bike in real life before, although the one I
inherited from Tommy was new when our cousin Dana
first had it twenty years ago. And anyway, I really don't
need such *luxus,* which is Mother's word for luxuries.
Modesty. That's part of life, otherwise you may get caught
out in a *bourgeois* existence and all the troubles of the
world will be visited upon you. Like greed, which is the
route of all evil, according to Father; and also what killed
his parents in Yugoslavia. *Luxus,* luxuries, is what David
and Betty buy their children *for Passover! Passover* is not a
gift-giving sort of holiday in our community. Sometimes
I wonder what our cousins even get for their birthdays,
probably a car for when they're grown up, or a trip abroad
or something.

I thought a skirt would also be too much to ask Ester
for, there's a nice one I saw in Tiberias. Ester buys all her
own clothes in the Jaffa flea market, which is why she
looks like a hippy, except when she wears whatever
Mother buys for her in the *Shalom* department store in
Tel Aviv, where the two of them go together every year for
Ester's birthday.

So, after all the thinking, I just say, For my birthday I
want peace to come to our country. They all smile a
condescending kind of smile, and Tommy says, *Nah nah
nahnah, nah nah nahhhh nah nah nah nahnah!* to the tune
of what I had just said, while nodding his head frantically,
twisting his face, looking like a retard, and meaning, *You
are a baby and an idiot. You have no idea about peace, war, or
anything.* Sometimes I hate my family. Tommy especially.

But mother ignores him. Good for you, darling. Oscar,
did you hear what Abbie's just asked for her birthday?

Father says, I did. And I think, Abbie, it's wonderful

that you think this way.

But Tommy hasn't quite finished showing off by showing me up. He says, Well, it's stupid to ask for something—something which is just—juts a tower floating in the air. You may as well say you want the Messiah to arrive on your birthday.

I say, Who needs the Messiah? And why *shouldn't* peace come, Tommy?

Because… Tommy puffs his chest, takes a deep breath and raises his voice like some passionate politician. Because to have peace means you have to have a partner for peace. And we haven't got one. Every Jewish person in this country would do anything to end all conflict. Like they say in this play we've been reading in class, mothers would rather their sons were born without the trigger finger.

Ahhh, Arthur Miller, says mother, *All My Sons…* And I can tell she's preparing to tell us all about it, she's always trying to Widen Our Horizons.

Quickly, I interrupt, Anyway, Toto, that's what Josh thinks, I've heard him talk about it before, and you're just a plain old parrot. Why don't you think of something new to say?

I know it isn't fair but he's just so annoying.

But I believe it too, he answers, voice squeaky now. The Arabs aren't bothered about living in peace with us. They'd rather have perpetual conflict than accept it that we have a right to be here.

Then Ester says, Because their women don't love *their* sons as well as *ours* do? Tommy has no chance against her. He shuts up.

Well, Mother says, *I* think peace is a distinct

possibility. We just have to work harder at it. And keep hoping… She links her arm with Tommy's. He tries to shrug her off, but she hangs on; she loves to embarrass him like that, pretend he's still her Little Man. Smiling at him, she says, Maybe Tommy won't need to go in the army—okay, that's probably too soon, but Abbie—yes, who knows what will happen in the next four years.

We'll always need to have an army; even in peace time, Father says, but, you know, your mother is right, I believe there's reason to be hopeful—what's the matter with you, Tommy?

Tommy is walking almost sideways, like a handcuffed prisoner attempting an escape from Mother, who is ignoring his awkwardness. At last she lets go. Father, who hasn't realised what has gone on, gives Tommy a look. Father says, I mean… look at Europe in 1945, war-torn. Bleeding. And look at it now: peace and prosperity. Even the British are to join the European Community. And soon, you'll see, it will be the United States of Europe.

We reach the bottom of the steps that lead up to the Dining Room. Mother stops, even though we're late because of watching the Arab film on Ruth's television. She stops to let Father finish what he's saying. Father is pleased. He says, The same can happen here, too. No doubt about it. The question is, how much blood; how much blood has to be spilled first, before this happens.

We climb the steps, one united family. But before we reach the doors, Ester says, Well, all I will say is… She hesitates because she and Father aren't supposed to discuss politics, Mother has forbidden it, they always get too heated, Father gets upset and Ester's visit is ruined. Mother's hand is hovering over the door handle. Will she wait for Ester as she has just done for Father? She also hesitates, and Ester says, Abbie, it's true what Tommy said; people on both sides need to want peace. To *really* want it. Not in a slogan kind of *Peace, man*, hippie kind of way. That won't do it. They need to want it so much they are willing to give up some really precious things to get it.

Like land, I say, I think we should do that. Give back the 1967 Territories.

Yes, land, Ester goes on, but not just the Territories. That's land we don't need… Mother pushes the handle and is through the door, and we follow her into the bright fluorescent lights of the Dining Room. Ester knows what needs to be done. But Father thinks she's a dreamer, playing at politics, planning The Revolution with her *comrades in arm*, all twelve of them, he says. And Uncle David, he calls her *The Loony Left*, which makes Betty's laughter burst out. Ester is a Communist, but why is that so bad, or funny? I haven't yet found out half of what people like Father and Ester know about peace and war.

We walk over to our table by the eastern wall, late for the Sabbath meal as usual, the Arab movie doesn't finish till eight o'clock. My parents don't have a television so on Fridays we go next door to watch it on Ruth's. Ruth says, Look, look, that *Mahmud*, he's peering right at her bra, what do you say to that, Rifka, should I tell Abbie to look away? She laughs.

She calls every Arab *Mahmud*, likes to talk about how lucky she is to have got away from Iraq when she did. Oh, to live in a civilised society where rules are rules, isn't that right, Rifka? Although *this* is no bed of roses either… The wars, oh, when will there be peace at last? And the Arabs, you know, you just can't reason with them. *They* don't care whether there's war or peace, whether they live or die, even! They are all the same, you know, and I should know, yes; no respect for women, all the husband has to do is say, *I divorce you*, and the wife is banished, out on the street. Not to mention taking two or even more wives. Primitive, don't you think, Rifka? Oh, I tell you, this movie is going to end badly, very badly; there'll be tears before we're done here tonight.

Usually, there are. Usually, the heroine dies of a broken heart, and the hero is sorry for having abused her so. He sings one last heartrending song, at the end of which he is sprawled over her grave, his two young motherless children looking on solemnly.

Then Mother and Ruth wipe their eyes; they're smiling, satisfied. The Egyptian film industry has delivered. And it doesn't matter that Ruth was talking practically throughout, we just read the translation subtitles, except for Mother, who's Hebrew reading is too slow; but she says it doesn't matter, she understands, they are that predictable. Besides, sometimes these films are remakes, she says. So tonight's movie was based on William Shakespeare's *Othello*, one of Mother's absolute favourites, she simply can't wait for my English to be good enough to read all his plays by myself. My favourite Shakespeare character so far is Bottom, he reminds me of Leo's older brother Abe.

Abe loves acting, like Bottom; and he has a screw missing in his head, also like Bottom, a small but crucial screw, says Aunt Betty, because of being born bottom first. Well you wouldn't believe the mess the hospital made of Abe's birth, mother says. It was before people knew they had legal rights so that same doctor was still there when

Mother went into labour with Ester and saw him at the hospital, and even though Ester was coming, she shouted that she would walk out onto the street there and then rather than be attended by that scoundrel after what he did to Rita and Ezra and Abe, which he never apologised for, and no one could calm her down, not even Grandma Rose who came on the bus from Tel Aviv, and in the end they had to bring another doctor to deliver Ester safely, got him out of bed in the middle of the night.

Now Abe works in the gardens, and he even has a girlfriend, sweet and smiley but not as beautiful as Titania Queen of the Fairies. And I am a girl-lover, Hermia or Helena, confused, running through dark woods, swaying between desire and disgust, not knowing friend from foe, donkey from human. Mother promised to take me to *A Midsummer Night's Dream* in London when she finally, *finally* gets permission from the Community to visit her family.

27 November 1973

The reason Jacob and Ruth have a television is that Jacob is seventy-three per cent disabled after stepping on a landmine by the Suez Canal in 1956. He also has a telephone, a car and a week in a health spa every year. So they don't need to ask the Car Steward to borrow a Community car or wait to find out whether there's one available. If you drive a Community car you have to give other Members a lift, even if they're going somewhere quite out of your way. That's the beauty of our Community, but, Mother says, it's the trouble with it too. This happened last spring. Father took Tommy and me to the Holocaust Memorial Museum in Jerusalem, a three hour drive each way, quite enough for one day, Mother said. But we went *via Tel Aviv*, because Ella was visiting her daughter in hospital. That's mutual assistance gone absolutely ludicrous, Mother said. But father didn't mind, he'll do anything for anybody. I just wish you could say No sometimes, Oscar, before people start taking advantage.

No one is taking advantage, Rifka.

And I worry about you when you're out so late. Is it too much to ask that you stop at a payphone and let Ruth know when you'll be home?

Rifka, I wouldn't bother Ruth and Jacob over a trivial matter.

It isn't trivial for goodness' sake. This is just like the time you—

Mother stops. We all remember The Time—the War of Attrition, 1969, when Father disappeared during a bombardment. He'd been out and went straight to the headquarters to see what he could do, and they put him on guard duty till morning. When he got home, he couldn't understand why Mother was fuming. She had spent the night wondering where he was.

Father smiles, is a bit embarrassed about that night. He says, But Rifka, why worry about a little diversion on the way to Jerusalem?

I'm sorry, I can't explain it, she says. When Mother starts apologising unnecessarily you know there's trouble. It's the English in her, coming out to get you. It's a fundamental issue, Oscar, and if you don't understand, well… she wonders, she really does sometimes wonder, whether there's any common ground between them anymore. Oscar, I need you to try and understand. Well, do you? Her voice is raised now, which is definitely not allowed. Oscar, do not walk out on me now… She chokes on the last word; but it's too late, the neighbours will have heard.

Father is putting on his coat. I'm not walking out. I'm going to see Solomon. To check he's fully aware of what you think about me taking Ella to her daughter in hospital, and whether he has the complete picture on the state of our marriage according to you. I'll fill him in, if necessary, he's a little hard of hearing.

But when I leave to go back to school at bedtime he's sitting in the dark on the front lawn. When he sees me, he gets up slowly.

Are you okay, Father?

Yes, Abbie, I'm okay.

Mother, she doesn't appreciate you, always having a go when you haven't done anything wrong.

Don't say that, Abbie. Mother does her best, and so do I. Then he mumbles, Let's hope our best is good enough.

I certainly had no idea what to say to that. So I asked, How was Solomon?

Oh, fine, fine. He's a good friend, but, hmmm. I didn't stay long, wanted to sit quietly, here.

The children laugh at Solomon sometimes, I say. He can't keep control.

Yes, well. He is highly intelligent, you know. Have I told you, he saved my life, in the War of Independence?

Yes, Father, you have.

Why is there so much talk of war? When will there be peace?

2 December 1973

It happened last night, four weeks before my fourteenth birthday. We were sitting in the Big Room, which Mother calls The Living Room. Josh was here, he and Tommy had been playing chess on the floor, but they stopped when Father told the story of how Solomon saved his life in the War of Independence. They are both obsessed with anything military, can't wait to be called up by the draft-board. They go to the firing range, know every military rank in order and can identify any weapon, any type of ammunition, any airplane in the sky by its silhouette.

It was I who asked to hear about Father and Solomon. I'd been trying without success to write about how Father survived the holocaust, and Queenie said maybe I'm overwhelmed by the enormity and sadness of it. So I thought, this was something else to practise on. Something exciting. Father was happy to retell his story, and we were glad he was, even though apart from Josh we'd all heard it before.

In 1947, Father was nineteen. Solomon, who's two years older, was his unit commander, a sergeant. They were called to take part in a reprisal operation against an Arab village in Lower Galilee.

Reprisal for what? I asked.

Well, there had been attacks on Jewish farmers. The week before, three men were killed while working their fields, Father said.

So—So did they know the killers came from that village—

Oh, shut up, little one, Tommy snapped, who cares! Let us hear the story. He is always so rude in front of Josh. I sat quietly, fighting back tears.

Father said, There was a war on, you see. It was them or us.

And then! Then it happened. Well, not all of it, yet, but—Josh said, Don't worry, Abbie, I'm sure the High Command had their reasons. They wouldn't have taken such a decision lightly. I looked up quickly, forgetting my probably-red-face and definitely-watery-eyes. He was looking at me as he spoke, I just caught him before he looked away again.

That was the first momentous thing to happen last night. Josh had never started any conversation with me, till then. Whatsoever. Well, never more than a word here, a half-sentence there. Never even looked at me longer than was necessary to avoid bumping into me. If you didn't know he was Tommy's best friend and comes to my parents' room at least twice a week, you would probably assume we were complete strangers.

There was one time, on the day of the funerals, just after the war, when he and I walked side by side by the river, and I felt there was something, an energy between us holding us fast. An invisible shackle. But then I realised this had been a figment of my imagination. Wishful thinking, as Mother calls it. Probably he wouldn't even know what I was talking about, should I be enough of a lunatic to mention it. Which I'm not. I may have kept my unrequited love for Josh going for years, I may have given him my heart though he doesn't know it and wouldn't care if he did, but I still have my dignity. It's so hard to love someone who constantly, persistently, ignores you. Until today. Two sentences. Just for me. *And* in front of Tommy and my parents. *And,* he said my name! My cheeks felt even hotter now. I wanted to shut my eyes, shut everyone out and savour the moment Josh spoke to me. I knew it was silly. Nothing to celebrate, really. But... it felt good. And I lowered my head, so the others didn't see me smile.

Father carried on his story. His unit was providing back-up while another platoon entered the village with orders to find the perpetrators and blow up their houses. This should have taken an hour, but instead of leaving as soon as the mission was complete, the soldiers went around looting and ransacking, taking cigarettes, antiques, narghiles, tea-sets, anything. Meanwhile nineteen-year-old Oscar, watching over the proceedings down in the village, lying on the ground in his vantage point, fell asleep.

Mother was laughing, Well, of course, it *was* nighttime and you know how tired your father gets after nine o'clock. You know, Oscar, if we ever leave this community, I think you could start a business teaching people how to relax in every single situation. There's bound to be call for that sort of thing; maybe from rich, highly strung stockbrokers; or, even, their equally rich, neurotic, social climbing, gold-digging wives. You would be a great success, you know.

Yes, well... Father was smiling. And so, meanwhile the villagers called for reinforcement from Nazareth, and the reinforcement arrived, and we had to go into a quick retreat. But I was still asleep and didn't hear the command, there was so much noise from the battle going on all around us.

Mother was holding her head in her hands. Oh, Oscar, wake up, wake up already! I can't bear it, my love. You know you might have been killed there and then! This is such a frightful story, are you sure the children should hear it?

Of course we should, Mother, Tommy said urgently. We're not babies, you know; at least, Josh and I aren't. Tommy is truly an idiot. He couldn't even tell Mother was actually joking. I hate him.

Anyway, Father continued, my unit started retreating under fire, and after about twenty metres Solomon realised I hadn't moved. He shouted but I couldn't hear him. It was too dangerous for him to go back, so he threw stones at me; one hit me on the shoulder, and I woke up. And that's how Solomon saved my life. Father sat back with a smile.

Well thank goodness for that. Mother was fanning herself with *The Jerusalem Post*. What a roller-coaster tale! And thank goodness for Solomon. He is the best neighbour anyone can have; I will never say another bad word about his gardening. Not even to Betty.

After that Tommy and Josh wanted to know what sort of gun Father was using, how many rounds of ammunition he had and other such boring details. Then they went back to their chess board. Tommy lifted a pawn and was about to make a suicidal move which would put Josh in check. Then he changed his mind and put the pawn back, but Josh said the pawn had already touched the new position. Which meant Tommy had to make that stupid move whether he wanted to or not. Tommy said he hadn't touched the board. In the end Josh said it was fine, he was going to beat him anyway, so they carried on and that's when Tommy remembered it was his turn to feed the horses; he shot off in a panic because it was almost dark already and Gideon would slaughter him if he's late. On his way out he said, Abbie can finish the game for me… I've had enough anyway.

So Josh was still on the floor by the chess board, but I stayed sitting next to Mother and Father, who were discussing the Members Committee meeting coming up next week, which will decide whether Mother may go to England in June. Aunt Rachel's daughter Isabel is getting married in London and Mother should be there, it's a normal thing, isn't it, to be at your niece's wedding? Mother was drawing up a list of every Committee member and trying to guess which way they would vote, totting up the votes in three columns, one for Best Case, one for Most Likely and one for If Worst Comes to Worst.

I was thinking Josh would leave now Tommy has gone, but he stayed on the floor by the chess board. He sat so long Mother asked him if he wanted something to drink and he said, No, thank you, and carried on looking down at the board. Because he was there and clearly listening, Mother spoke in a hushed voice, so quietly Father couldn't hear a word, and was annoying Mother by asking her to repeat everything; it was impossible, Father should get his ears tested, she had said that so many times already. At last Mother asked whether Josh wouldn't rather sit on the sofa, the floor is so cold, he might catch something nasty; but he said Thanks, I'm fine down here. Mother likes Josh; she says he might be the closest to a true English gent you can get in Israel. Which is the top-most accolade she ever gives. But right now I could tell she was wishing he was gone, Outstaying His Welcome which is her convoluted way of saying the same thing. So then we all sat in silence, the three of us looking at Josh, wondering what he was still doing on the floor, when he turned towards us, *towards me*, cleared his throat and said, So… ummm, do you want to finish off the game for Tommy?

Did I want to finish off the game for Tommy? Well, no, not really. Unless, of course, it was Josh I was going to be finishing it off with. Or against, but who cares! The evening was turning into the best in my life so far. I don't like chess. Father had tried to teach me when I was younger, but we never got far. I just hate the simmering slow aggression of it; can't be bothered with the endless calculations and strategising. My mind wanders. But Father did insist I should know all the rules before allowing me to give it up, and tonight I was grateful for his persistence. So I was able to keep the game going, despite Tommy's bad start, for about ten more moves. Or fifteen. Before I was check-mated and, together, Josh and I (*Josh and I!)* put all the pawns in the box. Then he got up, looking as though he was about to go back to school, and I told Mother I would wash the dishes.

But he sat on the sofa and asked if he could have a look at today's papers. Father said, of course he can, and they talked about Gerald Ford becoming Vice President in the U.S. of A. The question was, according to Father, was the appointment going to be good for the Jews or bad for the Jews. Josh said that in his opinion, at this difficult post-Yom-Kippur-War time, it was appropriate for the American Jewish Lobby to step up the pressure on the Nixon administration, and did Father agree? Yes, Father did, we should make the most of our friendship with the Americans without whose ardent support, frankly, we would be in grave danger of losing our foothold in the Middle East; it's as simple as that. I didn't catch what they were saying President Nixon should agree to; but did you ever? Josh is fifteen years old, and he's sitting like King Solomon Wisest-of-All-Men himself, discussing current affairs. With Father!

I finished washing the coffee cups and cleaned around the sink, so Mother doesn't tell me off. Then I announced into the room that I was going back to school. It was eight o'clock and I thought I would do some homework, (well, probably not if I were honest) and go to bed early, to carry on reading the brilliant, the amazing, *Gone With The Wind*. I gave up adoring Gilbert Blythe now that I know Rhett Butler. Gilbert was a childhood infatuation. I loved him because I loved Anne Shirley and the two of them were meant for each other. But he wasn't very interesting, not really. Unlike Rhett, who told Scarlett he loved her even though the world around them was collapsing. And other things like courageous people don't need a reputation. I wish I could think of lines like his. Can you imagine anything more romantic? I don't think so. Oh, will the two of them ever work things out? I hope so.

So I headed for the door when Josh said he was going now, he had homework too. I wasn't sure whether to wait while he put his coat on or not. It was true he had just spoken to me directly for the first time, and true we had just had a half game of chess together (without talking). But did that mean we were on walking-back-to-school-at-night-together terms? It was confusing. In the end I decided not to wait, it would make me look desperate. But I did walk slowly, not so that he could catch up with me, I knew that wouldn't happen, but because I felt like it. Really. I told myself to calm down, stop being stupid, not get my hopes up. Besides, what happened this evening meant nothing. Nothing at all.

Chapter 3: Devon, England

January 2010

Here lie / Abigail Aswan-Boskovitch 1960-2008 / And her beloved daughter / Tamara Aswan / 1983-1986

Yasmin and Omar stand in the graveyard on the hill overlooking the sea. Father and daughter, they stand over the grave in which her mother Abbie and older sister Tamara are buried. Abbie died two summers ago, Tamara twenty-five years ago, when she was just a toddler. Yasmin herself was born soon afterwards. It had been Abbie's wish, expressed from her hospice bed, to quite literally join Tamara in the ground when the time came. Much better to double and triple up than to rest in solitude, she had told Omar and Yasmin who were sitting on plastic-covered chairs next to her bed. Besides, she added with a wry smile, seeing that the two of them were slow to embrace her plan, I'll have you know family graves are an old English tradition. Go to any churchyard, you'll see I'm right.

Omar protested, Since when do you abide by what the English have to say about anything?

He was only half joking.

In a minute you'll tell us you want a cremation, then what? I mean, what next? Drying dishes with the soap left on? Flowers in baskets hanging by the front door? Will you start complaining about the weather now? For all her physical weakness, Abbie was determined. Just because I don't sheepishly follow every local custom, she sighed, massively understating the case.

She stretched out a thin pale hand to Omar. Darling, just because I follow, you know, follow my own path doesn't preclude me from adopting the customs I do like. And I like this one, she smiled weakly. I like it, so do it for me. And at that she closed her eyes, the matter settled. She was forty-nine and didn't see her fiftieth birthday.

Now Omar is home for a month. He will return to Beirut next week. In his absence, Yasmin had to take care of the headstone, which has only just been put in place. Better late than never, Omar sighs. Abbie had asked for the writings to be in English, Hebrew and Arabic. The three facets of her life. Which was a huge palaver to organise in deepest Devon. After a few false starts, Yasmin made an executive decision not to squeeze the new script onto Tamara's old gravestone, instead having a new one created for the two of them. You had no right to do this on your own, Omar says crossly, I'm still the head of this family. Oh, don't be ridiculous, Dad, Yasmin retorts, you know you sound like a cave man. He has no idea how difficult it has been for her, managing everything without him. Without Mum. Since when do you speak to your father like that, he snaps. And who's paying for all this? Not you I dare say. But his voice is mellower now. Quietly, he says, you should have consulted me at least, Yassi, you should have picked up the phone. But it is so difficult to get a hold of him when he's away for months on end. And Yasmin didn't imagine he'd be at all sentimental about the old gravestone. Why would he, when they don't even have any photographs of Tamara before she died. Not one, and Omar seems not to mind this at all. That's not so strange, Yassi, he says, my parents didn't take photos of me as a baby either. Yasmin says, I expect they didn't have cameras in Sheich Jaraach in the sixties. Hurt that his priorities again seem opposite to hers. Though it's true what he says, Tamara would have had plenty of photographs had she lived.

The silence is easy between them. I had a letter, she says, from Grandma Rifka. That's good, is she well? Did she find Tamara's photograph? No, she doesn't have one either. She wrote that Tamara was the most gorgeous baby with her fair curls and big blue eyes, always watching. They called her Shirley Temple, Grandma wrote, where did she get that fair hair, those blue eyes? Omar is quiet, then he says, You know Yassi, to lose a child is… your mother for a while—a long time—she was unravelled. Both of us were—but then, and you were born into all that grief but you were the apple of her eye. No one could wish for a better daughter.

Side by side they stand, facing the grave and the grey sea beyond. Yasmin puts her arm through Omar's, and they stand some more. She says, did you know I'm the same age *Imma* was when I was born? Yes, he says. They are quiet a while longer, it feels good to share the sadness. Shall we sit, *Abba*, she says and together they spread the chequered woollen blanket on the damp ground and sit a while in the heavy autumn air. Not wishing to leave, they lie down, looking up through long grass at a white sun in bright grey sky. Omar lifts his arm for Yasmin to rest her head on. Here you go, Yassi, he says, like the old days when you were little and only wanted *Abba*. You were away so much, she says. Hmmm, he grunts in assent. Soon, his arm slackens, and his breathing slows. Abbie was always marvelling at how easily he moved between sleep and waking. Now Yasmin finds his soft snores bring comfort to the rage and longing she feels at the cruelty with which their family is shrunk.

She knows so little of her mother's life. Abbie had kept diaries when she was a child and a young woman living in Israel. And she kept all the letters she received, even had copies of letters she herself wrote. Like Sir Winston Churchill had done. But the writing was mostly in Hebrew which Yasmin could not read nor understand. Even so, Yasmin felt more connected to her roots. Israel, Palestine, the Middle East. Having parents on both sides of the Conflict, she used to imagine that her and Tamara's very existence was some kind of a peace offering. Consequently, she grew up believing her role was to be neutral. But now it seems she has been naïve to think it possible to sit on the fence. Her father, of course, is always happy to tell her what she should believe; *from the river to the sea, Palestine shall be free.* But what does this mean? And where does it leave the Jewish side of her family? Where does it leave her? She wants to make up her own mind. To make sense of it herself.

About three years ago, before they knew that her mother was ill, they talked about going back to Israel together. Soon. When you see the Community, when you're there you'll understand, Abbie said. There was even mention of Omar joining them. Come with me, Abbie pleaded, I need you, I can't do it alone. After all these years, surely the Security Services wouldn't bother to arrest him anymore. They must know he's no longer a radical? Not any kind of a security threat, but a common or garden Professor of Middle Eastern Studies. Every Arab is a security threat, Omar said, they think we're all terrorists. But he would look into it, talk to the embassy. Soon. Of course, they thought they had all the time in the world. Then the cancer was diagnosed, and everything escalated. Downhill, like an avalanche.

Yasmin raises herself onto one elbow. She sits cross legged, her eyes following three sailing boats across the bay. Now she's thinking of the latest business, her correspondence with Abbie's old friend. Joshua Pasternak. His letters, written laboriously on transparent airmail paper, explaining in crooked, misspelt English that he is coming to London and wishes to visit Abbie's grave. Strange that he wrote to Yasmin and not Omar. Well, why not? At twenty-four years old she is a grown woman. And in any case Omar will be away. Still, she wonders, why hasn't she told her father? About this Joshua? Should she? With excitement and trepidation she offered to meet Joshua off the train and drive him to the graveyard. But in his next letter he was no longer sure. He had thought that Abbie was buried in a Jewish cemetery. Had never heard of Natural Burial Sites. This changed things for him, and so he will consult his rabbi. Seek permission, if you please! Yasmin supposes he's some religious fanatic. She is pretty sure Ordinary Jews like her grandparents and mother don't have their own rabbis to consult with, and in any case don't care about such things. She realises how ignorant she is, regrets that as a child she never listened when her mother talked about their heritage. That it didn't bother her to know next to nothing about the Old

Testament, who fathered whom out of Isaac, Jacob and Abraham, what the Twelve Tribes were, or the Ten Afflictions of Passover. Though she did always look forward to the holiday of Chanukah with its candles, *latkes* and doughnuts.

Joshua also asked if he may have letters from among Abbie's things. Letters Abbie wrote him in the seventies. This was Curiouser and Curiouser. She wondered whether Omar knew this man. She should ask him. Maybe. Perhaps now Omar can be persuaded to help her open Abbie's shoeboxes in the attic. Perhaps together they will find Joshua's letters. When she asked him before, he was not ready. It's too soon, Yassi, he said, but you can go ahead without me, it's all yours now anyway. As a child Yasmin would sometimes spend an afternoon rifling through the incomprehensible letters and fishing out old black and white photographs. And Abbie would tell her who this or that person was. But now it felt unbearable to open those dusty archives, crammed with mountains of tightly scribed letters. She couldn't do it alone, the task was too big. In any case, with an almost non-existent Hebrew she wouldn't make head nor tail of any of it. Omar said *his* Hebrew wasn't up to scratch either. But how can that be, when he grew up outside Jerusalem, is super-clever with a PhD and three professorships? Most probably, he's finding excuses. Apparently, he's behind schedule to submit his book for publication and that's why he has no time. No time to spend with Yasmin or face the past. Apparently. Honestly, *Abba*, are you scared of some dark secret lurking in these shoeboxes, Yasmin asked. He said, Of course not, Yassi, now you're being silly. Quite seriously, not realising she was only joking.

Chapter 4: Jordan Valley

5 January 1974

The night before the Sylvester celebration we took the bus to Tiberias, Saffi, Anya, Sara and I. We were going 'shopping', which Saffi said was what sophisticated teenagers do, especially before a big party like Civil New Year. Sara had money to buy a skirt, but the rest of us only had enough for half a pita and falafel, which we ate standing in the busy, dirty street, feeling sorry we didn't think to wear anything on our feet. Except Anya, who had on her winter shoes. But we did have a nice time trying on clothes in the shops and watching Sara choose an embroidered shirt. Afterwards, we went into the *Mashbir* department store and got the makeup lady to show us how to apply the special-offer eyeliners. Our plan was to keep it on for the party. In the end, Anya did buy one eyeliner, blue. She was just too embarrassed not to, she said, after the lady had spent half an hour with us. But this meant there wasn't enough money between us to catch the bus home.

We sat by the lake, the Sea of Galilee, feet dangling off the pier, and watched the windsurfers and pleasure boats. Sara got out a Time cigarette. She'd stolen it from her father. It was a little squashed and bent from being in her pocket, and she got a light off a waiter who was standing outside a restaurant behind us. We shared it, taking a drag then passing on. Except for Anya. It's disgusting, she said. Unhealthy, too. But she did try it, the smell reminded her of *someone*, she said. Who, we all asked. She smiled mysteriously, You don't have to know *everything*, but it was clear she was bursting to tell. Sometimes she meets with a man she can't tell us about because he is old, maybe thirty. There was a shocked silence, my heart was in my mouth and Micah floated into my head. I pushed him away. Then I said, Noah, it's Noah Katz, isn't it? I was just guessing; Noah Katz works in the dairy where Anya also works after school. Anya said, This is top secret if people find out his wife will leave him and take the children with her, and it will be my fault. Saffi said, Anya, they will send *you* away like they did Tovah after she had that abortion, sent her to another school in another Community where it was too far for her to visit home. I can't help it, I love him, Anya whispered through tears. We sat quietly watching our shadows darken the pier and the moored boats till it was time to go back.

So then we stood at the bus station and tried to hitch a lift home. There were a lot of soldiers, also hitchhiking, or waiting for the bus, trying to get home for the weekend. We were stuck for an absolute age. Just because they were soldiers in uniform, drivers assumed they deserved a lift more than we did. In the end, a car slowed down, the driver, wearing dark Ray-bans, looked through the crowd of hitchhikers as he came to a stop. The soldiers crowded him like bees around a honeypot, but he told them to go away and pointed toward us. Saffi was the first to notice it was her brother, Micah.

Why does the sight of him give me such a sinking feeling? Anya, Sara and I climbed into the back, Saffi went in front, smiling ear-to-ear, breathless, excited. They chatted all the way, ignoring the rest of us. I was weighed by gloom and just looked out of the window as the beaches of the Sea of Galilee rushed past. The water was grey in the weak, late afternoon sun and the Golan Heights rose darkly beyond the eastern shore on the far side. Micah had borrowed the car for the weekend from a friend who owed him favour. He promised to take Saffi for a ride the next day, to look for cyclamens in Upper Galilee, or whatever. Saffi was squealing with excitement. Which made me feel even sadder.

I didn't feel like Silvester-partying in the evening, but it seemed even more depressing to be the only one going to bed early. The party was in the Dining Room. The tables had been pushed against the sides, leaving a big space in the middle for dancing. I like circle dancing, it was good, but when the band played couple-dances, there was no one to stand up with. Hardly any of the boys dance, they only like heavy rock and the like. I begged Leo to give me one dance, just one, he's good when he wants to be, but he wouldn't. Tommy also refused and walked out with Josh and the other older boys. So I was sitting by myself on a table, legs dangling back and forth, keeping time with the music, when Micah came over and asked me to dance. It was fun, despite what I said about him earlier. It's true he held me too close and kept breathing right onto my face. But still. I was excited. I love dancing and now I had a partner. When the music stopped, he didn't go off to sit, but stood with me waiting for the next one. The next dance was one where you swap partners and when it finished, he came looking for me again. And so we kept dancing—mazurka, waltz, paso doble—circles of sweat appeared on his shirt around his armpits, but I didn't mind. I breathed in the smell of him, sweat and dust and cigarettes.

And when the band was packing up and the rock-and-roll music played, I went outside to find Leo and the others, Saffi gave me a funny look, but I ignored her. I sat with them, Josh was saying we should accelerate the government-funded building projects in the Occupied Territories, especially now we've been found to be so vulnerable in the last war. Daniel tried to interject, What's the point in investing in the Territories, Josh, if we have to give them back as part of a peace agreement? But Josh just laughed, anyone who thinks the Egyptians, or the Jordanians, are going to be handed the Jewish Settlements back on a plate is nothing short of naïve. The Settlers are the new Pioneers; their settlements are buffer zones to protect us in the next war. We should be grateful to them instead of promising to hand them over to the Arabs. We talked quietly or listened to the older boys, until Alice Cooper played *School's Out* and we went back in and danced the night away with Status Quo, David Bowie, The Who, also Simon and Garfunkel—my favourites—and the Bee Gees, who Tommy says are castrated and that's how they can sing so high.

Until twelve o'clock came and a new year started with more music but this time it was Led Zeppelin and *Stairway to Heaven*, and a few couples did slow dancing. I sat among my friends, watching. Leo asked Anya to dance, and they went off into the semi-darkness; and Daniel asked Saffi, but she said no. What about you,

Abbie? I also didn't want to dance, thank you. I wasn't desperate enough to be a replacement for Saffi!

Daniel went back to where the boys sat and Saffi said, He sounds soooo ridiculous with his *wa-wa-wa* English accent, doesn't he?

So I snapped, Shut up, Saffi, my Mother has an English accent. Why don't *you* try living in a foreign country and learn a new language?

Okay, okay, don't bite. I was only joking. She looked away. I said I was going to bed. It was two o'clock. I was a little sorry for saying no to Daniel, I liked him. Did it really matter so much that he had asked Saffi first? Answer: Ummm, yes, probably. I had planned to wait to the end of the slow dancing in case Josh asked me to dance. He was standing with the other boys, by the windows, looking on. But it was too late, I'd had enough. And besides, what's the point? I may as well face it. Grow up and face the facts.

I was almost at the door when Micha caught up with me. Annoyingly, my heart skipped a beat. He said, Finished dancing? I said I was going to bed. That sounds exciting. I ignored him. He seems to take pleasure in embarrassing me. Why? He was still walking beside me. Was he going home himself? That's how strange it is, our so-called relationship, or whatever you call it. He said, I've got a car, it's parked by the gate.

I know.

Oh, yes, I gave you girls a lift today. He chuckled. Anyway, would you like to come for a ride?

Now?

Now. Or a bit later, if you prefer.

In the car, with the engine revving, a feeling of panic

rose in my throat. Why did I agree to go with him? Where is he taking me? It was so exciting.

So, Abigail, where would you like us to go? I'm in your hands. He was smiling, his blue staring eyes bored into me. The moon was high up in the sky.

I don't know.

You don't know?

No.

So, shall I decide? Would you like me to do that?

I suppose.

Okay, I've got somewhere in mind. Somewhere special.

We turned onto the main road, then right towards the eastern shore of the Sea of Galilee, then right again, up the Golan Heights. It took about twenty minutes, he was chatty, asked what I was reading; *A Tale of Two Cities*—Oh yes, I read all of Dickens when I was your age, told me what he was reading; *One Hundred Years of Solitude*— Marquez is a Genius. You should try it, it'll blow your mind, have I seen *A Clockwork Orange* yet? No? Well, you must. It's a classic. He told me about his girlfriend, named Galia, as if I wanted to know her name or anything about her, how she let him kiss her the first time they went out, even though she's only four years older than me. I sat there, not knowing what to say, wondering whether this girlfriend might be wondering where he was right now.

When he stopped the car and we got out, he said, Hang on. Don't look until I say, and I put a hand over my eyes and walked a few steps, with him guiding me by the arm, his fingers felt rough on my skin, warm too; he held me gently. And he said, Look now, and the view did nearly take my breath away. The Sea of Galilee, big and black below; and all around it lights from villages,

112

Communities, hundreds, thousands of lights reflected deep into the water. And over on the opposite side, Tiberias, crowded, extra busy lights wrapped round the marina and creeping up the hill, away from the water. Like a chain of diamonds.

Like a diamond chain, he said, but he was looking at me instead of the view. I continued to look down, willing him to stay where he was, but he was getting nearer, standing close, too close. Do you like it?

It's the most beautiful thing I've ever seen.

Abigail, turn towards me. His hand was on my shoulder. I turned but kept my head down. He put two fingers under my chin and lifted it towards him. I've missed you.

I smiled. I couldn't help it. He *missed* me? No information about what stopped him from seeing more of me in the last two and a half months.

It's… it's complicated, he said, was he reading my mind? I didn't answer. Eventually, he continued, It's Galia, she wants to see me at the weekends. Also, Saffi and you, being friends, you know.

I understood. And yet, here he was, standing too close on the edge of the Golan Heights at three o'clock in the morning. I felt lost. It would be good to go back now. I was dead still.

Let's sit, he said, my legs were tired, and so we sat on a big flat rock nearby. I looked ahead at the beautiful view below and tried to ignore his hand on my shoulder and back, his fingers tracing the line of my spine, up and down. It felt nice, but I did want him to stop, so I sat statue-like, still, hardly daring to breathe in case the movement encouraged him. But he didn't need encouragement, his hand carried on endlessly, endlessly stroking, up and down, left to right, up the back of my neck, down again. Forever. Then he leaned towards me, his hand on my chin and turning it towards him. He said, You know it's my birthday today? I said, How old are you? Though I knew exactly, he is twenty-six, the same age as our State, born a few months before Independence. He laughed. Let's just say, old enough to know better, and when he kissed me on the mouth I lay back and let him. Aren't you going to wish me a happy birthday? he said, gently, slowly pushing my clothes out of the way. I was still playing statues, and so everything after was because I didn't snap out of it, because I said, Happy birthday instead of, No! Stop! I want to go back. I know he would have stopped, he's that sort of person. It was up to me, what happened next. I'm okay now.

10 February 1974

My birthday. Mother looked sad when she handed me my present. They were two, wrapped as one—a pair of trousers, lilac, my favourite colour; and a green sweater she'd been knitting. Usually, one present is considered plenty in our family, but Mother wanted me to have something extra, because I have been looking sad lately. I hadn't realised I was sad, but then maybe she was right, maybe it was that thing with Micah on Sylvester night; which, by the way, I've not told anyone about; and which, also by the way, I've been thinking about a lot. Even at lessons time.

One good thing would be when my period comes, and I can stop worrying about having to tell Mother or having an abortion. Was it the abortion that made them send Tovah away? Saffi knows but how to talk with her about it, she will think I'm a gossip, or want to know why I'm asking. Was it that Tovah was meeting with a married Member? Or was it that he was a grown man like Micah? And what if we're found out and his girlfriend leaves him, this quiet and sweet looking girl called Galia, sometimes I feel so sorry for her and sometimes jealous, if she leaves him will that be a good thing? Or will it be my fault like Anya said it would be her fault if Noah's children are taken away? Sometimes I imagine him asking if I would like to be his girlfriend, would such a thing even be possible? But I know that is how it's supposed to be, instead of—what does happen. Which is, he will see me but only when he feels like it, and expect that we will do the thing which is hard not to find quite disgusting sometimes, and all the while not to show—I don't know—he keeps me hanging and confused.

The way I imagine it, he would ask, would you like to be my girlfriend just like Josh had asked Anya last year, and I would say no. Politely. Then he might ask Why not? Why not, when he is in love with me. Then I would say, I cannot love him. Just that, not that he's twelve years older and maybe that's too much. Nor that I want more. I won't say I don't like his smell, or his hard fingers against my skin, or the way my stomach churns when he's near. This dread is mixed with excitement, longing, hope—I wouldn't dream of saying *that*. All these thoughts going round and round, it's exhausting. They come into my head uninvited and stay like unwelcome guests. Father says if you don't want to think about something you should replace it with a happy thought. I can't think of anything happy right now.

Even my birthday came and went, almost unnoticed, on a dark, rainy day; everyone looked gloomy under effortful smiles. By everyone I mean Mother and Father. Tommy, on the other hand, was annoyingly cheerful. Something about a song he and his band, confusingly called The Band, are working on. Apparently, it's brilliant. Daniel has written the words and Josh the music. They're going to perform it on Independence Day.

Ah, says Mother, Lennon and McCartney! You're Ringo Starr of course, Tommy; but who's going to be George?

Tommy said The Band is nothing like The Beatles. It is an original band, Mother, creating original music. Anyway, Led Zeppelin is nearer the mark; mixed with Bob Dylan.

They're looking for a singer; asked Tali already, she's the best singer in our school. But she can't perform on Independence Day, which is the day after Fallen Soldiers Remembrance Day. It'll be the first Remembrance Day since the last war, the first year her father is on the Fallen list, she'll need to be with her family. Daniel suggested asking Anya, but the others weren't sure, she has a good voice but might look awkward on stage. What did I think, Tommy asked. I tried not to feel hurt he didn't think to ask me, not for the singing, but I've been playing the flute for five years already.

The idea of Anya in rehearsals, down in the dark, dank, cramped bomb-shelter, spending long evenings with all those boys, is hateful. I know I can't dictate who he sees, when and where, but—

No buts, just a full stop.

For my birthday, Mother baked a cake but there was no card. Tommy turned up in time for eating and joined in with birthday songs. When it came to *Happy Birthday*, which, unbelievably, is the only birthday song that exists in English, he remembered he hadn't seen to the horses yet and disappeared in a flash. I could tell Mother was upset. He has a negative attitude towards England, hates it when she speaks English. Although he does enjoy it when there's an American film on Jordanian television, and Ruth asks him to be a translator, then he can show off by explaining the plot and eating as many of Ruth's biscuits as he wants.

So Father, Mother and I sang *Happy Birthday* and Father did a harmony, and afterwards offered to get his mandolin out, Mother loves it when he plays. But instead of feeling pleased, she fought back tears and apologised for crying on my birthday, which is a happy day, brings back such wonderful memories of when I was a new baby and the nurses on the maternity ward made such a fuss of my thick curly hair and big blue eyes, it was only a few weeks later that each blue iris turned a different colour, one brown and one grey, which I hate so much, no one wants to be different. And when I was born Grandma Rose came to stay, and that was such a comfort for Mother, having her own mother by her side. Father gave her a sideways look, he doesn't like it when she cries in front of the children, it was a little embarrassing because she hardly ever does.

Mother has been upset since the Members Committee refused to approve her request to go to England for Isabel's wedding. A niece's wedding is not a reason for an approved trip abroad, according to Protocol. Mother's parents came here from England to join her and Uncle David. Aunt Rachel, who was already married and settled in Hampstead, stayed behind. So we have Grandma Rose to go and stay with in Tel Aviv, and to come and visit us with presents of books for me, and football magazines for Tommy. But it means Mother can't now tell the Community she needs to go to England to visit her parents, which *is* an approved reason to travel abroad once in seven years. She really wants to see her sister. Community Members don't think weddings are important. But they *are* important to some. To her. To Darling Rachel and Isabel. Grandma Rose would buy her the air-ticket and they would fly out together. So there's just no reason she can see not to go. Whatsoever.

Poor Mother. Father said if she'd stayed living in England, she would have been a top surgeon by now, she's that clever. She did think about studying medicine here, the Community would have allowed it. It would have been hard because the University is such a long way. Why do we have to live quite so far, in the back of beyond? she moans when things become too much. She would have done it, though. But the University said no. And *that's* because Mother has a British nationality and so she must study in Britain, there are only a few places for medical students in our young and impoverished Country, and these are kept for people who don't have other options, who cannot swan into an English medical school, all expenses paid. Well Mother couldn't just swan over to England. Not without taking Ester, who was only five at the time. Mother even contemplated doing just that, but in the end, she could not contemplate life without Father. He is her rock. The best man any woman could want, and

118

so on, very embarrassing. So she stayed. Also, she is a Zionist and does love our Country. Most of the time. And Father's life is here. He has no other. And then Tommy and I were born and the whole idea was taken off the agenda.

And now, this. Honestly, what if she just packs up and goes? What will they do? Slap her wrist? Throw her out? They won't dare. Will they? No, Father says. It would be embarrassing, if she went without permission. But they wouldn't throw her out.

Oscar, do you or don't you support me? Will you stand by me if I fly to England for the wedding?

Father doesn't want to take a stand, not until the appeal process. There's no point thinking about it until then.

13 April 1974

I've been meaning to write more about Oscar and how he came to survive the Holocaust when practically all the other Jews of his town didn't. Every now and then, Queenie says she's still waiting to read his story. Last night I dreamed I'd already written it. In the dream, I wanted to show it to Queenie but couldn't find my plastic-bound diary. I stood by the stopcock outside my parents' Room, helpless, when the door opened and out came Tommy and Josh. They walked away, talking and laughing carelessly. Then something dropped to the ground behind them, but they didn't stop. It was my diary, lying in the slushy mud. I woke up wondering whether my life was worth living, now Tommy and Josh knew everything about my deepest, most secret thoughts. Freud would have had something to say about it, I've no idea what it means.

But it did make me think of Oscar's story again.

A few days later, Mona told our class we're doing a project for Holocaust Memorial Day. We have to interview someone who is a holocaust survivor. And write a report. Mona said it has to be an authentic report of first-hand experience. She is relying on some good work being produced because she would like to choose the best extracts to be read at the Memorial Day ceremony. Is this my chance to be an author? An author needs an audience, if I never show my work then I can't be one.

So I consulted with Mother. Her family left Poland in 1935 when leaving was still allowed, Grandpa Arthur realised the Jews had no future under the Nazis. They settled in London, Hampstead, learned English, opened a small legal practice in Golders Green with Grandpa Arthur as the lawyer and Grandma Rose as everything else. At the end of the war, when they found out everything that had happened to the Jews, they decided not to go back to the continent. Mother suggested I might want to talk to Grandma Rose about being refugees in England. She herself is too young to remember. But I decided to talk to Aunt Deborah, Father's older sister.

So on Saturday afternoon Father took me to Haifa to Aunt Deborah and Uncle Aaron. She told me about the train they took from Belgrade, which travelled to Hungary and northward to Turkey, then in a taxi to Beirut and a boat to the port of Haifa. But most of the time she and Aaron talked with Father about this and that, mainly the problems Mother is having with the Community. Aunt Deborah said it is absolutely ridiculous. Madness! Father doesn't like to speak ill of the Community, even to his own sister, and especially not in front of me. This is the situation: there's no hope the Members Committee would change its mind, now Mother's appeal has been rejected. The only avenue still open to her is the full Community Assembly, the ultimate democratic tool. Well, says Deborah, let her go ahead and do it. Why shouldn't she? Sometimes all you need is to get away from the narrow mind-set of committees and protocols; let the people have their say. I guarantee the outcome will be in Rifka's favour.

But Mother is undecided. The thought of publicly begging to be allowed to go home makes her sick to her stomach. And people will stand up and speak about her case. *Her case*! As though she's a problem, *a thing* instead of a person. A whole world of a person. And the things they'll say: Why should one Member go, just because her family can pay? And that other argument, the one used every time something new is introduced in the Community, that says, This is going to spell the end of our way of life. The end of socialism.

For example, the huge outcry when Rita's father Jonathan wrote his name with a marker pen on his work-shirt collar. He didn't like sharing it with whoever happened to arrive at the laundry first after it's been washed. That was in the old days, when the penny piece still had a hole, probably. But nowadays, everyone's clothes are marked, no one must share, and the Community is still standing.

And when Solomon came back from studying in France, and brought home the first radio, and the radio had to be put in the Dining Room so everyone could share it, and also in case listening to your own radio in your own room was such a depraved, bourgeois habit it would bring about the end of communality *and* of socialism.

And now. Now they're saying, If we let you go, we'll have to let the next person that comes along do what they want too, and the next, and before you know it there are no rules, no Community, no solidarity, just people like the Rest-of-the-World. And they say, What about Members who don't have family abroad? Why should they never get to go? To which Mother says, Let *them* live away from their country, their families, everything they grew up to expect and love! See how they feel about it after eighteen years! Of course, most of our Members are immigrants, just like she is. But unlike Mother, they don't have homes or families in Europe. Mother knows this, and she *is* sorry for those who lost so much, Father knows she is; but does the fact *they* can't go back mean that *she* shouldn't be allowed to? No, Father agrees it doesn't.

Aunt Deborah, who has strong opinions on everything, says, Well I must tell you, this could not be simpler: Rifka wants to see her family. What's the harm? Seriously, Oscar, would anyone die if she went to England for a short holiday? I just don't know why people must be so small minded. And so on.

Then it was the nearly equally difficult issue of Ester. Aunt Deborah was sure Ester will soon come to her senses, she'll realise the whole notion of Revolution is a tower floating in the air, and then she'll go to university as a clever girl like her must and give up the silliness of being a proletariat who must do factory shift work if she isn't to betray her class-brothers. By the time they'd done all their news and talking it was late. Father stood, he had to be up at four o'clock the next day, but Aunt Deborah said, You go and telephone Jacob, Oscar, ask him to tell Rifka you'll be late, and I'll make a quick start with Abbie while you do that.

When the Second World War started, Yugoslavia was not yet taken by the Germans. Not until the spring of 1941. Our Mother, Irene, was a volunteer with WIZO. You've heard about WIZO, Abbie, haven't you? It stands for Women's International Zionist Organisation. And in 1939, she used to work with, I mean take care of, Jewish refugees escaping Nazi-occupied Europe. They came into our town by boats on the Danube River. Our mother would arrange for families to put them up, and she brought many home to us as well. Speaking to the refugees, she began to understand what was happening to the Jews in the occupied countries. It was a much bleaker picture than the one painted by the radio reports. Mother was always listening to the radio, she even taught herself English so she could listen to the BBC. So then she became determined to leave Europe and join her sister Rosa in Palestine—that's your great aunt Rosa, the same, yes.

Mother was convinced that something dreadful was going to happen in Europe. But our father objected, he had been born in Stuttgart and had great nostalgia for all things German. You know what nostalgia means don't you Abbie, yes? He would say it was madness to leave a peaceful country only to go into a war zone, oh yes, there was much trouble here then, worse than now. Also, his business was flourishing, he was selling woollen blankets to the army at a time the army could not have enough woollen blankets. He was a Zionist, yes. But, like many Zionists he preferred to, you know, talk about Zionism rather than do it. It's always been the same, We're about to go up to Zion. Always, just about to go, just as soon as this and that happens, as soon as the children start school, as soon as they leave elementary school, business picks up, business slows down... truth was he was not ready, and Mother had to stay with him. But she decided to send us away anyway, Oscar and me. On our own to Palestine. We would go to boarding school and stay with Aunt Rosa during school holidays. And they would follow us as soon as possible. That was the plan.

On our way to Palestine, at the train station in Belgrade, Mother came on the train with us. I think she couldn't bring herself to say goodbye, and she came with us as far as the border. While we were stopped at the Hungarian border, she told me to go into the toilets and stay. When I came back to our seats Mother wasn't there. Gone. And she never said goodbye.

On our way home in the car Father talked about the time before he and Hermina, which is what he calls Aunt Deborah, left their parents in Yugoslavia, never to see them again. His father had been opposed to sending the children to Palestine on their own. He had tried to persuade Irene, but to no avail. Everyone who knew them thought she was wrong, irresponsible. She was the talk of the town. Palestine was in the grip of a three-way war between the native Arabs, the pioneering immigrant Jews, and the occupying British. It was a dangerous country: poor, violent, uncivilised. And at the same time the British were preparing for a German invasion from the African front, via Egypt. Their Aunt Rosa's husband Shalom had joined the British Army as an officer. And back in free Yugoslavia all was quiet and peaceful.

When their travel had been arranged, Morris had asked Oscar to tell his mother that he didn't want to go away, that he wanted to stay home and safe. His mother would let him stay, Morris said. She wouldn't force him to go. If Oscar did that, Morris said, he could have anything he wanted. Even a bike. But Oscar had already told his friends he was going to Palestine, and it would be embarrassing to tell them he wasn't leaving after all. Also, he wanted to go, it was an adventure.

It's difficult to imagine being eleven years old and wanting to leave home, go to an unknown country where you know no one and can't even speak the language. Lucky Father did. Otherwise, he wouldn't be telling this story now. Because Deborah and Oscar never saw their parents again, because Irene and Morris were murdered along with all the Jews in their town. In 1941 a battalion of Hungarian sword-bearers came into the city of Novi-Sad ahead of the German army. They took the Jews to the banks of the Danube. Then they drilled holes in the ice over the water and shot them, and they fell into the river, one by one.

17 April 1974

Mona chose Aunt Deborah's story for reading at the Holocaust Memorial Day ceremony. I hardly changed anything from the way I wrote it the first time. Mother said to leave it raw and that it would be more Authentic (Authentic is a word I don't know, but Mother won't tell me what it means, Look it up in the dictionary, she says). Father was not sure about having his story read out to everyone. He said this to Jacob and Ruth who came round the evening of the ceremony, before it was time to go to the Dining Room. I wore shoes instead of sandals, and a white shirt. Readers must look smart out of respect for the dead. Ruth said I looked lovely in white; she could see me as a bride already, Oh, won't she make a most beautiful bride, Rifka? Which of course set mother off crying again, thinking of how the Committee Members won't let her go to Isabel's wedding.

Ruth is a kind woman, but you do need to spell things out to her or she doesn't notice them, so she was just going on and on about how lovely I have become, prettier even than Ester, and how Father would need to be careful, men will be queuing at the door, he must keep that M-16 under his bed oiled and ready. Neither of my parents responded, they never give us compliments, especially not on our appearance, which you shouldn't think about, it's shallow. It's not that they are a disapproving sort. They just don't want us to become proud. Or vain, which is worse. Although I know I shouldn't care about such things, Ruth's words left a warmth in my chest.

To change the subject, Father asked Jacob what he made of the latest in the Watergate affair. Was the noose not tightening around President Nixon's neck? Is his position not untenable now? Jacob agreed. The U.S. of A. is the greatest democracy in the world, a system with checks and balances, where even the President himself is accountable. Yes, the Senate will bring Nixon to book, Father said. He will be gone by summer. If not before.

You see, says Jacob, we have so much to learn from the Americans. About how to hold politicians to account. Father says, Hold on, Golda Meir has just resigned, after the blunder she made over the Yom Kippur War. Isn't that accountability? But Jacob disagrees. The Prime Minister is a scape goat. She shouldn't have resigned. The failure to predict the war was an Intelligence failure, not her fault. And now she's replaced with a bloodthirsty General, who's surely going to give us more conflict and wars, mark Jacob's words. But Father has high hopes for Yizhak Rabin. And so on and so on.

Ruth was telling Mother about what happened in Dov's shoemaking workshop. She is a big woman, you know that, and her steps are heavy. So, she wears out her work shoes more quickly than some, so what? In the Dining Room kitchen, I'm on my feet all day, Rifka, you know that don't you, and the work shoes wear out. So when she goes to Dov for a new pair, he says nothing, even though by Community Protocol, new work shoes are only given every two years. Dov is a gentleman, a lovely man! What a lovely little family he and Clara and Josh make, don't you think? Such a shame Clara couldn't have any more children after that tragedy, oh, but isn't Josh a nice boy. I've been telling my Maya, I said, Here's a boy for you, they would make such a lovely couple, don't you think Rifka? And you, Abbie, don't you think Maya and Josh are well suited? But her questions are Rhetorical because she doesn't wait for a reply. And she says, but do you know, she won't listen to me, that girl. Tells me she doesn't even like Josh! Can you credit it? I said, Darling, you don't have to *like* him. When I was a child in Iraq no one spoke about *like* or *dislike*. You counted yourself lucky if you got to set eyes on the boy before your wedding day, I said. Then Ruth looks at me sideways, and continues. Besides, darling, I tell her, you're too young to understand the human heart. Isn't she Rifka, don't you agree?

I mean! *All* I'm saying is she should get him now so no other girl can have him. I know she'll thank me later. Oh, if only Tommy would bring Josh to our room sometime, Maybe Maya would change her mind. And if not her, then Shira. Or Gali. Oh, but Gali is too young to think about such things. Do you think you could have a word with Tommy, Rifka? He and Josh could come over, they would have coffee and cake, watch the news on our television, or an Egyptian film. You can come too, Abbie, sit with Shira. Oh, but there's no point, I should save my strength. Maya is so stubborn; I don't know where she gets it from. And now she is walking out with that boy Daniel. I don't know a thing about him. Except, he is too lazy to learn Hebrew. But at least this means Maya is improving her English, that's something, isn't it Rifka, you know about such things, isn't it?

Mother doesn't respond. There's never any need to with Ruth, not when she's in the flow. Lately, though, Mother is becoming more and more quiet. For a moment Ruth is at a loss. Where was she? Oh, yes, in Dov's workshop. Here she is returning a worn-out pair of work shoes that is less than a year old, and Dov is measuring her for a new pair. So, then *Someone* walks in who shall remain nameless in this company. Dramatic pause. So, this *Someone* says, Oh, Ruth, you're having a new pair of shoes, *again!* Did you ever, Rifka? Bold as brass, that, that... excuse me, Abbie... She's whispering now. That *parasite*... who last winter took so many illness days that when she finally went back to work the toddlers had forgotten her! Yes, I heard they all burst into tears and that's the truth! And now she's making out that *I'm* a dancing princess who needs new shoes every night. And then—then she says, do you hear, Rifka? She says, *I* haven't had new work shoes for *three years*. So I told her, I told her straight. Are you listening, Rifka, I said, Yes, but how many new *slippers* have you had? I said that, what do you think?

128

Now Mother's smile creeps up her cheeks, she's smiling and then she's laughing. And she's gasping for air like she so often used to. Oh, Ruth... How many new slippers... that's brilliant... Ruth is smiling, a little bemused. And Mother has tears down her cheeks, she's shaking silently, and Ruth is giggling. I love it when Mother laughs. She sees hilarity where others don't. I'd love to be able to laugh with such abandon. Mother says, Oh, Ruth, well done—you stood up to her...

And she's no longer laughing, but her tears are still flowing. Now she's crying. Oh, Ruth, I'm so sorry... I'm all mixed up. And to me, I'm sorry, Abbie, I'll be alright in a minute, I promise. It's... people can be so very mean and petty sometimes. And Ruth is also crying now, she didn't mean to upset Mother. No, no, Mother is grateful. Ruth has cheered her up. Truly. And their arms are round each other, they wipe their tears and actually do seem quite cheerful.

Jacob says, Well, we seem to be ready for the ceremony. I hope you haven't used up all your tears, Ruth. You'll need them in a little while.

She will, says Mother, When she hears what Abbie has written.

1 June 1974

Queenie is dead.

She died two weeks ago, on Independence Day.

The same day terrorists infiltrated the Lebanese border and killed twenty-one children, 71 injured in a school in Ma'alot. Queenie's car crash was unconnected, but the roads were blocked and the ambulances all busy elsewhere because of the hostage-taking. By the time she arrived at the hospital it was too late, she'd lost too much blood. She had two weeks in hospital having operations and blood transfusions. Everyone in the Community donated blood for her. Those who could.

Children under sixteen are not allowed to donate blood.

Not even half a portion.

She is buried in the cemetery, overlooking the Jordan and the palm plantations.

She'd been expecting her first baby.

26 years old and studying to become a school teacher.

That's all I can write.

8 September 1974

Today is the day Mother was supposed to return home from England. After a whole month being away. Father said he needed to talk to Tommy and me, it was important, so we stopped our Rummikub game, and Maya and Josh went away. I thought maybe something terrible had happened to Mother, maybe she died in a plane crash and is lost forever, like Queenie. And how awful that the last time we spoke, the last time we were together my words were mean and angry.

Back in August, she woke me in the nighttime. Sitting on the side of my bed, in a hushed voice so as not to wake the others, she told me she and Grandma Rose were flying to England together. Father was going to drive her to the airport, leaving in half an hour. Even though the Members Committee forbade it. I had to understand, she simply had to go. Tommy, he'd known about this for a while. And said nothing. Ester also knew, so I was the only one they did not trust with the knowledge that Mother was leaving us for a whole month. I was the only one given only a few minutes to say goodbye.

So I said it was selfish to leave Father in the lurch, to face the Community, the criticism, the talk. He'd be the one having to defend her, and no one will understand. While she would be trying on hats in Harrods; and taking tea with Aunt Rachel at the Ritz, which is all she's been writing to me about since she's gone. Hats and biscuits at Harrods, tea and cake at the Ritz. She would never ever let us buy anything when we were out in the city. Not even a cup of tea. Not in our country. Only in Marvellous Old England is such a luxury permitted! I hate her. And when she tried to hug me, I pulled back. And when she had to go because Father wanted to avoid the traffic rush hour in Tel Aviv, I didn't say goodbye, just let the wild anger and fear bunch up like a pair of fists between us. The longest I'd ever been without Mother was last spring, when Quills went on a five-day seminar on Arab-Jewish relations.

Since then, she's been writing and writing, how she loves or misses or is thinking of *our country*, how *breathtakingly* beautiful it is and no wonder we have so many wars, simply *everyone* wants a piece of it. Well, not *everyone*. Because *she* doesn't. She doesn't love it as she should, and she doesn't want to come back to us. Mostly, Mother writes about how wonderful London is, how blissful the weather, how beautiful the scenery, Hampstead in all its colours, so many shades of green, not like our own scorched yellows and burnt browns. And she writes how absolutely marvellous everyone is, her family has taken her right back into its bosom, our cousins are so well mannered, *sporty* and talented. Oh, and of course, Isabel's wedding, the wedding, the wedding! For which they need flowers from John Lewis, a dress from Selfridges, guests from London and Manchester. And they have a thing called Seating Order because the English aren't trusted to find their own seats for their lunch, and *that* nearly caused a pre-wedding divorce. And not forgetting the bridesmaids who are girls in pink dresses, the page-boys who are boys wearing miniature men's suits, the Rabbi, the synagogue. And there's the day-time dress, including a hat; the evening-party-dress, which is different to the daytime one but with no hat. Everything, according to Mother, everything about England is better than here. Some of her letters are sent to all of us. But she also sent special letters just for me, where she writes more of the same, but also pleading for me to write, or to come to the phone next time she calls. I haven't written back, though I have read all her letters. Many times.

And now, Father was saying, Anthony has telephoned the Community Secretary's office at lunch time, and Father was called to the phone from the Dining Room. Anthony said Grandma Rose had a fall. On her way down the steps to the taxi which was waiting to take Mother and her to the airport. She is now in hospital and Mother and Rachel are with her. They missed their flight, and we don't know yet how soon Grandma Rose will be able to travel.

Tommy and I said nothing. I suppose we were relieved nothing worse has happened, though we did feel sad for Grandma Rose, a fall at her age is serious. Eventually, Tommy asked why Mother had to stay in England.

Rachel can look after Grandma Rose, can't she, she's her daughter too, isn't she. Father said Mother wouldn't walk out on Grandma Rose in this state; no way would she have stepped over her and taken the taxi to the airport herself. Why not, Tommy asked. And how will it look if after all that's happened, she doesn't come back when she said she would? Father said not to worry. She may catch the next flight, tomorrow. But Tommy persisted. She must go to work, you know. Ezra has been managing in the henhouse without her long enough. People are making comments. Even Leo told me that, because of Mother, Ezra injured his back, he's been working too hard. Can't they see, she's sprinkling salt on their wounds, by staying longer! Tommy was upset. He was talking for both of us. In the end Father had to go and speak to Ezra, to let him know Mother won't be back in the henhouse tomorrow.

5 October 1974

Mother is staying with Grandma Rose at Aunt Rachel's house. For the time being. At least till after Chanukah. She was so very thrilled to receive my letter. And grateful, and sorry too but oh, never mind darling, let's not dwell on the fact that I've abandoned you. That's the implication, anyway. What she writes is, *But these are trials and tribulations which we will not be defeated by, darling. They are a consequence of living so far away from ~~home~~ where I used to think of as home.* Just like this, with the word home, *our* home crossed out, and that is a Freudian Slip which is a concept she herself told me about. Now that it's holiday season and the weather is cooler, she misses our country even more, she writes.

133

Well, it *is* holiday season, tabernacle next week, then Chanukah in December. Autumn is the most exciting feeling, the smell of rain in the air, armies of migrating birds stopping by on their way to Africa where they will spend the winter: the Community yard is awash with hoopoes, starlings and wagtails, but storks, cranes, sparrow hawks and eagles don't land here, Father has to drive us to see them congregating by the fish farms in Bet Shean Valley, but he hasn't offered. Mother used to love bird spotting, she knew all about their silhouettes and calls. She isn't here now. But gone are the mosquitos and the tedium of waking before dawn to work in a hot grapefruit plantation which makes school feel like an actual rest. And Saturday Saffi and I went looking for squills, there was a mass, a white sea of them all along the disused railway track by the main road. We stayed a while and talked about how the British built a railway here before they left us to our Independence. And the trains passed right here on their way to Beirut and Damascus. Hard to imagine a time when such journeys were possible. Mother used to miss living in a place where peace and crossing borders are taken for granted. Where it's normal to not go to war with your neighbour. Well now she *does* live in such a place. Oh, except she's just heard about a terror attack in a city called Guildford, four dead and fifty injured. Probably, it's *those ruthless Irish nationalists*.

Mother's letters are long-long, they probably take her all day to write, she and Grandma Rose bought me a coat for winter, which is on its way by sea-post, and now I must write a thank you letter to Grandma Rose whose money paid for the coat. And I have to send her a get-well letter too, Grandma is very unhappy in the hospital, she cannot understand the nurses' accents with her bad hearing, half of them are foreign and the other half are from The North, and all of them too busy or too rude to do their job properly. And now Grandma has offered to buy airplane tickets for me and Tommy so we can come to England over the Chanukah holiday. Mother is so excited; she has written that I must help her persuade Father to agree but why should I?

At Jewish New Year David and Betty celebrated the coming of autumn with us here in the Community, they had never done that before, probably they were trying to support Father who is having the worst time. It was bad enough that Mother ran away to England without permission but then when she didn't come back even their good friends lost sympathy. You get to know who your real friends are, Father sighs. He won't discuss this with me, but when Ruth and Joseph come by that's all they talk about, how unfair it all is. Especially furious are the Members Committee, the ones who refused Mother permission to go in the first place, they even brought a Resolution before the Full Assembly meeting, to condemn Mother's lack of discipline. Father was so upset about it he didn't attend the meeting, he said so that he doesn't have to watch the Members vote. Yes, it was a horror, Ruth said, like a Hitchcock movie, you know the one where the woman was stab-stab-stabbed, just like that, a stabbing in the back is what it was. Poor Rifka. But you know, Solomon stood up and spoke in Rifka's defence, and in the end the Resolution was only passed by the slimmest of slim majority. Father doesn't want to know. And yet he does. It's such a disgrace, how did things come to this, he simply cannot understand. And yet. How do you continue living in this small Community after a thing like that? He can't bear to be told who voted how. But wouldn't it be better to know? Know where you stand with people? What they are really thinking? One thing he *can be* sure about, Ruth and Joseph stand with him. All the way.

16 November 1974: Micah

We were sitting in the parents' Room last night, waiting for it to be time to go to the Dining Room for Sabbath Reception Meal. Ester was helping Tommy and me make a list of things we need for going to England. Father was taking no notice. Ever since he agreed for us to go to England, he hasn't spoken of it. He can't face the reality of it, was Ester's explanation as she unfolded the newspaper. Though he did talk to Shosha in the post room, who ordered us blue passports from the Home Office.

Tommy still says he won't go. He has a performance with The Band. Also, he has a girlfriend: Maya! Ruth was so busy matchmaking her with Josh, asking Tommy to bring Josh over to watch their television, or to eat her Iraqi biscuits, and sending Maya over to us every time she saw Josh walking over. Even though Maya told her she wasn't interested, Ruth didn't give in. Not until Maya told her about Tommy. He's crazy about her, I can tell though he won't admit it. He should be grateful to Ruth and her meddling. Without it, Maya would never have noticed him. And another reason he won't go to England, he is angry with Mother. He hates it that people disapprove of our family. And Father says not a word, so no one realises he really hadn't realised Mother was thinking of staying away. And maybe she wasn't, who knows. Father thinks Tommy will go to England in the end.

At seven o'clock Micah came in. Hello, I've heard Ester was here, was what he said. He ignored me, that's usual, though I knew he would come for me later. He and Father talked about farming, milk and egg quotas, water shortage, inflation 35 percent. Then he and Ester started on politics. Last week's infiltration, terrorist massacre in Bet Shean, a town only fifteen kilometres away. Four people dead and twenty injured. After the terrorists were killed by our paratroopers, the town people abused their bodies, Father won't say how. So now the death-through-terror toll for this year is sixty, not counting the terrorists. In Micah's view the answer is simple. Return the Territories, go back to the 1967 border in exchange for peace.

What about East Jerusalem? Ester asks. And Father looks about to walk out. He thinks Ester's views are extreme. But then he changes his mind, settles back in his chair.

Jerusalem is ours, Micah says, We cannot give it back.

Ester says, Then you have fallen at the first hurdle. Even if the rest of it were plausible, which it isn't. The Jordanians won't have it.

Micah gives her the narrow eyes smile I know. Do people see him look at me this way? He says, You know, in *Time* magazine, it says we are A Nation Sorely Besieged. That's how we look in America. Terror is rife, the PLO gaining strength; and now Yasser Arafat has observer status in the UN.

Ester says, Ah, you're following the news. She can be rude when she wants to.

He's rattled, the cat-smile fades. He says, What's your solution, since you are such an expert?

Ester says it is a One State Solution—Palestinians and Jews living together.

Oh, you agree with Arafat, a Secular-Democratic Palestine! Kind of him to allow us into his fantasy state. Are you going to bring back all refugees as well?

Of course. Do you expect them to be refugees forever?

Then we'll have a Jewish minority. Can you live with that? Micah sits back as though he's just punched his way to victory.

Are you saying we are more capable of running this country than the Palestinians?

Yes. And, personally, I would oppose anything dreamed up by Arafat. Seriously, that unshaven bandit, that terrorist—a *Prime Minister*? With an Arab *Chief of Staff*? He smiles. Ester smiles back. He says, Also, the refugees aren't coming back. How would that work? It wouldn't.

Ester says, Well, we've not shown ourselves so adept at running this country. Five wars in twenty-five years and a refugee crisis. Are you proud?

We didn't create the crisis, Micah said. *Or* started the wars. Except in '67; in which case we were provoked.

Ester sighs. Look, I don't like to see anybody killed, any more than you do. But terrorism is how the Palestinians keep their cause alive. We are leaving them no other option and we shouldn't be surprised at what's happening. Now she's gone too far. I looked over at Father. Ester did too. Normally, he would be telling her to watch herself, not to defend the terrorists, not in this house. Or he would walk out in protest. But today he did nothing. And when nothing happened Ester went on. We must negotiate. Instead of which Rabin has announced his government will never talk to the PLO. That's his idea of diplomacy.

Micah said, I say again we should hand back the Territories. In return for peace.

Ester laughed, but only to make a point: King Hussein doesn't want the West Bank back! With a million refugees and no infrastructure it's at best a liability, at worst a barrel of explosives. Not to mention the Settlers. Fanatical immigrants, turning up here in the name of Zionism, given every tax break we can't afford, sent off by the Government to colonise the Territories. The same government I expect you voted for, and my father too.

Father raises his hand. He opens his mouth, about to protest, he didn't vote for Rabin. But he changes his mind, his hand floats down onto his lap, slowly, like a fallen leaf. Ester doesn't notice the side show in Father's chair. Once she starts on the Settlers there's no stopping her. This is what our supposedly left-wing government is doing by populating the Territories with religious zealots—you've heard of demographic warfare? Micah looks like interjecting, but she ploughs on. Every new settlement makes it more difficult to hand the Territories back. And everyone's a loser; not just the Palestinians, but all of us. Especially you, she points at Micah, fighting this unsustainable war, and soon Tommy as well.

But Micah isn't stationed in the West Bank. And he's glad to defend our country against its enemies. And then it was time for Sabbath Reception meal. Tommy rushed ahead on his bike, and I walked with Father, my arm in his, in silence. While Micah and Ester continued arguing. He was frustrated, and I was glad. I've had enough of his games, enough of the secrets and being ignored in public. I'm fourteen years old and three quarters, not a child anymore. I wondered whether next time he comes for me, probably tonight, I would say something. Something like that.

But I didn't. When he asked to walk me back after supper I said Okay, and when he turned towards the graveyard and continued through the grapefruit plantation I continued alongside him. When I talked it was to answer his questions, I let him be in charge. And I let him hold my hand. When he mentioned the debate, he and Ester had earlier I thought perhaps he'd ask me what I thought, who was right and wrong. But he didn't and instead said he had trouble concentrating on the discussion because he'd noticed early on I wasn't wearing a bra. Sometimes I think I worry too much about Micah. Maybe I should let him kiss me again. Etc. That's what he wants. It's like a bridge we've not crossed, and he can't see me properly until we have. If I cross that bridge with him, maybe he would feel that we are going somewhere, that we have a future, and he would maybe begin to think I was a girlfriend, someone who has views worth listening to. Maybe that's how older people have relationships, they can't get going until they've done the sex? And it wasn't so bad, after all, last New Year's Eve. Plus, I'm much more grown up now! Practically fifteen. Probably ready for that kind of thing anyway. Or should be.

But last night I had the paralysis again. Having him close was heavy, so oppressive all I could do was be still and hope he would give up soon. Which he did, after doing the light strokes, gently, patiently, and now I wish I could look forward to seeing him again very soon. But that won't be until two months' time, when I come back from England and I am nearly fifteen.

24 November 1974: Josh

I was walking back to our boarding house from my parents' last night. It had rained earlier but the sky was clear again, the moon large in the sky and glittering upwards from the puddles. Above the swimming pool, between two cypress trees I saw a shooting star. Automatically, I said the usual wish, that Josh would love me. I don't believe in this kind of nonsense, but always make that wish anyway, to be on the safe side. It's just a silly game. But, tonight, just then, Josh came up behind me on his bike. He jumped off next to me. At first, I thought he may have fallen off, I was so unprepared for the possibility that he would choose to fall into step with me. But it turned out he hadn't, that is, he did. I mean, he did choose to walk with me. And he hadn't fallen off.

Hi, he said, a little breathless, Going back?

Hi. Even though since last year Josh had occasionally spoken to me, I was still not used to talking back. The bike he pushed with one hand was on his right, on the narrow pavement, to avoid dragging it through the puddles; and I was on his left, which didn't leave much room for our swinging arms. And so, our coat sleeves brushed each other before I put my hand in my pocket, elbow braced against my waist. There was silence in the narrow space between us, screaming in my ears, this was my usual Josh-reaction. My throat pressed onto my stomach, and my right arm, the one next to him, got hot and sweaty.

After years of longing for Josh I had at last managed to

persuade myself to move on. I don't want to be a victim of unrequited love, end up like a shrivelled Miss Havisham. I had consulted with Queenie about this. It was a week before. The last time we had a proper conversation. Before she was lost to me forever. I asked her if she thought it's ever possible to stop loving someone. She said, Why would you? And I said, Because he doesn't love you back. Queenie said she wasn't sure what I meant by love; she was always choosing the most complicated, philosophical answers. She said she believed true love is independent of whether the other person loves you back. If I want to stop loving that person, it probably means I've already done that, that I don't truly love him; then she added, Or her.

So I was beginning to feel a little easier when I saw Josh. But that was when there were other people around us. Unlike now. Now, we were walking towards our school, alone. He chose to get off his bike, to create this opportunity... for what? It was dark and no one else was using the pavement. I tried to conjure a feeling of an easy, familiar-kind-of-friendship. It's what we should have anyway, we see so much of each other because of his friendship with Tommy. Breathe more easily, in two, out three. Relax. That's it. Casual friends. But I could not think of a single thing to say. Even if I could, I was far from certain of being able to physically produce the words. Looking ahead at the trees behind which lay our school, I thought, *don't let's get there, not just yet*. And then this chant: *not just yet, not just yet, not just not just not just yet...*

I saw a shooting star just now. His voice was startling in the thin darkness.

Yes, I blurted, hoarsely. *Say something longer than one*

syllable, silly girl! Silence again, for the longest time. But I could hear his breathing, and I heard him take a breath in a way people do before talking. He did this twice but remained silent. Was he nervous, too?

Ummm, he started. He was holding on to the tension that had been between us. This eased some of the weight in my throat, and the words spilled right out before I could catch them: Did you make a wish? The heat in my right arm climbed to my face. A drop of sweat made its way down between my armpit and ribs. He didn't answer straight away, and I cursed myself for being so ridiculously unguarded. Of all the things I could have said, of all the things *anybody else would have said…* anybody with half a brain.

But then he said, I did, yeah. Well never in a million years was I going to ask what his wish was. Or tell him mine. But he went on, I… I asked for courage. *Ah, courage,* I thought. *I see, courage, of course.* It wasn't disappointment, not really. I'd never imagined he would have wished for something else, something related to me. He wants courage, it's natural; he needs courage because… well, probably because, like Tommy, he is obsessed with being a fighter-pilot. Next year, when he joins up. And, failing that, because most do fail at that, he wants to be a navigator. Or an officer in a crack unit. Like Staff Patrol.

We reached the crossway where his class house was turn-left and mine keep-on-straight. And we stood still for a moment. I thought maybe he was not sure how we should part. And then. Then he took another breath, another breath-before-you-speak, and opened his mouth slightly. And he said, Ummm… I have to go and lock the gate in the garden below the graveyard now… Ummm…

And I waited, for him to keep talking, keep talking to me. I didn't mind. I was used to waiting, good at it. I would have waited longer, an hour or two, but I didn't have to. Because it seemed as though, a moment later, at long, long last, my waiting was over. Because, Reader, he said, Would you like to… to come?

This has been the most momentous occasion in my fourteen-year-old life so far. Writing this down, a day later, I'm re-experiencing the stomach-churning, heart-pumping feeling I had then. I've just finished reading Jane Eyre, last Friday, having been able to do nothing else for three days. I even took the book into lessons, reading it on my lap under the desk. And one romantic situation (Jane's) put me in mind of another (mine). Though, now I think about it, *Reader, I married him* doesn't have the same ring as *Reader he asked me out*. Oh, well. And, besides, unlike me, Jane was in love with the wrong man, whatever Mother says about tall-dark-and-handsome Mr. Rochester. But still! Oh, I wish I could write like Charlotte Bronte.

Standing at the crossroad, with Josh at my side, I wanted to say, Yes; also, I'd like that very much. But a stone was pressing on my voice box again, and an evil hand had opened a floodgate behind my eyes and it was as much as I could manage to fight back the tears, *Don't cry, you idiot! Give him an answer or he'll walk away…* and I was fumbling in my pocket for a handkerchief though I was sure there wasn't one; and in the end there was no choice, I had to press my hands hard against my eyes, and sniff for everything that my life from now on was going to be worth; and, miraculously, was able to blurt, Yes… and, Sorry, and sniff some more; and then, at last, regain composure, long enough to look up, look him in his dark eyes, and smile. Sorry, I said then, in a nearly normal voice, Sorry, yes. I do.

Okay, Josh said. Did he sound cheerful, relieved even? I just have to drop off my bike and get the key for the gate. Then I'll be ready. So we turned left and walked to his boarding house and the silence between us wasn't so heavy. Not comfortable, but warm, like I imagine having a bath (I did have a bath once when we stayed at David and Betty's house after Passover, but it was a long time ago).

I stood in the shadows, outside Josh's house, waiting for him to come back out with the key, when Tommy appeared on his bike, racing it downhill. He parked it under the bike-shelter and nearly walked into me. Oh, hello, little one, what are you doing here? he asked, but didn't wait for an answer, just walked on by, disappearing through the wide-open doorway into the fluorescent-lit corridor. I could hear his heavy footsteps on the marble floor; his voice, saying, Hey, Josh, I'm going down to the bomb-shelter; making music, want to come? My heart sank, but Josh's voice said, No, he didn't, he was going out. Then Tommy's voice disappointed. Out? Out where?

Just out. His voice floated nearer.

Where, Josh? Tommy seemed lost.

See you later! Josh called behind him and was through the doorway, walking towards the shadows. Towards me. The bright neon lights framed his head, for a short moment giving his long limbs and wild, wispy hair a stranger's look. Let's get out of here, he said.

We fell into step, walked down to the end of the pavement, then down the steps towards the river up to the parameter fence. The gate was locked, all gates are, at night time. Josh's voice was quiet, close. Shall we climb over? There's a gap on one side, see, the barbed wire has been pulled away. Or we can walk around the other way, if you prefer. I said it was fine to climb the gate. He went first. Reached up, pulled himself to the top and swung his legs over. Crouching now, he readied himself to jump, though it was too high. There was the sound of tearing cloth, followed by a thud of landing and a groan. He lay on the ground, motionless.

Are you all right? I whispered. No answer: just quiet moans. Josh, what happened? His silence was more alarming than the fall. Then his moans turned, and I thought for a moment he was crying; but he wasn't. It was laughter. Laughing quietly, fiercely, like Mother sometimes does. Did. What? What is it? What's funny? I was embarrassed, cross. Is he playing a joke? Are his friends going to jump out from behind the reeds? Will they jeer at me for entertaining the thought, for being so naïve? For daring to believe Josh Pasternak would seriously consider asking me out? I felt my cheeks burning, my eyes too. I should walk away now; save what scrap of tattered dignity I had left.

But he was talking again. No, nothing, it's nothing… He was still struggling to speak through whatever the joke was, wiping his eyes, pulling a handkerchief from his pocket to blow his nose. He sat up, legs out in front, leaning back on one hand. I'm sorry. I'll explain, promise. Come on, your turn. I'll help you down. And he stood, a little laboriously, he was hurt. And when I was at the top of the gate he was up there too, holding the length of barbed wire away so I could climb through. I realised with alarm that when I turn round to go down the other side my bottom would be just about face-high for him. I could hear Mother's voice, *Il faut être toujour très élégant!* But as I swung my leg over the top he was already down and waiting, and when I was ready to let go with my hands, his hands were on my waist, and he nearly carried me down, so it was not so much a jump as a lovely Cinderella dance float to the ground.

Thanks, I said, turning towards him, standing close, but not too close.

He smiled in the moonlight; close but not too close.

He said, Did I embarrass you? Laughing?

It's okay, I said, his friends were probably not there after all.

It's just that I had this image. Of jumping over the gate, you know, he chuckled. I was going to do it like the Sundance Kid. With a swagger, you know. You were watching me, and I thought I'd impress you. Then he took a breath. I realised it was the way he nearly always started talking. Breathe, then open his mouth slightly, inviting the words to come out, giving them a head start. My heart ached with the beauty of this small detail. He went on, Instead, I landed in a heap. Ummm, and now my trousers are torn.

He was laughing again, and I did also, walking together under clear winter sky. My head was floating above my neck like a helium balloon with the joy of it.

And I relaxed so much that, when I heard my voice say, Oh, never mind, I love you anyway, for one anxious moment I wasn't sure whether it was in my head, or I'd spoken those words and it was too late to take them back, they were out and between us, and all was lost. But no, I hadn't spoken, because, next, I heard my own, actual voice, and my voice said, But are you hurt?

I am. But not mortally. We smiled then, two Cheshire Cat smiles, floating in the night's shadow. How to transcribe so much happiness onto paper?

In the garden there is a stone bench and some bushes. We headed for it without talking; there was a couple already sitting there in the dark. We stood still and silent, then I felt his light touch briefly on my shoulder, and we walked up through the narrow snaky path, up amongst gravel and sleepy flower beds. Josh locked the gate behind us. They'll have to walk back another way, he said about the couple on the bench.

We walked to the big old ficus in whose branches there used to be a tree house. We sat against it, looking up through the branches. And it seemed a good time to talk about how we might meet like this again; just like this. To say how glad he was to have at last dared to ask me out. But instead, he was quiet. And panic rose in me again. Could it be that he did just feel like company, that anyone would have done tonight? Maybe he feared the cemetery in the dark and was too embarrassed to admit this to his *real* friends. He knew I wouldn't ask questions. Has probably worked out years ago how I feel about him. And even if I did find out that he's scared of the dark, of ghosts, whatever, what would it matter? It's only me, Tommy's little, practically invisible sister. No one important.

I felt so upset, with the frantic confusion in my head, that I missed the beginning of his speaking. He was saying, Well, does silence mean yes or no?

What? I blurted, rudely.

I said it's my turn to lock up the gates every night this

week. Would you come with me tomorrow also? It's fine if you don't want to—

What? *Shut up with the stupid Whats already! Speak sense, quick, or he'll disappear in a puff of smoke!* I said, Yes, ah, no, I mean—*Come on, spit it out!* I mean yes, I'd like to. Yes, please.

Well, there's no need to say please. Or, if there is, it's me who should say it. His voice smiled. As though enough wonderful things hadn't already happened tonight! I smiled too and didn't pull back, only held my breath, when he seemed to move towards me. But he was only leaning on one hand to stand up, then stood there beating the slightly muddy earth off his trousers, remembering too late he'd hurt himself earlier, Ouch, but his Cheshire cat teeth were still shining in the moonlight. Well, I need to go back now, it's workday tomorrow, five o'clock start. He stretched his arm to help me up. But I was already halfway to standing, and it collided with my head. Sorry, Abbie. Are you okay?

Was I okay? I was. More than okay. Did it hurt? Who cares! At fourteen and three quarters my dreams were coming true. I thought of all the heroines I know. Poor Jane, loving cold Mr. Rochester; and Mrs. Rochester, heartlessly abused; Miss Havisham, cobwebbed in her wedding dress. And Scarlett, she never did get Rhett to settle down. I pitied them. All. Because I now had what they had longed for. Or I was going to, soon. I wasn't sure what the thing would be. But it was coming. And it was going to be wonderful. Yes, I said out loud, yes, I'm fine. Just fine.

25 November 1974

Well, I could hardly sleep at all the night Josh asked me out. First, because of being so excited about what had happened. And then, when it was already late, I worried about what he would be thinking. About the things I said, how stupid I must have sounded; and the things I didn't say. How awkward, ignorant, naïve, boring, infantile, ugly am I! He's bound to rethink about calling for me tomorrow. Probably, he just said he would because he couldn't think of anything else to say; because I was so boring; because he wanted to fill in the silence, the silence I had thought was pleasant, friendly, but which to him was uncomfortable. Wasn't it? *Wasn't it?* And so on, till morning-chorus.

So, in the morning I decided not to worry, there was no point, I was too tired anyway. And the day went by quite pleasantly. We're studying *Lord of the Flies* with Mona. I already read it in the summer. Just picked it up at random off the shelf in the library. Never heard of William Golding before. Couldn't believe it! That such a work of genius could have been unknown to me. It went right through me; I was bowled over, as Mother would say. Gripped to the end. The bitter end. The island setting was familiar, too. The boys were our boys. I can just see Ralph chairing our school assemblies, presiding over decisions such as, Should we have a girls-only hour in the communal showers? And Piggy; even Jack. Although their situation was extreme, of course. And that's why it all went wrong.

How marginal adults are in our lives, here in our community. Except for Queenie, who was our

150

cornerstone. I still miss her many times each day. So this is my case: I've been living with my classmates, since I was born; have only ever spent two nights at my parents' room. I care about my family, sure. But I'm closest to my contemporaries. And of all the adults in the Community, Queenie had been the main woman in my life. Morning, noon, night. Breakfast, lunch, afternoon cake. She supervised our bed-making, shoe-shining, dishwashing, floor-cleaning, tooth-brushing. She was the one; the exception that proved the rule. The rule which says that in our society adults and children don't mix. Which is lucky because now that Mother has left for England my life goes on as before. Nothing changes. I still go to bed, have lessons, eat in the Dining Room, visit Father's Room. Homework, flute practice, committee meetings, choir, sitting around with my friends till midnight, whatever. It's all just the same. Except she's not here anymore. Neither of them are.

Anyway, this is about Josh. A happy chapter, it turned out. Because when the evening came I was sitting outside our boarding house with the girls, watching Ori, Leo and Sara playing five stones, Sara was on her first go and already at Bridge, and the boys were looking on glumly, knowing they were losing before they started. We were cheering her on, and also talking about which is the best film, *Butch Cassidy and the Sundance Kid*, or else *The Sting*, and who's better looking, Robert Redford or Paul Newman—well I think it's Paul, but the other girls disagreed—and right in the middle of this passing-the-time-of-night, as Anya was saying *Fiddler On the Roof* is the best film, and Paul Michael Glaser the best looking, and no one agreed and she started singing *If I were a rich man*, she has such a lovely voice, and someone joined her with the *Yabadibi Dams*, just then, Josh was standing between her and the pavement, looking in. Everyone stopped to look his way.

Hi, Josh, Leo and Ori jumped to their feet, what's up? Leo said, they assumed, hoped, he had come over for them.

Hi, Josh said to no one in particular.

Ummm… Everything okay? Leo was by his side, ready to do his bidding.

Ahh-haa, fine. Still not looking my way. Should I get up? Now? I was paralysed.

So, what's going on? Ori asked.

Ummm, nothing much… are you ready? He looked at me now. At least, it looked as though he might be. Well, of course I was ready. Have been for years.

Ahh, yes. I was on my feet already, trying to control my smile, not look around, not look triumphant. I knew they were watching me. Watching us. With surprise. Shock, maybe, but I didn't care. It was as though by a trick of the camera they all went out of focus, and all that remained was the two of us. Like these schmaltzy wedding photographs you sometimes see, soft around the edges. Strange how schmaltz can be so true to life. If there was any more talk, I didn't hear it. We walked away, into the night. He might as well have been riding a white horse. He might have hoisted me onto it and galloped away. Into the sunlight. It was *that* romantic.

We walked in silence for a while. I still had my smile on and there was laughter in my chest which I thought better to keep in there, though it was pressing to come out, climb up into my throat. I had anticipated the joy of being alone with Josh once more. That's all I had wanted. But the feeling of triumph was so powerful. I hadn't thought before how overwhelming it would be to have him publicly acknowledged me this way. I wanted to cry with joy; wondered when the bubble would burst.

Uuff, he said at last, that was a bit embarrassing.

I'm sorry. We could have met somewhere else.

Oh, no. It's fine. I don't like hiding.

Of course, Anya had made him keep their relationship secret; and suddenly I didn't care about that anymore, the fact that she didn't really want him, that she didn't seem to care at all when he finished it, during the war.

Well, it was quite brave of you, walking in like that, with everyone watching…

Did you mind?

Oh, Josh, you understand me so little. I said, No, I wasn't embarrassed. At all. I don't care what anybody says. They can talk all they like. *Okay, don't let it go to your head. No one likes a show off.*

Okay, then, he said, and took a cheerful inward breath that put extra lightness in his step. Anyway, it's not like there's anything for them to talk about. We're just friends, right?

Right, I said. The bubble burst.

After he locked the gate, he asked if I wanted to walk longer and I said yes, I did, although I thought, *What about the just friends, just friends, just friends?* And so we walked to the cemetery. And among the graves he found the one with his little baby sister who was born with water on her brain and only lived a week. She would have been a year younger than me, born 1961, when Josh was three, he had no memory of her, except a hazy one of him and his father visiting his mother in hospital. His mother talks about her sometimes, remembers her birthdays, and occasionally Josh has gone with her to put fresh flowers on the grave. He said we mustn't dwell on the past. Other families have suffered just as much if not more. Families of fallen soldiers, for example. He said that when he went to the funerals of Alex and Ehud, who had died in the Yom Kippur War, at the funerals he had cried. He cried, not with pity or sorrow, but because of the enormity of the sacrifice those men had made. He was moved. And a little jealous too. He doesn't want to die, but at the same time he was jealous they were able to make the ultimate sacrifice for our people. To stand up to our enemies and be part of the victory. And now he wants almost more than anything to be a fighter pilot. Even though he is an only son, which means his parents have the right to stop him taking on a combat role. He's working on that. On them. They'll let him, when the time comes, he's sure. They wouldn't take this dream from him. He talked for a long time about wanting to make his mark, to be a war hero. And I tried to listen, but in my head the refrain kept beating, *just friends, just friends...* And then he said, Oh, but I've been boring you for such a long time now. You should have stopped me.

No, no, go on, it's fine. And it was. Because he was near, and he was talking to me. Nothing was ever going to feel anything other than fine again.

30 November 1974

But it wasn't fine. Whatever I tried to tell myself, and so I had another sleepless night, fretting over what Josh might mean by saying we were just friends and yet spend two evenings acting as though he was my boyfriend. Is it normal? Or has he changed his mind, regretting he ever asked me to join him. It was all so mysterious. Which made me fall asleep in history the next day and miss Solomon's introductory lecture on the background to the Masada rebellion. When I turned twelve, Mother told me nothing in my life so far will have prepared me for the agonies and ecstasies of being an adolescent. I wish Queenie were here to give me advice. Or Mother herself, even.

Anyway, the next day Josh came for me again, and the next and the next. All week. And we walked down to lock the gate, and found somewhere to sit and Josh talked. His father had nearly agreed to let him be drafted as a fighter, but his mother still refused to hear of it. He mentions it to her at least every other day, to get her used to the idea. He would rather die than be a 'Jobnik' soldier like Gideon. The disgrace of it would kill him anyway. He talked about what he'd read in the newspaper. Like the travesty of the United Nations agreeing to have Yasser Arafat, that terrorist with more blood on his hands than a butcher, letting him talk to its full Assembly. Next thing we know, Arafat is going to have his own seat at the General Assembly, with a PLO plaque and a vote! When something like this happens, we know we are up against it, and that's why we need to be strong, keep our forces in shape, invest in weaponry, stay ahead of the game. And keep in with the Americans, of course. Without them we are all doomed. As good as drowned in the Mediterranean Sea, which is what the Arabs would do to us, given half a chance. And that's why Josh will volunteer. If he can't be a fighter pilot, or at least a navigator, then he wants to be an officer in Staff Patrol or maybe another crack unit. He's already getting himself fit, working out in the gym and going for a run every day before school.

Josh knows so much about what's happening in the world. He reads the newspaper every day and listens to serious radio. Always, he has something to say, so clever with facts and dates and historical context, like Ester and her revolutionary friends. Except she talks of how oppressed the Arabs are, how we must withdraw from the Territories and let all the refugees from 1948 Independence War back in, live in peace, turn our swords to spades and our spears into scythes, recognise the PLO, be a Middle Eastern country instead of a U.S.A. satellite. While Josh, he thinks the Arabs only understand one language, the language of force. Which is why we must continue to settle in Judea and Samaria, hang on to them, create a *status quo* that will make a withdrawal impractical. And then again Father says we should hang on to the Territories but only so we can bargain for peace when the time comes. And Ester would have a fit if she ever hears Josh say Judea and Samaria instead of West Bank, or Territories. She says you mustn't use Biblical Jewish names as though they are part of our Country, The Promised Land. Naming them belies the fact they were taken by force from Jordan and Egypt and must be given back. And I find myself floating among these facts and names, unsure which way to turn; and all the while Josh was talking to me and I'm overawed by the fact that here I am, alone with him, in the dark. Are we really just friends?

And I tried not to spoil these precious evenings by fretting. Because having Josh call for me each day was almost more than I had dared hope for. And he was kind. It felt safe, without the confusion that Micah always brings. And another difference between Josh and Micah: when I speak he listens gravely, as though we're equals. And when he asks something, like how I feel about Mother having left, or about going to England, he waits to hear my answer. So I told him about Queenie, how I love her. And about my diary, that it's practice for when I become a writer. And he didn't laugh or even snigger. And about being angry with Mother, and not writing to her, except once, after she decided to stay in England as though Father and us haven't suffered enough. How I told Father I didn't want to visit her, and so did Tommy, and in the end, Father persuaded me but not Tommy, who still says he won't go even though everything is set for the two of us to fly on the first candle of Chanukah. And Josh listened and said he thought I was right to visit her, although he also understood why I didn't want to. He wondered whether I would write to him when I'm away. He isn't good at writing letters. But if I did want to write him, he will try to write back. That is, If I wanted him to. And that's another thing: he always makes sure things are okay for me. Which is the opposite of what Micah does. The total opposite.

And now I'm about to go to England, and the week of locking-the-gate-in-the-garden is over. Who knows when we'll be alone again? If ever.

7 December 1974

Yesterday we were sitting in my parents' Room. I suppose it should be called Father's Room now. It was our last but one evening, and all was gloomier than usual. Tommy and I were playing backgammon, which wasn't fun because all I wanted to do was sit quietly and think about Josh. And Father was reading the weekend papers. Then Micah came in, he said to see Father. And to tell him that he'd decided to join the standing army. Father said, Ah, good for you, Micah, and looked at us to check we've taken in this important news. Yes, Micah replied, I've thought long and hard. They say it's likely I'll be a Major within a year. A Major, well, well, Father said. Tommy also looked up from the board, he's so easily impressed. I continued to look down, as always, Micah was acting as though he'd never taken me for rides in his car, or to restaurants in Tiberias, or walks in the fields at night, looking up at the stars, breathing down onto me, his fingers on my skin, inside my clothes. About once a month, actually. Or whenever he happens to be down visiting his family and his girlfriend happens to be out of the way, or he doesn't have a girlfriend, I don't know, I never ask.

Then he and Tommy summed up the volleyball season so far, our team needs new blood, otherwise relegation is inevitable; and then they moved on to football, whether Maccabi Tel Aviv can get back into the National League (probably not), and what is needed for us to make it through the qualifiers in the next World Cup (a new manager). And all this time I'm sat like an idiot, waiting for Tommy to make his next move. Annoyance, irritation rising, climbing onto the top of my stomach and lurking like a big tight fist, then up past my chest and throat, and settling in my jaw. I was noticing this activity inside me for who knows how long, not listening to the conversation, when Micah's voice wrestled its way into my ears.

…trip, Abbie? His narrow-slit eyes on me. His smile searing onto my face.

Huh?

Are you all ready for your trip?

What trip?

To England.

Yep, I said, then I stood and walked out. I wasn't going to let him talk to me as though nothing. Not in front of my family. I walked out without saying goodbye. My feelings jumbled, and I continued walking, all the way round the perimeter fence. By the end of which I was calm enough to go back. Micah had gone and Father and Tommy were listening to radio, songs from the thirties, Father's favourite, and I listened with them, Louis Armstrong in the mood for love, Fred Astaire dancing cheek to cheek, then Tommy went over to see Maya and I also stood up to leave.

Abbie, wait, Father said. I stood at the door. Sit. Please. I sat on the edge of the sofa, facing the wall. He hesitated. For a long moment we just sat. Ah… what happened… earlier?

What?

With Micah. You were—ahhh—I was embarrassed.

I'm sorry. That I embarrassed you.

Alright. But what got into you?

Nothing. it was just—

Had Micah—had he done something to upset you?

Yes. I mean, no. No, he hadn't.

Because it seemed to me, he was being friendly.

He was. I—I don't know. I'm feeling a bit—

I know. Ahhh, I don't even want to think about you being away all this time. And your mother… he trailed off.

Well, I'm going to go now.

Alright, but—I think you should apologise to Micah. I expect he'll be in the Dining Room later; you can do it then.

Okay.

Okay. And don't worry, I'm sure he'll be fine about it.

I did see Micah later, in the Dining Room. Although I hate dishonesty, I would never normally break a promise to Father, no way was I going to apologise to him. No way. He came up to me after the meal, as though nothing had happened earlier. He has thick skin, like an elephant. He asked if I'd be at the disco later, unusually, not his pattern. Normally he turns up where I'm likely to be. Waits stealthily for an opportune moment; or for me to start walking home, then he approaches. Although actually, I'm not sure he minds it if people see us. Maybe he doesn't care. Oh, well, I nearly laughed. Was he asking me out for a date? I hate him for giving me secrets. I hate myself for keeping his secrets. And what would I tell, anyway? Josh doesn't know and mustn't ever, will I never talk about it? Never is the longest word.

Later, he drove us down to the Sea of Galilee where we sat on a low rock, looking out as the dark waves come lapping. My knees were hunched up under my chin, my arms around them in a tight grip. It was cold. He said, You were angry tonight.

Ah—yes.

What was it about?

I shouldn't have walked out. My father was embarrassed.

You don't need to apologise. I just want to know why you were so…

I'm not apologising. I'm just sorry my father was upset.

But you're okay about upsetting me.

No.

You're not okay about it?

No. I don't care.

That's not like you, Abigail.

What's not like me?

To speak this way. To be angry.

I'm not angry. And why are you talking about what's like me or not like me. You don't know the first thing about me.

That's not fair.

Why isn't it?

Well—we've spent quite a lot of time together, over the years.

But you've never asked me a single question. What I think. How I feel.

Abigail, I thought—

And you always ignore me. When we're not on our own. Acting as though you barely know my name.

He was quiet for a while. Then he sighed. Oh, Abigail. He reached for my hand, but I withdrew it. Tucked it away under my knees.

I'm sorry.

What?

I'm sorry. Really. I didn't realise you felt this way.

I sighed. Because you didn't think. It's not important.

You're right, I've behaved badly. I've been stupid. He paused. I said nothing, kept staring ahead at the sea. Didn't care how long the silence lasted. In the end he said, You know, I've always found you so… alluring. You're such a beautiful girl. I keep forgetting how young you are. I should have been more thoughtful. I'm sorry.

You should be.

So… do you think we can be friends, now? Start over?

I don't know. I'm not sure what being friends with you means.

Do you like me?

Do I like him? Not really. A lot. I said, I don't know.

Okay. That's fair enough, I suppose. You're not even fifteen yet, are you?

No.

And I'm…

Twenty-nine?

Well, if you must be literal about it, yes, I am. How about—what would you say if I come back for you in a while? Maybe when you're a bit older? How does that sound?

I don't know—

Because… I *really* like you.

I'm not sure, I'll have to see. And, but you'll have to treat me better. From now on.

I can do that.

And now, I want to go back. Please.

Oh, it feels nice writing this, as though it were all true.

Chapter 5: Devon, England

March 2010

Yasmin stood behind a stall outside the organic clothes shop at the top of the high street. Her frozen hands were clamped unfeelingly around a wad of glossy brochures. It was Friday, her day off. She was supposed to be presenting the brochures to passersby but could only bring herself to do this half-heartedly. People didn't want to be accosted in the street, even if it was for a good cause. Self-consciousness made her ineffective. Across the road, in the square, the Friday market was gathering pace. Chorizo, olives, Cornish cheeses, and bottles of Devon chilli sauce were exchanging hands, carefully placed in biodegradable bags; or carried away in shapeless cloth bags, home sewn and displaying variable environmental logos. *Don't Let Devon Go to Waste*; *Use me again and again and again*; *Transition Town Totnes.* People were milling, riffling through boxes of old LPs, trying on second-hand coats at first-hand prices.

Yasmin surveyed the familiar scene. The air was thick with the smells of fried onions and sour-dough bread. It was mid-morning, and a small patch of sun crept along the pavement towards her from outside the vegan chocolate stall. It should reach her spot in twenty minutes, she reckoned. She took a deep breath, savouring the smells, the freedom of not being at school, of no children coming at her at a hundred demands a minute. *Miss Aswan, Alfie said I'm four years old even though I had my birthday party yesterday. I told him I'm five, but he says I'm lying...* She closed her eyes. *Miss Aswan, James took all the potatoes out of the ground; the ones we planted today!* She loved those children. They were so open, and funny. But she was glad this was only a temporary job. In the autumn she would start her research project, by the end of which, fingers crossed, there will be another Dr. Aswan in the family. Now she let the children's voices float away. Ah, nearly time for lunch. She'll have it by the river. Before meeting the man called Josh off the train. Lifting her head, facing the patchy blue-grey sky, she readied herself for the sun's caress on her cold eyelids.

A couple stops by her stall. He is bearded, wearing an oriental cloth cap and shapeless old trousers. A sleeping baby is strapped to his chest, tightly wound inside a long floral cloth. The woman wears an assortment of skirts, layered, mismatched. Her long mousy hair is unkempt, matted in an attempt at a Rastafarian look. Yasmin makes no judgement. She looks away. Across the road Sebastian has abandoned his stall of Indian leather-bound books. He is heading towards her, carrying two steaming mugs. Seeing she has potential customers; he stops on the edge of the sunny patch. He will wait unobtrusively until they move on. Yasmin gives him a quick look, then turns towards the couple. A young girl, a teenager, may neglect to wash her hair in this way and still look attractive. But this woman must be in her forties. Someone ought to tell her. At the very least she ought to try smiling. A sour face is terribly ageing, Yasmin's mother would say. Would have. Her mother died two years before, and the memory of such mundane things, idiosyncratic phrases, still squeeze at her heart with violence. Yasmin's eyes feel watery, like two Dartmoor springs. She holds her breath once, twice, in an effort to reverse their flow. Purposefully, she turns her attention back onto the couple standing before her.

Anyway, how do I even *know* it's fair-traded? the woman is saying. Adam? Adam! she insists when the man doesn't respond. She sounds cross, as Yasmin knew she would. Yasmin smiles. Yes, it's hard to tell, Adam says vaguely. His voice is deep, melodious. It hits Yasmin in the pit of her stomach. Is he her husband? Brother? Baby's father? He is inspecting the label on a bottle of organic olive oil, tossing it lightly round and round with one hand, then stretching his arm away to get the small print into focus. Too vain to wear glasses, Yasmin knows the type. Good looking, though, even through his beard. Long, delicate fingers, she likes that in a man. She watches the way he gently places the bottle back on the counter, then grips a jar of honey made by Palestinian bees.

Yasmin allows herself a quick look at Sebastian, but he is gazing dreamily down the road, his own huge, fleshy hands dwarfing the mugs they cradle. The woman is nervously fingering through bags of za'atar grown in Jerusalem's mountains. She picks up a box of olive oil soap made in Nablus. Yasmin edges nearer. You never know with such people. Sometimes they have a lot more ready cash than appearance suggests. How do you *know* it's fair-traded? She's looking at Yasmin with fierce, expectant eyes.

Ummm… says Yasmin. She decides not to reveal it is

not her stall. She only stands in for a friend on Fridays; has never previously been called on to discuss such matters.

I mean, it could be anything, couldn't it? Anything at all, and we wouldn't know... The woman's tone is accusatory, aggrieved.

Yes, I suppose you're right... Yasmin falters. The woman's frown intensifies. Three vertical lines deepen in the middle of her forehead. Yasmin blinks. She says, But, ahh, the—the company, Sindyanna of Galilee, they are, you know, they're a Fair-Trade—you can look them up on the—

I don't know, the woman turns towards Adam. Should I feel reassured?—I mean, there's so much fraud around... She trails off, picks up a large ornate basket, traditionally weaved by Arab women in the Galilee. And what's this about? she asks the air between Yasmin and Adam.

Well, this basket is made of palm-fronds, Yasmin says. That's an—an agricultural waste product. They— Sindyanna of Galilee, they empower Arab women; give them employment, and skills—

Mmmm... the woman studies a brochure. Okay, she raises her head. Okay, can I taste the oil?

I thought you might need rescuing from the Rasta woman, nearly came over sooner to help you get rid her. Sebastian was standing too close, and Yasmin took a step back, sipping the lukewarm milky tea he'd handed her.

Oh, it was fine. They spent a fortune in the end. Bought all the olive oil. Took my phone number to order more.

Really? That's great!

Yes, they're bringing a car round to pick it up in a minute. Then I'm done. I'm meeting someone off the train.

Yes, I know. The Israeli guy. Your mum's friend.

How do you—

We talked about it, remember? Do you still want me to chaperon you?

What? No! Since when do I need a chaperon?

You did! You asked me to come along. He said he was religiously barred from hanging out with you.

Ah, yes. Seb was right, she had forgotten. She said, He did very weirdly ask that we shouldn't be alone together since we weren't married. A woman not his wife, was how he termed it. Never have I been defined by not being someone's wife. She laughed. But, Seb, I haven't asked you to come along. I believe I decided to ignore him. If he doesn't like riding in my car to Mum's grave, he can jolly well get a taxi.

Well, I've already planned to leave the stall early today. I could come along; keep you two friends company?

First, he's not my friend. I've never even heard of him until a couple of months ago. She remembered the strange note paper he used, lined and baby blue, with little clouds in the corner; the sort of stationary little girls might have kept in the days before email. Anyway, she said, you've got your stall to run, and—I expect he'll get over it.

But I've been looking forward to this outing, Yasmin.

You have? she regarded him doubtfully.

Yes. It was going to be the closest we ever got to a date. Such frankness, and it wasn't even midday. Yasmin blushed, embarrassed. Sebastian was a good deal older than her, probably in his late thirties while she was just twenty-four. He had dark, rounded features, hairy arms, a soft middle, and a ready smile. They had met in the market a couple of years before and initially developed the sort of shallow friendship that tends not to go beyond the scene of its conception. More recently, though, he had pursued a more rounded, deeper acquaintance. She had found this new state irksome, then irritating, and then just mildly ludicrous. He made frequent, persistent references to their lives outside the market, and took a keen interest in her family, studies, work. She liked him well enough but had consistently rebuffed these attempts at familiarity. Anyway, he was saying, everything is arranged, so... he petered off.

Everything?

Yes. Mark is going to look after my stall. I think even he can handle the two or three customers I'm expecting today, sell a leather-bound book to one of them. Come on, Yassi, it will be fun!

And why not, she thought. He seemed genuinely keen, almost desperate. And she did enjoy his company. The thought of the afternoon ahead, on her own with the stranger named Josh Pasternak made her, if not anxious, then at least uncomfortable. Seb would help defuse tension. And why indeed is she always resisting him? She wondered whether her resistance had simply become a habit. Had she been hasty discounting the possibility of him? She faltered, in itself an irritating sensation. No, she said at last, I can manage on my own. And she added, But thanks for the offer.

How callous of you to stand me up at such short notice.

Oh, don't be so ridiculous. This isn't a date, Seb. It's some freakishly religious guy my mother had never seen fit to mention, asking me out of the blue to take him to visit her grave. I'm going to pick him up from the station, drive him there and back. I'm planning to give him about three hours of my precious Friday; he doesn't know I've just sold all my stock so I wouldn't be working this afternoon anyway. I'm doing him a big favour and he's in no position to make demands as to who will be part of the entourage.

Okay. But Mark will be disappointed.

No he won't. Because you haven't asked him, have you?

Well, no. But, you know, I didn't need to. He would do it, I know he would. I just didn't want to get him over excited. In case it doesn't work out. What with you being so feckless and inconsistent.

Yasmin smiled her full-width smile, the one her uncle Toby called The Yas Charm Offensive. Thanks for the coffee, she said, and, shoving the empty mug in his hand, she turned away.

Chapter 6: London, England

10 December 1974

Almost the best thing about London being so very strange and new is writing to Josh. I want to share all of it with him. Yet it feels strange to write to him, and I wonder why. Am I wrong to make so much of the evenings we spent together? I think of him receiving my letter, opening the envelope with long delicate fingers, reading it once, twice. And I see his hay-coloured hair falling onto his eyes and him sweeping it back every now and then. I see his hand hovering behind his head, ready to scratch the back of his neck. These are the nice thoughts. The others are of him tossing the letter to one side. Or worse, showing it to his friends for a laugh.

My impressions so far are that this country is cold. The first three days I couldn't leave the house. Which is enormous, maybe the biggest I've been in. The English themselves don't care about the cold or the rain. They are used to it. Yesterday Toby offered to show me Hampstead Heath, and I said, but isn't it raining? He laughed and said if they stayed in every time it rained, they'd never go out. I'm not sure yet if I like Toby, or if he likes me. Everyone is obsessed with the weather, there's even a special weather programme on television! I found that the English language has a whole treasure of ways to describe rain. Proper rain like we have in Israel is called a Shower, or Cats and Dogs. And the usual rain here, which is light and persistent, is a Drizzle. But they don't have our special words for the first and last rain, and no wonder, it falls here all year round. What's wonderful is that when the sun comes out, everyone is very cheerful, they don't take it for granted like we do.

I'm back from a shopping trip with Toby as my guide, and there isn't enough ink in the pen to describe everything I've seen today. So many people and so much order! First, the Underground. When the train stopped a man's voice echoed through the station from powerful tannoys—Stand clear of the doors, it says, and people do, just like that. And on the long-long escalators they stand to one side so others can rush past them. Everything is so efficient, but no one gives up their seat to old people, in our country you'd get beaten up with a walking stick if you don't!

The richness of the garments in shop windows, the elegance, like a movie set. And the mannequins, instead of standing straight and majestic as they do in our country, look willowy and shy. Standing like question marks, as Father would say. Quite unsettling how they look out at you all the way along Oxford Street. Sure Ester would have something to say about how society's attitude to women is reflected in its mannequins. Ester has a view on everything. Whereas I'm a sponge, absorbing everything, not sure what to make of it all.

In Selfridges, the smartest shop in the world, Toby pretended he was about to buy the most expensive clothes, and I had to try them on, we laughed so much. Some shoes I could hardly stand in, the heels were that high. Then the two of us had a Cream Tea. This came with jam and a kind of thick white cheesy thing Toby said was to be spread like butter. Disgusting. It felt so grown up to sit there, looking at the street outside through steamed-up windows. Toby held my hand. Like an old married couple, we are, he said in the strange croaky voice he calls his Cockney, and we laughed. Toby has so many funny phrases, like Tally Ho! and Not on your Nelly. Also, When the going gets tough, the tough gets going, which he shouted before jumping over the tube station barrier. It was a nice afternoon.

Mother says life's too short to hesitate, she's trying to persuade me to stay in England with her and Grandma Rose. They are staying *for the foreseeable future*. Of course I think it's a terrible idea. But I do agree that life is short, and plan to no longer hesitate; when I go home, I will let Josh know my feelings.

It's great getting to know my English family. Especially Toby, who is home for the Christmas holidays and takes me out every day, sometimes twice. We go all over London, and he makes me laugh a lot.

Last night was New Year's Eve, the Christian one. We had a big meal, which Aunt Rachel and Mother cooked. At twelve o'clock everyone linked hands and sang *Old Lands Eye*, or something like it, and that was it, the adults went to bed. Toby said he wanted to show me something out in

172

the garden, so we wrapped up warm, it had started to snow, and when we walked out, I stood still, face up and the snow came down so cold and sprayed my coat with white flakes in the moonlight. I told Toby how exciting this was. I'd never seen snow falling, the only time I'd seen any snow at all was when we once drove for hours to Mount Hermon up by the Lebanese border where we did plastic-bag-sledging on the slushy, muddy slopes. Toby said fantastic, he was really happy for me, but he was beginning to freeze and would I please come along. And he refused to go in and tell Tommy about the snow. Instead, he held my hand and pulled me along, giggling and stumbling, towards the bottom of the garden.

What is it? Toby, hang on, it's too dark.

Don't worry, I've got you. His disembodied voice ahead sounded determined, like a military leader.

Where are we going?

Right here. He stopped. We were in a corner of the garden, a dark thicket of old fruit trees, overgrown. Father, if he were here, would have hard pruned them without delay. Stand still, Toby said. Back a bit. There's a tree branch right behind you. You can sit down. The branch made a perfect bench. Toby sat next to me. His voice turned to whisper in a Scottish accent. Right, then. Are you sitting comfortably? Or Irish. I'm not good at telling them apart. He was rubbing his hands and blowing to keep warm.

Yes, I am, I said, but you're acting strange, even for you. And I'm getting cold, Toby. But I was smiling. He makes everything seem like a game.

He went quiet for a few seconds, and when he spoke again it was in his own voice. Oh, well, I suppose—If I'm being strange and you're getting cold, I suppose we should just head back now. I wanted to introduce you to an old English, I mean Scottish, custom—a special New Year tradition—but—maybe now isn't a good time—never mind, there will be other New Years—and it's way past your bedtime. He stood up.

Past my bedtime, indeed (as the English say). I haven't had a bedtime since I was twelve!

Wait, I said. What tradition?

We heard Tommy calling for me from the door. Mother wanted to say goodnight; and do I know where Toby is. We didn't move. I whispered, What's the tradition, then?

Oh, nothing—

Well, it was something.

He turned towards the house. I had this crazy idea of kissing you at midnight. Under the mistletoe.

I'm never sure with Toby, whether he's serious. You have mistletoe?

No. I was going to pretend. He started towards the house.

I stood up. So, where is it? This pretend mistletoe?

He stopped. Well, where do you think? He walked back towards me, a strange, shadowy form, closer and closer until the cloudy whiteness of his breath was mine. His big soft hand warm against my icy cheek.

Chapter 7: Devon

March 2010

Yasmin is going to meet a man. A man named Joshua Pasternak. Josh, in brackets. He is an alien from another world, a blast from the past. Her mother's world, her mother's past. What is he like? What does he look like? After he had contacted her by a strange, out of the blue, letter, Yasmin had gone up to the loft and opened the tattered old shoebox where her mother's photographs and letters were stored. She had been through them before, many times, as a child. The photographs, not the letters, which were both private and mostly in Hebrew. Mummy, look! She would plead. But her mother is too busy, no time to delve into the silent, black-and-white, dusty world of the shoebox. Abbie is cooking supper, writing an article for the local paper, standing on her head in a yoga pose. There is always a reason not to join Yasmin's *projects*, as she calls them, not to answer her million and one questions. Who's that, Mummy? Who's that in the photo? Sometimes, Abbie comes closer and peers over Yasmin's shoulder.

Don't touch, Yassi, she warns, we don't want finger marks on the photograph. Let's see, that's my friend Saffi, dressed as a clown. Saffi is sucking her thumb, her head tilted to one side. And who's that, Mummy, who's the teddy bear? That's me, I was Teddy No-No. Remember him? Of course I do, he got lost and no one helped him because all he could say was no-no-no. You do remember, Abbie smiles, I used to love that story. And so did I! Yasmin says, see we are the same, aren't we? Abbie smiles again, and Yasmin feels powerful, a happy almighty little girl.

And who's that, Mummy? She points at a man in army uniform, a long black gun hanging off his shoulder. He is on the edge of the scene, turned from the camera. Ah, well, that's… that's Saffi's brother, Abbie says, everyone's heading for the Purim costume parade. Yasmin says, Is the soldier also going to the costume parade? No, darling, I mean, he is dressed as a soldier because he really is one. A real one? With a gun that shoots bullets? Yes—Jewish Israelis join the army when they finish school. Yasmin asks, Do they join for three years? And the girls for two? Did you? You know they do. Abbie is distracted now, impatient to get back to whatever she was doing before Yasmin interrupted her. Mummy, did he, what's his name? Micah. His name is Micah. Did—*Micah*, did he give back his gun, after three years? Abbie says, Well, as it happened, he didn't ever leave the army, he stayed and stayed and became a big general, until. Until what, mummy? Until— until he—she peters out. Yasmin is enchanted with the possibility of perpetual soldiering. She says, I wouldn't give back my gun. I'd stay and be a general too. Why would you want to do that, darling? Just in case. Just in case, what? Yassi, guns are dangerous. They're not something to keep just in case.

But Yasmin has moved on. She is searching for her

favourite Purim photograph. Abbie poses for the camera, unsmiling. She is about nine, a little older than Yasmin herself. Her plaits stick out at right angles; large freckles have been painted on her face. She wears men's boots and odd socks pulled up over her knees. Abbie the mum straightens herself to standing. She is walking away. Yasmin waves the photograph at her, like a flag. Look, Mummy, you're Pippi Longstocking! Was this also a Purim Parade? But Abbie continues her retreat. What else did you dress as, Mummy, for Purim parades? What other people?

Abbie stops. Characters, darling, she says, not people; she never can resist correcting Yasmin's English. She sighs. Oh, well, my favourites, you know, from books. Which ones? Well, one year I was Noddy, and Saffi here, she was Big-Ears, Noddy's friend; then another year I was Queen Ester and Leo was the king. He wore a velvet gown and I a long pink dress, but we both had to wear our own brown lace-up shoes. Yasmin is outraged. You did? The high Doc Martins, your everyday ones? Yes, darling, but I didn't mind. And I got to be on stage. Was it exciting, like being Mary at the Christmas play? Well, almost. But not quite? Not quite, darling, none of it was ever quite like Christmas. Or being Mary.

Yasmin imagines Abbie the girl, majestic in a jewelled crown and pink maxi dress. She tries not to think of the brown lace-up shoes peeping from under the hem. Did you get to hold a baby, like Mary? No, Yassi, Abbie is moving away, Queen Ester didn't have children. But she did save all the Jewish people in her land. Yasmin calls after her, a last-ditch attempt to keep her close: Did Aunt Ester get to be Ester the Queen? Did they let her because of her name? But it's no good, Abbie has had enough. I don't know, darling, I can't remember what Ester did, she says as she disappears through the doorway.

Twenty years later, Yasmin hardly knew any more about Abbie's childhood than she did the first time she had opened that box. She hadn't been up in the loft for years, not since the time she and Jeremy, both sixteen, would sneak up there for what Jeremy termed *exploring Newfoundland*. Her mother had thought he was helping Yasmin with maths O Level and rarely bothered to check how they were doing. A few weeks in, as their *explorings* turned from breathtakingly thrilling to pleasantly predictable, one afternoon her father returned home from the Middle East unannounced. How she panicked as they yanked on their clothes, hastily arranging the old blankets and cushions they'd just sprung from into something that resembled a studying space, scattering books to the sound of his voice and his approaching, galloping footsteps up the stairs. Although they weren't found out, the episode was so traumatic Yasmin resolved to avoid sex altogether afterwards. For the time being. She told Jeremy he couldn't visit her at home until her father went back to Beirut, where he was completing a course of lectures on Islamic Law and international treaties. Within the week Jeremy began visiting another girl, Natasha, whose parents had put a small outhouse at her disposal and didn't care who she spent time with.

Yasmin hadn't minded, apart from the humiliation of finding out about Jeremy's defection from a mutual friend. She had been quite obsessed with the idea of him, the firmness of his limbs, the smoothness of his skin, the sweetness of his breath. She loved his awkward gentleness and giggling at his gawky jokes; the charming way he looked as though he'd been lost and was hugely relieved that she had found him. He was easy to please. She liked that. Now, though, she was surprised how little she missed him. She didn't date anyone else for about two years. Apart from Toby, her uncle. Or, rather, her mother's cousin. Which, in the circumstances, made the situation more palatable.

Toby was a bachelor and an eccentric. He had inherited a big house on the edge of Hampstead Heath. Yasmin's grandmother, Rifka, and her sister Rachel, Toby's mother, had grown up in that house. When Yasmin was fifteen, she stayed with him on her own during the summer holidays. On the first day he took her round the London sights. Then, in the evening, they walked to the bottom of the big house garden where he lay her tenderly on a soft picnic rug and relieved her of her virginity. Yasmin knew she ought to be scandalised, probably report him to her mother, or, worse, her father. But she'd been wondering for a while how best to launch herself into this aspect of the grown-up world.

And she liked Toby. He made her laugh, was skilled at imitating accents. And even though he was a little thick around the middle, had nasal hair and an unattractive sniff, even though he was only a year younger than her father, she sort of enjoyed having sex with him. He was a gentle lover with large, soft hands. And, as he seemed incapable of taking anything seriously, was never going to make heavy work of what they had together. So, when the time came to go home to Devon, Yasmin asked if she could visit again. Toby laughed and said she ought to take care, that he was sensitive, and middle-aged. And anyhow, he said, what was it about the Boskovitch women that made them so determined to steal his heart? Unable to contemplate what that statement might allude to, Yasmin was not deterred, but proceeded to make regular occurrences of what Toby called their *delicious adventures*.

Intermittently, this continued until—she wasn't sure there was an *until*. It has been a while, two years perhaps since she last saw Toby. She wondered whether she was inclined to contact him again. But whatever it was she had with Toby didn't count, never had. Their *affair* was so well compartmentalised in her mind she didn't consider it an actual relationship, never contemplated whether to mention it to boyfriends. Of which there had been a few. Now, though, sad to say, the most romantic aspect of her life was Sebastian's persistent over-familiarity on market Fridays.

Two months ago, sitting in the loft, feeling the weight of the old shoebox on her lap, Yasmin looked around the attic. A spider web stretched across the skylight, a beautiful, intricate creation. She wondered if the spider was there, in wait for a lost fly. Beneath, a rumpled pile of musty old beddings still filled the corner furthest from the hatch. It occurred to her that it hadn't been touched since Jeremy hurled it there frantically that last time. She'd heard recently that he was married, had joined the Forces, was about to be stationed in Iraq. She pictured his wife and children standing in a straight line, waving him off outside a large house (Jeremy's father was a high court judge, the house was bound to be large). They were indistinct, fuzzy figures. She attempted to superimpose her face onto the woman's, but the image was slippery, evasive. She returned to the old photographs; would approach them with a new purpose. Something to do with the man Josh, his impending visit.

Would he be willing to talk about some of these photographs? He surely would recognise the people. It was exciting; may solve a problem weighing down on her since she resolved to find out more about Abbie's life. Ever since she realised her father was reluctant to help, or even let her. Well, *Yabba*, she pleaded with him the last time he was home, if it's too soon for you, let me have a go myself. No, he ruled, staring into his plate of Christmas turkey with Mediterranean condiments of hummus and tabbouleh. And then, uncovering the Lebanese baklava he had brought for her wrapped in underwear inside his suitcase: No, stop asking, Yassi, I'm going to do it myself. But why wait, *Yabba*? She asked, emboldened by the intimacy of his gift-giving. Why not just do it? But she should have known better than to argue. They shared the baklava and drank coffee with cardamom in silence. Later that evening, though, perhaps noticing she was hurt, he said more softly, But you may help me, Yassi. You may help, when the time comes. The next day he flew back to Beirut, where there were no Christmas holidays, and his PhD students awaited supervision.

Well, the man Josh was a sign, an opportunity. She can do her own research. Her father would understand, wouldn't he? She considered telephoning him, but he was always on edge when taking long distant calls. Growing up as he did where money was often scarce, he never got used to spending it, despite being quite prosperous now. During his early days in London every phone-minute to his family in East Jerusalem had cost a full hard-earned pound. And even though prices have tumbled in recent years, his attitude hasn't changed.

The photographs were buried beneath wads of light blue aerogrammes, mixed in loose sheets of long, incomprehensible letters. She picked up one, a black and white baby Abbie, lying in a line of six babies on a blanket. Here is Abbie the toddler, standing inside a cot with five other toddlers. Here is little Tommy, sitting on a tricycle, and Abbie perching on a platform behind him, holding onto his shoulders. Both gaze solemnly at the camera. The pose is curiously static, disconnected from the playful activity. Here is Abbie the child, the teenager, the young woman in staged family photos. They line up, shortest to tallest, oldest to youngest with Uncle Tommy, long haired and gauche, Aunt Ester, willowy in shorts, and Grandma and Grandpa, impossibly young and handsome.

Yasmin looked for other people-photographs, a sign of the man, Josh. Is he one of the toddlers? The boy sitting with Tommy on a tractor trailer? The soldier in Ray-Ban sunglasses, standing at a bus stop? The soldier smiles toothily at the camera, his right hand held up in a half salute. Behind him a mountainous scene of white-bricked town houses. Jerusalem? On the back of the photo something is handwritten in Hebrew. Yasmin once more regrets that she hadn't heeded her mother's wish to teach her the language. She places the photo of the soldier carefully on the floor.

Guilt creeps over her at the thought of sharing her mother's things with the stranger named Josh. After all, her father had said they would look through it all together when he is back from Beirut. Her father. What was he afraid of? How he clamped up at every mention of the letters. Not now, Yassi, it's too soon. And, Don't keep on, Yassi, we'll do it when the time comes. Well, she reckons the time *has* come. She brings out another photograph. A teenage Tommy and another boy, sat on a tiled floor, a chessboard between them. Tommy holds a pawn between finger and thumb, mid-move. The other boy looks away, only partially visible. Josh had written that he was Tommy's contemporary. She places the photograph on the pile.

She picks another. Black and white, grainy, faded. A teenage Abbie is lying on her front, close up, her left cheek to the ground, a stray strand of hair across her face. She is smiling at the camera, irises caught by what might be the last of an evening sun. Even in black and white Yasmin can tell one iris is darker than the other. What is she wearing? No clothing is visible on the fraction of arm and shoulder in the corner. Behind, the ground slopes to a dark river, dotted with a spread of darker boulders. On the back of the photograph are hand-written words and a date: 20/1/1976. Abbie's birthday. In 1976 she turned sixteen. Yasmin scrutinises the image. There is something intimate about it, though she can't say what. She adds it to the pile on the floor. Who is the amateur photographer? Grandpa, she knows by Abbie's earlier childhood photos, had moved to coloured some years before. And the poor quality indicates a different hand, or a lesser camera.

What is this man who writes strange, awkward letters? What is he looking for? Had he and her mother been childhood sweethearts? Had they been lovers, even? Swiftly, Yasmin backs away from the thought. As far back as she can remember, as far as she knows, her mother didn't have a love life. Although, of course, there was her father, Omar. But any conventionality within their marriage had been over by the time Yasmin was aware that most of the children she knew had two parents living at home. Dr Omar Aswan was an associate professor of politics at the University of Beirut. He'd been living there, apart from a few weeks each year, since Yasmin was a little girl. When she was a teenager, during long and lonely evenings in their isolated Dartmoor cottage, while her mother was out volunteering with the Samaritans, or practising yoga in the village hall, Yasmin sometimes spent a quiet hour searching Abbie's things. Being at that age quite obsessed with the possibility of sex, she searched for signs of company her mother might have kept while she, Yasmin, was not home. What had she thought she might find? An extra toothbrush? Unknown aftershave in the bathroom cupboard? A second mug of coffee in the sink? She even inspected her mother's bed for dents and pillows. But there was only ever one pillow, neatly arranged in the centre of the bed. And as for dents, Abbie had never, not once, come downstairs in the morning without first making the bed, covering it completely with an ungainly old orange and green ribbed bedspread.

Once, Abbie came home early to find Yasmin rifling through a pile of bedding, searching for clues the shape and colour of which she daren't articulate. What are you doing, darling? Oh, I lost a coin, and… Her mother looked at her sideways and Yasmin was aware of not having bothered to finish the lie she'd started. But then Abbie continued talking as normal. This, the shame of being caught, or nearly, made her determined to take a more direct approach. The next day she braced herself during supper and asked whether Abbie was seeing anybody. Do you have a man-friend, she added by way of elucidation when Abbie looked at her blankly. Darling, *of course* not, she had protested. Your father and I are together. Emboldened, Yasmin said, You're not really, though, are you? Well, certainly, yes, we are, Abbie retorted, where did you *get* such a notion?

But you never see him. Why don't you go over to Beirut and… But Yasmin knew the answer; the party line taken by both her parents throughout her life. An Israel-born Jewish woman could not swan into Beirut university, start choosing curtains and painting the walls of her staff-issue home, marriage certificate to a professor or not, British passport or not. Later, though, this explanation had begun to sound off. Yasmin said, And why won't Dad find work somewhere else, where we can all be together? Her mother sighed. It's just the way things are, darling. *Ç'est la vie.* Sometimes Yasmin thought her parents had planned it, so they didn't spend time together. Although, now Abbie was dead, and Omar's grief so abundant, so overwhelming, she felt guilty for having entertained such thoughts.

Josh knows Abbie. Knew. How well? Strange, the thought of her mother having a life that did not include Yasmin's own, or even Tamara's short-lived one. Abbie the child, plaits bouncing about her shoulders, playing with a boy called Josh. Are they skipping? Riding a bike? Lying on their backs in a field of daffodils? The field slopes to a row of eucalyptus trees with the Jordan beyond. There is always a river in Abbie's childhood. The daffodils are small, and white, and few. The youngsters' heads incline towards each other without touching; they look up through the green stalks at a perfectly blue sky. Abbie is singing. When she was Yasmin's mother she was always singing. But then her illness came, and she had stopped. Instead, she asked for music. Any music, to start. Then opera became intolerable, the voices too high, too loud and garish. And as the weeks went by more of the pieces she had loved were banished. Even Chopin, her all-round favourite, began to grate at her nerves that last month, and in the end only Bach's cello suit in G could satisfy her, give her peace.

Time glides over the two youngsters in the field. The sky is pinky-red. Let's go swimming, she says to the faceless boy named Josh. She jumps to her feet and runs off towards the trees. Josh props himself on one elbow and watches her figure bouncing away. He squints in the still-bright evening sunshine. Abbie stops. A silhouette. She turns towards him. Come on! She shouts, laughing. Come on Josh, don't be lazy! Her bare feet are planted on the earth. She belongs to this land, and the land to her. She shifts, leaning onto one hip. Tilting her head, she tugs absentmindedly on a plait, wrapping it round her wrist. Josh stands. He's walking towards her. Don't shout, I'm coming, but Abbie doesn't hear. Her back is turned, and she is running down the slope.

Yasmin shudders. These scenes come uninvited. They are irresistible. Or is it that she doesn't want to resist? She looks at the shoebox. Does it hold a trace of him? Abbie had never mentioned a Josh. There was a Leo, Yasmin remembers, had he died in a war? She remembers a Daniel, a soldier named Micah, was he a colonel? No more.

She picks up a last photograph. A group of teenage boys stand in a line at the top of a shallow hill. Tommy,

186

Leo, Daniel, Micah, Josh? Tall thorns surround their lean, bare legs. Behind, a ruin; a half demolished, ancient looking stone house. Each boy brandishes a large stick, warrior-style, like a primordial, conquering army. Yasmin adds this to her pile. It's time to go.

As an afterthought she rummages to the bottom of the box, fishes out a newspaper cutting: Seven men marching, chanting, arms linked. Behind them, another marcher holds a loudspeaker, pointed backwards towards an invisible crowd. A protest march; no clue to its nature. When, years before, she had asked her mother about it, Abbie had only sighed, looked out of the window, and said it looked like rain. The man Josh would read the caption for her, maybe explain its significance. Yasmin places the cutting on the pile.

Chapter 8: Jordan Valley

20 January 1975

Fifteenth birthday. I've been back from England a week. Mother telephoned me in Ruth and Jacob's room, said happy birthday and to expect a present in the post. Then Ruth arrived with a cake. Father put on a brave face. Tommy and Maya also came round. Tommy gave me a china mug from London, saying Mind the Gap. And Father gave me a Simon and Garfunkel record. Then I went to my bedroom. Anya is away so I had the room. I found the card Toby left on my bed in Hampstead before I left. It had been strange, saying goodbye, and his words made me cry.

1974 was not a good year. I did have a wonderful time in England with Toby. But it was heart-breaking, leaving Mother behind and now it is clear she's not coming back. Father acts almost as though she's dead; doesn't talk about her. Ester says he's *in denial*. She visits often.

Everyone is helping. But in the end, it's the three of us on a Saturday, sitting in silence, wondering each to ourselves what brought Mother's desertion on. I should have been a better daughter. I should have written to her, then she would have missed me more. She would have known I need her. Just because I live in a boarding house and she doesn't have to do any washing for me, or cook or kiss me good night, just because I can manage alone doesn't make it okay to leave me behind. I told Father this, and he said, Nonsense, Mother loves you more than... but then he stopped, lost in his own sadness. I'm wondering how you get from loving your children to abandoning them. That was 1974.

January 1975, we got home from the airport. Josh came round the first afternoon and sat with Tommy and me. Then Tommy left to see Maya, he'd been a massive sulk throughout our time in England and now we're back you couldn't wipe the smile off his face. I thought Josh would leave too but he asked if I wanted to play chess. I'm such a poor player, he only took five moves to win. I thought he would leave then, but no, he stayed, and we played backgammon and draughts and cards. I had wondered how it would be, seeing him again after all that's happened—London, Toby—it turned out Toby *had* been serious in the garden on New Year's Eve, under the imaginary mistletoe. But then I saw Josh, standing uncertainly in the doorway, peering at me from under dark eyebrows, his hair longer and spikier than before; I saw him and the feelings came flooding in like old friends. Then Father went to check the irrigation meters, he'll also look in on the cows afterwards, see how they're taking to the new silage. So Josh and I were alone. I asked if he wanted coffee and he did.

As we settled to dunking biscuits at the low table, I remembered the Cream Tea I had with Toby in Oxford Street. And I said, Look at us two, like an old married couple! But the joke didn't work. Josh looked mortified while I laughed, nervously. We both turned helplessly red in the face.

After a while, he said, So, how was London?

Great. I wasn't going to be the one to mention that I had sent him a letter and had no reply.

Yes. I read your letter. So he did receive it. I thought, I don't need to fret around Josh anymore. It felt fine. Yes. Ummm, he said, sorry I didn't write back.

It's okay, I said. Only this. I was a cool person now.

I did mean to. Sat down a few times to make a start, even. But every time—I don't know. I mean, what would I write? School's the same. At work I've been moved to the bananas now. Not really headline news…

Don't worry, it's fine.

Well, I did worry. And I did think. About you. Quite a lot.

I tried not to break the silence, not to disturb the Promise that was all at once tumbling ceiling to floor between us, the little grey moth of a promise careered down and down through the air, then recovered, stretched its delicate wings and, uncertainly, fluttered around the room. But as the moment stretched, I worried that Father would be back, open the door and let the Promise fly out into the night. I asked, What sort of thinking?

I—I was wondering about your cousins. You got on well?

Yes, I said, watching the Promise, its wings translucent against the mosquito net.

Especially… one of them specially?

Toby?

Tommy said you and he, I mean your cousin, you were always together. He said he hardly saw you. I sat up. *By my life, is he jealous?*

190

I said, Ah, yes, Toby, he showed me round London. Tommy didn't want to come out. Anyway, you said you'd been thinking.

What?

Thinking. While we were away.

Yes, well, that's it. You see, I was thinking—thinking— I mean, how would I feel if you meet this great guy and— I know he was only your cousin, but… And I thought, it might be too late already. *So he is jealous!* I felt calm and collected. Ha! He said, And I only have myself to blame. That's another thing I realised. Recently. His hand was spread on the sofa between us. I put my own hand next to it, forefinger nearly touching. I thought of Mother, how she said life is too short to hesitate. And I willed myself to look up, into his eye. And, just for good measure, and to be sure we were clear, I said, There's no one else. No one at all.

Chapter 9: Totnes, Devon

March 2010

Yasmin stands at the railway station, waiting for the London train. On board the train is Joshua Pasternak, a visitor from her mother's past. How will they know each other? Will he recognise Abbie in her—dark thick hair, long thin face, different coloured eyes, one green and one brown? She should have written his name on cardboard, held it up as taxi drivers do at airports. Pasternak—the name is familiar; doesn't sound Jewish, Abbie would have said. Her mother was always pronouncing on such matters. The Paddington-to-Penzance train arrives. A man standing next to Yasmin watches anxiously as the doors open, then quickly moves towards a woman who emerges with two children in tow. The children see him and run into his open arms, squealing as he swings them round, a human carousel. Teenagers with low-slung shoulder bags and plugged-in earphones skip down the carriage steps. Behind them a smart suited man clutches a partially open briefcase. Is it him? He is the right age, a contemporary of her mother's. A fearful excitement rises in Yasmin's chest, through her neck, round her jaw, and into a bright welcoming smile as she watches the man stride along the platform towards her.

Watching, but without staring; ready, but without expectation. Here he comes, black curly hair, a ridiculous goatee, a beer belly resting over a thin pair of legs. She looks at him and lightly opens her mouth to greet his approach, but he rushes past and disappears into the carpark behind her. Still on the train, a bearded old man in a long black overcoat and top hat struggles to open another carriage door. Finally successful, he climbs down to the platform, an army surplus canvas rucksack on one shoulder, an enormous suitcase in tow. The whistle blows. The train moves off. Next stop Plymouth, and on to Cornwall. The platform, which a moment ago was frantic, is quiet again. Only Yasmin and the old man are left. He sits on his massive suitcase, not looking around, not searching for anyone. He takes off his greatcoat, places it in his lap and rummages inside the khaki rucksack. Finally, he retrieves a small black book. Holding it up with both hands, he opens it and reads. Never once looking around. Reading, his body sways, backwards and forwards, backwards and forwards; praying, oblivious to the world.

Yasmin scans the deserted platform. Just the two of them. It *must* be him. Extraordinary, that he should ignore her so determinedly. She feels irritated; then indignant; then irate, as minutes pass and he continues to sway peacefully.

Then, gradually as she watches, a tenderness engulfs her, a kind of compassion. Compassion for—what—his innocence? Yes, for the vulnerable, almost childlike figure he cuts. There's something delicate, graceful even about him; about this bearded, top-hatted, conspicuously dressed, black-and-white, clearly Orthodox man.

Feeling she is intruding, Yasmin looks away. The

display on the station clock flashes eighteen degrees Celsius and she unravels the pashmina from around her neck. She rummages inside her shoulder bag until she finds the letter—a single sheet, penned laboriously, as though by a diligent child.

By the grace of G-d... Miss Yasmin Aswan... your mother Abbie... Kibbutz Community... sincere condolences... deep part of the heart... everything that happened...

Yasmin scans the familiar words. She thinks of the car journey she and this man will take, driving south to a graveyard in a field overlooking the sea. The roadside hedges will be laden with bluebells and cow parsley. Shame there won't be time for a swim.

Miss Aswan? Yasmin? She jumps to her feet, the letter hot, disconcerting in her hand. Hastily, she slips it back into her bag. How long has she been sitting here? The old man stands three yards away, hands in the pockets of his greatcoat.

Yes, that's me... she says, are you—?

Josh. Josh Pasternak. He seems distracted by something high above her head.

Ah, pleased to meet you. She smiles, stepping forward and holding out her hand. But he remains still. Yasmin lets her own hand drop by her side.

You are ready? His heavily accented voice is that of a younger man, fifties rather than the seventies his greying beard and old-fashioned clothes suggest.

Yes, my car is over there. She points, and starts towards the exit. He doesn't follow.

We don't walk? He asks.

Patiently, she says, No, It's too far; on the coast.

The cost? He mispronounces.

Yes, the coast, she repeats. My mother wanted to be buried by the sea. It's a half hour drive.

At length, he starts, It's kindly of you to come—for take me to… he peters out.

Oh, it's fine. She smiles. I often go there anyway; I like visiting my mother and sister. Usually I have a swim, too, while I'm there. Shall we go? She starts to walk away, but he doesn't follow. What now?

You know, he says, still addressing the same spot high up above her head. You know, she like the water also. Rain or hot, always she go swimming.

He followed her out of the station. When they reached Yasmin's car he walked over to the driver's door. Was he expecting to drive, she thought irritably. Ah, sorry, he said, and his face lit momentarily, in my country the driver, he is sitting on this side. Of course. She mustn't be so quick to judge. Looking more closely, through his beard, long scraggly sideburns and top hat, he didn't seem as old as all that.

Struggling to squeeze his suitcase into the boot of her car, Yasmin spent a flustered five minutes making the back seats lie flat. Instead of offering to help, the man turned his back on her to face the road. People wouldn't know they were together. Was the age of chivalry truly dead? She wondered. I'm sorry, I'm not sure how this works, she said at last.

Don't be sorry. You want that I do it? he asked.

Would she like him to *do it*? Would she? Yes, indeed,

she would like him to have *done it* right from the start instead of standing back like an invalid. Yes please, I'd be very grateful, she said. He set to it and was done seemingly before he even started. Gosh, that was quick, she said, genuinely impressed.

I used to look after this car. I mean, not *this car.* One the same.

You're a mechanic? She looked at his delicate white fingers, clean fingernails.

Long ago, he said. She waited for an elaboration but it didn't come. She had feared things will be a bit awkward in the little Renault. That his long, gangly limbs wouldn't fit into the small space and he would be forced to lean against the gear stick, adjust his position with every gear change. But when he got into the passenger seat his large frame appeared somehow to shrink. He kept his knees firmly together and pointing away from her, wrapped his arms tightly around his army rucksack, held on to it as though for dear life.

They drove along country lanes, towering hedges teeming with the joys of spring flowers on both sides. Mostly, they were silent. When she pointed out various landmarks, he responded with noncommittal grunts. She decided he was indifferent, was about to give up when, driving over the brow of a hill, the view opened and they could see over the hedges down to the distant sea. He sat up, his head colliding with the ceiling. Oh, he said. The sea. I didn't know we were close. It is the North Atlantic Ocean? It was the first question he had asked. And he still hasn't looked at her.

Ah, yes, I suppose it is. Hang on, sorry, I think actually it's the English Channel, the one between us and France.

You don't need to apologise.

Sorry?

Don't apologise. It is un—un-necessary. He sounded cross. What was the matter with this man? *And* he still hadn't thanked her for picking him up from the station. For driving him to Abbie's grave. Come to think of it, he hadn't mentioned Abbie. Neither of them has. It was a test, she decided. *He* was a test.

She said, No, I wasn't—I mean… The water, it's all connected. If you look at a map. It's the same—same water as the ocean.

He craned forward scanning, she thought, for more glimmers of the sea. But the hill was behind them now, and the only view was straight down the hedge-bound road.

After a while he said, Stop the car. Please. There was urgency in his voice, quite new. She said she would, as soon as they come to a passing place. Did he have a bladder problem? Older people often did. Not that she was interested in his bodily functions; but, if he were ill, that would explain his pallid complexion. I'm sorry, he was saying, voice strained, weak. Please stop now. She did, in the middle of a narrow lane. The sound he made as they ground to a halt made her turn sharply towards him. His hands were cupped around his face and he was leaning forward, retching. Acrid fluid oozed through his fingers onto the rucksack and his lap.

Oh, for crying out loud, Yasmin thought as she ran round the car to open his door from the outside. He swung his feet out, and continued to retch onto the roadside while a small number of cars congregated in front and behind them. The thought went through her head to place the palm of her hand on his forehead, supporting, stopping him from throwing it forward as he retched. Abbie used to do that when Yasmin was a child and sick over the avocado-green toilet bowl. She remembered the firmness of Abbie's cool hand. How welcome it had been. Should she step forward to help him? Would he flinch? It would be embarrassing, if he did. But what if it was? Finally, he seemed to be done. He continued sitting, though, elbows on thighs, head down.

Ah, we have to—have to go, she almost whispered.

Huh? he swivelled his head towards her.

I need to move the car, she said, more loudly. The others—they can't get through.

He looked at her; his gaze unfocused, remote. Did he not understand? She was about to explain, was searching for simpler words, when one of the waiting cars tooted its horn. The man Josh sat upright. He swiftly swung his legs back into the car and Yasmin ran round to her side, waving apologies at the other drivers. The queue in front was backing away slowly towards a passing place in the distance and they set off again. Are you okay? Would you like some more air? she asked, and wound down her window, hoping to dilute the sour smell.

Yes, okay now, he said, although he didn't sound it. Thank you.

That's fine. I'm sorry you're not well.

I didn't ask you to stop—enough early. I'm not used to this—bushes, by the road.

Hedges, she corrected.

Yes. It was too much last minute. I think you can stop

quickly. When I say.

I'm sorry. I didn't realise—

Don't apologise. There he goes again, telling her how to speak.

I wasn't. I was just—I was saying I wish I'd stopped sooner.

I think I should say sorry, instead of you.

Honestly, there's no need. Was she telling *him* how to speak now?

I—your car, it is dirty, I will clean her, of course, he was mumbling.

Don't worry about it…

I am very, how do you say?

It's fine. Really.

Dishonoured. *Ashame?* I feel, ummm—

Don't. Please, don't… First he wouldn't say anything at all, now she was begging him to stop. When they got to the parking area outside the gate to the burial ground, Yasmin turned off the engine and searched for the bunch of daffodils she had placed under her seat for safe keeping. But then the man declared a change of plan. He was too dirty. Not right to see the grave. He needed somewhere to wash and change his shirt. Yasmin couldn't believe it. Why didn't he say so before, when they had passed through Modbury? She said the nearest place to wash was the sea. They could walk to the beach from here.

Walking down between hedges bursting with wildflowers, he seemed more ready to talk. Having been mostly silent so far, telling her nothing of himself, nor asking a single question, Yasmin now learned he was planning to catch the 6.11 train back to London. This gave them just about three hours to get back. She was to call him Josh, not Joshua; he grew up in the Kibbutz Community, a contemporary of her uncle Tommy. Tommy had been his good friend when they were children but after Josh *returned to God*, his actual words, after that he and Tommy had lost touch. When she mentioned Abbie by name, he went quiet. Then he said he was now married, and had seven children.

He asked if Yasmin had siblings and she said Abbie had had a baby daughter who died in infancy, before Yasmin was born. That her name had been Tamara, that Abbie was buried in the same grave as her so now they were together. Josh was quiet at that. To keep the conversation going, Yasmin added that they didn't have a photograph of Tamara, even though she lived nearly to her second birthday. Her father, Omar, didn't think photographs were important. He said you keep people in your heart, not on gloss paper. Then to stop herself from rattling on, she asked about his children. His eldest son was to have his *Bar Mitzvah* celebration the following month; thirteen. His wife was expecting twins in the summer. Oh, my goodness! Yasmin blurted. The man Josh looked at her. Their eyes met for the first time. His were light blue. Very clear. Why do you say it? he asked.

Sorry, I just, I was just—No—I mean I should have said, Congratulations. *Mazal Tov.* She smiled at him, apologetically.

Thank you.

It was very rude of me. I was—I was thinking it must be a lot for her. For your wife to—to cope with so many children.

In our country children are a blessing.

Oh, of course! It's the same here. I love children. In

fact, I—

From God, you know, he continued as though she hadn't spoken. If you have even more, you are more blessed. When you understand that, you don't think how many children should you have. You just have all the children that God gives to you. He was still looking at her sideways; so serious. She looked away. My wife, she think the blessing is three times. One for each twin and one more that they come together. In the same time.

The beach was deserted. She wondered what he was going to do. Wash his hands and face in the shallows? Have a swim? He seemed so reserved. For a moment they stood together, both looking out across the wide estuary. Then he said, In our country, there are different beaches. For religious. Men have their beach, and women also—

Oh, yes, of course! She gushed, her voice raised and earnest. She wanted to be broad minded, accept him as he was. She wanted him to know that this was the sort of person she was. Would you like to be on your own? You can go that way, she pointed towards the right of the beach, and I'll go over there, round that corner... You can walk over and get me when you're finished. When you're ready to... Ready to what? She wasn't normally that hesitant. He has rendered her incapable of completing a sentence. She said, Ready to go back. There, finally.

He was still looking across the water. But I think—if it ok—You know, we are not in our country now. I... I came here to... to visit the grave and... to meet the daughter, so... So they were going to stick together after all. In which case, why bother her with tales of separate bathing beaches, or the sinfulness of swimming in the sea within sight of a woman? She imagined a stretch of sand, dotted with neat little piles of black and white clothes, each topped with a wide-brimmed hat, and men with black beards and white skin wearing long-johns and running towards the water. She didn't understand him; no way near. And she resented the fact that although he has now referred to Abbie, he did so without bothering to use her name.

They walked along the river estuary to a bit of grass by the rocks, and settled, leaving what Yasmin hoped was sufficient distance between them. Josh stretched out his legs. He took off his brimmed hat to reveal a large black skullcap beneath. Then, still wearing his shoes and overcoat, he lay on the sand. Is it okay? We stay a little? His voice was low, as though emanating from his belly.

Oh, fine, she answered. I love the sea.

After a while he said, Abbie, she love the water also. She waited for him to continue but, again, he didn't, and she realised he had fallen asleep.

What do you want to do for your birthday?

Josh, you remembered! How sweet!

Of course I remember. Why wouldn't I? Tommy had told him a parcel had arrived from her mother the day before. *Again, he said, Why wouldn't I? Was he picking a fight? It wasn't every day your girlfriend turned sixteen.*

Hmmm—

Why hmmm? He felt panic. When she wasn't happy, it was as though the sun had disappeared behind a cloud.

Well, hmmm, because you're always preoccupied.

He was?

Thinking of, you know, important stuff. War and—and politics. I didn't think you cared about small things. Like birthdays.

Well, that's not true. I've just asked you what you want to do. Relief. She was smiling again.

Well, if you really mean it—

Of course I mean it. Let's do something, you know, special. He knew what special thing he wanted to do today. And every hour of every day for the rest of time. It had been a year since they started walking out together. He'd waited. Patiently. Now it was time. He planned to make it happen. Today.

What sort of special thing?

Oh, I don't know. We could go somewhere, or, or just… But he couldn't say it. He could never ever speak about such things.

You're teasing, Josh. You think I'm a baby, fussing about a stupid birthday.

You're wrong. I'm not. Blood pumping in his ears. He hated blushing; been practising a control exercise he'd read about in an army magazine. A technique used by Swedish soldiers. What would she think, if she knew?

But her smile was carefree. *Okay,* she said finally, *let's go swimming in the sea. You can drive us.* She meant the Mediterranean. Even though it was winter. Cold water didn't bother her in the normal way. And so he raced around the yard trying to borrow a Community car; he'd only just passed his driving test, had not yet been in sole charge of a car. But all the cars were being used and they walked down to the river instead. He felt humiliated at being unable to take her where she asked. But she was happy and chatty and held his hand once they were outside the perimeter fence—she knew he was self-conscious and refrained from showing signs of *intimacy in public. Though, as for herself, she didn't care what anyone thought; and when they walked through the field of new reeds she turned towards him and her eyes, one grey, one brown, made him think of drowning again. She said, Are you looking at my eyes being different, Josh? She said, Don't look at them, it's my birthday.*

And he wanted to say how, when they had been children, he'd been afraid that if he looked at her, at her eyes, he would get stuck, and stare and stare, and people would know she made him feel like drowning. The children would share knowing smiles and so would she. And so he had learned to avert his gaze from her, and in time it became easy, and sometimes he would forget. Forget how he had longed to stare into those eyes, just check that one was still brown and one still grey. No, he said, I love it that your eyes are different. Tears in her voice, Well I hate them. And she smiled and put a hand onto his neck, a sign, and the saltiness of her lips made him think of the sea and drowning again. Which gave him hope. For later.

Turning left at the bridge, downstream, there was a hidden patch of beach, screened by clumps of reeds, where they sat on the hard black ground. He had got close before, but That Thing, it was yet to happen between them, the thing Josh knew about, quite a lot, but even in the privacy of his own head could only ever refer to as It. Or That Thing. He had read the magazines Daniel bought in Tel Aviv and kept under his mattress. Nonetheless, he was ignorant. Because how can you know about something you've never done? Like trying to imagine the sea while living in a land-locked country. That Thing, dreams of which having been familiar in his night-time world, has now begun to occupy his days as well. He couldn't concentrate. Not even on newspaper articles or the news. It was a nuisance. He was unable to progress, to move towards his goal of being a fighter pilot; and, afterwards, a career in politics, perhaps.

It was ironic. Knowing Abbie was there, her devotion, had given him the peace of mind to ignore her most of the time, to get on with what he considered the important things in life. But now, her very presence, the possibilities she presented, were hampering his ambitions. There was only one way to resolve the situation, which he had set his mind on doing. Today.

He might have got there before, with more determination. More resolve. But something had stopped him, every time, told him it was not right, or too soon. Leaning against the large eucalyptus tree outside the cemetery, lying together on the soft earth under a grapefruit tree, sometimes huddled on her single bed, for hours. They were opportunities he had not taken. Are you coming in? She sat up, away from him. Standing, she took off her clothes. He blinked. Soft lines, unimaginably smooth. He tried not to stare, though she was unconcerned. Talking and laughing as she let each item fall to the ground. Another sign.

He busied himself by gathering eucalyptus leaves and twigs, creating a model bonfire on the ground. Then he got out his camera, the Pentax his parents had given him for his eighteenth birthday. He liked handling it. Heavy yet compact, a textured, bumpy grip. The sound of the film advance lever, a reluctant, drawn out pull. The satisfying heavy crunch of the shutter release. He put his eye to the view-finder. Everything was fuzzy. Was it okay to watch her, now that she was out of focus? Hey! She laughed. Put it down. Don't shoot! Wearing nothing but the buckled brown leather sandals his father made for all the Community children, she waded into the river, stood *still a few moments, then disappeared in a splash. Oh, she cried, reappearing midstream, It's freezing! And a little later, It's wonderful! Come on Josh! Put the camera down!*

Get up, Josh, don't be lazy! she called, and the words, pearly and light, tumbled out of her like a smile. Come on, the water's lovely! But he was shy of her knowing what the sight of her had done to him. So he stayed still, and mumbled about being fine where he was. But it's my birthday! Sweet Sixteen! You said we would swim together. Josh!

Chapter 10: Jordan Valley

21 January 1976

My new year's resolution for 1975 was to write more but it's been a year since and I've not written a thing. Josh and I started to walk out together on my fifteenth birthday and I haven't thought about writing much. But yesterday was my birthday again, and a new beginning. Josh asked what I wanted and I said, swim in the Jordan. So we did, and then sat on the bank and watched the sun disappear behind the mountains. Then raced back for supper. Later, after the nine o'clock news, he came to my room, holding a newspaper, talking as he walked in.

Well, good news. Rabin interviewed on U.S. television. We need the world to understand why we couldn't participate in the Security Council talks. They must wake up to reality.

Nothing about what had just taken place by the river. I said, Josh, what are you talking about?

The Security Council. Their *Middle East Problem* talks. Last week. He threw himself on Anya's bed, settled with his head leaning on one hand, feet hanging off the end.

Middle East Problem?

Problems, you know. Refugees, Judah and Samaria, wars, terror? By the way, I've got you a present.

Oh, thanks. And for changing the subject. Can I see it?

You know, it's important; so why are you being ironic?

I wasn't. Although it's funny how you walk in with this story and I don't know what you're talking about.

Okay, listen. Rabin explained it to the Americans; why we had to boycott the Security Council talks. You with me?

Of course I am. I watch the news, you know.

Right. Yes. Although newspapers are much more instructive. Anyway. The Security Council debated the *Palestinian Question.*

And we wouldn't join the debate? That's stupid.

It's not. So listen. Hang on, I'll find the article—the *so-called PLO*, they can't take part in the talks because they're terrorists; full stop.

Okay, we don't like them. But we should still talk to them. Otherwise—

That's just it! We don't have to. Here, Rabin says, the Palestinian issue is only part of the Arab-Israeli conflict, it cannot be resolved in isolation. See? Wait a minute—it says, we shouldn't negotiate with every—*any splinter group* that might come up, or there will be no end for it. He let the paper drop to the floor. I was still reeling from the river, but he was behaving as though nothing. And I know the PLO isn't just *any splinter group.*

I said, But we shouldn't let something like this get in the way of peace. Why not give them the West Bank and Gaza, their own country?

You mean Judea and Samaria. And there's not going to be a Palestinian State there. We can't tolerate such a hostile entity so close by.

Oh, Josh, must we talk about this now? Can't we have

a nice time?

Well, we are having a nice time. Aren't we?

Why do you always talk as though everything is so—us-against-the-rest? Don't you want peace?

Of course I do. But remember there's no peace without security. Everyone knows that. And, it *is* us-against-them. Give the Arabs a foothold and they'll demand to go back to their old houses. Do you want the people of Abudiya to come flooding back?

Why not? I hate to think of them in refugee camps, dreaming about their old village by the Jordan.

Abbie, don't be naïve. These people hate you; they want to throw us all into the sea. He's always having the last word. And I dread the time, next autumn, when he joins the air-force. Since he found out about being accepted on the pilots course, he's been walking around with his chest puffed up. And he never hangs on to bad feelings, so after a few moments he said, I went to Tiberias today, for your present.

Oh, you didn't need to.

Well, it wasn't difficult. He sprang up and sat himself next to me on my bed. I had a lift with Ezra, and on the way back Micah Ashkenazi picked me up straight away, I didn't have to wait at all.

Oh. My stomach lurched. What's he doing here midweek?

How should I know? He looked at me quizzically but I said nothing, hoping he will change the subject which luckily he did. Anyway, you don't want your present, and you don't care about the Security Council, fine, let's think of something else to do. And he smiled through pursed lips.

I laughed. Ah, no, I can't think of anything else. Better open that present.

I don't know, I've kind of lost interest in it now; what with you acting so ungrateful; and it being such a stupid present. I don't think you'll like it.

Oh, no, I will! Truly, I promise.

Ummm, I don't know. Not sure why I chose it.

Come on, Josh, please. I want to see it.

You do? He turned. You're sure you want to see it?

Uh-huh, but only if *you* want to show me.

I want to. He smiled. Definitely. His breath was on my face. It smelled of damp earth. And I thought of the hard black slope where we had lain by the Jordan earlier that afternoon. How warm the shady ground had been against the skin of my back, how gentle his hands, his fingers on my arms and through my hair. So different from what I had known before—the greedy, grasping, puzzling touch, always cold, never cool, or warm.

Abbie, are you crying? Josh asked through the dust that floated on the sun's rays. His concern for me was so unfamiliar and made the contrast starker. What's wrong? he asked, and Are you sorry? For what we're doing?

No… are you?

Me? No. I've been—been—waiting. Thinking about it for—for a while. I could hear the blushing in his voice. But you know, he said, you know we don't have to— Don't be sad.

I'm not, I said and dislodged a pea-size stone from digging into my spine. Not sad. The tears, they're flowing on their own.

Abbie? Back in my room, Josh's face was against mine. I asked if you are sure.

Sure?

Yes, sure.

What of?

He inched forward, close. We waited. Are you sure? he asked. You know I don't want you to—feel—you know. Pressure. I thought I would forget to breathe, lost in the thin air between us. His long fingers through my hair. My cheek against his palm. Does anyone deserve so much happiness?

1 November 1976

I picked up Josh's letter, heart racing, then went into the Dining Room. Got my food quickly and sat alone, planning to read while I ate. But here's what it's like to live in a place like ours: people kept coming up, asking who the letter is from, wanting a full report on what Josh is doing, etc. I said he's still in general training but starting in the air force in a few weeks. And Ella Mulkin, Ah, I thought he was already an officer, Rita has told me, and, Oh, he would make an excellent pilot! As though she has a way of knowing this! As though her sheer trust can carry him through the gruelling months ahead. Well, that's being a Son of the Community for you. And by the time I got to read the letter my soup was cold; or colder, it was only lukewarm to start.

Training Base X. 22nd October.
Abbie, thank you for your letters. I know I promised to write

sooner, but there has been no time. Anyway, here it is. The first day, Daniel and I took the bus to the draft centre in Tiberias. Then they put us on an ancient bus with small, opaque windows, you know the type that smells so bad you only want to throw up. When we got here, they lined us up, very efficient, issued with uniform and a kitbag. Now I'm a soldier, Personal Number 3539470. Then into another kind of big shed place, where they gave us injections, right and left shoulders, then face down on the treatment bed and another shot, you know where. All with not a word of warning or explanation. Vaccinations, we supposed it was. Everyone came out limping and sat lopsidedly for the rest of the day. You would have laughed. But wait till you see me next: my uniform doesn't fit at all. Made for someone much shorter. Hope Miriam can have it altered when I'm home next. Which, by the way, will be in two weeks. I must go now. Please write soon. Josh.

p.s. I like to remember our time in the Sinai last summer. You loved swimming and snorkelling over the reef. But for me it was the desert. The vast expanse of it, wild and silent. And I find myself longing to see it again. Lights are off.

I told Father about this, how frustrating to have no privacy in the Dining Room. I thought he'd laugh, maybe say how Ella loves to talk—I know he sometimes switches to a different pavement when he sees her coming. I thought he'd sympathise, because he himself has greater need for peace now that people are talking about Mother, what drove her away, is she ever coming back, etc. Ester says he is *withdrawing*; but from what, I'm not sure. Last night he and I sat in his room, and not a word passed between us for an hour or more. I was glad when finally

Solomon came round and they chatted a while over coffee—Jimmy Carter has beaten Gerald Ford to the Whitehouse, the Republicans have been punished for Watergate, Carter is Good For the Jews, he hardly mentions the Middle East. And now that Anwar Sadaat has offered to negotiate, we might have peace with Egypt within the year.

Anyway, so the other day. I thought my father would understand. But he said it's not for me to judge Ella, or any of the Veteran Members. Do I realise how many people live in such alienation that they might lie dying in their house and no one would know? Because no one would miss them? We must be grateful, all of us. It wasn't idle curiosity that drove them to accost me with their questions. It was love, and camaraderie. Hmmm.

Well, Father had been so extra-silent lately, and suddenly, this torrent. Of course, he's right, and I felt wretched. I wrote to Josh about it, but then threw the letter away. I want to impress, not lay my flaws before him. Like hanging out one's washing in public, which one mustn't do according to Mother; her letters are brimful of such pearls-of-wisdom since she's left London, moved to Devon, and *found Jesus*.

In other news, I've decided to take the Matriculation examinations. Which means moving to another school. I know I'm going to university, eventually; I don't want to just come home to the Community after the army, work in the henhouse like Mother, or otherwise walk in the Pioneers' footsteps. Being *The Future Of The Community* is not enough for me. It doesn't mean I'm going to leave forever; if Josh wants to stay, become a Member, work in the banana fields, that's fine by me. It's just I want to do other things first. Which I can with a Matriculation Certificate. And it will be easier to get my studying done now Josh is not here, too near, distracting.

Now there are no more night-time wonderings—swimming in the Jordan, stargazing, lying under the old eucalyptus tree; sneaking into my bed in the dead of rainy nights, hoping Anya doesn't wake up. Now it's me always first to bed and she's out all hours. What is she doing? She won't say, only that it must be a secret or else. Or else what? We never mention the conversation about Noah from two years ago and meanwhile he has a new baby, is she still meeting with him? Is that why she sometimes cries under her duvet when she thinks I'm asleep? Or else nothing, she says, no one must know and that includes you Madam Boskovitch. Josh's weekend leaves are short. So much longing. Of course, it's worse for him—the line ups, the drills, the humiliations—he says he didn't expect it to be a holiday, and it's not. I don't know how he can keep going on two or three hours sleep a night. Daniel is there too; they share a bunk and that's some help. And he's made a new friend, Isaac, who lives in the Occupied Territories and has ten brothers and sisters, compared to Josh's none.

Everything is set for me to start at the new school. I feel no regret about leaving—everything seems empty, desolate since Josh left. What a row they had at Members' Meeting over whether to introduce the Matriculation examinations at our own school. Mona thinks it's time we prepare Our Youngsters, Our Future, for life in the modern world. Not everyone is going to be a farmer. Anyway, even farmers need to be educated nowadays. That's what she said at Community meeting. But the opposition was too strong. Solomon threatened to resign, he will not be party to our children's education being degraded by extraneous constraints, their creativity restricted by mark-scoring. He spoke passionately, Father said; at the end of which no one except Rita voted for Mona's proposal. Rita is trying to persuade Leo to move with me to the other school. But he resists, no doubt afraid of having to do homework instead of windsurfing in the Sea of Galilee every afternoon.

So, a fresh start in September. And I'll be mixing with the rest of the Jordan Valley population—should be quite a shock.

And meanwhile, Mother has declared I should live with her and go to school in Devon, where she now has a house. English education is the best in the world, she says. Of course, Father won't hear of it; and nor will I. Still, she persists. But who would want to live in a remote, windswept cottage where your nearest neighbour is a kilometre away and is an old farmer whose accent is so strong communication is near impossible—even Mother herself has trouble understanding him.

22 February 1977

On my birthday, Josh telephoned the Dining Room phone from his air-force base. Luckily, I was there eating supper. I was so excited and grateful to hear his voice, but what could we talk about, with me standing in the corridor and people walking up and down all pricking their ears, and Josh with a queue of people behind him. And am I wrong to bother him with my fears and confusion, my doubts about whether his feelings have changed now he's going through so much and with his father's health as well? I get so excited about his next leave, make plans, imagine what it will be like. Then when it turns out to be different, I can't help wondering what's wrong. I know he needs to catch up on sleep, see his parents and friends, but I do want more of him for myself. So then it's another three weeks during which a short letter, really a note, arrives in the post. Sometimes.

My dear Josh

How are you, I really hope this letter finds you in good spirits? I'm well. My mother has taken up knitting again, which explains the balaclava enclosed. There's a matching scarf and gloves waiting for you at home. She sent a whole load for you brave soldiers, all knitted by her Sunday Prayer Group; hence whoever wears them shall have plenty of good luck, she says. Which reminds me, I saw your mother this morning. She will stay in Haifa while your father has his tests. And, Josh, she asked me how you were. But surely, you've written to them too?

And meanwhile, I'm going to Tel Aviv with Saffi, staying in her brother Micah's flat. Also Sara, Anya and Shira are coming. It's the first weekend of Passover. Micah will be away in the army, probably. So excited to go to the cinema, trying to decide which film to watch, my choice is All the President's Men—*you know how I feel about Robert Redford; and do you remember Dustin Hoffman too—in* The Graduate *last year? I don't! It was the first time you and I watched a film together, and all I remember is, well, you.*

If Micah is back in time, he'll take us all out to eat on Saturday, he said. He can afford it now he is an important army officer, a Major with a big salary. Of course I won't go if

*you're home that weekend, I'd much rather be with you. I'm
counting the days till I see you again. And the hours. Till then,
I will let you get on with defending us from our enemies.*

All my love, Abbie

*p.s. please don't speak of my mother's 'Jesus phase' to anyone.
Seriously embarrassing! And if my father finds out people
know about it, I don't know; it might be the straw that breaks
the camel's back.*

1 March 1977

Josh's leave is cancelled. Not for the first time he's in
trouble; he's wretched and that's why. He said my last
letter cheered him up, not much else does at the moment.
They had night training all week, some of the men were in
tears. Exhaustion, I supposed, but Josh says it's the
shouting and humiliation, being made to eat dirt. He's
worried about the religious guy he's made friends with,
Isaac; writes about him a lot: Isaac may not make it
through the training, he has no experience of physical
work because his father is a rabbi, so it's been schoolwork
or else studying the Torah all his life. Apparently, his
family all think him mad for volunteering to be a fighter,
but he says he doesn't want to sit around while others risk
their lives defending his. I suppose this is commendable.
What a life! And meanwhile, Josh says coming home is a
light at the end of his tunnel; the mere thought of getting
out of base makes him breathe more easily. And now, this.
Grounded for the Sabbath.

When his letter arrived, I decided to visit him. Of
course there are no busses, so I asked Tommy if he would
drive me, which he would have done, any excuse to borrow

a Community car. But Father said if Josh is grounded, he won't be allowed visitors. Josh had asked me not to tell anyone, Members would frown upon impudence to a superior, which is what he did. Even so, I couldn't lie when Father asked me straight why his leave was cancelled. But he won't tell; he hardly talks to anyone anymore.

Josh's letter came inside a parcel—a completely surprising and only slightly late birthday present, I cried as I opened it. I've no idea when he got a chance to buy it, and how he knew how much I love Sylvia Plath; that I adore every word she ever wrote. And to have my own copy is really special. I read my favourite lines, some of them weird and wonderful. Coincidentally, she also lived in Devon, and would have been about Mother's age had she not killed herself. The two of them might have been neighbours; they could have passed the time of day together, commenting on the weather and the price of beef, the sort of things the English talk about. I wonder whether Mother would have offered to have her "very talented musician son" put some of Plath's poems to music; would she have had the nerve.

Tommy said, Stop moping about the place, it's worse for us. By 'us' he means The Band. They are planning a revival and had scheduled a grand rehearsal to fit in with Josh's leave. Tommy has been going on about it non-stop for a month, boring us all nearly to death, asking me to give Josh endless messages, be ready, make sure he's not too tired, what does he think about this and that chord, etc. As though I'm his secretary. And it's nothing to him that by the time Josh has visited his father in hospital, practised with The Band, did his washing and other chores there would be practically no time left for me. To properly thank him for my birthday present. I said I'm not moping, if I were it would be none of his business and he can get lost. Then I walked out before he could come back at me.

When Josh's news came, I wrote him a letter, and asked Daniel to deliver it when he gets back to base after the weekend. Also a cake from Ruth. She ran off and brought it as soon as she heard. Said to say hello, and that they're going to visit his father the next day, and take his mother out too, give her a break. Father and I will visit next Sunday. And afterwards we'll meet with Aunt Betty's brother Manu, who lives in Haifa with another man. It's to keep in touch with Mother's side of the family. I used to enjoy Betty and David's visits, loved Passover celebrations at their house. Mother and Betty were friends, always laughing together. Manu too. But now I wonder whether any of this was real. I suppose it wasn't difficult for Mother to hide her feelings; she only had to put on a brave face for three or four hours in the afternoons, while Ester, Tommy and I were with her, away from the children's houses.

22 March 1977

Last night, a surprise! I woke and Josh was hovering over me. My heart swelled, right after I screamed. I had just been having one of these awful dreams, a variation on a theme, in which Josh is gone and I am looking for him, in vain, with the added complication of having no clothes on. So waking to him being right there, so unexpectedly, was extra-confusing, a rare happy ending. Luckily, Anya was away again. Oh, I wanted us to stay up all night; there was so much more to be said. Much more love still to be made. But we fell asleep, and I didn't even hear him leave.

He'd been given an eights hour leave, which really isn't long enough to come home. And to top the inconvenience, a journey back to base, setting off before dawn with Ezra! Ezra had given me a lift once. *Once* being the operative word as Toby used to say. He drove so wildly I had to ask him to stop the car so I could be sick by the roadside. *Very* embarrassing. He took it completely in his stride. Probably it happens all the time. He took quite a pleasure in telling me how he was once stopped by a traffic policeman. He'd said, Hello, Officer, was I driving too fast? And the policeman said, No, you were flying too slowly. What I'm wondering is, why has he only ever been stopped once.

Ezra normally has the mildest manners—Father says the man's a saint, the way he puts up with Rita. But get him behind a car wheel, he turns into a demon, a Dr Jekyll. And yet, he won't let Leo near motorcycles, which he says is the Angel-of-Death's cousin.

Excited to be going to Tel Aviv next weekend. Josh said nothing about us staying at Micah's apartment. I had wondered if he would.

25 March 1977

I spoke with Josh on the telephone today. He is so unhappy it's hard to bear. What are they doing to him? He won't say. Then we argued about *everything*. He has a week's leave and he's going to spend it at Isaac's house in the Occupied Territories. So they are Settlers, why is he making friends with such people? He hung the phone up, then he wrote to apologise.

Abbie, I'm sorry I hung up. That's all. You were unfair about Isaac. I put the receiver down, without thinking. Then the phone swallowed my last token, and the queue behind, so I walked away. If it weren't for this stupid pay-phone. Yes, Maale-Adumim is in Judea, which technically makes Isaac a Settler. But Settler isn't a swearword, you know. He's a Settler and a good person, both. We don't have a veto on each other's friends, do we? If we did, I would first of all stop Micah Ashkenazi always hanging around you in the creepy way he does. Fair enough, you say he's just a friend and I must accept this. Let us not argue any more. I will try to telephone you in the Dining Room tomorrow or the day after, I daren't bother Ruth and Joseph two nights running. Josh.

4 April 1977

On our way back from Tel Aviv the bus broke down and we had to wait for another one. Oh, the brutality of queuing! If I hadn't been to England, I would have thought it natural. In London, I took a photograph of people queuing single-file, the civility of it was so enchanting. Well, *today* was no such experience. Everyone was trying to get home for Passover. Us girls hung back, fearful of being bashed by fierce old women wielding baskets and walking sticks; or endure full body contact with fat sweaty men striving to improve their positions. Of course, standing back meant we didn't get onto that first bus, and had to wait an hour for the next one.

Then, in Tiberias, no one stopped to give us a lift. We

even tried the old trick of hiding behind a ditch while Sara hailed passing cars on her own. Her being the prettiest. That didn't work either, drivers stopped, but then moved on when they saw us scrambling up the bank. We decided to walk, it was so hot, we thought we'd never get home, but then on the bridge over the Jordan Joseph Mulkin stopped for us, he was driving Josh's father Dov home from hospital.

Anyway, Tel Aviv was just great! Friday evening, we walked along the beach all the way to Jaffa. The old city lights are a sight, we couldn't get over its beauty. We sat at a café with sticky chairs and dirty tables and floors, and had Turkish coffee with cardamon and too-sweet baklawa. All around were narghileh-smoking, backgammon-playing Arab men. We got talking to some young guys, they were quite friendly, and offered us a smoke. Then they said let's go down to the sea together. Sara said, Why not, and we tagged along, but Anya was scared so we grabbed Sara who was surrounded by the three of them, and said thank you and goodbye. They followed us down the road shouting and swearing but Saffi shouted back to leave us alone and we ran all the way down the road, laughing, quite hysterically.

Saturday Micah was home early. He drove us to a beach south of the city in his grand army issue black number plate car. He and I went swimming; we were the only ones in the water, apart from a couple of sunburned tourists. It wasn't cold, we stayed in a while catching waves. Then we swum round the corner to a smaller, even more beautiful and deserted beach, and stayed talking there for ages. It was beautiful on the warm sand, in the mild sun, looking out to sea. Then his hand was on my back and I asked, Why don't you speak to me when we are with the others, and he said, Maybe it's because I love you. How do you answer this, I didn't, and there were just the waves breaking gently and the yellow sand rolling underneath back and forth, back and forth. I said, You know, what I would like is, I'd like us to be friends, just normal friends, and he said, Galia, that's his girlfriend, she's pregnant. If she doesn't agree to an abortion we'll get married in the summer. Why is he telling me this? In the end I got up and said, Let's swim back. As we waded in, a walker stopped and stared. What's the water like? she asked. Micah looked at me and said, Delicious. You're both mad she said and added, Oh, what it is to be young and mad, and walked on. Mother swims every day of the year in a freezing Devon river called The Dart. Now, that *is* madness. She also swims in the Ocean with *like-minded* Wild-Swimmers. The highlight of their year is a New Year's Day dip. In January, not our September new year.

In the evening we had pizza in Dizengoff Centre, and watched *Rocky*, a film about a boxer. No tickets left for *All the President's Men*, which I was glad about because Josh wants to see it and maybe we will watch it together on his next leave. Unless he's determined to visit his new friend Isaac, the religious guy he seems so concerned with half the time (Micah said the town, *Maale-Adumim*, where Isaac lives *is* in the occupied territories; which makes him *a Settler*). But when I asked Josh about it he put the phone down. He won't listen to me.

23 April 1977

Parliamentary elections next month, and I've volunteered

to help with the Labour Party campaign. Labour have been in power since Independence, but now Solomon says they are in graver danger of losing than ever. We must do everything to keep the ex-terrorist Menachem Begin out. What would the world think of us if he were to become Prime Minister?

And, speaking of what The World thinks, the Security Council has condemned Israel's Occupations of the Territories. Josh says the UN can get stuffed. I don't like to contradict him—he knows so much. And it's true that I'm also upset with his new Settler friend, this Isaac person whom I've never met, and who is the reason I won't see Josh at Passover. Josh sent a postcard from the Territories where he's staying with Isaac, a picture of beautiful panoramic views over the Settler town of Maale-Adumim. It's as though his words are not his own. I'm so confused that he is writing this way.

It is the Promised Land, or part of it. From here you can see the hills of Jerusalem to the north and west. To the south and east is the desert; and in the distance, beyond the Jordan River, the mountains of Edom and Moab. Abbie, the Green Line that separates Judea and Samaria from the rest of our country is an artificial border, pencil-drawn in the aftermath of Independence. It's fiction. Here, with Isaac's family, I feel real. This land is as beautiful as our own Jordan Valley—and every bit as much ours. If you ever visit here you would understand: the people, how they love the land; you would never want to leave, or give it up.

He feels real. But I want him to want to spend time with me. I long for us to be together; not just on Friday evenings when he is dead-tired; not just a Saturday when he has to be packed and ready to catch the first bus to base. Does this have anything to do with my view on the Security Council? I *do* have my own opinion about such things. It i*s* wrong to Settle the Territories. It's an obstacle to peace. Josh won't discuss it, any of it. Sometimes I think he doesn't want to know what I think about anything.

30 April 1977

Two weeks to the Elections. The newspapers are predicting another Labour Government, so no worries there. Today, Solomon took ten of us to the highway junction, where we stood for two hours, waving *Labour* and *Rabin for Prime Minister* banners at passing cars. Some drivers stopped and talked to us. One got heated, a right-wing Opposition supporter, said we're wasting our time, that the next Prime Minister will be Menachem Begin, not Rabin. Well I never! Leo held his own, I couldn't have done nearly as good a job. But Josh would have. He'd have brought up facts and figures to shut him up.

Now Josh. He has started as a Flight Flower, and it's becoming more difficult to sustain my correspondence with him. Mostly in my letters I create a kind of fiction. A parallel reality. Because, Reader, and I don't want to sound melodramatic, he has changed. A recurring dream: I'm sitting on the shore of a lake, like the Sea of Galilee, but bigger; water all the way to the horizon. I'm looking up at Josh standing over me, and I'm blinded by the low evening sun. He walks away, towards the water. I hear the crunch-crunch of his bare feet on the tiny shells and stones, crunchier than sand. With every step I see a glimpse of his soles, white, not pecan-brown like the rest of him. I want to stop him, hold on to his waist, my cheek flat against his back. Instead, I stay seated, paralysed by indecision, fear, lethargy. He reaches an old abandoned fishing boat, without sail or oars, drags it the short distance to the water, and pushes off. He drifts away. That's how I see him now.

On the positive side, Josh says he's enjoying the maths and science lessons in pilots training. After hating both at school. I went to visit my own new school last week. They said I will need to take my studies seriously, apropos of nothing; our own school's reputation must have preceded me. Father was with me. He's still being harangued by Mother, who insists I should go live with her; I suppose that's why he's taking an interest.

Ester thinks I should go to England, grab the opportunity. But—I don't think I want to live so far from my family. And the Community, which is my family too. Mostly, Josh. If I leave him to his own devices, he's bound to meet someone else, maybe one of Isaac's sisters, and consign me to the dumping ground of history... Then there's my father. He's only got me now, with Tommy doing National Service, and joining the army soon after.

So that's two things to worry about—my future schools and will I be abandoned by Josh. Now the third: his first solo flight; keeping fingers crossed for next month, the last day of May!

2 May 1977

Yesterday was Mayday, also called International Labour

Day. Red flags adorned the yards and pavements, interspersed by our country's blue and white ones, which have been up since Independence Day. At the parade, Mona made a moving speech about workers' rights. Through our Way of Life we strive for Equality. She spoke of the Zionist dream to metamorphose the Jewish people; turn us from pale shop-keepers and pen-pushers to a nation of strong, sun-kissed farmers. All for one and one for all. And, Workers of the world, unite! These slogans are no dream. They are our present, our reality! The Zionist vision is realised here every day, not just on Mayday, etc.

It was rousing; everyone said so. Except Ester. She said talk of Jewish national Self-Realisation leaves a bad taste in her mouth. She's only just recovering from the annual trauma of Independence Day. Ester has a talent for spoiling things, for making you feel ashamed of enjoying such special occasions. As children we would spend the days before Independence Day stapling hundreds of blue and white flags onto string, tying them high between tall trees; making the yard look festive. We would wear white socks and shirts, and decorate our bicycles with strips of crepe paper, threaded through the wheel spokes, round-and-round the cross bar and handle bar. There would be a bicycle procession, a parade from the Big Lawn, to the Granolith Square by the Dining Room, where everyone would gather. And the flag would be raised from its half-mast of the day before. The day before Independence Day is Fallen Soldiers Remembrance Day, when we commemorated those who gave their lives so that we can live ours, The Silver Tray on which the Jewish State was gifted to us, as the poem goes that everyone knows. And raising the flag to full-mast marks the end of our mourning, and signals it's time to celebrate Independence. There's dancing and singing, and the next day a fun fair, and barbecue. It's nice.

But now, Ester, listing the reasons why we shouldn't rejoice, draining the fun out of it all. Her lecture is about the Arabs; some of them are citizens of our country, but they surely don't celebrate Independence. For them, it's the day they lost the war. The day their own dream of a Palestinian state was dashed. The day their neighbours and relatives ran away and became refugees. Part of me doesn't want to know. And part of me already knows. And another part doesn't understand how I'd failed to see this before.

At home, Ester said, people like Mona always leave out that we are not alone in this 'Promised Land' in inverted comas. The early Zionists called it 'Virgin Land', inverted commas also, which it most certainly wasn't, but they chose to ignore this and still do. Of course, the Situation is more complicated now than it was early in the century. We have the Territories, she was really getting going, workers from across the Green Line, tens of thousands, cross into Israel every day. They work in construction, in agriculture; all those jobs Jewish people can't be bothered to do anymore. Then they cross the border again. Back to their refugee camps in the territories. So much for building our Jewish land with our own fair Jewish hands. And she leaned forward in her seat, ready for more.

You're exaggerating, Father told Ester. No one ever thought Palestine was Virgin Land, not even at the turn of the century. Ester said, Father, I'm not exaggerating, of course they realised there was a native population here.

228

But they dismissed it as irrelevant, swept it under the carpet.

Father said the Zionists were keen to treat the Arabs fairly; to be good neighbours. That's when philanthropists like the Baron de Rothschild came into such prominence, buying land off Arab owners and handing it to Jewish Pioneers. Ester said we didn't need a history lesson right now, but Father wanted Abbie to know such things, as though we haven't learned it at school already. He said the land we settled on was acquired legally. Did you hear that, Abbie? It was all done by the book.

But Ester said, The land owners who sold to the Zionists were fat cats sitting in Beirut and Damascus. They sold the land under their tenant farmers' noses. And those poor peasants woke up to find the land they'd been farming for generations wasn't theirs anymore. Could that be true? Father said, Well, that was—that was unfortunate, of course. But these things happen, Ester. Legally, we were in the right. These things happen. They do.

Then, Ruth was in the room. No one answered my knocking, Oscar. Oh, hello, Ester; you're home, how lovely. Father said to come in, of course, and carried on talking to Ester. You see, it's easy to criticise, with the advantage of hindsight. In those days there was no such thing as a Palestinian nation. They had no—no national identity. The Pioneers assumed things would work out. Remember the Jewish state was just an idea, a dream; more like a fantasy—There was no—no one planned to dispossess anyone—And so on, for quite a while, because Ester always has an answer. Until eventually Ruth got up and left.

Ester asked, What was Ruth doing here? Father said, Doing? Ester said, She comes in, sits down, then she leaves. Father said, Oh, that, it's her routine nowadays. It's because Tommy and Maya sit at Joseph and Ruth's Room all afternoon watching television, he explained, and in Ruth's words, *More than hold hands*. So rather than tell them to stop, she goes out. Ruth doesn't want to risk upsetting Tommy, even though her first choice for Maya was Josh. Mother used to call her *Mrs Bennet*, because her obsession with finding husbands for her daughters, tall-dark-handsome-and-extremely-rich or not. In fact Mother called her *Mrs Bin-Bennet*, which is more appropriate for our region, she said. This always sent us into fits of laughter, Ruth too, although she has never even heard of Jane Austen. Father would say it's Ruth's Iraqi roots, where such things were more important. Why he should think that, Mother had no idea. How many Iraqis does he know, anyway? Ruth is the only Community Member born in an Arab country. Everyone else is European. Father is going to have a word with Tommy, this can't go on.

After Ester left, Father and I continued talking. He said, Yes, the Arabs who are citizens of our country have equal rights. Ester's views are extreme. Would the Israeli Arabs like to emigrate to one of our neighbour Arab states? No. Why? Because their lives would be much worse there. Because we are a Democracy. Here there is law and order, technological advances, a welfare state. But, you know,

Ester doesn't believe in Democracy. That's why Father doesn't argue with her. And he sat back, smiling. He seemed quite relaxed today, almost cheerful. I had thought the news that Mother was coming back or visiting (don't know which) would upset him. Instead, it seems to have had the opposite effect.

8 May 1977

I received a letter from Micah Ashkenazi, that's never happened before. He writes that ever since the time we stayed at his apartment he's been thinking of me a lot. He saw me at the Mayday Parade and wanted to come over but I was surrounded by people, then he looked for me in Father's Room and in my room at school but I wasn't there. He wants me to stay with him again. Says he will buy me another pizza. Also that he is coming to the Community again the last weekend in May and wants to see me. I don't know what to think. Maybe I need to tell Josh about what is happening? What would I say *is* happening with Micah?

My dear Josh,

I have been missing you more than usual. When you next come home, I'd like to tell you something, which I've been meaning to talk about for some time. I fear the knowledge of it may upset you, and make you think less of me, and this is why I haven't told you before. I love you. Abbie

10 May 1977

I decided to walk over to the post box, to send the letter I wrote to Josh straight away, before there's time to reconsider. Which I did even though my shaking hand almost refused to let go of it. Like Tess of the D'Urbervilles sliding her letter under Angel's door. But I regretted it straight away. What was I thinking? Men like Angel Clare, men like Josh, cannot fathom such things. And how will Josh understand what even I can't—the hold Micah has on me?

I posted the letter after the post-van had gone so there was still time to salvage the situation. At six o'clock the next morning, as Joel Littani shuffled his way to work, I waited for him outside the post office. I explained I needed to retrieve the letter I'd sent the night before. Joel is never happy, and today was no exception. I don't know how Mona can stand him. He muttered about irregularities and Members' time being wasted, people were lucky his post box, *his* post box, is not a regular city post box, if it were there would be no retrieving of letters, rules would be rules and people would stick to them. He took an age to get the key from a locked box inside a locked drawer, shuffling across the room, his elbows pointing backwards and up behind him, as though trying to pull his stooped figure upright, there's something quite wrong with him, maybe arthritis, I don't know. Then he stood still for an unnecessary age, contemplating the key and inspecting the lock on the back of the post box before finally opening it and letting the post tumble out into a cardboard box. I tried to pick it up for him but he said, no, no, stand over there, and he stooped further forward, lifted the box only a fraction off the ground and in this impossible position shuffled all the way back across the room where he set it down on the desk, and back to the post box to lock it and take the key over to the box that was placed in the drawer that was shut and locked. One thing after another, he mumbled, yes-yes, all in good time, and I thought, no wonder you have to start work at six when the post van doesn't even arrive till noon.

Then he started to search for my letter; I felt my hot cheeks, he now knows there's a problem between Josh and me. But his face was poker, just mumbled, Pas-ter-nak, Jo-sh Pas-ter... Every syllable a stab, the blood was up in my throat, I wanted to cry, or shout, shut up, but no way would I ever in a hundred years, not at a Pioneer Member. He kept mumbling as his dry long fingers travelled nimbly, mortifyingly, through envelopes. Finally, he picked up the letter and looked it over. As though such inspection was necessary in any way; examined both sides with vindictive thoroughness. And only then, a million years later, handed me my letter, still frowning and grumbling about the lateness of the hour and the bother some people are.

11 May 1977

A barrier is growing between Josh and me. I wrote this about what happened the other day:

After the Sabbath Reception meal, they walked out through a hole in the perimeter fence. Hand in hand, down the hill and across the river, over to the abandoned Arab village, Abudiya. The village had been a thriving fishing and farming community, stretching all the way to Wadi Fijas. But the inhabitants went away during the War of Independence, and not one came back. All that was left of these former lives were the ruins of stone houses scattered on a thistle-covered hill. She hadn't been up in the ruins since that day more than five years before, just after the Yom Kippur war, the November morning when the children were let out of the bomb shelters. Not sure what to do with their unaccustomed freedom, a group of them had walked out, down the rain-soaked hill and across the swelling river. Abbie recalled the prickliness of the thistle leaves; her fingers dismembered them gingerly to reveal the delicious soft white insides; the muddy lumps on the soles of her winter shoes which the children called 'lady's heals'; the squelch of their march along the track; and Josh. Magnificently grown up at fifteen years old, the oldest of their little group and its undisputed leader. He had been the object of her deepest longings and most fervent wishes. And she remembered the moment, just after they had crossed the bridge, when Josh had fallen into step with her. At least, she thought she could remember it, though sometimes she wondered what, if anything, had actually passed between them in those brief moments. On the face of it, nothing more than walking along in silence, side by side, all the way to the foot of Abudiya hill. Nonetheless, at the time she was nearly overwhelmed by the suggestion that Josh Pasternak, tall-and-achingly-handsome, smart, charismatic, might have sought her out; albeit casually; covertly; offhandedly. At the time, she had written about the episode extensively in her blue and white diary. Childishly, even by the standards of the thirteen-year-old she had been, she exaggerated the significance of his gesture.

And tonight, five years later, walking along the same path, most remarkably, miraculously, Josh was by her side. Spring was morphing into summer and the night was starry, cool enough to keep away bloodthirsty mosquitoes. As they climbed the mound towards the ruins, picking up wood for a fire, she asked him whether he also remembered that walk on the day the war ended. He did not. Think, she persisted, we rushed home afterwards; there were three funerals that afternoon, fallen soldiers. Oh yes, he remembered the funerals. Alex Levi, Ehud Applefeld, Noam Baum. Ehud had been a navigator and the last one to be buried. It was while listening to his commanding officer's eulogy of Noam Josh had made his mind up to be a fighter pilot when his time came to join up. No, he couldn't remember anything else about that day.

He lit a fire in one of the ruined stone houses, and they lay together on her ribbed orange cotton bedcover. Afterwards, they sat, her right leg stretched along his left. He told her about his first weekend in the air-force. His parents' visit, and how when they went home, he was left with unbearable loneliness. Saturday evening, after he'd finished cleaning the kitchen, he had walked to the high security fence, had looked out like an Alcatraz prisoner. He had picked up a stone and threw it over the fence. In the night's silence he could hear it land on the other side. And he wished more than anything he could be that stone. And he cried, looking out through the fence, knowing that being a stone was better than being him. Cried like a baby, he said.

She said, You're not a baby. Men are allowed to cry. And she held his hand as her own eyes welled up. There's no shame, she said, her voice a watery gravel.

But he looked at her sharply and the moment was ripped open. He said, You don't need to feel sorry for me. That's not why I told you.

At that, she was lost for words. Still, she said, It's just… it's because I love you.

235

Sometimes I wonder whether you can, you know. I wonder if I even deserve it.

She almost cried in alarm, Why? Why don't you?

I don't know. I think there is something wrong with me. I don't know. I don't know what it is.

She wanted to tell him he was perfect, that she loved everything about him, down to the smell of his sweat. Instead, she said, Josh, there's nothing... nothing wrong with you.

When he talked again it was a different melody, like there's been a switch from minor to major key. He said, Oh, well, enough of that, aren't we here to enjoy ourselves? Because, I was thinking just now, before the conversation turned so sombre... He turned towards her, his face a hazy moon against the gloom, his eyes dark, wide. The farrows he'd been sketching on her thigh were deeper now, and longer.

This is how things are between us. Joy and doom in a confusing salad. Here, for example. Fast forward. We're still in the ruined house. Still Friday night.

Later. The fire had gone out. They lie on the ribbed cotton bedcover, her head on his arm. He is humming a new Eric Clapton song. He's going to work out the chords on his guitar later. Clapton is a genius. Are you alright, she asks, still shaken by earlier. He tightens his grip. Quietly, he is singing, And then she asks me, Do you feel alright, And I say Yes, I feel wonderful tonight.

She says, Do you sometimes wonder about the people who made love in this house, years ago?

What? No. Of course not.

Well, I do, and the lives they lived here, you know—

I don't know. He sits up. Do we have to think about this? Now?

I think of the children born on this floor, maybe. Where they are now.

Oh no, Abbie, don't—

But, you see? People somewhere, in another country, are right now thinking about this village. Their village. I can't imagine how awful I would feel if I could never see home again.

He said, Why are you always talking about this village as though somehow it's our fault the people aren't here. We didn't dispossess them.

I heard they still wear their old house keys around their necks. It's a kind of amulet; they pass it down the generations.

Josh ignored her, he said, Come on, I want to have a swim on the way back. And they hurried down to the old mill where the river bend meanders around the foot of the hill, racing to take off their clothes, but keeping their sandals on to step over the sharp pebbles. She walked in ahead, bursting with joy and anticipation and he followed. The full moon was low, heavy in the sky, its bright light bleaching their skins as they waded to where the water was thigh-high, deep enough to swim. He said, Careful you don't head-butt a boulder, I'm not carrying you home. Careful yourself, she laughed, I'm not carrying you home. And she plunged in and he followed, shrieking at the coldness on their backs. Then, conscious of their voices carrying far through the wilderness, they spoke instead in sighs and whispers between holding their breaths underwater and floating, face up to the stars, watching the white moon as it crept towards the village, counting out constellations, pointing, there's the Great Bear, and Orion, slowly turning in the gentle current, here's Cassiopeia, the North Star, Little

Bear. Till the moon disappeared and was illuminating the ruins behind the hill and they waded out shivering, teeth chattering, eyes smiling at their night swimming adventure.

Walking home, hurrying up the hill, he said, Everything that's happened here, everything, was because the Arabs tried to drive us into the sea. Or, you know, their leaders did. Still do. If we hadn't pushed their armies back in '48 there would have been no Jews in the Middle East today. Ask yourself, why did the Arab countries not set up a Palestinian state after the War of Independence? They could have done it with the land that ended up in their control. Instead, Jordan seized Judea and Samaria, Egypt took the Gaza Strip. Why? Because they didn't want a Palestinian state. Why? Because they don't want peace and prosperity, no. What they want is to keep the refugee problem alive. So they can keep the crisis going. Forever.

He always has the last say; my own words run out. I'm scared. Scared of what's happening to us; I know life will in fact continue even if there is no us, but what sort of life? Not one I want to imagine.

Chapter 11: Devon

March 2010

After a while he said again, Abbie, she love the water also.

Yasmin waited for more but none came. She said, I'm going in now. Then added, Swimming, by way of clarity. He didn't stir. She looked at him and realised he had fallen asleep. Still, she turned away from him as she stripped to her pants and bra, and wrapped herself in the old sheet from the boot of the car, only letting it fall to the sand at the last minute, by the estuary edge. The water swirled icily around her ankles. Standing in the shallows, the tranquillity was already absolute. Well nearly so, she thought, dismissing the image of the man's supine figure behind her, with his shoes, overcoat and skullcap still on, baking in the high sun. Determinedly, she waded in—knees, crotch, waist, no point hanging about. You may as well go for it, get the initial shock out of the way. Deep breath, plunge. She gasped as the water engulfed her hot shoulders. A few deep, laboured breaths are good for coping with the tight cold that grips your chest. She forced the air right into her lungs, then out; in and out. Then more slowly, quietly, in out. Ninety seconds is how long it takes for the body to adjust to the low temperature, for the burning pain on your skin to subside. Then it's all good. She looked around her, out towards the beaches either side of the estuary, the cliffs engulfing them from behind. Further down river, ahead, she could see the sea. Her limbs relaxed now with the joy of it; a familiar, unique peacefulness, an ease hailed by the initial assault of the icy water. Another word for it was bliss.

The tide was coming in, voluminous seawater forcing its way up river. She tried to swim against the current, kicking hard, sweeping water with cupped hands, but was soon losing ground, swept backwards, back up the estuary. How long before high tide? She must watch out they don't become marooned on the beach. She remembered a day, years before when she was still a child, a hot sunny day like this one. A rare family outing here on their favourite beach. She and her mother had been in the water, probably floating on their backs playing Cloud Pictures, a game they made up together; or else they'd been looking for shells, or lying in the shallows and letting the gentle waves roll them to and fro. Then her father was running towards them. He had his shoes and socks on but had hitched his trousers hastily up to his knees. She remembered his wet shoes as he ran splashing through the water to tell them they had to get back, There's a tide, he said in his low urgent voice, and she was grateful no one was there to hear his imperfect English. He waved his arms impatiently. Come on, we need to go. Omar, your shoes are wet, her mother said, holding Yasmin's hand as they walked towards their little camp at the back of the beach. You didn't have to walk into the water. But her father would never have raised his voice, of course he had to come right up to talk to the two of them, hence his wet shoes, there wasn't a choice. He has never been seen outdoors without "proper" trousers and shoes, and certainly never in shorts or sandals. And much to her mother's *chagrin*, he was passionately averse to seawater, on account of his childhood, spent in Jerusalem, a place as far away from the coast as you can be in Palestine. Never so much as laid eyes on the sea until he'd graduated school at eighteen, when in celebration his family spent the day in Jaffa. When else would you leave school, if not at eighteen, Yasmin would wonder before she knew he was the first in his family to make it that far. You see, Yassi, although Father and I are from the same country, we were raised worlds apart. Worlds apart, yes indeed, her father concurred, it was something they agreed on. By the time the three of them were ready to walk back the water along the estuary beach was mostly knee high. Still wearing his shoes, his trouser legs stuck to his shins, sandy and wet, her father was silent, doggedly marching and carrying nearly all their belongings under his arms, while she and her mother were laughing and chatting as they waded barefoot through the river. Oh, darling you'll be fine, she told him, stroking his cheek and the back of his neck till he seemed to relent. Come on, Omar-like-the-actor, she laughed. That was what she called him when the moment was light or tender. Come on, she said, the water won't hurt, you're not made of sugar, are you?

Now, Yasmin looked up the estuary. There was time enough to walk back, even if the water comes up quickly. She had been flustered earlier, up at the graveyard gate, by the sudden change in their plans. That's why she didn't check the tides timetable that was always kept in the gloves compartment. No, it wasn't the change of plan that had unsettled her. It was him. The man Josh. His silences, his bursts of speech. His accent, so much stronger than her mother's had been. Similar in a way, though not quite the same as her father's; and again very much stronger. His strange, off-centre vocabulary. His reactions… did he even understand half of what she said? His clothes! Conspicuous, incongruous in black and white; the long coat, that hat! Truly, he was a time-traveller, an alien. And there was something about his manner. What was it? A detachment. A strangeness, even an oddity; yes, she decided it *was* oddity.

And yet. There were moments she almost—almost what? Moments—in which she felt—drawn to him? The thought startled her. It had been so much easier to criticise, even despise. Rejection fitted, suited his unsympathetic ways. She tried to dismiss these thoughts but they persisted. Yes, there had been brief moments, such as—such as standing by him in the narrow lane, cars gathering front and back, drivers waiting quietly, grudgingly for them to move, watching him retch onto the tarmac. Then, uninvited, a tenderness had come over her. It pushed aside the irritation, the disgust, the resentment she had harboured. And there was an urge to put her cool palm on his creased, clammy forehead.

And then again, when they came down onto the beach and the two of them stood silently, looking at the sea and he was still, and steady, like a pillar of salt. Then she had felt a peacefulness coming over her, some energy radiating from him and filling the space between them. Now the memory of it was crisp, palpable, sensed distinctly although she hadn't known a thing about it at the time. The air that separated them had been dense, almost hot. And she had become calm and silent also. Two strangers.

Two ancient pillars, looking on to sea. Hours, days had passed as they stood, the silence engulfing them like a breeze. Then once more, just now before she got up to swim, there was an urge, ludicrous yet real, to stretch out next to his long lean frame as he lay carelessly sleeping on the sand. Briefly, she imagined the delicate pallor of his limbs beneath the layers of coarse garments. And the feeling this conjured was longing.

Unsettled, she wondered if he'd noticed it too, or had it all been in her own head? She hoped it had. A shoal of small fish floated past her hand. The fish ducked sleekly underneath her. Trout? Or salmon? She never could tell them apart. She gave up struggling against the current and followed them as they glided gently, easily down river, until they disappeared under the seaweed, into the murky depths. She let herself drift down some more. Floating on her back, her ears filled with water, she looked for animals in the clouds. Cloud Pictures: a flock of sheep. A human head, open jawed, breathing steam. She felt euphoric; swimming always did that to her. Like stepping into another world. The day was turning out well. She took a deep breath, the head in the cloud was spitting fire now, a dragon. Hello dragon, what have you had for breakfast, her mother's voice said. She smiled. Her foot brushed against a mound of sand. The current had taken her onto the shallows. She sat up. In the distance, way up river she could see that Josh was still sleeping. Two black shoes sticking out from behind a rock, toes pointing skywards.

As they walked from the grave he said, The Sabbath is coming in. He called it *Shabbat* but she knew what he meant. When she pulled out of the parking area he said, I cannot travel in the *Shabbat*. Can't go on the train? she asked. Are you sure? She'd been looking forward to dropping him off at the station, saying goodbye to this strange man, this apparition, getting back to normal. Having him around was a strain. But on the whole she reckoned she ought to congratulate herself; her conduct had been dignified. And now, what! Some random religious law preventing him from taking his leave. Apparently, the Holy Day would be defiled by any kind of work. And bizarrely, sitting on a train counted. She ought to ask him to stay at her house; that would be right. But she really, truly didn't want to spend the evening with him. Worse, the next train he was permitted to catch would be on Saturday evening and that was more than a whole day away.

I'm sorry about the mess. Yasmin rushed in ahead, hurriedly picking up a pair of shoes, scarves, a half empty mug of tea. Hanging on to those, she gathered the clean, ready-for-folding clothes left on the sofa pending a moment of domestic inspiration. Struggling to keep hold of her load with one arm, she rearranged the throw over the sofa, an oversized Palestine flag coloured red, black, white and green. Her father had brought it back from a lecture tour some years back. Sit yourself down, she said over her shoulder as she walked into the kitchen. I'll get a cup of tea. She rushed around, throwing dirty dishes in the sink, piling leaflets and posters on the kitchen table. Do you take milk and sugar? she shouted over her shoulder at the front room. His response came from

244

startlingly close. Two spoons. Not milk. Thank you. He stood in the kitchen doorway. She said, Go and sit down on the sofa, like she was talking to one of the children at school. Was it okay to speak to him in this manner? Did he notice? Yet she really wanted him out of the kitchen. Why was he hanging around her as though he needed something from her? As though he *were* a child? She said, I'll bring your tea through in a minute. Ignoring her, he sat at the kitchen table.

Silently, she made them tea, got out biscuits she suspected were stale but didn't care. When she took the tea through to the front room, he followed her and sat on a cushion on the floor, surprising her by how athletic he was, how nimbly his long legs folded under him. He looked at ease. It embarrassed her that a middle-aged man was on the floor in her house. Her father would always make for the most comfortable seat in the room like the Alpha Male he is, though if she called him out he wouldn't have the first clue what she was talking about and deny it if he did. She needs to talk to him about his lifestyle, Mum was always going on about it, which he pretended to find irritating, but was secretly grateful for. Or so Abbie said, who never had sugar, sweets, biscuits or any other kind of *poison* in the house. Always cooked everything from scratch, waging a war against disease and his expanding waistline.

Won't you sit down on the sofa? Yasmin asked. It's okay, he said, no problem.

But you'll be more comfortable, she insisted. What was the matter with her? She had only just met the man and here she was, nagging him like a mother, or a wife. Where did you get this from? he was pointing at the sofa. Oh, I'm not sure. She sat, also on a floor cushion. I think it came with the house.

Mmmm. He raised his eyebrows. You know, it's a flag… he paused. Oh, you mean the throw. No, no that didn't come with the house. She laughed nervously, I thought you were asking about the sofa. Yes, it's a Palestine flag; but of course you know that. My father, he brought it from Beirut, I think, years ago. Was he offended? Was that why he wouldn't sit on the sofa?

Yasmin knew that some Jews were opposed to Palestine having a national identity. But she'd never come across one before. Come to think of it, she didn't know many Jews at all, not personally. Having a Jewish mother, she was also one herself. But growing up with a Palestinian father who has made a career out of researching and teaching Middle Eastern politics, she thought she felt most empathy with his side of the divide. Her mother had not been nearly as opinionated, but seemed to accept as given the idea that it was up to the Jewish state to rectify the wrongs done to the Palestinian people. For her own part, Yasmin had never taken the time to get to grips with the ins and outs of the conflict, much to her father's disappointment. There was so much yet to learn. But where to start?

Would you like a biscuit? she asked. I'm going to make some calls, find you a hotel for tonight.

Two hours and twenty phone-calls later Yasmin, desperate, resorted to calling Sebastian. He was about to go out, but would help Yasmin out, certainly. It was *quaint*, and *so authentic* that Yasmin had to ask him to host her mother's friend, he said. That the man wouldn't stay in her house because she was a woman. It made Seb even more excitable than normal. Nothing was ever straightforward with Sebastian, who claimed to have no spare bed, besides which his flat was tiny, not suitable for a non-intimate guest. And so they agreed he would spend the night at Yasmin's, and Josh would sleep in the tiny flat on his own. On top of that, he managed to bully Yasmin into giving them all supper, which, he claimed, was the simplest way to go about eating tonight all round. Simple for you, Yasmin said. All right, she added, but it'll be pasta. I'm not going out shopping now. Sounds delicious, he chirped, I'll bring wine. See you in a minute.

When Sebastian arrived, Josh relaxed. A little, but noticeably. Whereas with Yasmin he was constantly averting his eyes, he greeted Sebastian with a handshake and made conversation. He asked Sebastian about his work and family in what certainly passed for a normal way. And he became animated when Sebastian inquired about his own life, talking about his work as a car mechanic and reciting the ages of his children. Even his English seemed more fluent. It was hard for Yasmin not to feel a little resentful. She had been so accommodating. Had tried her hardest to engage him in conversation. Had even offered to put him up for the night, and arranged for alternative accommodation when he rejected her offer. All of which he was yet to thank her for, she thought as she served up the dinner plates.

Listening to their conversation, Yasmin learned that Josh had spent three years in the Israeli Defence Forces, which he referred to as *the army*. He had started as a trainee pilot, a highly selective and prestigious programme, according to Sebastian, who seemed to know an awful lot about it. Josh lasted nine months on the course before being ejected and joining the paratroopers, where he trained as a medic. He was discharged after three years, but was called up again when war broke out in Lebanon. Was he in Beirut during the Sabra and Shatila massacres, asked Sebastian, whose knowledge was astonishing! Yes, he spent months in Beirut. Yes, he had been stationed a few streets away from one of the camps. During the massacre the night's sky had been alight with fires and illuminating flares. They could hear shooting and shouting from the direction of the camps. What did they think was happening? Sebastian asked. Josh didn't answer. Yasmin looked from one man to the other. How come you know so much about this? she asked Sebastian, who was watching Josh intently. What's all this about, she asked. What massacre?

Josh continued to sit impassively, as though in meditation. Sebastian said, Sabra and Shatila, they were refugee camps in Beirut; ghettos for Palestinians. There had been an assassination in Beirut. A Christian politician—what was his name?

Bashir. The voice came from Josh's chair. Bashir Gemayel, his face, it was everywhere. Big posters on every building.

Yes, Sebastian said. Bashir Gemayel. He'd been elected president but killed in a bomb explosion. And the massacre in the camps was retaliation. It lasted two days. No one knows how many died, two or three thousands. Palestinians.

Who did it? Yasmin asked. She ought to know about such things; was glad her father wasn't there to witness her ignorance.

Josh said, Christians, it was the Christian militia. Phalangists, they were called, he added, and fell silent as though this should explain how a Lebanese civil war is relevant to Josh Pasternak the paratrooper.

And, so? she prompted.

And so? Sebastian said, So the Israeli army was occupying Beirut. Controlling access to the camps.

They let the militia in?

That's right. There was a big outcry about it back in Israel.

Seriously, Sebastian, you're a veritable expert! How do you know all this?

Well, I was there. He paused, allowing Yasmin to process this news. I was at the Peace Now demonstration in Tel Aviv. Four hundred thousand people were there; a tenth of the population. We demanded answers, and a Committee of Inquiry.

We? I mean, Sebastian, who's *we?*

Well, I was living there at the time. My father, he's Jewish, you know… She didn't. Why hadn't he told her before? …when I left school, I didn't know what I wanted to do, so Zionism—the idea of—my roots, of doing my bit for the Jewish state, well, it filled a gap. I lived in a Kibbutz community. Stayed for two years.

My mother grew up in a Kibbutz.

Did she? Where?

In the Jordan Valley. Near Tiberias. That's where Josh comes from too.

Is it? Well… But I was in the south, by the Dead Sea. Worked in the palm plantations. He sat back and looked up, sighing in reminiscence. Mile upon mile of dead-straight lines of trees. An amazing sight. We had to start work at half past four, finish at lunch, by which time it was too hot to continue. You wouldn't dream of leaving the house without a hat. And the work was back breaking. And *so boring*. He laughed. Good grief, I had no idea time could pass that slowly. Sometimes it would literally ground to a halt... hmmm. He fell into contemplation while they ate in silence. Then he said, Well, I stayed and stayed; sort of got used to it, the physical work, the off-handedness of the locals. He glanced at Josh. Yasmin was unsure whether Josh was following their conversation.

Go on, she said.

I don't know, Yassi, it's not very interesting.

It is, honest. She asked Josh, Are you bored?

Hmmm? He seemed to wake from a reverie.

Do you mind if Sebastian continues with his story? He thinks he's boring you.

Oh, he said, no, very interesting. What is the name of your Kibbutz?

Ein-Geddi. Do you know it?

Oh yeah, sure. I was there once. He turned to Yasmin. Your mother too.

Really? They both stared at him. Yasmin wondered what she needed to do to get him to tell her more. What—Ah, did you go there on—on holiday?

Well, he started slowly, There was a music concert in the Salt Sea. I mean Dead—the Dead Sea, is what you say? They didn't reply and he went on, All the best artists were coming; Israel ones, not—well, you know—and I was—I really liked music, you know rock n roll, jazz, reggae, blues, classic rock. He smiled as though embarrassed to admit youthful follies. And I was in a band, boys in school—nothing, really, but—you know, we thought sometimes, maybe we have a future. We write our songs— He petered out and Yasmin willed Sebastian not to interrupt, watched with relief as he shovelled forkfuls of pasta into his mouth. Sebastian was too well brought up to speak with his mouth full.

Finally, Josh continued, So it was summer holiday, we go, to the concert. Six or seven, maybe. Tommy, your uncle, he was also in the band. The Death Sea, it was far away. We stay a night in Jerusalem, on floor of a girl from our Community. In the morning, there was a bus to the Death Sea. We get there at noon time. It's hot, the lowest place in the world. More hot than Jordan Valley, we didn't know what to do in so much heat. Your mother, she was pale, said she going to faint, the sun was so strong, you know. We think to go swimming but the Death Sea water, they are too hot also. So *Ein-Geddi*, we know it is nearby, maybe two kilometres. We know there are trees for shade, and cold water to drink, maybe even we can swim in their pool. Every Kibbutz has a Dining Room and a pool. So we decide to walk. We walked straight in, no one at the gate. He sniggered and Yasmin caught a glimpse of the mischievous boy he had been. We didn't know somebody... someone... I mean no one, he continued. But, you know, because we are from a Kibbutz also, we think it okay to go in. Like a family, but not so close. All the Members was on siesta, you know, no one around. And we find the swimming pool. I remember the water, they were nice; very cool. Your mother, she was fine after. And there were big trees around, ficuses, I think they were. Very unique to have much green in the desert.

Yasmin listened intently, trying to absorb every word.

She wished she could grab him by his broad shoulders and squeeze it all out of him; all these memories, this knowledge. Was it likely he would agree to help her sift through her mother's papers? Would he want to? Would *she* want him to? She was so deep in thought she hadn't noticed Josh had fallen silent again. She had to keep him going now; before Sebastian took over the conversation, which she could sense he was readying himself to do. When? she blurted. When did you and my mother go to the Dead Sea?

I think it was—maybe 1976. Or 1977. Maybe. Yasmin was about to ask something else; something that would make him talk about her mother for longer. But Josh turned to Sebastian. He said, But you were speaking about time in our country.

Oh yes. Sebastian perked up. Well then, summer started in earnest and I had to get out of the furnace that *Ein-Geddi* had become. For at least five hours in the middle of the day it was simply impossible to move; impossible even to sleep; with every breath the air would singe your throat, the insides of your lungs. The locals, they were hardy. He looked over at Josh. They had a huge capacity for drinking water, like camels; and they had their siestas which I never could manage. But even so, everyone slowed down in the heat. We were like lizards. I would dream about swimming in the Atlantic Ocean, which normally I find too cold. I'm not a water baby like Yasmin here. Well, I needed a break; had to leave. But I'd just got together with this girl. Kerren, she was called, oh, she was a beautiful woman, older—*Very* experienced—yes. So then I asked to attend an *Ulpan*, a language school. To learn Hebrew. It was in Tel Aviv, by the Med, where the weather was more bearable. I stayed for the summer months, then went back to the desert in autumn.

Yasmin couldn't believe it. How long had she known Sebastian? Five years? And he'd been half-courting her for the last three, at least, though she's given him no encouragement. He knew her father, and yet had never told her he had even been to Israel, let alone that he could speak Hebrew. Let alone that he had a Jewish father. Why? She asked, So, are you—fluent—in Hebrew?

Well, it's very rusty, but when they finished with me, after three months, well, yes, I kind of was. I tell you, he chuckled, they jolly well know how to run military-style operations. There was no messing around; whatsoever. You go in, barely able to string a sentence together, and come out chattering. Yes. He smiled in Josh's direction. You people have this language assimilation thing down to a fine art. But I'm going on and on—this is all very boring for you.

No, Sebastian, I'm really, absolutely fascinated. Why have you never mentioned any of this before? You knew that's where my parents are from.

Certainly, I did. He averted his eyes, looked at his arms, folded tightly onto his chest. He reminded her of an awkward, shy teenager, though by a quick calculation he must be in his early forties. At least.

So, why didn't you say?

We'll talk about it another time. He glanced at Josh. Yasmin followed his eyes.

Are you all right, Josh? she asked.

Yes, I'm fine. He looked at his plate.

You haven't touched your food! Has there ever been a more awkward house guest, she wondered. I thought you said tuna would be fine with the pasta.

Yes. I'm sorry. It not allowed to mix the fish with cheese. Not Kosher.

Oh, sure, she cried, I mean, don't worry about it. It's me who should apologise! How thoughtless of me! I just threw the cheese on your plate without asking. Without thinking! Actually, she had at some point that afternoon wondered whether he would eat anything at all at her house. Didn't these people have separate dishes for meat and cheese products? Some of her uncle Toby's rich Jewish neighbours in North London even had two separate kitchens. To prevent contamination. And why should she care, anyway? Why was this graceless, aged man making her want to feed him? To care for him? It's fine, she said as she whisked his plate away. Look, Sebastian will have your pasta as seconds, won't you Sebastian? And I'll get you a fresh plate. There's plenty more in the pot. And she rushed in and out of the kitchen, and sat to watch him finally wolf down his food as though he hadn't eaten for days.

Thank you, that was very nice, he said, ignoring her mother's napkin next to his plate and wiping his mouth with the back of his hand.

After supper, the two men got up to walk to Sebastian's flat. I'll be back in ten minutes, Sebastian said. Yasmin followed them to the door. There was something she needed to say. It felt as though by morning it might be too late. Josh, she called after him. He turned. I know it's late now, but tomorrow, before you leave I... I wonder if I could show you some of my mother's photographs?

Abbie's photos?

Yes. I have a box. She wrote a lot.

She had diaries. His tone was noncommittal; did the idea of it bore him?

If you don't mind. I would be very grateful. Only a few photos. Her words hung between them, like stardust. Finally, he said, Yes. I… we will do it. In the morning.

Standing in the doorway, Yasmin watched their receding figures. Josh's was lean and tall, and appeared still in the dark though she knew he was walking. Sebastian's was rounder, shorter, and swayed with every step. She stood watching until they disappeared around the corner.

Chapter 12: Jordan Valley

15 May 1977

I hate his friendship with Isaac, that religious boy he met in the Air-Force. It's fine he's religious, though how can you be friends with someone who is so completely different to you? But it's upsetting Josh doesn't mind him being a Settler. Settlers are the greatest obstacle to peace, Ester says. And Father agrees with her, for a change. Josh says I shouldn't use the word Settlers in a derogatory way. And I didn't know there was a non-derogatory way.

If you mention the *Territories*, or the *West Bank*, Josh will correct you. He'll say they should be called by their proper Hebrew names, *Judea* and *Samaria*. The other day he and Leo had an argument about it. Josh said, We won Judea and Samaria fair and square in the Six Day War, and we're not giving them back. It would harm our national security to return them. And so again he has the last word. National security is the mother of all justifications. Who doesn't want to be secure?

Well, you wouldn't think it such a big issue. But it is. With the elections coming right up, all we hear on the radio are debates about The Conflict. Can Labour's Shimon Peres become Prime Minister even though he has never been Chief of Staff? Solomon says voters will not entrust our national security to him. Though Father thinks these fears are exaggerated, time has come for a moderate, non-military leader. Politics is all around.

Example: last elections there was one vote in our polling station for the right-wing Likud party. Everyone thinks it was Nira's husband Dani. Nira had never had a boyfriend even though she was in her thirties and then Dani turned up and they got married, but even so their baby was born first and so technically he is a bastard, Ruth says, though no one cares about such bourgeois concepts here. Dani doesn't fit in, and so everyone suspects him of being the right-wing voter. But when we were talking about this, just casually, well, Josh's reaction. We were passing the Friday night, lying on the not-so-clean cushions in Tommy's room, smoking Nobles cigarettes and drinking Turkish cardamom coffee. Josh was quiet, but that's not unusual; he doesn't gossip. So the talk was of Dani and how odd he is, always last into work and first out, someone saw him standing over his son, screaming and screaming, there's something wrong with the man, no wonder he supports the right-wing opposition, etc.

Suddenly, Josh. It's narrow minded to talk about people who support the right as though they're scum; we've been brainwashed, think we're so superior. A thick silence followed. Maya and Saffi stopped their pop-song discussion and turned to watch the unfolding drama. Josh said, Besides, the two main parties aren't so far apart as you think. The watchful silence turned to embarrassment. Everyone looked away, anywhere but at Josh, staring at our hands or out the window at the black night. Menachem Begin was Labour's enemy, *The Enemy*. Josh looked at us, his audience, defiantly.

I said, Josh, what are you talking about? I wanted him to take it back, to dismiss Likud's supporters as the politically-illiterate, semi-educated, probably-not-a-fighting-soldier-among-them, racist parasites they are. Who else would back Begin, the man who in the days before Independence headed a terrorist organisation? But Josh ignored me. He paused, contemplating his next move, then shook his head slightly, as though getting rid of an annoying thought. He turned his face upwards and ploughed on. The difference between the parties is not whether there should be a Palestinian state. Neither party will ever agree to that. Also, neither party would ever agree for Jerusalem to be divided again. Also, neither would go back to the 1967-borders. There's only one difference, and we should listen carefully because we might learn something. It is that the Labour Party says we should be ready to give back part of Judea and Samaria. Not to the Palestinians, but to Jordan.

That's not true. It was Leo, who also reads the papers every day and knows things. Probably this was the first time he's ever contradicted Josh.

Josh looked at him in mild surprise. What's not true?

In 1967, when we first took the Territories, Rabin said we'll hang on to them, but not make them our own. He said we'll hand them back in exchange for peace.

Tommy said, What are you talking about? Rabin wasn't in the government in '67. I don't think he likes Josh's new stance; still, he tries to defend him. The other boys joined in.

No, he was Chief of Staff.

No, it wasn't Rabin. It might have been the Prime Minister, what's his name?

Ben-Gurion?

No, dummy, he was already dead.

Don't be an idiot, he's only just died, two years ago.

What? Ben-Gurion dead? Why didn't anyone tell me? That was Maya.

We did, but you weren't listening.

Of course I was listening. Oh… and he'll never do headstands on the beach anymore… Tommy, did you know about this? Maya moved over, was practically sitting on top of him, and sharing his cigarette.

He died after the Yom Kippur war, Tommy said, that's why it wasn't so much in the news. But we did watch the funeral on the television in the Dining Room. Didn't we, Josh?

Josh looked at them with distaste. He stood up and said, It was Moshe Dayan who said that thing about using the… the conquered land as a bargaining tool for peace; he was the Minister of Defence. The Prime Minister was Levi Eshkol. But they've changed their minds since then, Labour politicians. You only have to look at the Settlements they've built to know they have no intention of giving them back. Abbie, I'm going now, are you coming? I said, Yes, Okay, and stood up; but he had not quite finished. Anyway, who are we going to give this land back to? In 1948 King Abdullah of Jordan invaded this country, killed our people, destroyed our synagogues, and occupied part of it. So the territories, as you call them, didn't even belong to him in the first place. He looked around the room, but no one spoke. Not even to say, What's all this about synagogues, synagogues are not what the Independence War was about. It was about whether seven Arab armies would push us all into the sea, or

259

whether we would fend them off instead. In the end the latter happened and that's how we got ourselves a country. But no one said a thing, and Josh turned around and walked out.

I followed him down the external staircase. He reached the pavement in seconds, almost flying down. I wondered whether he was upset, whether he'd stormed off and didn't mean for me to come along. But he stopped, turned back, and looked up. I stopped too, on the half landing and leaned over the banister to watch him. The night was mild and still, except for a muffled Mick Jagger behind a door upstairs, he was getting no satisfaction, even though he tries and tries and tries. Josh broke the standoff. His voice was a lovely, soft smile. He said, Come on; and stretched his arm towards me. I said, I thought you were upset; that you walked off without me.

What are you saying? I don't know what you're talking about. His arm dropped. Come on, it's too late for a balcony scene.

You're right, we're way past that stage, I said, walking down, slipping in between his long arm and lean body. We walked by the moonlight, on the narrow, cracked concrete pavement. Like lovers do.

What did you mean by that? he said at last.

What?

Way past that stage?

Way past what stage?

That's what I'm asking. You said we're way past that stage.

Oh, nothing. I was agreeing with you. That we were past the balcony scene stage.

What balcony scene?

You brought it up, Josh. I laughed. You said it's too late for a balcony scene!

You were leaning over the balcony.

Ah. *I* was thinking about Romeo and Juliet. You know, the night of the day they met?

Ah, yeah. Well, no. They weren't on my radar; you should know that. I was just saying, please come down so I don't have to shout. Tightening his grip of my waist, he laughed. By my life, does anything ever happen to you that you haven't already read about in a book?

I thought about the book I want to read in which the girl sees off her old pursuer and lives happily ever after with the handsome prince. I said, Ah, not sure… I don't think I've read the book with you in it yet.

Sure you have. You know about the time I led us all around the city of Jericho, and the walls came tumbling down?

Oh dear, I don't like to think of you leading that battle.

Why not? It was the pinnacle of my career. Do you want to stay out or shall we go to my room?

I don't mind. What do you want to do?

We'll go to mine; listen to my new Eric Clapton.

Okay. What were you saying?

I said, what's wrong with leading the battle of Jericho?

Well, the people of Jericho didn't do anything wrong, did they?

No. Except, they were in the way, you know. It had to be done, I'm afraid. Orders from above. Highest authority.

You were told to invade the city, but did it have to be completely destroyed?

Well, that's life, you know, brutal and bloody. It's

human nature. Hang on, did I leave the key above the door? Walking in, he said, Ah, I'm dead tired. He put on the Eric Clapton LP he and Daniel had clubbed together to buy. Saved from their meagre spending money, which Josh hates spending as he disapproves of luxuries. Except cigarettes, but he gets those mostly on the budget, four free packs a week. If you don't mind Nobles, which are deadly strong. But he does love music; is never happier than when playing his guitar. And he needs to stay up to date with world music, he says. They are keeping The Band going, even though most of them have left school now. There are winners and losers, he was saying. If you don't make sure you're the winner, you become the loser.

You even put a curse on the city and anyone who rebuilds it.

Did I? Well, that was good thinking. You have to admit it made sense.

So it's about two in the morning, Eric is singing, *Layla! you've got me on my knees, Layla! I'm begging, darling please, won't you ease my worried mind*, and Josh sits on his bed. I go over to lie down. My head is resting on his thigh. I know not to talk in the middle of the guitar solo. I drift into sleep; when I wake the music had stopped. Josh is standing by the door.

Mmmm, I sigh, blinking in the harsh light of the naked ceiling bulb, what's the time? Where are you going?

You were asleep. I didn't want to disturb you.

I'm awake now.

Okay, I won't go out. Are you sure you're awake?

Ahaaa. Why?

Just checking. You're not tired?

Well, yes. But... you know...

What? He slipped the Clapton LP it into its sleeve. Is Led Zeppelin okay for you? He put on the new record and sat on the bed. So… you were saying?

Josh, don't tease me. You know what.

I'm not teasing.

You are. You're embarrassing me.

I wouldn't do that.

You are though. His breath was on my face, and Robert Plant was shouting, *Gonna make you sweat, gonna make you groove.*

The night was turning out fine. Josh was home. He was lovely and gentle. How could I have doubted him? Why do I always have to complain?

He took off the elastic band that held my plait and unlaced it with the fingers of one hand. Don't, Josh, I wanted to keep it for tomorrow.

Sorry, he said solemnly, can't be helped.

I wanted to look nice for you when you came home. Saffi took ages to plait it.

Well, you did look nice. More than nice. Now, stop fussing. You know I like your hair down. There. Isn't that better?

Mmmmm. If you say so.

I do say so.

Then it's better.

Abbie…

Yes?

What's funny?

Nothing.

Come on, out with it. You're putting me off.

It's just, your beard.

Does it bother you? He pulled away.

263

No, no. It's just—new. I said, pulling him back towards me but he resisted.

So it does bother you. He looked grave.

Well, no, it doesn't, really. I mean, not at all. You look different, that's all.

Different? How?

Only the obvious, honestly. Older. More serious, probably. But I quite like it. It's, you know, sexy.

Sexy.

Aha. Also quite useful, see? I laughed, pinching the hair on his cheek and pulled him towards me. Now, where were we?

Ouch, let go, he snapped. Let go, I said! He grabbed hold of my hand.

Okay, fine, I said in alarm. What's the matter?

He looked at me fiercely. Nothing. You hurt me. That's all.

I'm sorry. I didn't mean to. I'm sorry.

I know you didn't, it's all right. Don't cry. His voice softened, but my tears were in flow. C'mon, Abbie, it's okay.

Robert Plant was still shouting for a woman to hold his hand, make him a happy man. We lay quietly while Jimmy Page went all out on his guitar. Then Josh sighed, You're right. I'm sorry. It wasn't that—ummm—I can't lie to you.

He didn't explain and eventually I asked, What is it, Josh, what's wrong?

I don't know. Not really. Sometimes, ummm, I feel it's wrong for us to be... to be so, you know.

You do? Well, that's news. I sat up.

Yes. I've been thinking... I've been thinking more

about, about religious stuff. Oh no, I thought. My heart sank. Yes. I mean, not very seriously, just… thoughts, really. And reading, a little… I've started… doing some small things, too…

What sort of things?

Like, you know, not shaving, and… and not smoking on the Sabbath.

Silence. He had told me he was going to let his beard grow over a week's leave, because it was too much bother to shave every morning. A practical thing, he had said. Lots of guys are doing it. And the smoking—when I asked if he had given up—I don't know, he might not have answered. But he hadn't denied it. And now it turns out he hasn't given up at all.

Silence. Then he said, Until now, I haven't spoken to anyone about it. Only Isaac knows. You know, there was hardly anything to tell. Just ideas, really. I was worried you would be—I don't know—upset. I curse Isaac, silently, and all his family. Hope their house burns down.

So you are? Upset?

Yes, ummm—Oh, I don't know—I just don't know. Mostly, I'm worried about losing him.

Well, don't be. Upset, I mean. Or worried. It's still me. I'm the same person.

So, are you saying—I mean, do you believe in God now?

I've been thinking about God, sure. But I don't know what I believe. It's been… it's helped me, following the edicts. It's helped me cope with… He petered out.

Like what? What other edicts are you following?

Not much, just the smoking and shaving; and blessings before meals—I've been joining in with that at the base…

and obviously eating kosher food—everyone does.

But not at home.

No, not at home… but I was thinking of maybe giving up meat, just when I'm here. It will be something…

Josh, a Repenter? Well, it's not the end of the world, I thought. He hasn't announced he was dying of cancer. Or that we were splitting up. But it felt as though he was dying, or leaving. The old Josh was. I don't know any religious people. They don't mix. Because they eat different food, Kosher food. And pray three times a day, have to rest on the Sabbath. There are religious rules for every single thing you do. And they hate us. Once, before the last war, we had a class trip to Jerusalem, and entered an ultra-orthodox neighbourhood. Us girls wore long trousers and long-sleeved shirts, so as not to offend them. Even though it was June. Some of their young men saw us approaching, and came running at us, shouting and throwing stones, shouting that we were worse than Arabs. We ran away. Queenie explained that these people believe Jews were chosen by God and are superior. They think non-Jews can't help the way they are because they don't know any better, but Jews who choose not to live by God's law, people like us *should* know better; which makes us, to them, the worst kind of people.

I do know that not all religious people are fanatics who throw stones at children touring their neighbourhood or at cars driving when it's Yom Kippur. Some just live and let live. Some even join the army, although they are exempt. But who knows what kind of religious person Josh is thinking of becoming? I thought of Tovah, Miriam and Uri's daughter. She's the same age as Ester, and they used to be friends. Tovah had been like everybody else;

sweeter than most, Mother said of her, although she did have to go to another school for a few years. After her army service she went backpacking in South America and rumours came back to the Community that she took illegal drugs and was even seen dressed as a clown, performing in the streets for money. Imagine!

So she had some mental illness and became a Repenter because of that, everyone said. And now she's aged thirty, living in a Settlement in the Territories with five small children, plus one on the way. She wears long dresses and a tight head scarf, so you can't see whether she shaves her head or not. And she married another Repenter, whom she met on her wedding day, or maybe just before. Repenters are unlike other religious people, who are born into religious homes. They discover God as adults and must marry other Repenters, because the religious communities look down on them as lower class.

In the end Josh broke the silence. It's not like I've turned into another person, you know. I've been thinking about this for a while now. I don't know where it's going to end… just didn't want to hide it from you. Because, you know… Because I love you. And…

And?

And—oh, nothing. Just, we belong together.

We sat on the bed, side by side, neither of us talking for the longest time. Has everything changed? Or nothing? I waited for him to make a move, but he didn't. At length I said, So, shall I go back to my room now? He took a while to answer. He held my hand, squeezed it a little. No… please don't go.

No?

No.

Then on the deck Jimmy Page was lonely, but by the time the lady was buying a stairway to heaven, it was as though this conversation never happened and I was beginning to hope I'd dreamt it all up.

Josh?

Hmmm?

Are you okay? You know, with… with—

Yeah, I'd say so.

You said it felt wrong.

I know I did.

Well?

I'm not ready.

What does that mean?

It means I'm just talking. I'm not ready to walk this road. Not yet.

Okay, but… so… so, what?

Does it look to you as though I'm ready?

I don't know, what does *ready* look like?

Not like this, he said, and Jimmy Page's head was humming, the piper was calling, calling him to join in.

Anyway, now Josh was nearly whispering, we could get married.

What?

It's just an idea.

A sudden one.

Do you want to? When you're eighteen, I mean.

Is this about you not wanting to make unmarried love?

Partly. But, so what? People get married for different reasons.

Religious people. Not us. Not people like us.

I thought, neither Tovah nor her husband have jobs. She's too busy having babies, and he studies the Torah all day! And the government pays for this lifestyle. Shamefully, father says. Of course, Ester says, this is Demographic Warfare, encouraging Jewish families to have more babies so we can maintain a Jewish majority. And Tovah, she hardly ever visits, because they can't travel on the Sabbath. Also they can't afford a car big enough for their oversized family. And if they do manage to somehow get themselves over here, they can't eat in the dining room, the food isn't Kosher. And they can't eat in Miriam and Uri's Room, except food they bring with them, from their special Chief Rabbi-approved shops. They even bring their own plates and cutlery. All very awkward, Miriam gets upset, any mother would, Ruth told Mother, and Mother agreed. Once, Tovah agreed to having apples from Miriam's fridge, after they were washed with soap and water. Uri was about to cut them up for the children, but Tovah said, No, don't use this knife, it hasn't been made Kosher with boiling water or whatever, and they watched the small children struggling to get their little teeth into the big Granny Smith apples. In the end, Tovah also couldn't stand it, so she bit some off, spat the pieces onto her hand and handed them to the children! Miriam had to leave the room, Ruth said, so they couldn't see her tears, she was that frustrated. Such a graceful, elegant lady.

Another time, Miriam got chocolate for the children, went to Tiberias specially to buy it, to make sure it's the right kind of Kosher, brought it straight home in a bag so Tovah won't say it's been sullied by lingering on our Community store shelf. But when she offered it to the children, their father snatched it out of her hand. Then he read all the small print on the wrapper. And eventually he declared they couldn't eat it. The reason was that *his* Rabbi didn't recognise the inspector who issued the Kosher certificate for the chocolate. Something to do with different Kosher inspectorates, and righteousness and sitting nearer to God in heaven. Absolutely ludicrous, even Tovah thought so. She tried to persuade him to let the children have the chocolate, it was perfectly Kosher, but he wouldn't listen; in their culture women have no say.

Mother said, Oh, and Tovah was such a lovely, sweet girl; but now she is lost; lost in a cloud of prayer and procreation. And Ruth said, Rifka, you are so right. I don't know what I'd do if this should happen to one of my girls. Poor Miriam! They act as though she's going to contaminate her own grandchildren. You've no idea how careful she is around them, or the husband would forbid them to see her altogether. He's already stopped them seeing his own parents, no contact for over a year before Tovah fortunately persuaded him to reconsider. Imagine.

But, listen to this, Rifka, now his father won't talk to *him*. Refuses to have him in the house. Apparently, the husband, whatever his name, he was spotted on the television news; someone saw him, in a group of protesters. Demonstrating against the demolition of a Jewish Settlement in Gaza, they were, an *illegal* settlement, did you ever? Miriam told me all about it, yes, on the television. *Greater Israel is ours* they were shouting, *Two banks to the Jordan,* that kind of thing, and abusing the poor soldiers who were there trying to keep the peace. Oh, Rifka, the *shame* those parents must have felt. And Tovah, too. The two mothers fell silent, shaking their heads at the gravity of it. Those poor children, living in a tiny flat, they love to come here where they can run around, see the cows, the horses. And Tovah is worried, how will they cope with more children. Because, of course, she'll keep having them—or words to that effect; it's been two years since this conversation. Mother has been gone that long.

You're exaggerating, Josh was saying, his strong arm engulfing me from behind like a rescue rope, a lifeline. People always have their own reasons to marry. My parents told me they did it to be given their own room by the Community. They all did in those days. And he said, Look, the way I see it, it's not about what anyone else thinks. Has he been reading my thoughts? Have I spoken them out loud and now he knows the contempt I feel for religious people, the shame of it? But he said, Abbie, do you love me?

You know I do.

Well, then. And I also. I also love you. And his arm was tighter round me and the safety of it made me feel sleepy and peaceful. But, anyway… He released his grip and slid back to the far edge of the iron framed bed. Anyway, let's not worry about this now. It's not really a good time to talk about marriage.

You brought it up.

So now I'm bringing it down. Now stop all this talk, or we'll never get to sleep.

Sorry. I laughed, and wondered if we were back to normal.

It's okay.

Thank you; for your forgiveness. Turning towards him, I slid my hands under his shirt, am I still allowed onto his hot smooth skin? May my fingers wonder up the farrow of his spine and down the way he likes it? He is still and silent. I say, Josh, are you—

271

I'm here. He pulled me close. Still here.

Oh, Jimmy, I wish I could believe in your Stairway to Heaven, believe there really are two paths and time to move between them. But yours are just words. Far away, foreign words. You know nothing of here, of this beautiful, war-torn country. Just words.

Chapter 13

From Rifka Boskovitch, Jordan Valley, Israel
25th July 1982
My dear Rachel,
  Everything has been so traumatic and chaotic since I arrived here last month. I only just found a quiet moment to write to you, to explain. When I heard that Tommy was called up and was heading for Lebanon, I could not bear to spend another night in Devon, could think of nothing to do but pack a bag and go back home to the Jordan Valley. I know you understand, and please thank Anthony for so kindly offering to arrange for my things to go into storage, and to sublet the cottage. You have both been kinder to me than I could ever have hoped for.
  Well, here we are, with a war on our hands, and one of our Community Sons, a contemporary of Tommy's, dead. He died on the first day of the war, died with five others, capturing the Beaufort, a castle on a mountain in Southern Lebanon. And would you believe it, the next morning the Prime Minister Menachem Begin stood by the castle, a blue and white flag flapping behind him and told the world we took the Beaufort without casualties! And Daniel, not yet twenty-four years old, in his coffin. I simply cannot express how sick I feel about it.
  All day long army truck convoys snake north-bound along our highway, heading for the Lebanon border. All our young

men are up there. Tommy managed to telephone us a couple of days ago, but we've heard nothing since. His girlfriend Maya promised to let us know if she gets any news, but she's not heard anything either. It's strange, knowing her as an adult after my years away; she has turned into the spitting image of her mother, Ruth—you remember our Iraqi neighbour?—but with reverse colouring. Like a black and white negative, one of those inside-out figures Oscar used to hang in his photography lab. I always say mixed marriages like Ruth and Jacob's make the most beautiful children. What she's still doing with Tommy no one can understand, according to Ester! But she must watch her weight before it gets out of hand. If it does, she really will be like Ruth.

Dearest Rachel, I cannot sleep for nightmares, I'm even contemplating moving back in with Oscar. But I won't. It feels fitting I should instead be living on the edge of our Community, outside the perimeter fence. The fringe of Society. Metaphorically, this has been the case for years, though I haven't always known it. As you very well know, I was never good at conforming, and conformity was required. I've tried, God knows; for Oscar's sake, for our children. And there were times, years even, when I thought I'd finally adjusted, forced my misshapen character into the communal mould. It didn't last.

Here, in this tiny, one room building, a kitchenette at one end, a bed under the window, here I can turn my back on everything. And with Tommy far away and in so much danger, I'm even greedier for space, to be alone with my thoughts. All those years of 'together', can you understand? Being part of something—a family, a community. Even this country, I realise, encircles us with its tight embrace, demanding this and that, like a queen, both adored and tyrannical. In England, one can live alongside the State and not have much to do with it. Certainly, there is the Greater Good, but nationalism is viewed with suspicion. One knows what it did to the Germans. But this country—it seems nothing is ever enough for her. We sing her praises, build and cultivate her, conquer, kill and die for her. So now, instead of being 'a part,' I'm 'apart'—do you pardon the pun?

But don't think I'm a complete recluse. Not quite. I see my old neighbours Ruth and Jacob, they come over "for coffee" for which read afternoon tea. Also my friend Clara, Josh's mother if you remember her, when she takes time off from looking after her husband, Dov, who has cancer. The poor woman is exhausted, and the business with Josh I told you about doesn't help. Oscar, of course, has been over often, fixing anything that needs it, a broken mosquito net, a blocked basin. At first, he assumed I was coming back to the marriage and when I didn't, he refused to enter the house. Gradually, though, he relented. He now wants to plant a lawn for me and started setting up sprinklers. But I'm tired of his incessant fighting against nature. I like the barrenness here.

I hope you visit me one day. Perhaps when the situation is more settled. We can sit on the door step, look out onto the valley, the Jordan, the eucalyptus grove, the bridge and in the distance, the abandoned Arab village on the hill. I could sit here all day. Sometimes I do. Something about this view connects me to the past, makes me feel whole.

26th August 1982
Darling Rachel,

I don't understand what we're doing in Lebanon. Granted, people in the north of the country suffered missile attacks; and there was the matter of the London ambassador assassination attempt. I accept we need a security zone, forty kilometres deep. But Beirut is way beyond that. Haven't we learned already that bloodshed always leads to more bloodshed? And they call it not a war but an Operation! Peace of Galilee Operation, if you please! A war for peace? I am not fooled! I'm terribly anxious about Tommy. Who will it be next? Whose mother will answer her door to grave-faced military news-breakers?

Oscar says wars are part of life, that I should accept it. But how can I? It is the sort of gap that makes us incompatible. Although I miss him terribly and wonder sometimes... you know, yesterday he asked me again to come back, while we were waiting for his x-ray results in the hospital. But of course I haven't told you how we got to the hospital! Well, I was reading the newspaper, a story about a woman whose son was in Lebanon. She answered the door to two Parachute Regiment officers, fainted, thinking they were news-breakers, fell over backwards and broke her skull. It turned out the officers were her son's friends who had come to give her his regards. She's in recovery, if you want to know. I was reading this story when Oscar knocked on my door. When I saw him standing on the bottom step, I was convinced he was bearing bad news about Tommy. I stood in the doorway, paralysed. He asked, Are you all right, Rifka? You look as though you've seen a ghost. And from his tone I knew he hadn't come about Tommy. He was holding a large pipe wrench for fixing the drain. I was literally overwhelmed by relief; my legs gave way and I collapsed onto the marble floor. Oscar was so alarmed he dropped the wrench and that's how his toe was broken. Two hours we waited for him to be seen in the hospital, and the whole time he was bemoaning how he had come to do a job *wearing sandals instead of shoes, and I was telling him he mustn't stand in the doorway that way again. Not until Tommy is back. Oscar must rest now for two weeks; no doubt he'll be back at work tomorrow, though he can barely walk. The cows won't cope without him! I have asked Abbie and Ester to tell him to take it easy; I'm afraid he won't listen to me.*

I'm sorry this is a gloomy letter. But these are gloomy days. Every evening on TV they announce the latest casualties. Photographs show them young, brimful of life. They beam at the camera—at officers training course, at a graduation ceremony. Flanked by elated parents, proud wives, children. Or they hold a baby up to the camera. Of the fate that awaits them they are ignorant. We, all of us, walk blindly through a furrow ploughed by others.

Hugs, kisses and all my love to you, Anthony, Toby and the girls.

Yours as ever,
Rifka

30th February 1983
My dear Rachel,

I'm sorry that our last telephone conversation was so rushed. As you can imagine, we were in utter chaos. Organising the wedding was so much simpler than calling it off! And I'm so sorry about your plane tickets going to waste. And thank you so much for having Abbie to stay with you now. What a time she's having; what a time we all are!

I promised I would write you as soon as possible, to explain. But the truth is I can add very little to what you already know. Abbie has told us nothing, gave no reason for her decision. However, here is the chain of events that led to that frantic telephone call. The night before, on the Thursday, we had all been to a mass demonstration in Jerusalem. I wonder if you've heard about it, a man was killed when a grenade was thrown into the crowd. The protest was about Sabra and Shatila, the two Beirut refugee camps where thousands of Palestinians were massacred back in September. To cut a very long story short, our forces were in occupation in Beirut, and yet they did nothing to stop the slaughter, which lasted three days. There has been a huge uproar about it over here, hence the march. Well, the grenade went off and we all dispersed. It was awful, though so much has happened since I sometimes forget all about it. We all got back to our coach, except Abbie, who didn't arrive for a long time. Eventually, she turned up, escorted by an Arab man. He had found her sitting on the road. Completely coincidentally, he is also in London now, studying for a doctorate. Such a small world, they met again on the plane.

Well, Abbie did look shaken when she got on the coach. This wasn't remarkable; we were all traumatised. Even so, I wonder whether that's where things started to go wrong for her. The next evening, Friday night, she cancelled the wedding. Without explanation, not even to Josh I believe. It's been absolutely fearful.

Such a lot happened in so short a time. Our whole Community is in shock—first the grenade attack, then the wedding. And in the hours between, one of our friends nearly died and is probably disabled for life. He grew up with Ester, is friend of our whole family, an army general. Terrible! Oscar was the one who to find him the morning after the march on his way to work. He was lying under an olive tree and at first, Oscar thought he was dead. Which he would have been, but for modern medicine. A stroke, they say, but there's more.

According to Oscar it looked like he'd been beaten up, beaten black and blue, and left for dead. However, he won't say a thing about it. And Abbie was first to visit him in hospital! Even though she has her own crisis to deal with. Seems like a small thing, I know, but I've been puzzling over it. I hadn't even realised they were such friends. Though, looking at it favourably, perhaps she's just being kind.

Well, darling sister, I will sign off now. As you see, things are difficult here; and the war, of course, is ongoing. I will write a longer, hopefully more cheerful, letter soon. Take care of yourself and your family. And thanks again so much for looking after Abbie.

All my love as ever, Rifka.

Chapter 14: Devon

March 2010

When Sebastian came back, he found Yasmin sat on the Palestinian flag-clad sofa, looking through the envelopes of photographs she had taken to the station the day before. Your friend's quite a nice bloke, he said, but odd. Very. He asked me to turn off all the lights before I left, said he wasn't allowed to do it because of the Sabbath. I left him in complete darkness, standing in the hallway.

Oh, I expect he has some candles in that great big suitcase of his. He would have anticipated this problem arising.

Why would a candle help? If the idea is not to do any work on the day of rest, then it's easier to flick a light switch than light a candle.

I suppose, she said. Would you like a drink?

I most certainly would, he said, draining the bottle into two glasses and joining her on the sofa. What's this? He peered at the photograph in her hand. Let's have a look. He moved closer. Yasmin was irritated. It had been a long day and now felt a bit late for company. Sebastian should have asked permission before sitting so close, barging in on her privacy. He was practically nestling into her, had no respect for personal space. Oh, is that your mum? He pointed at a six year old girl perching on the arm of an armchair. On the other arm a younger boy was balancing, legs asunder. In between them sat an old woman, diminutive and stooped, a pearl necklace around her neck and a swaddled baby in her lap.

I don't think so, she said. It might be my aunt Ester, and this one my uncle Tommy. I suppose my mother would be the baby. And this, she pointed, is my mother's grandmother Rose. I remember her from when I was little. She lived in London with her daughter, my great aunt Rachel. Then again, Yasmin thought, it felt nice to have him there, close and warm and smelling of the cigarette he'd had before coming back in the house. He made no other comment but waited for her to cue him in. That also felt good. Besides, he had heard her asking Josh, a stranger, to look through the photos the next day. Why wouldn't she want to share them with a friend? She realised that she did.

Sebastian, why did you not tell me you were Jewish?

I'm not, strictly speaking. Only on my father's side. That was the problem I came up against when I asked to stay in Israel; to join the Forces. They said I may not qualify; one can only become *properly* Jewish through the maternal line. They wanted *proof of Jewishness*. I mean, how is this even possible? I was summoned to an absorption centre. The man was pleasant, an immigrant himself, from the U.S. He said, you need to give us your parents' *Ketubah*. Sebastian put on an American drawl that was distinctly Dalas. I said, What's that? He gave me a look that meant this wasn't the response he'd been hoping for. A *Ketubah* is a Jewish marriage certificate. I said, As far as I knew my parents got married in a register office. He said, That's fine, just show us a letter on synagogue letterhead from a recognised rabbi of a recognised Jewish community, who knows you to be Jewish. I said, I don't know any rabbis; I've only ever been to a synagogue once, on a school outing. He said, Well that settles it, my friend, you must convert to Judaism. I said, Fine, I'll convert, show me where to sign. Hold on, he said, not so fast. First you must talk to your rabbi. Again, I said, I don't know any rabbis. Well, you better get to know one and start attending synagogue while you're at it. Attending synagogue? Do you mean on a Sunday? No, my friend, that's a Christian custom. Jewish men are expected to attend three times daily, but for our purposes, once daily will be sufficient. Depending on your rabbi. You need to show that you are sincere, my friend; that you are committed to mustering Jewish knowledge and to becoming strictly observant. Then you will be sent away. Sent away? Do you mean turned down? We do not encourage anyone to take on the Jewish faith; in fact we discourage it, actively; and if you come back, you will be sent away again, three times. That's the tradition. Remember Ruth and Naomi? Who are they, asked I. Never mind, he said. If you come back after that, you will be considered sufficiently determined to adopt the faith. Then you will be called before a panel of judges who will inquire into your suitability; a rigorous, in-depth assessment. Then, if you pass, you can embark on the process of conversion. Are you circumcised? Well, circumcision will be your first step. Don't worry, my friend, I have attended several adult circumcisions and the experience has been both spiritual and positive. For the convert. Oh, and the wound should heal within a week or so. Sebastian laughed.

Oh my goodness, is that right? Yasmin said. There was something so engaging about the way he told a story; something that drew you in.

Absolutely verbatim, I swear. Well, you can just imagine me listening to all this no doubt well-meaning stuff. I fell at the first hurdle. Gave up on the idea of becoming a *proper* Jew. Don't worry, they said, you can still join the army and fight in Lebanon. And if you want to marry your girlfriend, you may do so in another country. Most people hop over to Cyprus, our nearest friendly neighbour. There, a registrar would be glad to perform a civil ceremony. That should give you and your children practically the same rights as everyone else. The only difference would be when it comes to matters under Orthodox controlled religious establishment. What matters are they? Oh, life events; marriage, divorce, burial, that sort of thing. Sebastian laughed, he moved away from Yasmin and was watching her reaction.

So, you were lost to Judaism, Yasmin laughed too. Life events, ha? I suppose it's their loss.

I doubt they see it that way.

And what happened next?

Well I got involved in Israeli politics... attending demonstrations. Like, you know, the one in Tel Aviv; we talked about earlier; 1982, after the Beirut massacres? Need any more clues?

Oh, yes. I mean, I know the one you mean, Yasmin said, smiling. She felt warmth in her stomach at the way he so often made her smile. It wasn't that he was a really funny guy. She just liked his turn of phrase; the way he raised his eyebrows and the half serious smirk that came with it.

Ah, okay, he went on, so the war was going on in Lebanon, and at the same time I was in touch with people back home, in England. They were seeing really disturbing images of the war on television; which we in Israel weren't shown. Mass destruction; civilian casualties everywhere, not just in Beirut. And I was—I suppose I became disillusioned. And I got involved with the anti-war campaign. Then came the other Peace Now march. This one was in Jerusalem. A man was killed. Emil Grunzweig, his name was. Killed by an extremist Jew. It was a kind of turning point for me, and I went back home to England. I did intend to return but... Gosh, is that your mum? He picked up the photograph uppermost on the pile.

Yes, that's her.

Oh—she's pretty, he said, then added quickly, not as pretty as you, though. He glanced at her sidelong. Yasmin ignored him. The photo showed Abbie and Tommy as teenagers, sixteen or seventeen, sitting on a sofa. The sofa was neither low nor soft-looking. It had a kind of utilitarian air to it, with sharp edges and plain corduroy upholstery. It was the sort of item Yasmin imagined would have stood in doctors' waiting rooms in those days. But this was someone's house. Probably her grandparents'. Another boy, the same age, sat between them. Dark paintings hung on the wall behind the sofa, and a coffee table, also sharp edged, square and dark, stood in the foreground. Abbie was wearing a skimpy vest and short shorts. She had one foot on the sofa, with the knee down to the side in a half lotus. She was slouched over her bent leg, elbow resting on the inside part of her thigh, and hand raised to support the side of her head. Two dark plaits hung over her shoulders. The two boys were also wearing shorts. Tommy's hair was as dark as Abbie's, nearly shoulder length, tousled, with a side parting and an overgrown fringe swept diagonally over his forehead. Yasmin smiled. The other boy's hair was fairer, shorter; it shot out in all directions, putting Yasmin in mind of a hedgehog. His face, though, was lean and smooth, with thin lips and prominent cheekbones and eyebrows. He seemed chiselled, like a Greek God; a handsome lad, if you liked that look, which Yasmin did. All three were gazing in one direction, watching another person, who was sitting just outside the frame on the right-hand side. The unseen person was wearing long trousers, tucked into high military boots. Only the shoe and half a calf were visible, hanging in mid-air. The effect of the booted, dismembered, hovering leg was surreal, as though the three teenagers on the sofa were witnessing a supernatural phenomenon.

Hmmm, Yasmin said, I wonder what they're looking at.

Perhaps they're listening to the soldier man outside the frame. Or they might be watching the telly.

Well this should be—late seventies? I don't know when they got televisions in their houses, Yasmin said. She flicked the photograph over. On the back was a date, 4/7/1976, and writing in Hebrew. Yasmin gazed at it. In 1976 Abbie would have been sixteen and Tommy eighteen. She recognised a few of the letters, but in no way could begin to decipher any of the words.

Operation—um—Operation Entebbe, Sebastian said.

Huh? Yasmin was lost in thought.

Here, see? he pointed to one word and then the other,

Operation—Entebbe. Shall I read the rest?

You can read it?

Naah haah! Yes I can.

How, Sebastian? How come?

Haven't you been listening? I went to *Ulpan*, Hebrew school. It was a residential course; three months, with two hours of homework every evening except Saturdays.

And you came out chattering, yes I was listening. But I didn't realise you could read as well. I mean, isn't it so difficult to learn? And this is hand-written, without, you know, without vowels—

Yes, they taught us both print and hand scripts.

My mum tried to teach me to read when I was little. She showed me the printed script first, so I could read books, printed matter. And I never did get to grips with the other set of letters. But you, you can do it! Oh, Sebastian, why didn't I know any of this about you?

Well, to be honest… he started.

…And, come on, tell me. What else does it say? Oh, sorry, I interrupted you. To be honest, what?

No, it doesn't matter. It says—hang on, it says here… *Josh—Josh nearly a soldier.*

Josh? Does it say Josh?

Ah, I'm pretty certain it does.

Then that's him! Yasmin was surprised at her own excitement.

Which one?

The blond one, in the middle. The other boy is my uncle Tommy, I'm sure. It fits, you see: 1976, mum was sixteen and Tommy two years older, eighteen, and so was Josh. He said in his letter he was Tommy's friend. So I reckon they were at school together. And so if they were

eighteen, then in July they'd just finished school and…
well, that means they were about to join the army.

Well, yes, that would make sense.

Oh, Sebastian, this is amazing! You're amazing!

Am I? Well—

Yes! How lucky that you should be here! Thank you,
she put a hand on his arm, to show she really meant what
she said. But, don't—don't think I'm asking you to do it
all; translate everything. I'm not. It's going to be a big job
for someone—it's just—it's so exciting to understand
some—any of it. It's quite… Her eyes welled, her throat
tightened. It's moving.

Oh, Yassi, of course it is. Look here, don't cry. There,
there. He patted her gently on the shoulder, then put his
arm around her, pulled her closer, quite awkwardly,
breathing in, and she let him.

It's fine. I'm fine, really, she said. I'm quite happy, you
know… it's a happy feeling. I'm just… I've just been
carrying these photos with me—for years now. I mean,
not literally, just in my head… sorry, have you got a tissue?
Sebastian dived into his pocket and fished out a crumpled
serviette, the one they'd used at dinner earlier. She blew
her nose, trying not think about what it was doing in his
pocket, taking care not to unfold it. Thanks—and, you see,
I haven't realised how much it bothered me that I couldn't
access all this… all this information. Mum was a writer,
you know. She hardly ever had anything published; a few
articles in local papers, but she was always writing, from
when she was a little girl.

Well, I'd be happy to help you. If I can. If you want me
to. He was stroking her black curls, lightly, gently, no
longer awkwardly. She let him.

But she wasn't done with the photo yet. She sat up, away from him. She said, So, what was the other thing written here? Some operation?

He took a while to respond, but she knew he would come round. If he'd thought this was going to be the night he finally gets her to go to bed with him, he must have now realised he'd been mistaken. It was true that their closeness on the sofa had been quite delicious, which had taken her by surprise. And the smell of him close—strangely familiar, sensuous, even. Yes, sensuous was the right word: a blend of sweat, cigarettes, leather and deodorant, quite light, none overpowering, not at all. And none had she previously found particularly appealing in Sebastian. But tonight, somehow, the balance in him was right. In fact it was just right. She turned her head towards him to take a deep breath, hoping to recapture the experience. Before getting on with what she really wanted of him. He was too old for her. Wasn't he? Nearly her mother's age.

As she turned towards him Sebastian watched her on the sofa. Unsmiling, he held her gaze with his dark eyes and she wondered whether she'd been too abrupt with him. If he were to walk out now, she wouldn't blame him. She'd been taking him for granted. All those months and years, and yet he'd always been there for her, if only she'd bothered to notice. Then Sebastian collected himself. He picked the photo out of her hand. Turned it over. Let's see... what was it? Entebbe. Operation Entebbe.

I've never heard of it, she confessed. Have you?

Well, yes. And I dare say you would have done too if you weren't so ridiculously young. He smiled, tentatively. How old are you, anyway? Oh, don't say, it would only depress me. Entebbe, yes. You know it's in Uganda. It was in Idi Amin's time. You've heard of him. Ruthless dictator? A plane heading for Israel was hijacked. Well, the Israelis sent a rescue force to Entebbe, where the plane had been diverted to. It was incredibly—dramatic, yes. Amin, he believed Kenya had colluded in the rescue, so in retaliation he massacred hundreds of Kenyans.

Oh, that's terrible! And had they? Had the Kenyans colluded?

I don't know, Yassi. What do you take me for? Wikipedia?

You seem to have a *Wikipedic* knowledge of such matters.

Not really, I'm just old. I remember it being on the news. 1976. I was nine or ten. And, don't forget, Israel-related stories were big news in our house. He was ten in 1976! Only six years younger than Abbie! What was she doing?

Well, I wish I had your memory, she said. There was no harm in boosting him up a little. She held up the photograph. So, here they are, what?—watching the news on television? And on the back Abbie writes, Josh nearly a soldier. But Tommy was the same age as Josh; and he also went in the army, didn't he? Didn't they all have to go? How little she knew about her own family. Sebastian, she said, I reckon… I have a feeling… I'm wondering if Abbie and Josh were a… a couple? Why else would she not mention Tommy as well?

I don't know. Sisters can be so annoying to their brothers. I can say that with authority. And vice versa, I'm sure. Maybe she chose to ignore him.

But then, why mention Josh? Unless he was special.

Well, I suppose—maybe that's why he's traipsed all the way from London to Totnes to see you; but you can ask him tomorrow.

I don't know. I find him—I don't know—reticent; difficult to talk to.

Do you? I suppose that's understandable.

Why? Don't *you*?

Well, no. I found him friendly, considering he's in a foreign country, and his English isn't very good. I would think he's not used to talking to women. He told me he'd been an Orthodox since he left the army. That's probably more than half his life. In fact I'm surprised he felt able to travel in the car with… just the two of you.

He did more than that. We walked down to the beach in Wonwell, and I swam and he went in too. He was in the water for ages; great long strokes—really quite—quite elegant. I'd assumed he was asleep on the sand before, but now I'm wondering whether he might have been avoiding looking towards the estuary—at me—while I was in. And he waited for me to come out before going swimming himself. Then we had to wait while his clothes dried up on him.

He went in fully clothed? Ha! Well, I'm not surprised, in Israel they have separate beaches.

He did take his skullcap off. And socks. Lucky it was sunny or he would have frozen. That's why we were late back. Why he missed his train.

Yes, they can't travel on the Sabbath; don't really go on holidays in the way we do. Plus they tend to have massive families, and can't afford big enough cars.

He said he has seven children. And two more on the way.

Good grief! That would be a minibus, then.

So… Yasmin was turning Sebastian's words in her mind, So—would you—would you say he's being—I don't know—subversive, coming here?

Certainly. Visiting the grave of an old girlfriend, travelling in a car with a young woman who's not his relative, frolicking with her on the beach.

Seb, he wasn't! She laughed.

So you say—then coming into this house, eating your food—

No meat, and we didn't make him eat tuna with cheese!

That's nothing. You've no idea how strict their culinary rules are. He would not even be supposed to eat off plates that have previously been used for non-Kosher food.

So… do you think he's in trouble?

Who knows what goes on in people's lives? Whatever, I expect these things do happen. He'll go home to his family and pick up where he left off. No one over there need know about it.

But maybe—maybe he's having doubts; thinking of giving up his religion. And he's trying it out here, away from everyone he knows? After a while, when he didn't answer, she said, Seb? What do you think?

Think about what?

About Josh! Is he planning on leaving his old life and becoming… I don't know, *normal* again?

Do you know he was *normal* before?

You know what I mean—well, is he?

Yassi, I'm tired. It's way past my bed time. And—I suppose this sofa is where I'm sleeping tonight? And this Palestinian flag is my sheet? When she didn't reply, he went on, So, well—unless you'd like to share it with me, would you please get me a blanket, and after that jolly well shoo off to your own bed?

In the morning Yasmin woke early. She was lying on the very edge of her bed. One foot was on the floor, guarding her slumbered self against an otherwise certain fall. One arm and half a shoulder hung off the side as well, suspended mid-air, and her head was sloped awkwardly onto the bed frame. She had to make a decision whether to let herself down onto the floor boards or make the effort to pull herself back onto the bed. The first would be easier but spell an end to the sweet drowsiness she wished she could hang on to a little longer. The latter seemed impossibly challenging. She chose to stay on the bed, and, after some consideration, grabbed a hold of the headboard and used it as a lever to shift her position. With effort, she swung her arm behind her. But it turned out the headboard was not where it should have been, just above her head. She searched for it. If it cannot be located in this way it might become necessary for her to open her eyes and then she really would be fully awake. She must have moved a long way in the night. Her hand was on something. Something too large and hard to be a pile of pillows or a bunched duvet. As she prodded it gingerly, it gave slightly to her touch, rocking away before resuming its original position. Then it grunted. There was no mistaking it. Sebastian.

What in the name of the god of human mishap and folly was he doing in here? There was no going back to sleep now. She relaxed her body, giving in to gravity and sliding onto the floor. There she sat a moment, her back against the foot of the bed.

Her head hurt. Was it a hangover? She had been known to become rather reckless when drunk. But she didn't think she had drunk too much. Last night was beginning to come back: Sebastian settling on the too short sofa, his feet and half way up his calves dangling over its high arm. There was no way he would be able to have a good night's sleep there. She offered to sleep downstairs herself, and for him to have her double bed. He refused. Finally, somehow, they ended up here. She was pretty sure there had been nothing more to it than that. Now feeling lighter, relieved, she went downstairs to make a cup of tea. As she walked across the living room there was a knock at the door. Who could be knocking at this time? Probably the postman. Her dad was always receiving parcels sent by registered post. She thought she ought not to answer in her pyjamas, was about to go back upstairs for her dressing gown, but the postman would already be writing a slip she would then have to take to the post office. Plus, she didn't want to risk waking Sebastian. She wasn't ready to face what she feared might be a new awkwardness between them; at least, not until after she'd had her cup of tea. And besides, her pyjamas could probably just about pass for joggers and a shirt.

So she opened the front door. It was Josh, who seemed to recognise her clothing as pyjamas straight away, because he averted his face abruptly and continued looking away as he spoke. Oh, I'm sorry to disturb. I will come back later. And he turned and was already walking away before she collected herself and called after him. He needn't go. Coming in now was fine. He stopped and turned back, still looking somewhere to the side of her.

She was just about to make tea. Or coffee, if he preferred. But now he's here, she'll nip upstairs and get herself dressed first if that was okay with him. Yes, it was, he said, though he sounded doubtful. She left him standing there and walked away quickly. As she entered the bedroom, she heard the front door shut downstairs and a cough from the living room. So he decided to stay. She supposed he was now standing stiffly on the edge of the carpet, waiting for her to come down again. It occurred to her that perhaps she ought to remove the Palestinian flag from her sofa. Maybe that's why he has refused to sit on it, its red-black-white-and-greenness conjuring an animosity in him. Well, if that's how he feels, let him. Let him keep standing in his inelegant, artless, bigoted way. She's not going to help him out.

She wondered whether Sebastian was awakened by the commotion downstairs. Hoping fervently he wasn't, that she would not need to face him as well as Josh right now, she looked over at the bed and found he was lying on his back. His jaw was hanging loose, the partially open mouth revealing a surprisingly smooth, pink tongue. Like a puppy's. His face was slack with deep sleep. She realised he had been snoring resoundingly for a while. Still, she turned her back on him as she changed.

Josh was sitting cross legged on a cushion next to the coffee table. He was staring at, but not touching, the photograph at the top of the pile. The black and white close-up of her mother on her sixteenth birthday.

It's my mother, she said, hovering over him.

I know, he said, admonishment in his voice.

Yes, of course you do, she mumbled. It's—I think it was taken on her birthday. Sixteenth. The date on the back—

I know, he said quietly.

Yes, she said. She started slowly towards the kitchen. I'm going to make a cup of tea now. Would you like one? Or coffee?

No, tea is good, thank you.

Sure. Her voice was unnaturally loud and high, jarring against his quiet, deep one. Once inside the kitchen she looked back into the living room. She could see his back and the table beyond. He still hadn't moved a muscle. She took a deep breath, willing herself to sound calmer, less frantic, and called out, You're welcome to look through these photographs. If you want to.

He got up abruptly and walked over to the kitchen doorway. Sorry? he said.

I was saying you're welcome to look at the photographs. As the water boiled, she turned her back to him and poured it into the two mugs. I got them out to show you, she said to the window, I... I wondered if you would be interested to—maybe tell me what some of the writings on the backs say. I can't read Hebrew, you see... She fished out the tea bags and added milk to one mug. Her words hung loosely over the gentle steam, hovering, ready for him to collect as she put a sugar bowl on the tray and walked past him to the living room. But he followed her towards the coffee table where Abbie was smiling on her sixteenth birthday, a strand of hair cutting darkly across her face, and the evening sun forever caught in her eyes. Who was she smiling at?

Yasmin handed Josh the tea. He was still gazing at the photo; so intently, and yet he hadn't picked it up. She had to ask again. Would you like to have a look?

Yes. Thank you, he said but still he made no move to

touch it. Instead, he put a hand on the table, next to his mug of black, sugared tea, as though contemplating his next move. Did his hand shake momentarily?

There's writing on the back of this one. I wonder, would you tell me what it says? Were her words getting lost in translation?

He was quiet for the longest time. She sipped her tea. He picked up his mug with two hands and then put it down without drinking. Finally, he said, It's written, *Remember this, remember me.*

Yet he hadn't touched the photograph. Had he turned it over when she was in the kitchen? *Before* she'd given him permission? She picked it up herself. Her mother's eyes had been on the camera lens, now they were on Yasmin's; what were they saying to her through the years? She turned her over. Something didn't fit. There were too many words; several more than would be needed simply to say what Josh had told her. Even allowing for language differences. As she looked up, she saw he'd been watching her, but averted his eyes, as though caught out. Handing it over to him, she asked, Is that all? Are you sure?

He winced. His hands were still on his thighs. But he did glance at it, then said, It is written, *In my hour of need you gave me days of pleasure. Remember this day, as I always will. I give you all my love.* Then he added, *Josh.*

Josh? she asked in a small voice.

It is written here, *Josh.* Without touching the photo, he pointed to the last word.

It says, *Josh?* Something missing, she was scrabbling around. Is it *your* photograph?

I… he was searching for the word. Finally, hesitantly, he said, I *photo'd* this.

Yasmin couldn't speak. Josh—the photographer of this intimate, beautiful, possibly nude photograph—one of the same? Though why be so shocked? Hadn't she already guessed something of the sort? That he had been more to Abbie than a childhood friend? And—oh, that he had inscribed it with a romantic, soppy teenage message—all my love? As in The Beatles? The two of them—lovers? She felt weak. This man was too devout to look at her. He would almost certainly be ostracised by his own community, were it to be known they were sitting in her house right now, on their own, Sebastian sleeping upstairs notwithstanding. Lovers—they must have been lovers. Was he ashamed? Ashamed now of his love? Of its sinfulness? In *Fiddler on the Roof*, people didn't even meet before their wedding day. Is that how Orthodox Jews live nowadays, too? Is that how he had met his wife? She knew she couldn't expect a full and frank confession, even if she had felt strong enough to receive it. But here was an opportunity. Blink and you'll miss it. Quietly, almost whispering, she said, Would you like to see the others?

Silently he picked them up. He still hadn't touched the birthday photo and it occurred to Yasmin this might be hard for him too. Looking at the Entebbe scene she and Sebastian had talked about the night before, he smiled. I never see this one. He flipped it over, and seemed to catch his breath. Yasmin remembered, it said, *Josh nearly a soldier*. He collected himself. Ah, Entebbe. 1976; yes, I know. But… I don't remember—

So it's you, in the middle? She asked, trying to reconcile the handsome fresh faced black and white youngster with the bearded man sitting before her.

He nodded. And here it is Tommy and Abbie. And

this... he pointed at the dismembered leg on the right, Ah—I know! and his face fell, or did she just imagine it? It's—Micah. Micah Ashkenazi. He went on. This—he was a... a kind of... He was older than us. And he went to Entebbe, you know to bring the people home, it was something... Yes he was with, how you say... Commando? And this, he held up the photo, it is after. And he is talking about it. Army shoes, you see? I wanted to be a soldier, like him and—but I was very young... he petered out and seemed deep in thought.

Well, these were more words spoken in one go than practically all she'd heard him say before. This new animation could only be a good thing. So, they were not watching television, the teenage Abbie, Tommy, Josh. They were listening to this—Micah. Was it one of the names her mother had mentioned? She wasn't sure. Josh put the photo down and picked up another. The one with a soldier at a bus stop, smiling broadly in front of a city of uniform white houses sprawled over a hill. Yasmin had wondered whether this was Josh himself. But that was before they met. The soldier looked short for the army uniform he was wearing. Only the tips of his fingers were visible, protruding from the long sleeves. And the slither of something white on the top of this head, Yasmin realised was a skullcap. His toothy smile, long nose and oversized sunglasses gave him the comical air of a dressed-up bird, a crow maybe. She remembered a line in a poem about someone being a crow, a line Abbie used to read to Yasmin at bed time. It's a Ted Hughes, she used to say, a fellow Devonian though he had been born in Yorkshire. And this was one of the poems which almost redeemed his bad behaviour towards his wife Sylvia Plath.

Almost, but not quite. This bad behaviour Abbie forever held against him.

Yasmin watched Josh as he studied the photo. Hmmm, he said, finally.

Do you know this man?

It's my friend, Isaac. We were in army training together. He turned it over and looked at the inscription. I don't know what it's doing here, he said, as though to himself

What's what doing here?

This—this photograph. Isaac gave it to me. And Abbie—I don't know why she has. She didn't like him. Maybe it was by accident—

Didn't like him? Why? Why didn't she? Surely, he was mistaken. Yasmin thought of the lengths her mother had always gone to see the best in people. Her intrepid insistence that everyone was *doing their best* had been a family joke, and became a mantra. Here they go again, doing their best, her father would comment while watching one or other disaster on the evening news.

Oh… I don't know, Josh was saying, She didn't know him, but… she said he was not a good friend for me. He was religious, you see, Orthodox you say—and—and she didn't feel good I was also liking the religious. His family—they lived in Judea. And Abbie, she didn't like the Settlers, not—not them, she say they doing their best, but she didn't like that they were Settlers, you know what they did. Difficult to explain. In Israel, everything is—is politics. You can't, how you say it? Sit on the fence?

Yasmin felt a little hurt. The idea that Abbie was intolerant, that she judged people by their lifestyle choices, their political leanings. How rude of the man

Josh to criticise her. But she let it go. His talkative mood couldn't last much longer. What does it say, on the back? she asked, again feeling like a voyeur.

He say, Josh let out a chuckle, He say, *See you—see you the other side.* He mean other side of border. You know, Lebanon border.

Do you mean the Lebanon war?

Yes, 1982. We had, how to say, Holiday; time at home; from the army.

Leave?

No, we didn't leave, just send home for a week. Before going to war. And I visit, at his house. This is his town. He pointed at the white city behind the soldier Isaac.

I thought it looked like Jerusalem.

Hmmm, well, it quite close. Maybe you right. Maybe they use Jerusalem stone for the houses.

So, are you still friends, you and Isaac?

He died.

Oh, I'm so sorry!

Sniper. In Beirut. He was quiet for a while and Yasmin waited, wishing beyond wishes that Seb stays out of the way so she can complete this conversation in peace. Josh said, We were on patrol; big apartment blocks search. They found weapons in one apartment; three men hiding in a cupboard. It was—it should be, was—should be safe. Well—not safe, exactly, but, you know. We were joking and laughing. Isaac in front. One of the others, it was his birthday and we pretend that he take us here, to Beirut, you know to have a party. We pretend that's what we were doing there, and in a minute we'll go to a bar where the girls are dancing, and then we go swimming in the sea. We can see the sea through the houses. We start to sing,

300

you know like a birthday song. Singing loud. Maybe too loud because you know I didn't hear the gun. Isaac, he fell, and I went to him, but the fire, the guns, it was from both sides and another guy fell and there was nowhere for, you know, to cover, so I drag him to another street, I drag him into a building where the stairs were and we hide and I say, it's okay, it's okay, don't worry, everything is going to be okay. But when I look down, he is dead. I think he die straight away when the bullet hit him in the neck. I was just too—panic, you know, chaos all around. I didn't have time to look. I think he die straight away.

Yasmin said nothing. The man had been through an unspeakable experience. What did she have to contribute? Which facet of her own charmed life would she utilise by way of comparison? Finally, she said, I can't begin to imagine what it must have been like. To be there. I don't know how you coped.

No, he said. No, I didn't, you know, I didn't—cope. Not good. He smiled a half smile, a sad smile. His eyes shone. He was done talking.

Would you like to have this, I mean, his—Isaac's… photograph? You're very welcome to take it.

Thank you. He slipped it into an inside pocket. He was still wearing his coat. Actually, he rummaged in his pocket, actually, I have something for you also. He got out a thin blue plastic booklet.

What's that?

Oh, this here just my—my identity card. I'm not showing it to you, he chuckled. He opened the booklet and she glimpsed his younger self looking out of a passport-size photograph. He was bearded and wearing a skullcap but his hair was cut short and it was possible to see the shorts-wearing teenager lurking inside him. He pushed one long finger in behind a clear plastic sheet on the inside cover, and fished out another passport-size photograph. A woman and a small child. A baby. He held the photo between finger and thumb, contemplating it at length. Was he going to let her see it?

Were they his wife? And baby? The colours in the photograph had faded, and the two faces staring solemnly at the camera, were ghostly white; how old was the baby now? The woman's eyes were dark, and her hair long, with black curls; but the baby's eyes were light, maybe blue, its hair fine and almost white—his father's colouring. He handed her the photograph and she took care not to contact his hand. Looking at it closely, her stomach lurched. Here in her hand, watching Yasmin from across the years was the young woman her mother had been. And a baby. Not Yasmin herself, with her dark eyes and thick black curly hair. Who, then? Everything was jumbled up.

Tamara, he said, and the way he pronounced the R, harsh and throaty like Yasmin's parents did, made her eyes feel swollen.

Yes, she mumbled. Yes. Her sister Tamara.

Josh said, You—you said you have no photograph.

No, we—but what... she started, but didn't know how to go on. Where did you... She tried again but gave up. Her hands shook as she settled the small square on the palm of her hand, where she could continue to watch the two people whose absence from her life was unimaginably deep now, an infinite abyss torn right from inside her chest. She didn't mean for him to see her cry. Thank you, she blurted as he handed her a handkerchief. Surprising that such an unkempt man carried a beautifully laundered, perfectly white handkerchief. I'm sorry, she said again in a strangled voice.

Don't be sorry, he said kindly. It's okay. He sat quietly, peacefully, without stirring, while she sniffed and choked and blew her nose.

No, I am sorry, she said, finally. Such a spectacle... She smiled at him and was grateful no one else was watching; grateful Sebastian had not yet woken up. Not yet. So... well, thank you so much for letting me see this. It's really... She handed the photograph to him.

Oh, no, no, he protested, you keep. It's for you.

Really? But... she didn't want to give him reasons to change his mind. Well, thank you so much. It's very— you're very kind.

No sweat. He smiled. I have another copy.

You do?

Yes. He was looking straight at her now. We—we did it in—what do you call—hmmm—like a room with a camera.

A studio?

No, no, ah—a little room. You put a coin in the machine. It was Paddington. Paddington Station—

A photo booth.

Yes, yes, a photo... he was having trouble getting his mouth around the long *oo* and the soft *th* of *booth*; seemed to be able to pronounce one or the other, but not both at the same time. She tried not to let him see that she'd noticed. In the end he shook his head and laughed. I have to exercise to say this word. He was laughing at himself— Yasmin hadn't realised he had a sense of humour. Anyway, yes... he went on, it come out of the machine and there were four, you know? All together. He spoke as though a photo booth photograph was a marvel she was unlikely to have experienced herself. And Abbie—your mother, she wanted one for herself, but we didn't have, you know, scissors. And I was going away in a minute. Back to Israel, you see, I couldn't stay. So I took them. I took all four in my wallet. I said I'll cut them when I get home and send her one in a letter. And she promised she send me another photograph, one when she is older, Tamara. I want to see her even if she did live here. In England. I ask Abbie, I said please you should send me one on her birthday, when she one years old. And she said yes, she said she would. But she never did... so—so I never did too. I never send her this photograph. Just carry it in this wallet all the time. All the years.

He paused, as if waiting for a response. Maybe he was expecting her to rebuke him. To judge him for depriving her family of the one photograph they might have had; although how should he have known? But she didn't. She didn't condemn him. His story—something didn't fit, and she was trying to work out what. She wished she could record his words. Perhaps they would make more sense on second listening. Her father had an old tape recorder somewhere in the house, and she wondered about telephoning him to ask where it was. He should be home on a Saturday morning. But they hadn't spoken for over two weeks and it would be difficult to keep the conversation short. He would want to know why she needed it. And how would it sound? Dad, there's a Jewish-Israeli man sitting in your living room. An old boyfriend of mum's. We're just looking through some photographs together... No, that wouldn't sound right. This whole scene wasn't right. Like something out of a surreal artist's sketchbook. Take a bearded, black-and-white orthodox Jew, and a non-orthodox woman wearing a colourful t-shirt and jeans, long curly hair falling untamed about her shoulders. Put them in a room, on their own, make them face each other across a low coffee table, sideways on to the camera, deep in conversation. To finish, place a Palestinian flag centre stage between them… No, forget about the tape recorder.

You know, Josh was saying, in Israel you are not allowed to go outside without identity card. If police stop and you don't have it you can go to the prison. So this wallet, you see—they have been with me. Always. He seemed to assume she knew something she didn't. A man visiting his ex-girlfriend and taking a photo of her and her new baby wasn't that unusual. But there was something puzzling, disturbing about the story. He went on, I know it was, hmmmm, wrong. That I didn't send the copies as I promised. Maybe I shouldn't be talking with you like this. Hmmm?

Oh, no! Yasmin protested, though she wasn't sure of it herself. Please. Please go on. I'm… I'm very grateful. If you don't mind.

Well, but I thought she probably had many others. I didn't know it was the only one. And then. Then Tamara had her birthday, and she, Abbie, she didn't write. I was angry you see. I said, to myself, she didn't do what she said so I don't need to do what I said. And I'm sorry. About that. I know it was difficult for her. I understand now. Stupid, no? That half laugh again. You see, she was already, I don't know… she was knowing your father when I visit…

Knowing my father?

Well, maybe not *knowing*. Maybe is the wrong word… She talk about him. I think they were friends, maybe… She said that they met at the demonstration. She tell you? Peace Now march where the man was killed—Emil Grunzweig? He looked up, maybe expecting her to show recognition. Had she heard that name? It rang a distant bell; but no, she had never heard of this Emil Grun—

Emil what?

Grunzweig. Peace Now? He glanced at her again, having realised he'd been giving her more credit than was due, mistaking her for someone more knowledgeable. Well, I don't know if is interesting. He sighed, lowering his head.

Yes! she said and realised she was nearly shouting. Lowering her voice, she added, Yes. Please go on. I mean, please explain. She worried he was losing momentum. That the moment was about to pass, and he would return to his previous, incommunicative form. The strain of speaking so much English was showing; he was becoming more halted, taking longer to search for the right word, sounding more foreign. How can she make it easier for him to go on? Should she get Sebastian out of bed? Ask Josh to continue in Hebrew with Sebastian translating? But she was fed up with translations; with second hand information. She wanted him to speak to her directly.

Peace Now, it's a… organisation? Like a movement. They were against the war. The Lebanon. The—the massacre in the camps, you know we talk about it, yesterday in the evening, it was the first thing, the thing that got the Peace Now starting. He waited for her to acknowledge that she remembered last night's conversation. They wanted heads to roll, it's a… saying, you know it? Well, they said chief of staff should resign, minister of security should resign, prime minister should go… Ministerial responsibility, is what they call it. That day, it was 1983. *Februar?*

February, she corrected and immediately regretted it.

But he didn't seem to mind or feel patronised as she'd feared, because he looked up quickly and said, February. Thank you. They were demonstrating in Jerusalem, march to the house of the Prime Minister. Abbie went. Also some friends. A group. Tommy too, your uncle. It was peaceful. A peace campaign. But then there were some others, anti-march people. They, ummm—they came to support our army, or, how you say—armed force, and our government. You know, it was a difficult time. Time of war. So both groups, they were there, one against each other. But then. Then few people started to throw thing. Tomatoes, eggs, mostly. They were throwing them at the Peace Now march, in the crowd. And a few… very few, they were throwing stones. Then someone threw a—a grenade.

A grenade? Yasmin said in alarm. Was anyone hurt?

Few, yes. And the man, Emil Gruntzweig, he was one of Peace Now people, he died. So that's who he is; was. Yasmin thought of the newspaper cutting, the men marching.

Yes, Josh went on as though she had spoken aloud, Yes, I saw your picture… It's in this—here. He spread the photographs on the table, picked up the newspaper cutting, the line of men linking arms. He pointed at a short man with a receding hairline at the centre. That's him. Very famous, in our country. Is the last picture of him.

Oh. Yasmin felt behind the pace again. I thought this man, with the beard… She pointed. He reminded me of my father. I thought perhaps he was a relative and that's why my mother kept it.

No, he pronounced abruptly, This is Emil Grunzweig. And these are his friends. Your mother, she was nearby. She never tell you?

No. The word tumbled out, lonely, like an oversized playing cube, its pointy corners scratching the roof of her mouth. No, she never did.

Well, it was—it was when she met your father. When she met Omar. She didn't know him, at the start. That's what she told me… He scratched under his skullcap, then absentmindedly rearranged it at the centre of his head, like a cathedral dome. Omar—he was at the protest, he went on. They were marching, against the government, against the war. It was chance. And then, that was when the, the grenade—it explode and people run, they were running, you know, in every direction. And she fall. Her knee, it was. Blood, quite a lot. So she lost her friends, and you know; with the blood and the baby, people pushing all around.

Hang on a minute, wait… did he mention a baby? Josh looked up abruptly. She had interrupted his flow. His light blue eyes shone. Was he fighting back tears? Quietly, she said, You said, with the baby. What baby? A dread had come over her; did she even want to hear the answer.

He was there, Omar. It was chance. I think he saw her, and she need help. He hold her arm, that's what she said, after; hold her arm and they walk out, go away from the all the—the panic. Anyone would do that. Many people, anyway. It wasn't so special, but she told him right away that she was, you know, going to have a baby. No one else knew, not her mother, even.

So, so she was—pregnant? Before she met my father? What—what happened? What happened to the baby?

The baby? Well... she die—

She... When? Oh, poor mummy. It didn't bear thinking, that she had lost not one but two babies. It was too cruel. But why did Yasmin not know this? Why the secrecy? She blew her nose. So, who, who was... I mean whose? She began. But, looking at the stricken pose of the man in front of her, there was no need for an answer. They were both in tears now. Josh, the father of Abbie's first baby? Of her half-sister? This man—he was practically— practically family! No wonder he's been behaving so— well he *seemed* so odd. This must be so difficult for him. And she'd been so resentful, unkind even, quite unfair. She had been happy to manipulate him into giving her the information she wanted, and never mind the cost to him of revisiting his own loss. How could she do this to a man who had done her no harm? I'm sorry, she said, I'm so sorry.

Thank you. And I'm sorry you lost her also.

Well, it was hardly comparable. Even so, Yasmin felt this new version of events smack her right between the eyes. What happened? she managed at last.

Josh's gaze was on her now, searching. What... what happened? he repeated. It was, well, she told me that she... Tamara, she died in sleep. No one know why.

Tamara? But that's my sister's name! I mean, my other sister. The one—My father's daughter. It was her name on the gravestone, we saw it yesterday. She was also—also

309

young, when she… unexplained death, is what we call it. She stopped. The words dried up, as though someone had switched off a tap. Josh was watching her. When was that march again? A realisation was dawning on her; she looked at him, dumbfounded. He kept looking straight back, his blue eyes large, silent, yet speaking; they told her now, what her own parents never had. Quietly, hoarsely, fearfully she said, My sister, Tamara, she was born in 1983, September. She and I have the same birthday; but I was, I am, five years younger.

Twenty-four in September 1983, he said. It is when our baby was born. I came to London. Ask Abbie to—to come back. With me. I told her I change. A change man. I wanted us to be together. A family. Even I was preparing to stay here with them, find a job, if she want, but no. She didn't listen. I think maybe she found someone, another man, but she said no, there was no other. After I sometimes think it was his fault. Omar. I don't know. She say—she say she meet him again, in London. It was, how you say, an incident?

A coincidence, she said.

Thank you, yes, *co*-incident. They are, they were on the same plane, fly to England and she… recognise him, from that night, she say. It was only a few weeks, maybe two after—after they met. She say he stand next to her when she was waiting for her suitcase, to arrive from the airplane. Here in England. She recognise him. I didn't think she know him well. Not at all, I thought, she just mention, mention his name. One or two times. So then I went back home, to Israel; and I don't hear anything, not the photograph she promise… nothing. Then, he… your father, he telephone and say, he had to say me that the baby, she die. I don't expect to hear about a thing like that from him, and I ask to speak with Abbie, but he say she isn't talking, not to anyone, and she will telephone later, but she never did. After that I hear from Rifka, your grandmother. I hear that they were married, in London. And, I hear that you are born. I didn't know you had the same birthday.

After a time Josh moved in his seat, swinging one long leg over the other. Yasmin realised they had been sitting in silence for the longest time. She noticed with mild surprise that there was no awkwardness left between them. They were two warriors returned from a bloody battle. Athletes, at the end of a long-distance race. They were, the thought sprung into her mind before she could intercept it, they were lovers, spent after a night of passion. It was eerie, how easy it seemed to be sitting here with this strange bearded foreign man who'd just told her that he was the father of her long since dead sister (what did it make them, him, and her? Some kind of step-relatives). She had to get out. It was all too much. Too much information to digest. And then Sebastian was shuffling to and fro in the bedroom above. She got up. I'm going for a swim, she said. I'll be back soon.

Walking along the river bank, Yasmin replayed Josh's words in her head.

September the twenty fourth. Close to her death, her mother had told Yasmin how desperate she'd been for Yasmin not to be born on that date. She hadn't wanted Yasmin's birthdays to be marred by her sister's; by the pain of Tamara once more failing to reach that longed for second birthday. At one point it had looked likely Yasmin wouldn't be out till the following day. But at ten minutes before midnight, in a flurry of contractions, an exhausted Abbie, crouched on the living room floor, arms draped left and right over a chair in the recommended Natural Childbirth Trust position, bore down, desperate and screaming, and pushed Yasmin's dark, slimy little body into the hands of the midwife named Saskia.

And so the sadness, the heaviness, faint but palpable, that always hovered over her family as Yasmin was growing up, that which she later came to know as bereavement, used to thicken, somehow, on her birthday eves. Slowly, gradually, surely, the air would thicken and become more palpable. It would go on thickening until, in the morning as Yasmin would wake up, one year older, she would find that it had taken on a soup-like quality. Then the three of them would wade through the day. Yasmin would wear a flowery crown, blow candles, eat cake, all of them all the while smiling and putting on a brave face.

When she was quite small, Yasmin had taken this as normal. Then realisation dawned on her that other children's birthdays were purely happy, times to party, not mourn. To settle this confusion, this juxtaposition, Yasmin in her teenage years put the darkness of her own experience down to her parents' foreignness. She had once read in a book, or maybe an article, that in Japanese culture birthdays weren't celebrated at all; that it wasn't considered any sort of special occasion. It was never made clear to her whether in her family's case tradition was in fact being followed, or whether it was to do with her own parents' peculiarities, neither of whom had ever truly taken on board the English culture.

Her mother, for example, made no effort to produce any of the delicacies Yasmin coveted. She wouldn't even allow sausages at home, pronouncing them oversized and disgustingly fleshy. She was not vegetarian, and was fiercely atheistic, but had spent too long in a country where all meat was kosher. As a result she could not bear the taste of pork or the sight of blood oozing out of meat. Even shepherd's pie, Yasmin's very favourite dish, and the utterly harmless and wholesome macaroni cheese Abbie objected to on the ground that they were too rich. Besides, she would say, your father doesn't like it. Which was true, though irrelevant since he was hardly ever home. So Yasmin was brought up on a diet of small-cut-salad, tahini, and hummus with everything. If she had friends to stay, she would use her own pocket money to buy cereal and beg her mother not to offer them salad or omelette for breakfast. Her parents themselves were oblivious to the fact of their strangeness. She knew that because no one in their right mind would want to stand so much apart from their own community. Only complete eccentrics, freaks, would *choose* to be so different.

The river was in spate. It had rained the night before, and water was rushing off the high moor. She was glad Josh had declined to come along. Well, he hadn't declined exactly since she hadn't asked him. He had to get ready to travel back to London in the afternoon, he said. And he wanted to continue looking through the photographs if that was okay with Yasmin. Did Yasmin wish for him to write down who the people were, on the back, if he recognised them? Yasmin desperately wanted to be there with him. But she needed a break. It felt as though the past, her mother's, her family's, was charging at her, like a wave, careering forward with malice aforethought.

Plunging into the ice-cold water of the river Dart always sent her into shock. But soon, a calm would descend, a feeling that every worry is swept away. But today, as she fell into the icy, silky embrace of the river, and was swimming against the current so that she was neither advancing nor retreating, it was no good. No matter how delicious, how blue green the water; how magnificent the treetops above head, reflected in the depth; no matter how many dragon flies descended onto the water surface. Having practically run out of the house in search of this sanctuary she now longed to be sitting with Josh on the red-black-white-and-green sofa again, to hear his words fall crookedly, awkwardly onto her lap. There will be time enough to puzzle over Tamara. Later. They were still sisters, whoever their fathers had been.

Walking back to her car, Yasmin hastened her step, which wasn't easy since her feet were numb and stilt-like. She must have stayed in the water longer than she'd thought. Her fingers were tingling, her wrists ached. Yes, she stayed in too long. Sun rays penetrated the thicket of hawthorn and oak above head, dancing sluggishly to and fro on the ground as she broke into a half jog. Why was she in such a rush? She had no idea. Only that she wanted to be home. She would put food in front of him; ask him to stay another night. Two, if he were willing. Sebastian wouldn't mind playing host and staying over for a little longer. She quite liked having him around, anyway. Both, she liked having both around. Yes. She started the car, stepped a little too hard on the accelerator. It was surprising. But true, nonetheless. Josh was unassuming. And his voice was kind of deep and halting. She liked that about him, his halting quality, the way he seemed to contemplate each word. And he was handsome. Yes. Old, of course, and bearded, which wasn't her thing, but his eyes, light blue; even the fine wrinkles around them; they touched her, somehow. Handsome was what he was. She was ready to turn a page with him.

The front door opened. Sebastian. What are you doing, Seb? She was momentarily confused.

I'm opening the door for you. Just back from dropping Josh off at the station. And, oh, you're welcome.

He's gone? She panicked. Tears pushed up at her throat.

Yes. He said sorry not to say goodbye.

Why didn't he? Why didn't he wait? Her tone was accusatory. It wasn't Sebastian's fault.

He had an eight fifteen train. You knew that, Yassi. Where have you been?

Eight fifteen? But that's hours away.

It's half past eight now. Where have the hours gone? And what was Sebastian still doing in her house? What was happening today?

I thought it was lunch time. I felt hungry. I thought I was hungry because it was lunch time.

No, Yass. Come on, I've made us some supper.

You made supper? She walked in through the door. In my kitchen?

It's shepherd's pie, he said. Sit, I'll bring it through. Oh, and your telephone hasn't stopped ringing; like the clappers.

Oh, yes?

Yes. First Adam.

Adam?

Deep voice. Said you may not remember; he bought olive oil at the market yesterday; said he was there with his sister—and a baby—wasn't sure if you'd remember him—

The nice hands. She said, I remember, yes.

Yes, well, he has a spare theatre ticket for tomorrow. Asked if you might want to join him. Sebastian eyed her intently, though it was none of his business. He waited a while but gave up when she didn't respond. He said, And—yes, your uncle rang. From London? He said would you like to visit him next weekend. And to call back today. That he's been missing you. He paused again. Bit of a strange thing for an uncle to say, isn't it?

He's not my uncle. He's my mother's cousin.

Ah. That makes it completely different. It was uncharacteristic of Sebastian. Sarcasm wasn't his style. He was twitching, twisting his shoulders, shifting his feet as he watched her for reaction. Anyway... He turned, trying to hide his discomfort, the food can wait; if you want to call them back.

No, I won't, Sebastian. Let's eat.

So you're not going to call?

That depends. She smiled at him.

On?

On how good your shepherd's pie is.

Chapter 15

The 20:03 train to London was brimful of people. Josh marvelled at the efficiency with which passengers refrained from succumbing to physical contact. He placed his suitcase in the designated space between two carriages, found a seat and settled to gazing out of the window. Briefly, he wondered whether Yasmin would come rushing in through the station gate looking for him. He wanted to thank her. Was sorry not to have taken his leave properly. Being Abbie and Omar's daughter, he had approached their meeting with more than a little trepidation but was now pleased how well they got on. And she had been kind, needlessly so. As the train slowly pulled out of the station he felt for the envelope in his pocket, was relieved it was still where he had placed it a few hours before. He had found it in a pile of letters and photographs which the man, Sebastian, had carried into Yasmin's living room that morning. Josh, sitting on the Palestine flag clad sofa, had watched Sebastian stumbling downstairs, looking sleepy and worse for wear. Seeing that Josh was there, Sebastian stopped in his track and turned so that the papers were hidden from Josh's view. As though they were illicit, private, or secret. Then, after some hesitation, Sebastian mock-carelessly continued across the room and placed the pile carefully on the dining table, as far away as possible from where Josh was sitting. Relieved of his burden, Sebastian made coffee for both of them, acting, Josh noticed, as though the house was his own to play host in. They talked a while about this and that, mainly politics in the Middle East, after which Sebastian went out for a Sunday newspaper. As soon as he was alone, Josh had walked over to the pile of papers, letters and photographs. He still wasn't sure what had drawn him to it. Was it the shift in Sebastian's stance when he saw Josh? But perhaps there had been nothing odd about Sebastian's behaviour. Maybe Josh had simply been bored, as one often was, sitting in someone else's house with none of the usual things to do?

He didn't set out to take the letter. At the top of the pile there were old handwritten sheets and he recognised Abbie's tight urgent hand. Without picking them up, without touching, he read. A story. An imagined journey Josh took from that awful prison cell to his father's funeral. Standing very still, Josh tried to commit the forbidden text to memory. But it was impossible. The feeling that she was present, right there in the room with him overwhelmed him. He didn't believe in ghosts but here she was, standing behind him, looking over his shoulder and speaking the words on the page right into his ear. Wondering whether the densely inked paper still held her scent, he bent over to smell it. Naturally, it didn't. Just mustiness and dust. Then he picked up the sheet and held it once more to his face in case he'd been wrong about her scent not being there. And that moment he saw it, the letter. Topmost in a bundle of airmail envelopes, bordered with red and blue stripes and tied with string, it bore his name and address in the Community. Feeling no guilt, Josh slipped it into his pocket just as Sebastian was returning from the shop, his footsteps echoing in the little porch.

Now Josh felt the letter pressing hotly onto his hip, practically burning a hole in his trousers. The train pulled slowly out of the station and soon they were speeding along a grey sea front. In a moment he would read Abbie's letter. But then what? Would he finally understand what happened? Why she called off their wedding, would not talk to him or explain but took herself and Tamara across the sea and away from him? Did this letter hold an answer? Mechanically, trying not to think too much about what he was about to do, he took the letter out of the envelope. It had been written in 1983, shortly after Abbie's move to England. Shortly after The Flood.

My Dear Josh, I can only imagine how angry you must be. It is so difficult to write. Where to start…

12 April 1983, Hampstead. A midwife came to the house to see me yesterday. The pregnancy is going well, everything as it should be. Except it is anything but. Today would have been my wedding day by the Jordan and I am in London, lying in bed with my head under the Eiderdown. Keeping my eyes closed, I attempt to make a plan, so that today may pass like the others. On any other day I would be getting up now, have a porridge breakfast, clear, and wash to the sound of Rachel's protestations that I must rest and let her take care of everything. Then I would go out. I would walk along the Heath paths, up the hill, through green woods all the way to Ladies' Pond. I would change out of my warmest winter clothes and slide

into the dark silky water. Skirting the pool's edge under lush vegetation, the sharp chill on my skin never fails to give relief, to soothe my mind away from the constant whirring mix of regret and dread. Keep yourself busy, Rachel says. Keep busy and keep the wreckage of the past at bay. Also, the terrifying future. Even so, most days I'm glad I cancelled the wedding, glad I moved away. Can today be one of those days? But I suspect it may not be; it is difficult to imagine sitting up, never mind getting out of bed. No, this morning I will not run away. I will stay put and endure the catastrophic feelings, thoughts of the destruction of my former life, the looming disaster of becoming Mother. I turn in the narrow bed, will I fall asleep again? But sleep eludes me. What am I doing here? How is this grey and dreary country an appropriate refuge? How is it a suitable place for a baby to come into the world? I should be somewhere else, somewhere the sun comes out from behind the clouds more often than it doesn't, where neighbours and passersby are familiar, benign. A Community. A Motherland.

Memories flood, of a visit to England a decade before, when I was aged fourteen and stayed in this house for the first time. My love for Josh was already years old, and he had known nothing about it. Every day during my stay, I sat in this room, at the antique desk that still faces the window overlooking Hampstead Heath. Each day, for an hour or two I wrote copious letters to him, full of fervent longing and detailed wonders of London. The time I spent with Toby, what we did and how I felt about him I greatly understated, not least to myself. None of these bulging envelopes I ever sent. Instead, I tucked them among the sheets of my diary. Many times over the years

I considered rereading these letters, but always found myself unable to face the raw feelings of my younger self.

... Josh, I never told you how you dominated my mind years before you ever dreamed of looking my way. At the start, when we first walked out together, I was wary that my passion would scare you off. Then it became difficult to find the right moment to talk about such ancient history...

With effort I sit up in bed. The view through the narrow, deep-set window hasn't changed since my first visit. Now as then, the Heath is separated from the garden by large trees, oak, hawthorn, hazel, elder, a cacophony of soft rich greens, so very different from the thorny yellows and bare browns of the land I left behind. My land. My eyes rest on the Marc Chagall painting hanging on the wall by the bed—Flying Lovers. A terrifying scene with figures floating precariously over a tranquil pastoral landscape. Chagall painting his own refugee experience. My heart thumps as I imagine myself onto the canvas, and I too am floating, drifting alone, directionless in a world without gravity. When will I hit the ground? How hard will my fall be? I wonder, am I also a refugee? But I have no right to claim such a title, one that throughout my childhood was borne by the Holocaust Generation with so much weight and pathos. Their suffering had been unparalleled, incomparable to anything our little lives may throw at us. Father was one of these Survivors, though I never heard him complain or take the moral high ground, not once. But nor did he need to, as others carved into stone the Hierarchy of Suffering that would be unquestioned.

If there was one thing I knew that stormy week in

February, it was that I had to call the wedding off. Although I love you, our paths have split, we are too far apart. I know it, despite the hurt. Yet, I lie awake at night, sleep in the morning. How to un-accustom myself to being part of you? To you being part of me? It is as though someone has torn a piece of me away. And I am insufficient, incomplete.

Unexpectedly, Rachel's big old house feels almost like a home; though it isn't. Not *my* home. Even so, there's something comfortable, inviting about its rickety, musty, shadowy nooks and crannies. And I savour the contrast with the uniform, utilitarian architecture of the Community. Terrifying as the thought is of becoming Mother in this faraway place, on a good day I believe it will do as the baby's first home. And I begin to understand the attraction that this house, Mother's childhood home, held for her all those years ago, why she was reluctant to come back to us. Am I finally turning into her? Although she did eventually return to the Community, she never re-embraced her old life. And I see now that trying to go back to the past would have been hopeless. You find everything changed when you get there. And the thought of being her—estranged, eccentric, isolated on the fringe of the place that used to be her home, this once nightmarish thought now seems almost bearable. I will return. One day. Maybe.

You and I were raised not by our parents but a Collective. The Community reflected us to ourselves so we knew what we were: The Future, a tool, a vehicle that drives a Socialist Utopia down the generations. Which we believed wholeheartedly since no other voice was as distinct or stable.

But I have left this destiny behind, failed to carry out the promise I was entrusted with. And now the Knowledge of who I am is vanished. Do I even exist? Here in Hampstead the people are opaque, there is no reflection, or if there is it is so subtly coded I cannot decipher or make use of it. Surrounded by this grey void, how can I be Mother on my own? What thing of value can I give this baby, with no one by my side to help me find the way?

The pen has fallen onto the translucent airmail paper. I look down. At the top of the sheet the writing is urgent, dense, and blue. Below, the faint lines are pristine, expectant. What is there to say? How to explain the feelings I myself do not understand? When will I conjure the words? Not today. Today, my former wedding day, in bed under the eiderdown I will be mourning my girl-dreams. A white fairytale wedding, a handsome prince carrying me into an orange sunset. The prince of my dreams doesn't ride a white horse but a brown Arabian stallion. Perhaps he comes for me on a tractor or bicycle. Always, he wears Josh's features, mostly his teenage self— open, determined. Not the more recent bearded, downward-leaning face. How I loved the way his serious blue eyes would narrow against the distance. His scowl as he looked up and was about to speak.

The life growing inside me is awake, kicking or turning. Even so, I struggle to imagine her being here, being real. Babies are to be cherished and cared for, even now I must begin to love her, but how? This disconnection, this ambivalence, is it normal? I wonder what sort of childhood awaits this half-formed thing. A childhood in a cold, damp land where all things are abundant, and to have just enough is to consider yourself poor. Will we walk an hour to a park so she can run around the little fenced off play area? Will I take her to a steamy, bleach-saturated pool to learn to swim? I know nothing of heated pools, manicured parks or heading out in the rain because if you wait for the weather, you won't go anywhere at all. All I know is mountains to east and west and running between them, bare feet on black, sun-cracked earth. I know searching for mushrooms in the pine grove after rain, and picking olives on the slope to Abudiya. And teenagers in pairs along a moonlit river, searching for a place to rest their love.

Josh, do you remember? Woodpeckers high in the ficus tree on the western lawn, the quiet majesty of palms, the delicate beauty of the Judas tree? Do you remember autumn, intoxicating us with scent of citrus blossom? How the extravagance of the bauhinia flowers dazzled us in spring? These marks of passing seasons, this childhood, our baby will never know. the story of who we are already lost to her. Lost as I am.

Two months earlier: 11 February 1983, Jordan Valley. I am walking out of the gate in the perimeter fence. The Community is left behind me. Along the fence a line of tall streetlights carves narrow slices out of the starless evening. It's pouring down and my muddy boots feel their way along the dirt track. I'm making my solitary way towards the precipice over the Jordan where Mother's Room perches. Slowly, I advance through the storm. Raining cats and dogs, Mother would say. On any other day she would say it, but not tonight. Tonight, there will be more pressing things, we won't be commenting on the weather. If I take long enough Mother may go to bed and it will be too late to disturb her. I slow some more. But delay is useless. My mind is made up and the sooner she knows the better, or less worse. And here is the light in her window, shattered into a kaleidoscope of specks, each inside its own raindrop. When I walk in, Mother is knitting in her black wooden rocking chair. A.B. Nathan's Voice of Peace is on the radio, playing Songs of the Sixties. Knitting and rocking, she is humming along, *Oh Cecilia, I'm down on my knees, I'm begging you please come home.* Abbie, she lifts her head, what are you doing here? And, Oh Lordy, you're all wet, come, sit, I'll get you a towel. It takes a while to make her listen, and longer to persuade her I'm determined to call the wedding off. She asks what happened, wants to know why but I will not tell, not ever.

Mother says, We must let Father know, we must make arrangements. And soon we're both walking out in the pitch-dark, huddled under one umbrella, Mother and Daughter wading through deep puddles, leaning forward against the horizontal rain, following the pale flickering circle of torch light. We journey from Mother's isolated hut into the Community through a wicket in the perimeter fence, and it is as though we have emerged from the apple-wood wardrobe. On the outside we were the last people on earth, surrounded only by trees and mountains. Inside the fence, in the dim yard lights, are marks of civilisation—parked bicycles, children's swing—a Community. But the feeling of isolation, of being alone in the world stays with me and always will. A lifetime of communal living, being a bee in a hive, has rendered me unprepared for such solitude.

We arrive at the door of the Room that had been the

Parents' Room but is now Father's. Mother knocks. Even though Father asked her to walk in unannounced as the rest of us do she insists on knocking. But tonight, she doesn't wait to be invited. Instead, she ushers me through the door ahead of her, and already she is telling Father everything, and her entrance without waiting and the stream of words make no sense to him, what in the world is she talking about, over and over he says, What is this? What's going on? And Mother repeats the whole thing, and she uses Father's telephone to let my uncle David know. Then she calls Rachel in London even though it's not yet nine o'clock and will cost a fortune, then Mona who promises to make all the arrangements, or disarrangements, cancel the Rabi, the Kosher food, the Members' rotas. And all the while, Josh doesn't know, and I am a small child sitting passively on Father's sofa, letting my parents take care and praying to the God I don't believe in to make everything okay.

Tommy joins us with Maya and the twins. All are quiet when they hear the news. Maya, she puts an arm around my shoulders and I cry grateful tears for such a kindness. Then Tommy says, I will go talk with Dov and Clara, they must be upset, and Josh away so they are on their own. And I say in a voice that isn't mine, They don't know. And the whole room stares at me, even the twins stop their game on the floor and turn to look. Tommy asks, How do you know this, Abbie? Josh will have told them, surely, even though it's the Sabbath. Tommy doesn't realise how strictly observant Josh has become. He says, and if they don't know, shouldn't we speak to them ourselves? And I whisper in my smallest voice, speaking right into my lap, Josh, he doesn't know. They hear me, but think they haven't because what sort of person would do such a thing and so I must speak up and say, I haven't told him.

And that's when everything else stops, and Maya's arm around my shoulders becomes stiff and heavy, she must want to take it away and is unsure how to do so without seeming rude but who would do such a thing? Now Josh must be told without delay, before everyone else finds out, but he is with Isaac's family and it is Friday evening, they wouldn't break the Sabbath to answer the phone. No one can think what to do until Father says, Abbie and I will drive to Isaac's house in the West Bank, that's what we must do. Then Abbie will tell him to his face. Mother says, Come, Abbie, you need to leave now or it will be midnight before you get there. And when I do not move, she adds, Abbie, aren't you coming? And Tommy says, Abbie, come on. But my legs are clay, my body a heavy, useless vessel, I'm beyond coming or going. What am I? Not a grown woman capable of being a wife, of being Mother. Instead, I am an infant, a babe at arms, if I sit here long enough, Mother and Father will make it all better. I can do nothing for myself. If I do nothing, the Grownups, the Community, will take care, and everything will be made right. I am a child who cannot hold a pen never mind write coherent words. A child who cannot put a telephone receiver to her ear, never mind speak clearly into it, never mind make sense of what I've done.

Tommy will travel to the West Bank with Father. They will find Josh and let him know the wedding is off. And now. Having set the wheels in motion, and having left it to others to clean up the mess, I wonder, what have I done, where should I go? The questions come piling. Will Josh also stay away? Being so embedded among the Settlers, would he not have left some time ago if it hadn't been for me pulling him back? Perhaps it's but a small step for both of us to remove ourselves out of the old life and into the new?

No more delays, I must explain my actions. Here it is, Josh, our very own Flood...

Josh placed the letter on the folding table. Instead of turning the page and continuing to read he shut his eyes and listened to the faint click-clack-clicks of wheels over tracks. What was he afraid of? Deep inside he knew that through the years he had dreaded the truth, had even been complicit in keeping it hidden despite what he told Abbie or himself. Was he afraid that she knew what had happened when he came home to the Community after the march? This had been just a day before. Before Oscar and Tommy drove to Isaac's house knowing no one would answer the telephone on a Sabbath. Before they asked to speak to Josh and told him Abbie had called the wedding off. The day before, after the march, at dawn, had anyone seen him arrive in the Community? Had anyone seen him leave less than an hour later? Was he afraid Abbie somehow knew or even suspected what happened during that hour, what he had done? That it was that knowledge that made her give him up?

That awful business with the grenade was the reason he had pitched up in the Community that day at all. He had been staying with Isaac, and on the evening of the march the two of them had ridden the short distance to Jerusalem in a van full of hecklers and counter-demonstrators. On arrival, they all settled to throwing insults and eggs at the marchers and calling them out for the traitors they were. Then the man standing next to Josh, an unusually short man, bearded and wearing a large skull cap produced a grenade. For a moment the man stood perfectly still, a little smile on his face and staring quizzically at Josh. Staring Josh straight in the eyes as though saying, Watch this, brother. Or asking, What are you going to do about it? Josh had done nothing. Instead, he had lowered his eyes to the man's hand wrapped around the grenade, partially hiding it from view. He had noted the man's long fingers, the white almost translucent skin, and tufts of black hair above the knuckles. He had done nothing. The whole episode took a moment, five seconds. Ten at most. He had never spoken of it. Never told a single person that there had been a time when he could have said, Hey, what are you doing? Hey, man! Stop! Then the grenade was among the crowd and everything unravelled. Screams, paramedics, police. Emil Grunzweig dead.

After the explosion, Josh had walked away. He had been shocked, exhausted, couldn't face going back to Isaac's house. That's how he came to hitchhike home to Abbie that night. He imagined how he would surprise her, that she would welcome him, the two of them on her hard iron framed bed, her growing belly against his. An hour later he struck lucky when a Ground Force utility truck heading for the Lebanon border picked him up. They drove north through the night and arrived at the Community gate as dawn was creeping over the top of the Golan Heights. Now on the train, cruising along a grey sea front he remembered walking along the empty pavements, Members lying in their beds, sleeping behind thin plywood doors. He was approaching Abbie's room when her door opened and out came that devil, Micah Ashkenazi. Josh had stood still. He was so tired, deflated from the previous evening, the quizzical grin, the delicate fingers around the grenade, and now this? The devil who through the years had haunted Josh like an evil spirit, who had wrapped himself around Abbie like a poisonous snake. As though she somehow belonged to him. The man who had ignored Josh time and again, made him feel transparent, inconsequential. And through the years, Abbie would say, You're making something out of nothing, Josh. Sometimes she would retort impatiently, He's just a friend, and, he's done nothing wrong. Nothing to see here. Well, he was looking now, and seeing. This was not a figment of his imagination. The man leaving Abbie's room, his eyes nearly shut against the dawn light, slit-eyes squeezed so tight his face almost seemed like a smile. Hello Josh, he said jovially and continued to walk on by. Not even breaking his stride. Hello. Josh. Words cool as morning dew. As though he hadn't just come out of Abbie's room. As though Josh was just someone, anyone you happen to meet on the pavement.

Without giving thought to what he was doing Josh had turned to walk after him. Micah knew, he must have because he led them to the olive grove by the pool, a secluded spot on the way to nowhere. There, finally, he stopped and turned to face Josh. Now on the train, Josh watched as the view through the window changed from seascape to dense trees. What happened next? He recalled the Cheshire Cat grin, the slit grey eyes, but little of what was said. Mainly the question, What's going on, on, on, and the answer, I should have thought that was obvious, obvious, but don't worry, don't worry, the baby, it's yours,

yours, yours, or so she says, she says, says. This, Josh remembered, and the grin. And next he was on the ground, lying on top of the man who was also on the ground, the man's legs spread wide apart and Josh on top of him, both on the dusty black earth, one on top of the other like lovers, lovers of someone else, loving not each other, most certainly not each other. And Josh saw a pair of hands clasped around the man's neck, white-knuckled fingers clutching, gripping, hands he didn't recognise but were attached to his own arms, powered by his own heart. And finding himself squeezing a life out he held on. One-two and grip harder, one-two and hold. It was hard work, he remembered the exertion on his fingers, his arms, his temples beginning to sweat and drip onto the hands below, onto the neck between the thumbs, drops that made islands in the dusty skin. Then the grin was gone and the man made a noise like a cat's purr. Has he done it? Was that it? The relief he'd waited for didn't come, his hands let go. Was it too late? The man lay still as Josh stood up. Too late, his legs were spread wide, leave, get away, he was in shock, it didn't occur to him to check, just walk away out of the perimeter fence, and hitchhike all the way back to Isaac.

Now on the train Josh rubbed his eyes with two thumbs, blinking tears away and peering through the window where cows and sheep grazed in improbably green fields. If the man hadn't thrown the grenade, he would never have gone to the Community that night. But then what? His heart was racing as he picked up Abbie's letter again.

10 February 1983, Peace Now march, Jerusalem. Josh doesn't know I am here at the march. I told him I wouldn't be going, yet here I am. I had been beset by all day nausea and felt I could not bear the journey, the endless, undulating road to Jerusalem. Hours on a stifling bus brimming with the sweat of Community members, swaying like a boat in a storm, winding south along the Jordan Valley, south and down through the desolate wasteland of the West Bank, lower almost to the Dead Sea, then turn west to start the slow, dizzying assent up and round the interminable Judean Mountains and finally, Jerusalem. So I said I wouldn't go. Josh was on leave from the Lebanon, and staying with Isaac's family near Jerusalem. Naturally, he was pleased I wouldn't be joining the march. To him, the work of Peace Now, actually all opposition to the government, is reprehensible in war time. No better than literally stabbing our soldiers in the back, he said. But then. I thought of the baby I would call Tamara, how in years to come we would talk about her time growing inside me, and what we did together. I wanted to be able to tell her I had taken a stand. That I spoke out against the Beirut massacre in which thousands of Palestinian refugees were murdered while our army sat back and watched. And the morning of the march, I woke feeling almost fine, the nausea turned down to background noise. That was my sign to get on the coach.

…Josh, you didn't know the plan had changed but there I was…

We are marching, approaching the open space in front of the Prime Minister's house. All of us are here, Anya, Micah, everyone. My parents are a little way ahead with Solomon, Ruth, and Joseph. I can see the top of Father's blue brimless sun hat bobbing in the sea of heads. And I think of the obstinacy with which he insists on wearing this shapeless thing, despite my attempts to dissuade him. Let him wear what he likes, Mother said. That's all she wants, for everyone to please themselves.

Now the abuse from the sidelines intensifies. A line of bearded men in button-up white shirts and long black coats, chanting and swearing, arms waving like a troupe of menacing monkeys, their message unequivocal: we are traitors, Nazis, worse than Arabs. There's pushing and shoving into our lines and fights breaking out ahead. I am in the centre of a throng of marchers, their bodies protect me as we walk on. Then, something, a sight, catches the corner of my eye. Someone. A flicker, a streak of movement that holds my attention, and I glance over, not yet knowing what I'm looking at or why. I stop in my tracks and stand still as the others continue walking and disappear ahead. I stare at the line of angry, screaming men. Standing among this most unedifying of crowds is Josh.

And in the two or three seconds before my mind registers the horror of what I am seeing, my heart does what it always has at the sight of him: it skips with joy. Even after all the years he still affects me so. His face is towards me and at first, I think he has also seen me. He is shouting something I cannot hear and punching the air. Time is slow. The marchers keep walking past but my feet are planted in the ground, I am a tree in flooding river. I stand and watch him through the shifting crowd. And at length I realise my mistake. He is not calling for my attention. He has not seen me, but is shouting at me, at the marchers. He is not punching the air but hurling something into the crowd. An egg flies towards me and breaks onto my sandalled foot. My legs are splashed with sticky yellow yoke.

Did you throw that egg, Josh? I am afraid to ask, afraid to know the truth. Yet, I saw you and cannot now un-see the frenzy on your face. I saw you and cannot un-know the hatred that led to so much devastation.

I don't know how long I stand there without moving. A moment, maybe, or an hour. How long before the explosion up ahead, when everything turns to turmoil and people scatter like mercury droplets from a shattered thermometer. Not me. I cannot move or turn my head from the spot where Josh has been, though he is no longer there. And though I know I should get away, should follow the retreating crowd to safety, still I stay until my knees give and I sit in the road, right on the broken eggshells. There I sit until someone, a man approaches. He stands quietly for a time, then slowly sits on the road beside me and though he keeps a distance his serene calm feels like an arm around my shoulders, like an embrace. Then he helps me to my feet, and we walk to where the coach is parked. Be careful on the steps, he says, and turns to walk away. Thank you, I say, and quickly before he disappears, What's your name? He turns back. Omar, he says. Like the actor, Omar Sharif, you know? Yes, I know, I say and smile at him. Hello, Omar-like-the-actor.

Everyone on the bus was worried. Father and Micah had gone back into the square to search for me and brought news of the casualties. Where were you, Josh? Where did you go? Micah sat with me all the way home. We arrived after midnight, and he kindly saw me to my room. You know he collapsed the next morning? Of all people it was my father who found him in the olive grove. A stroke, they say, he may never walk again. I may have been the last person to see him before it happened. People on the coach thought I was lost in the chaos of the explosion. They still do. No one knows that I saw you there, standing with the hecklers.

Josh lifted his eyes and let the letter fall onto his lap. Was he relieved? All the years between walking away from the olive grove and now his greatest fear has been that he had brought his own downfall on himself. That Abbie found out what he did to Micah and could not forgive him. That was why he never insisted that she explains. Why he never asked, What were you doing that night? Why were you with this man when I am here for you and always will be? He peered out of the window. The fields were replaced by ashen tall apartment blocks. London Paddington will be the next station stop. He noted how smoothly the train was cruising, although the letter in his hand was shaking like a leaf. Abbie didn't know the worst of what he'd done. That was something, at least. Josh placed the letter carefully in the envelope. He rubbed his eyes again. Yet everything around him was watery, distorted by a film spread across his vision. Anya was right about his eyesight; he should get it checked. He will ask her to make an appointment for him. Yes, he will do that. As soon as he gets home.

Acknowledgements

Huge thanks to my early readers: James Gregory who read it first, gave me encouragement and said it was good enough to publish. Also Hadas Lahav, Anna Dunscombe, Debs Hedger, Jo Feloy, Angie Watson, Judy Marshall, Jo Barley, Clare Salkeld and Jane Jackson Rowe – thank you all for your feedback and support.

My writers' group was instrumental in helping me to develop as an author and supporting me to persevere with the rocky road to publication. Thank you Anna Lunk, Judy Gordon Jones, Sophie Pierce and remembering Cathryn Laing with love.